Cézanne's Quarry

Cézanne's Quarry

Barbara Corrado Pope

PEGASUS BOOKS
NEW YORK

CÉZANNE'S QUARRY

Pegasus Books LLC
80 Broad Street
5th Floor
New York, NY 10004

First Pegasus Books cloth edition 2008
First Pegasus Books trade paperback edition 2009

Interior Design by Maria Fernandez

Library of Congress Cataloging-in-Publication Data is available.

ISBN: 978-1-60598-060-7

10 9 8 7 6 5 4 3 2 1

Printed in the United States of America
Distributed by W. W. Norton & Company, Inc.
www.pegasusbooks.us

To Daniel, Roberta and Jae, in love and friendship

Acknowledgments

This first-time novelist owes many debts of gratitude. First thanks to Roberta Till-Retz who proposed writing a novel on Cézanne, Provence and geology. Elizabeth Lyon generously mentored me in matters of writing and publication. My agent, Mollie Glick, was exemplary for her editorial advice and her dedication to getting *Cézanne's Quarry* into print. Jessica Case was an encouraging and excellent editor. I also thank the many friends who were willing to read and talk about the manuscript in its early phases: Paula Rothenberg, Jeffry and Ulla Kaplow, Barbara and Tom Dolezal, Geraldine Moreno, Joan Pierson, Sue Choppy, Freddie Tryk, Pam Whyte, Patricia Phillips, Barbara Zaczek, Lisa Wolverton, Barbara Altmann, and especially the bi-cultural, bi-lingual critic extraordinaire, George Wickes. Keith Crudgington and Nora McCole stepped in with crucial technical assistance. And Daniel and Stephanie Corrado Pope gave consistent love, criticism and encouragement.

At the beginning of 1885 Cézanne's lonely contemplation of nature was interrupted by a violent love affair with a woman about whom little is known except that he met her in Aix.

—JOHN REWALD, *Cézanne*

Cézanne's
Quarry

Tuesday, August 18

Aix-en-Provence, 1885. A provincial town of 20,000 souls. Its glory days, when good King René reigned over a brilliant, chivalric court, were long since past. After Aix gave the great Mirabeau to the Revolution of 1789, it fell into a deep conservative sleep. As the nineteenth century wore on, Marseilles, only 30 kilometers to the south, more and more surpassed it in people, in industry and in learning. All that remained to Aix in 1885 were a few branches of the university, the law courts (bearing the high-sounding name the Palais de Justice) and, of course, its pretensions.

1

INSPECTOR ALBERT FRANC APPROACHED HIM about the dead woman in the quarry because there was no one else around. The Palais de Justice was closed for the summer holidays. Certain that nothing of import could possibly happen during the last two weeks of August, the officers of the court took off to the countryside, leaving the administration of law and order in the hands of Bernard Martin, a judge with little experience and no family or connections in the South of France.

Martin was alone in his attic room when the pounding began. Startled, he marked the page he had been reading in Zola's new novel and put it on the shelf above his bed. He pushed *Germinal* and Darwin's *The Origin of Species* hard against the wall, making sure that the black leather-bound Bible his mother had given him would overshadow them. He was not sure who was at the door. He did know that at this time, in this town, it was prudent to keep his radical political sympathies secret. Turning to his table, he shoved the letters from home to one side and swept the stale bread and hardened cheese that remained from his lonely meal to the other.

"Monsieur Martin. *Monsieur le juge!*" the voice on the other side of the door called out with mounting impatience.

With three swift steps Martin reached the door and swung it open. "Sorry, I was reading—"

"Thank God you're here."

The panting Albert Franc was not a welcome sight. Although not very tall, Aix's veteran inspector was broad and strong; a man known as much for his toughness as for his disregard of the finer points of criminal procedure. His bulk filled the low arched doorway. Martin stepped aside and gestured toward the wooden chair in front of the table.

"Thank you." Franc sat down with a sigh and began to fan himself with his cap. "Any water?"

Martin poured a cup from the clay pitcher that stood on the stand beside his armoire and handed it to Franc, who gulped it down and began to fan his face again.

Before Martin could ask, the inspector's breathless explanation tumbled out. "Sorry to disturb you, sir. But I had to. It's a dead woman. In the quarry. Murdered, I think. Since the Proc is not here," Franc said, using the courthouse parlance for the prosecutor, "I need you to go there with me."

"A dead woman, here in Aix?" Martin sat down on the bed. "Are you sure?"

"A boy just came to the jailhouse with his father to report what he had seen. She's in the old quarry. He thinks she was a gentlewoman."

"You're sure it's not a prank? Or a mistake?"

"No, no. You know me, sir, I'm good at that. Questioning."

Martin did know, only too well. The inspector's detainees too often arrived in his chambers bruised and terrified. "Softened up," as Franc liked to say.

"I was with him for about an hour," Franc continued. "I'm convinced he's telling the truth. He thinks he saw blood. And he even described the dress the woman had on. White with green stripes. Much better than anything his mother had ever worn."

A memory flickered across Martin's mind, but he could not quite catch it.

"The quarry, is it far?"

"No, sir, it's just off the Bibémus road, less than an hour away. That's why I'm here. I thought the two of us should go and take a look as soon as possible, especially with the heat and cholera and all—"

Martin's stomach lurched. Viewing murder victims had been the most gruesome aspect of his legal education. In the Paris morgue, they had lain gray and anonymous on cold slabs of marble. Martin could only imagine what this infernal heat would do to a body.

"There haven't been any cases of cholera in Aix, have there?"

"No, sir, but in Marseilles—"

"Yes, yes." Martin tried to sound matter-of-fact as he rose and went to his armoire. Whatever was waiting for him in the quarry, he was not about to show any signs of weakness to someone notorious around the Palais for telling tales. "Which of your men did you bring with you?"

"Most of them are still celebrating the Virgin's feast, sir."

Martin swung around. "But the Assumption was three days ago."

Franc shrugged. "They're good boys, and it is the middle of August."

Good boys! Franc liked to hang out in the jailhouse with the uniformed men doing God knows what. Probably mocking the priggishness of judges like himself. When Martin pulled out his frock coat and hat, the proper attire for official business, Franc raised his hand to stop him.

"No, sir, you won't want to wear that. Too hot. And who knows how long we'll be climbing around."

"Right," Martin murmured, "right." Priggish indeed. He grabbed the jacket and cap from his student days and looked around just in time to see Franc scrutinizing his lodgings.

"If you don't mind my asking, sir, do you have someone to look after you?"

"I have a day woman, someone from the country, but with the Picard family gone, she only comes in once a week." Would his living habits and the fact that he had to rent an attic room become grist for Franc's gossip mill? The veteran inspector surely knew that beginning magistrates earned a pittance, and he probably had heard that Martin was the rare judge without family wealth. "Let's go," Martin added with all the authority he could muster, as he reached over to close the shutters on his window.

"Of course." Franc put on his cap, bounded for the door, and held it open. As they hurried down the stairs, he told Martin that he had requisitioned a mule and cart. When they emerged into the blinding light, Franc gestured toward the end of the street. The notary, René Picard, owned one of the newer houses near what had been the northern wall of the city, only a stone's throw from the Saint-Sauveur Cathedral. The transport that awaited Franc and Martin at the entrance to the cathedral square was a simple affair, gray with age and splintery. Pointing to a handkerchief that he had wound around his left hand, the inspector cautioned Martin to watch out for protruding nails.

Once they settled onto the seat, Franc flicked his whip, urging the animal toward the great church from which the procession honoring the Assumption of the Virgin Mary into heaven had issued forth into the streets of Aix. Now, three days later, the only sign that remained of the holy festivities was a few blue and white flowers lying shriveled and forlorn upon the cobblestones. The narrow, winding streets that led them out of town were just as somber, the windows of the convents and houses resolutely shuttered against the late afternoon sun and the slow cadence of the beast's hooves.

Martin waited until they reached the main road to Vauvenargues to question Franc more closely about the day's events. How many boys saw the body? Exactly when did they find it? Did they find anything else?

There was not much to tell. Three farm boys, gone off for a swim. On the way home, they stopped to play hide-and-seek at the quarry, and they got the scare of their lives. Franc laughed, displaying a strong set of tobacco-stained teeth. Evidently, they found the body face down, and none of them had had the nerve to turn it over. They were convinced they wouldn't know a lady like her anyway. It was the oldest boy's father, Pierre Tolbec, who reported the incident to the police. Tolbec and his son, Patric, arrived on horseback around two, carrying a parasol and a little sack purse, empty save for a few coins.

Martin found nothing amusing in this account. His colleagues at the courthouse liked Franc because he took his police duties seriously, and he made their life easier. Most of the magistrates cared little about how the inspector treated the petty thieves, poachers, and prostitutes to whom they dispensed justice. Martin did care, although he tried to keep this to himself. If they really did find a dead body, he was stuck with Franc, and Franc was stuck with him, which, considering his inexperience and the potential importance of the case, was probably worse.

Martin studied his companion's profile. Franc's shiny dyed black hair and thick glossy mustache belied the years hinted at by the gray and white grizzle sprouting on his unshaven face. In the judges' and lawyers' cloakroom, Martin had overheard his peers joking about the inspector's surprising vanity and the excessive amount of pomade it took to keep up the impressive ebony mane. Yet they respected him. It was not only Franc's size, but his whole demeanor that manifested a rough-and-tumble authority. Martin was as tall as Franc, medium height, but much thinner. According to the rigid hierarchy of the

Palais de Justice, Martin was Franc's superior. Yet, sitting beside the physically powerful and self-assured man, Martin felt like a boy. He tried to quell these feelings by concentrating on his surroundings.

They made a slow, mostly silent ascent along the stony white road, past farmhouses with red tile roofs, yellowing vineyards, and groves of crooked, silver-leafed olive trees. In the distance, the luminous limestone hills jutted up toward a cloudless blue sky. Everything struck Martin as too bright, almost unnaturally so. It was nothing like the north where he had grown up.

At first it was a relief to turn onto the Bibémus road, which cut through a sheltering forest of pines and oaks. But the narrow stony road was steep, and as the pace of the mule slowed, Martin's anxieties mounted. He kept thinking about what lay waiting for them in the quarry. He loosened his collar. He was thirsty and finding it harder and harder to swallow. At last, the cart reached a plateau that was covered with rocks and brambles, and drew to a halt. Only a few misshapen parasol pines grew out of this barren plane, their trunks and feathery green branches bowing in one direction, as if in a permanent state of mournful submission to the *mistral*, Provence's fearsome winter wind. The only sounds were those of the insects, all about, screeching, buzzing, and whining.

"We're almost there," said Franc, climbing down. He looked around for a moment, then pointed toward a line of red-orange rocks and boulders. "This way, I think, sir. We'll need to carry the body back up, but don't forget to look for anything else a killer might have left."

Martin followed the older man's lead, steadying himself with one hand on the rough sandstone as they zigzagged down a path. The pounding of his heart had little to do with the exertion. But it was only after he slipped that he understood the full measure of his fears. He looked down, half expecting to see blood. Instead, he saw that the stones beneath his feet had been shined smooth by centuries of wayfarers like himself. Fortunately, Franc seemed too involved in the hunt to take note of his clumsiness. The inspector moved with the agility of an animal stalking his prey, sniffing and alert. At last he came up with something. Curled up amid the branches that jutted out from the rocks was an artist's canvas. Or, rather, a small piece of one. For as Franc unrolled it, they could see that someone had torn apart a crude painting of bent pine trees and great orange boulders. Franc studied the fragment for so long that Martin asked him if he knew who had done it.

"Not quite sure, sir, but I have my suspicions." Franc folded it up and put it in his pocket. Then he pointed to a second rocky path, which brought them to their destination, unmistakable in its eerie desolation.

Here it was not nature that showed the destructiveness of her force, but man. Below them, literally carved out of the plateau, stood gigantic geometric towers and caves, free-floating steps and walls, curved arches and tunnels; the remains of the greedy hunt to provide the material for Aix's great honey-colored houses. So fantastic was the quarry's jumbled architecture that Martin imagined that he was looking at the long-abandoned building blocks of some gigantic, ancient gods. The colors, too, were outlandish. The stones glowed orange and red and purple in the setting sun. Everywhere, branches strained and twisted to release themselves from the lifeless stone, reaching for the light in an array of black and yellow-greens.

Franc slithered down steplike indentations that had been excised by a quarryman's pick and began his search. It did not take them long to find her. The first thing they saw was her dress. White with green stripes, just like the boy said. With a start, Martin remembered where he had seen it. Across the cathedral square during the Virgin's procession, under a parasol. Undoubtedly the same parasol Franc would bring to him at the courthouse.

She lay in shadow and light, half-hidden by the remains of the quarrymen's work. As Martin approached, he saw an unmistakable sign that it was she. Her hair, unbound, shining under the rays of a merciless setting sun, looked like it had burst into flames. That magnificent golden-red hair, which he had always seen pinned up, rising gracefully from her long, white neck. Beneath her now, radiating from her shoulder to her waist, was a pool of dark blood, long dried by the heat.

Martin wanted to reach down to drive the buzzing flies from her body, but he could not move. By contrast, Franc paid little regard to ceremony. Putting his booted foot under her waist, the veteran rolled her over. And then Martin saw her face, that once-beautiful face, now locked forever in a grotesque death mask. *My God*, thought Martin, *this is not right*. The day's sensations, like the shooting rays of the sun, overtook him with furious intensity. Where he had once caught a whiff of perfume, he now smelled human remains. The heat, the odor of death, and the incessant rasping of the cicadas were making him dizzy. Afraid he would be sick, he let himself drop to a seat provided by a boulder.

"Did you know her, sir?"

"What?"

"I asked if you knew her."

"Yes . . . no, not really." Both answers were true. And what little he knew of her, he was not about to tell Franc.

"You know who she is, then."

Martin nodded and buried his head in his hands, willing his nausea to subside. Barely managing to raise his voice above the roar of the cicadas, he mumbled, "It is Solange Vernet."

Martin had met Solange Vernet early that spring at a bookstore near the Hôtel de Ville. He had gone to look for a recent edition of *The Origin of Species*. Because he did not yet know the political sentiments of the bookseller, he searched for it himself among the collection of books on science. He found Solange Vernet reading the store's only copy of the book at the back of the store. So concentrated had she been, her white hat hanging by a green satin ribbon around her neck, parasol leaning against the wall, brow furrowed with diligence, that she hadn't even noticed him until he was almost upon her. But she did not jump or back away. She smiled. A beautiful smile, warm and mischievous at the same time.

"Could you be looking for this?" she asked, turning her attention from the book to his face.

Martin backed away, demurring, insisting that—

"No, please," she interrupted. "We have a copy in English at home. I was only interested because. . . . Look here, see." With one white-gloved finger she pointed to the title page. "It is translated by a woman, Clémence Royer. I heard her give a series of lectures on philosophy and science in Paris."

"Yes," Martin answered, "very brilliant, isn't she? But also something of a scandal, no?" hoping that by conveying this knowledge he would conceal how much he shared the opinions of those who hooted and howled at the very idea of a woman speaking in public about such matters.

"You've heard her, then? You've lived in Paris?"

"Only for three years. I was at the Law Faculty, spending most of my time being boring, I fear, while studying for my exams."

He often asked himself why he had said so much. He kept coming back to the admission that he had wanted this woman, this beautiful stranger, to argue against his modest assessment. He remembered that her eyes, so merry and direct, were green, and that they matched the emeralds in her earrings. Never had he noticed this much about a woman before.

"Very well, then, you must have this," she said as she thrust the volume into his hand. Then she introduced herself and invited him to one of her salon gatherings on Thursday evening. "Cours Mirabeau, 57, second floor. At eight," she said. "Men of letters and learning of all opinions." Professor Westerbury, she explained, was the leading voice of the group. He was the Englishman whose name appeared on posters all over town, announcing separate lectures on geology for ladies and gentlemen. Without waiting for Martin's answer, which surely would have been some kind of an excuse, Solange retied her hat, saying that she had to go. Then she put one gloved hand upon his. "Really, you must come. You could be one of the interesting ones."

Neither her smile nor her eyes told Martin whether she was praising or mocking him. Now he would never know.

He had not gone to any of her "Thursdays." Since that day, he had seen her only from afar, always recognizable by the boldness of her carriage and the glimmer of that mass of shining, golden-red hair. Usually he had spotted her on the Cours. But he also saw her entering or leaving the Madeleine Church as he went to the Palais de Justice, or out for a Sunday stroll. The last time he had seen her was only a few days ago, at the procession for the Feast of the Assumption. He watched from across the cathedral square as she crossed herself and genuflected as the statue of the Virgin passed. What kind of woman reads Darwin and kneels before the Virgin?

"Sir?" Franc was addressing him and holding up a religious medal hanging by a thick white string cord. "Looks like a crime of passion. Someone tried to strangle her with this. I found it wrapped around her neck. And then he stuck a knife in her."

"But why?" Why? What a lame and childish thing for a judge to say, or even think. Fortunately, it did not give Franc pause.

"Who knows? That's what I was saying, sir. I've been keeping an eye on her and her paramour, that Englishman Westerbury, ever since they came to town. Never trusted him. Seemed like a charlatan. And her," he shook his head with distaste. "A loose woman with lovers, trying to set herself up as some kind of lady. And then she has the nerve to wear the Virgin's medal." He gave it one last look before he pocketed it. "We don't need that kind of Parisian behavior down here."

"How do you know she had lovers?" Martin hoped he did not sound too curious.

"That's my job, sir. To keep the town clean and quiet. So when people like that come in, I watch. I can probably get you the whole list of the professors and big shots that hung around their apartment. But I've also got my own personal suspicions." Franc patted the pocket of his jacket holding the folded canvas. "I saw her hanging around with the banker's son, Cézanne. The one who calls himself an artist."

"Mme Vernet and this Cézanne, alone?" Martin stole a quick glance at the body of Solange Vernet, a pious woman with lovers.

"Yes, at least once outside the apartment, and who knows what took place inside. I wonder what the Englishman thought about that."

"Or if he even knew," Martin added quietly.

"Right, sir. Or what he did when he found out." Franc gave him an encouraging look, as if to say, now you're on the right track.

Neither the buzzing in Martin's head nor the nausea had let up. Still, he needed to be in charge. "I take it you did not find the knife?" he managed to ask. "We should be looking for it while there is still some light."

Franc nodded his assent, and they began to search.

Martin was relieved to move away from the remains of Solange Vernet. They scoured the quarry for almost an hour. Finally they had to give up. There was no lamp on the wagon, and they needed to get back to town while they could still see the road. Martin told Franc to make sure that his men were in full force the next day and to send some of them back to continue the search.

Then the grisly task began. Franc took Solange Vernet by the shoulders, while Martin folded her dress around her feet, firmly holding her ankles together. Under Franc's less tender care, her head hung back almost out of Martin's sight. He was grateful not to have to catch glimpses of her swollen face.

Concentrating as hard as he could on keeping his footing and holding together the folds of her dress, he almost managed to block out the smells and sounds around him. It was with tremendous relief that he finally joined Franc in hoisting Solange Vernet's body into the cart, and covered it with an old blanket. After these silent rites, Franc began to brush the dirt of the quarry off of his clothing. Martin tried to follow suit, but his hands were so sweaty that he only succeeded in pasting the orangish-red dust more securely onto his jacket. Finally, they mounted the seat of the cart.

Martin stared straight ahead as Franc maneuvered the mule back onto the Bibémus road. He tried to calm his breathing and to block the image of what lay behind them. Fortunately, Franc was in the mood to talk. Martin was not sure whether the inspector's loquacity was an act of kindness, designed to take his mind off the mutilated body of Solange Vernet, or whether the veteran was simply attempting to impress him. It didn't matter. He was grateful for the diversion.

Franc had fought against the Prussians in 1870, which, he told Martin, explained why one murdered corpse did not bother him very much. Franc had seen things. Terrible things. Trees cracking overhead in the heat of battle. Comrades fallen. Women raped. Children hung on bayonets. Faces blown off. And you can be certain, he assured his listener, that he had made many a Hun pay for his sins. He recounted his heroic exploits in great detail.

Although Martin could feel their hideous cargo rolling from side to side with every jolt of the wagon, he tried to demonstrate an interest in Franc's war stories by reporting how, as an eleven-year-old boy, he had watched all of Lille panic when the Prussians crossed the border, and how hard his mother had cried when his father went off to defend their home. In the end, the German armies bypassed the fortified city, and his father, a meek, bespectacled clockmaker, never saw battle. He would die two years later, in his bed.

Compared to Franc's boastful stories, this seemed insignificant. But it wasn't. It only reminded Martin of the death that had done so much to determine the course of his life. He could still see his father, lying in bed, surrounded by the flickering wake candles. He would always remember the smell of incense, the odor of a sanctified death, and the sobbing relatives. He had not cried. It would have been unmanly. He had promised his father that he would comfort his mother, so he saved his tears for his walks in the woods, where no one else could see or hear. How he had missed their little private jokes, and his father's constant praise and embraces, and gentle admonitions to continue to do well, to do right always.

Martin's father had been a kind man. Perhaps too kind. He had not managed his property well. After his death, they discovered that far too much of his income had gone to indulge his wife's wishes and in loans to poor employees, which would never be repaid. His debts had made Martin and his mother dependent on her wealthy relatives. Martin glanced over to Franc. In a world of brute facts and evil deeds, there might be something to learn from a man of Franc's experience. A man who, unlike Martin, confronted death without being affected by it.

By the time they reached Aix, the town was already shrouded in darkness and the intrepid inspector was expounding on why it was important for them to solve the case before the other judges and prosecutor reappeared. Martin and he, Franc observed in a confidential tone, were both outsiders who had come to Aix to seek their fortunes. If it hadn't been for the war and the new world it opened to him, Franc explained, he would have never escaped the poverty of his native village. Solving this murder case could make him a *commissaire*, a man that everyone would have to look up to. That's as high as he could ever hope to rise. But Martin, Martin was young and educated. Even though he came from the opposite corner of France, there was no telling how far this case could take him. It could get him on the promotion list for a post in the north, near his family, or even in Paris, if that is what he wanted.

Martin was not sure what he wanted except, finally, to be his own man. He had not come from the opposite end of the country by chance. He came to escape the entanglements that threatened to pull him in directions that he did not want to go. His heart lay with the democratic ideals he once shared with his oldest friend Merckx. But Merckx's descent into anarchism and his increasingly violent harangues against the rich and powerful had become more and more troubling, even dangerous, for Martin, who had pledged to uphold the law. And then there were the rich and powerful themselves, the DuPonts, who had sponsored his schooling and expected him to ask their eldest daughter for her hand. This marriage would guarantee Martin status and wealth. As long as he was willing to accede to the reactionary opinions that went with it.

Martin fervently believed that he could find a middle way, a reasonable way between reaction and anarchy. Much to Merckx's scorn, Martin had chosen to be a judge rather than a lawyer dedicated to defending the poor, because the magistrature was a safer path for someone without family money. Unlike Merckx, he believed in the Republic. He believed that if everyone held on to its ideals of *liberté, fraternité,* and *egalité,* justice was possible for everyone, rich and poor alike.

These are things he would never say to Franc. Or anyone else in the snobbish inbred world of the Palais, where the Proc and the other judges regarded Martin almost as a foreigner, worthy of handling only the most minor and sordid cases. The inspector was right about one thing, Martin thought as the cart jolted to a halt in front of the massive courthouse: solving a murder case was a way to win respect. But at what price? To think of personal ambition while Solange Vernet's corpse was rotting behind him filled him with disgust.

"With your permission, sir," Franc said as he laid down the reins, "I'll let you off here and take the body to the prison myself."

"Fine, Franc. Thank you." Martin was grateful that the inspector was releasing him from the miasma of death and decay that was enveloping the stilled wagon. At least he had the presence of mind to ask Franc if he knew where Riquel, the biology professor who performed autopsies for the police, might be.

"If he's in town, I'll find him tonight," Franc promised. "As soon as I lay the body out on a slab."

The body. Already she was only a body.

"And I'll send the boys to find the lover first thing in the morning," Franc continued, in full command, eager to begin the investigation. "And I'll get ahold of Old Joseph for you." Franc had thought of everything, even Martin's clerk. The courthouse had quite naturally assigned its oldest and most decrepit *greffier* to Martin. As such, Joseph Gilbert was unlikely to be out of town.

Martin offered his hand, and Franc took it eagerly.

The handshake sealed their partnership.

Swaying as if drunk with the flood of images that the inspector's bluff conversation no longer deterred, Martin headed toward the cathedral. When he turned a corner, out of Franc's sight, he grabbed at his stomach. Unable to hold it in any longer, he bent over and vomited into a sewer. Then he wiped his mouth with his sleeve, leaned against the wall, and took several deep breaths. The gaslight lamps cast strange shadows on the narrow, empty streets, but his ears were no longer assaulted by the buzzing of insects. Instead he heard the comforting, civilized sounds of Aix's many fountains, gurgling, as they brought the city's famous waters up from the earth. Martin took advantage of this bounty at the side of the cathedral, cupping his hands and filling his mouth with the cool, clear liquid. He dipped into the stone fountain again and again, washing his hands and face until the water poured over his beard and ran in rivulets under his collar. He watched as the grit of the quarry swirled away from him.

"Ashes to ashes, dust to dust." So said the priests, and his mother, quite often. But even she knew it was not so simple a process.

Martin took a few steps back to look up at the great church and caught a glimpse of a smiling statue. When he was a boy, his mother had taken him to many churches, in an endless search for the right altar, the right saint, and the one prayer that would grant her a second child. At every stop she taught him lessons of faith and morality.

"Look, my boy," she once instructed, pointing to a beautiful figure on the façade of some great church. "She represents the impious Worldly Woman. Her smile seems so comely, so benevolent, but look here." She had made him twist around so he could see the serpentine figures etched on the back of the statue. "See those worms eating at her. It happens to all of us, of course, when we die. The body rots. But this, this is what happened to her soul—and the soul of everyone who touched her, who was corrupted by her, when she was alive!"

Martin smiled, remembering the nightmares that lesson had inspired. He had been too young to understand the allure of worldly temptations. So contrary to his mother's intentions, he had become far more frightened of the consequences of earthly death than of spiritual decay. Today he had witnessed that natural reality in the poor human body of Solange Vernet. Had he also seen proof of her spiritual corruption? As he turned toward his room, Martin wondered what kind of dreams he would have that night.

Wednesday, August 19

Judges of Instruction are a Pouncing sort of race.
—Nicolas Freeling, *Flanders Sky*

2

"Wake up, wake up, M. Martin." The rough hand of Louïso shook Martin into consciousness. "You must have had quite a night," the old woman muttered in her Provençal drawl. "Your bedcovers are all over the place." Martin struggled to focus on the gnarled, disapproving finger pointing down at him. As he lifted his eyes, he caught sight of an empty wine bottle and lump of stale bread held firmly against Louïso's ample chest. He groaned as he recognized the debris from his table. No wonder the Picards' day woman was in such a bad temper.

"I did not think you would want to sleep all day, so I brought you some bread from the baker and made you a bowl of *café au lait*," she continued. "I'll leave you so you can get dressed." Before Martin could respond, she turned and, swaying heavily from side to side, headed out the door.

Martin leaped out of bed and opened the shutters. The bright sunlight confirmed his fears. He was late. He slumped down in the chair in front of his table. His first murder case, and he felt terrible. It was that wine, drunk to get him through the night without thinking about the grotesque being that Solange Vernet had become. Martin grabbed the covers lying on the floor and flung them onto the bed. Even with the wine, Solange Vernet had still managed to haunt his dreams, mouthing soundless pleas that he could neither hear nor answer.

Martin's hand trembled slightly as he reached for the bowl of coffee and milk, but as soon as he got it to his lips, he drank greedily. Once he had consumed half the bowl, he set it down and began to tear at the bread, stuffing it in his mouth to settle his stomach. Today he must try to answer Solange Vernet's pleas. Today he might confront her killer. He needed all his wits about him.

Martin dressed, not even bothering to wash up, and dashed out. He deliberately avoided the cathedral district and the images it might evoke. While moving at a fast pace, he forced himself to clear his mind and remember: what were the main points of the lectures that he had attended on the art of interrogation? Put the suspect at ease. Make him think you are on his side. Listen. Take the measure of his character. If you know his character, you will understand the motive. If you understand the motive, then you will understand the crime. And when he makes a false step, pounce! Yes, and, most importantly, trust in your instincts. Martin was not certain how he was going to fulfill this last dictum. Reason and patience were what had always gotten him through. He often wondered if he had any instincts. Or imagination.

Martin's route took him past the open market in front of the Hôtel de Ville, where farmers and their wives proclaimed the virtues of their fruits and vegetables to anyone who would listen. Women carrying baskets bumped into Martin as they hurried to their favorite stands to inspect the produce and haggle over prices. After the quiet days following the Virgin's feast, it was good to see the town come alive again.

Unfortunately, the aura of renewed vitality did not follow Martin to the more sedate square that stretched from the great Madeleine Church to the Palais de Justice. The sight of the massive courthouse always made Martin's heart sink a little. His friend Merckx surely would have pointed out how much the broad pretentious façade, with its eight over-sized columns, resembled the entrance to the Bourse, the Parisian stock exchange where the nouveau riche made their fortunes by exploiting the labors of the poor. Of course, the builders of Aix's Palais de Justice had intended to convey a much loftier purpose, a courthouse dispensing the greatest legal system known to man. Yet social distinctions were impressed upon those who entered the Palais every step of the way. The wealthy arrived directly at the main entrance in their carriages via a narrow cobblestone driveway that arced around the back of a set of low stairs. Aix's lesser citizens reached the courts by climbing those stairs and crossing the narrow driveway designed for the privileged. As they made their way, the middling and poor were forced to pass between two large statues of famous jurists, forever seated in stony judgment of them and their woes.

Today, neither rich nor poor had been summoned to the Palais. The public entrance was closed for the holidays, so Martin headed for the back door, where a gendarme let him in onto the ground floor. A stair-case led him up to the grandiose main floor, and to more reminders of how the pretensions of the powerful overrode the egalitarian ideals of the Third Republic.

The majestic central atrium was a great open space surrounded by a two-story marble peristyle. The courtrooms rimmed the peristyle on the main floor. The second floor held the cloakrooms and meeting rooms for the judges and defense attorneys, as well as the magis-trates' offices. Martin's footsteps made a hollow sound on the marble floor as he crossed over to the grand staircase. If trials had been in session, he would have been threading his way through a crowd of self-important black-robed jurists, flying up and down the stairs and crisscrossing the atrium like a flock of cawing, rapacious crows. Martin hated the way they ostentatiously noticed and greeted only each other, while their prey—their poorer compatriots—sat anxiously on the benches outside the courtrooms, waiting to be defended, prosecuted, and judged.

Martin barely had time to shake off these dreary thoughts before duty confronted him in the hunched, thin person of his law clerk. Old Joseph was waiting at the top of the stairs to warn him that he had visitors. "A Mr. Charles Westerbury, sir," Joseph whispered in his ear. "M. Franc brought him in earlier this morning." When Martin straightened up, he saw Franc standing over a man seated on a bench, holding his head in his hands. Martin's first suspect.

The inspector left his charge and hurried over to meet Martin at the head of the stairs. "I picked him up, sir, about eight this morning, having coffee just as calm as you please, with the dead woman's maid. He's seen the body. Showed some shock, but I can't tell if it was fake or not. I tried questioning, but couldn't get anything out of him. I am sure you can handle his type better than me, sir, being an educated man yourself."

While Franc spoke, Martin gazed down the hall at the hapless suspect, who returned his stare. He was trying to remember if he had ever seen Westerbury with Solange Vernet.

"Would you like me to observe the interrogation, in case there are contradictions?"

"No," Martin responded quickly. "That won't be necessary." He did not need the inspector's help to do his job. Even if he did, he was not about to show it. "Have you sent the men to the quarry? Do you have the medical report?"

"The men went out this morning, and the report is on your desk. Riquel thinks that she has been dead no more than a day."

Martin nodded. That seemed right. The maggots had not yet taken over the swollen corpse of Solange Vernet. "And the material evidence?"

Martin asked without taking his eyes off the man who might be her murderer.

"I'll bring those up later. I didn't want to carry them along while I was bringing—" The inspector jerked his head in the direction of Westerbury.

"Yes, right. Good idea." Franc was full of good ideas. Martin was going to have to work hard to stay a step ahead of him. Martin took a deep breath. It was his turn. "Very well," he said, "we will talk later."

Even the bullheaded Franc should have recognized this as a dismissal, but he still had to offer one last piece of advice. He lowered his voice. "Don't forget, sir, to ask him about the money. They were living like kings." Then, with a little military tip of his cap, he headed toward the stairs.

Their conversation had given Old Joseph time to reach Westerbury. Martin saw the clerk's head of sparse, wispy white hair bob up and down as he explained something to the suspect. When Martin reached the door of his chambers, the Englishman stood up to meet him. They stared at each other for just an instant. Could this be the man who strangled and stabbed the beautiful Solange Vernet? Martin thought, before he dropped his gaze in order to conceal the excitement and disgust that had suddenly overtaken him.

He invited Westerbury into his chambers and asked him to sit in one of the two wooden chairs that faced his large mahogany desk. Martin passed a wall lined with law books on the way to the chair behind his desk, while Old Joseph took a seat at a small table in an alcove. The clerk sat with his back to the suspect and was ready almost at once to take notes. Martin, on the other hand, took his time settling in; getting out his pen, then ink, then paper, and thumbing through the documents on his desk. Of course, it was all an act. Even if he wanted to absorb what Dr. Riquel had written, he could not. The words on the medical report were swimming before his eyes. His performance was calculated to show Westerbury who was in charge, as well to give himself time to figure out where to begin.

He glanced up to find Westerbury staring blankly past him through the large window that opened onto the Palais square. From where the Englishman sat, there was really nothing he could see. His legs were crossed, hands sitting atop one knee. If this pose was an attempt to appear nonchalant, a slight trembling of the fingers gave the suspect away.

Westerbury's attire, a gray frock coat and matching top hat that he had placed beside himself on the second wooden chair, indicated that the professor must have been something of a dandy, perhaps even a lady's man. But now he looked ordinary, even bedraggled. He was taller than average, with fair skin of the English type, balding gray-blond hair, and watery blue eyes. A wrinkled striped silk cravat, which he or someone else had yanked loose during the morning's proceedings, added to the general impression of dishevelment. There was no dash, no sparkle. Martin would have to revive Solange Vernet's lover if he were going to get anything out of him. So he set out, despite the nervous fluttering in his own chest, to do as his law professors advised and put the suspect at ease.

"Mr. Westerbury," he began, in a tone of gentlemanly solicitude, "do you understand the French legal system?"

"I'm not sure I know what you mean." The Englishman mumbled his reply, barely opening his mouth.

"Well, let me explain. I am what in our language we call a judge of instruction. In your country," Martin said slowly in English, "I would be called 'an examining magistrate.' M. Gilbert," he pointed to Old Joseph's hunched back, "is my greffier. He will take down our interview, although I will also be taking notes. You will get to read his summaries later." Westerbury's gaze remained focused on some blank space behind Martin's left ear. There was nothing else to do but forge ahead. Martin cleared his throat. "Usually when making an inquiry into a violent death, you would first be dealing with someone like Inspector Franc, whom you met this morning. Then you might talk to a prosecutor. Since we are in the summer doldrums," he said with a shrug, hoping to convey a sense of shared sophistication about such matters, "we are skipping the middle man. In any case, you would eventually have to speak to me or one of my peers, for it is up to us to take down testimonies, examine all the evidence, and decide if the case should go to court—which this one surely will. We organize all the evidence into an official dossier and decide who will be charged with the crime. If the court determines that the murder was premeditated, the punishment will be the guillotine. If, on the other hand, we determine it was merely a crime of passion—"

"*Good God*!" Westerbury exploded in English. Martin could not decide whether this was for show or whether the man could have been so naïve as to not realize, until that moment, that he was a prime suspect. At least now he had the Englishman's attention.

"But of course, I'm sorry," Martin said, "you've had a terrible shock this morning. Are you all right?"

"The woman I love has been murdered and mutilated. Of course I've had a shock." The Englishman spoke in precise, clipped French, a red vein of indignation rising from his neck to his forehead. "Do go on. Let's get this over with."

"Of course." Martin uncorked his ink bottle, paused to gather his thoughts, then looked up at Westerbury. "Let's start with you. May I see your papers?"

The Englishman reached into his pants pocket for a thin leather wallet holding a tattered document. He stood up and gave it to Martin. The card certified that Charles William Westerbury had been born in 1845 in Liverpool. Occupation: Geologist. Emigration date: March 1875. The only other French residence listed was Paris. Martin removed the Englishman's identification card and handed the wallet back to Westerbury. "I'll need to hold on to this," Martin explained, "until the investigation is over."

"I don't see why. I'm not going anywhere until you find—"

Martin ignored this objection and, with a wave of his hand,

motioned for Englishman to sit down. This was Martin's first miscalculation. Westerbury obeyed, but his folded arms and grim pursed lips indicated that he had taken Martin's unthinking dismissal as an insult. So much for putting the suspect as ease. Martin needed to keep reminding himself that most of the witnesses in this extraordinary case would not be the humble and obedient sort that usually ended up in his chambers. He'd have to proceed with care.

"Mr. Westerbury," he began again, "did you study your science at Oxford or Cambridge?"

"No, not exactly."

"At another English university?"

"No. I am mostly self-taught."

Martin tried his best not to react, although this bit of information seemed to confirm Franc's accusation that the Englishman was a charlatan.

"But," Westerbury hastened to add, "I have heard the great Lyell himself lecture. I've studied Darwin. I can assure you that I know my craft."

"Yet your advertisements say 'professor.'"

"I thought we were investigating Solange's murder." The tone was righteous.

"Just so. But you have made quite a stir here. And I assume you also lectured in Paris."

"I may not have come from the leisured classes, *monsieur le juge*, but I do believe that I can play a role in the great controversies of the day." Westerbury leaned forward as he made this pronouncement, emphasizing Martin's title with unwarranted sarcasm. He sat back as he continued. "And Solange was going to help."

"Let's return to that later," Martin said dryly, making every effort to hide his irritation. If arrogance was an integral part of the Englishman's character, Martin was going to have to work hard to hide a nascent dislike for the suspect. "For now, can you explain exactly what your role in these controversies might be?"

"To reconcile the claims of science and faith."

Merely that, Martin thought, but did not say it. He waited a moment for Westerbury to explain. Evidently, however, the Englishman felt that his declaration of lofty ambition required no elaboration.

"Mr. Westerbury, if I may ask, why France? Why not teach in your own country?" Martin tried to say this without any hint of sarcasm or accusation. He did not want to put his suspect on guard.

But he was, inevitably. Great scientists do not ordinarily have to leave home to ply their trade in foreign cities. Changing his demeanor, Westerbury looked directly at Martin, as if he were trying to show his willingness to be completely cooperative and truthful. "I am, as you note, not from the best schools. I am self-made, not a gentleman. I never could rely upon family wealth to support my studies. In England, a man who knows about the great works of English geology is not a novelty. Here, in France, he is. It was a way to make a living and to do what I love.

"And quite frankly," he continued, "what I do may be more necessary here than in my country. Your women seem almost afraid of science. Of nature. It's the way they're brought up, all sewing and catechism. They instill in their children a fear of sin and death, even of life itself. This is a barrier to progress, to scientific thinking. This is why I offer courses for women as well as men. I want the fair sex to understand that nature is beneficent."

The image of the corrupting Worldly Woman frozen in stone passed before Martin's eyes. So did the much more vivid picture of Solange Vernet, flies buzzing around her flesh in the quarry. Beneficent indeed. Could Westerbury really believe that, after seeing his lover's corpse?

"And Aix? What brought you here?" Martin kept his voice even and low.

"Two things, really. The great geologist Sir Charles Lyell worked in the environs of Aix briefly when he was very young. I wanted to continue and deepen that work. And then, we—Solange and I—wanted to go somewhere where we could start up again."

Martin wrote down and underlined the words "start up again." His hand was so hot and damp that it almost stuck to the paper. He wanted to open the window, but thought better of it. Surely the heat would discomfort Westerbury more than him. Martin put down his pen and leaned back in his chair, striving for a pose of intellectual curiosity, which he hoped would lull his suspect into revealing more about himself.

"This Lyell—excuse me, I am trying to understand—is he a follower of Darwin?"

"No, no. Quite the contrary. It would be more accurate to say that Darwin was a follower of Lyell. It was the reading of his *Principles* that inspired Darwin to write *The Origin of Species*. Although I must say that in his later years, Darwin never gave Lyell the credit he deserved." This fact seemed to arouse Westerbury's indignation.

"And what was it that Darwin learned from Lyell?"

"Look, is this really necessary—or relevant?" Westerbury clasped his hands together and looked impatiently at Martin.

"To be perfectly honest with you, at this point in the investigation, it is difficult to know what will be relevant. Perhaps your lectures upset someone." Martin did not really believe this, but the issue was not *his* veracity. It was Westerbury's. And whether or not the Englishman had any real claim to being a scientist.

"Very well," Westerbury took a deep breath before launching in. "Lyell taught Darwin—and all of us—about time. That it is unlimited. That you cannot measure the earth's age in the thousands of years, but rather in the millions, perhaps even billions, of years. And that over this vast period of time, changes in life forms could, and did, occur.

"Lyell demonstrated through his own explorations, and his incomparable eloquence, that if you allow yourself to really *see* the clues the earth so generously provides—the strata of great rocks, the imprints of fossils, the way mountains lean to one side or the other—if you use your own hands and eyes, you can almost feel the earth constantly reshaping itself." Westerbury was gesticulating, shaping a rugged landscape with his hands as he warmed to his subject. Poor Joseph was bent over in his alcove, scratching away, trying to keep up.

"What religionists don't like about Lyell's *Principles*," Westerbury continued, "is that he proved, once and for all, that the earth's surface is not transformed by catastrophes, like Noah's flood or a vengeful God raining fiery comets upon us. Change is slow, very slow, inevitable, and regenerative.

"I came here to complete his great work. To prove benign transmutation by showing how this preposterously beautiful landscape thrust itself up from an ancient sea." Westerbury slowly raised an open hand, imitating this infinitely long journey. He concluded in a whisper, no doubt repeating the dramatics of one of his lectures, "The sea that was once all there was to Aix-en-Provence." The Englishman had brightened up considerably. Whatever the validity of his "science," he certainly relished talking about it.

"But Darwin—" Martin interjected.

"Oh Darwin!" Westerbury burst out, as if the very name irritated him. "Everybody knows and admires Darwin. Or is afraid of him. As if he were the first person to talk about extinct life forms. Even his famous 'struggle for existence' came out of Lyell's *Principles*. Only Sir Charles understood it differently, less anarchically. Even when, at the end of his life, he came to agree with Darwin that Man was not a separate creation, even then he held out the possibility that there was a plan, a set of natural laws put in motion at the beginning. In the end, he was more like your Lamarck. Sir Charles did not believe that transmutation came about by chance. He held that only the very best of what was in creatures was saved and built upon. And Man is the very best of creatures. For now. For Sir Charles, the main point was that the earth would keep regenerating itself indefinitely in the same way it always had."

Martin found these ideas astounding. An English Lamarckian. He had thought that after Darwin, only the French would defend the eccentric ideas of their countryman, and only because he was one of their own. But then he knew little about these subjects, which had certainly not been taught in the Jesuit school he attended. He was, however, getting to know a great deal about Charles Westerbury, who felt a strong kinship with overlooked genius.

"So this is why you prefer Lyell to Darwin—you think he offers a way of reconciling religion and science?"

"Yes, he didn't ask us to choose between God and Man. His views were larger than that. He was larger than that. He was, indeed, a greater man than Darwin. More generous, more able to change, to admit to others' insights. He didn't hole up in some country parish for most of his life. He traveled everywhere. Wrote for the common man. Talked to everyone."

"To you?" Now they were getting to it.

"Yes," Westerbury nodded. "Even to me. Once."

"And when was that? Were you one of his students?" Perhaps the Englishman had credentials after all.

"No. It was at a public lecture. I was a boy. A poor boy." Westerbury smiled to himself, as if recalling the innocence and possibility of that moment. "He patted me on the head."

"Oh?"

"Yes, my guardian took me to see him. My guardian was a vicar, who was, like half the clergymen in England, an amateur geologist, always tramping about the countryside collecting rocks and stones. I carried the basket." He smiled again. There were tears in his eyes.

"Were you an orphan?" Where, Martin wondered, did this amalgam of sentimentality, hero worship, and megalomania come from?

Westerbury paused for a moment, then came to a decision. "I might as well tell you. I am sure you have ways of finding out. My mother was his housekeeper. He took her in because she had been abandoned by the English sailor who brought her from France and left her pregnant, all alone, in the middle of Liverpool. Reverend Westerbury rescued her from the lying-in hospital. He was a very kind old man. He adopted me and gave me his name."

That explained Westerbury's excellent French. And his resentments.

"I see. Well, it's best we move on to other, more relevant matters." It was getting damnably hot. Whatever Westerbury's origins, his intellectual interests seemed quite sincere, if a little mad. It remained to be seen what part Solange Vernet had played in all this.

Martin loosened his own cravat a bit as he glanced at his notes. "You said before that you and Mme Vernet came to Aix to 'start up again.' Am I to understand that there was some trouble in Paris?"

"No, no, none of that," Westerbury gave him a defiant look. "I am sure you can check. And I'm sure you or your heavy-handed inspector will. But you won't find anything. Not even," more quietly, "not even trouble with the ladies. I've been entirely faithful to Solange. Entirely." Desperation clouded over his face. He took a handkerchief out of his vest pocket and wiped his forehead. His hand was trembling harder than before.

"All right, then, let's talk about your life in Paris for a moment," Martin said as he dipped his pen in the ink and wrote down a reminder to telegraph the *police judiciaire* in the capital, to see if they had anything on the suspect and the victim. "When did you meet Solange Vernet?"

"I met her five years ago at one of my lectures. Her real name was Sophie Vernet. She was born in some wretched village on the Seine, and she came to Paris to be a milliner's apprentice. When we met, she already owned her own shop." Westerbury paused at the end of this recitation. Then he added, "She had taught herself to read and write. She was really a quite remarkable woman."

From the little he knew of Solange Vernet, Martin had little doubt that she was, in some ways, quite remarkable. But if she had been a poor, uneducated country girl, how did she become the beautiful sophisticate he had seen in the streets of Aix?

"You say," he began, "that she was born in a wretched village and that she changed her name. Do you know why? Was she escaping some trouble?"

Westerbury opened his mouth, as if considering what his answer should be, then he shook his head. "All I know is that she preferred the name Solange. She never spoke of her native town."

"Yet you were together five years. I presume you wanted to know something about her past. Certainly she knew about yours, didn't she?" Martin prodded.

"Yes, I told her everything. But she always said that her past, her town was uninteresting," Westerbury mumbled, "that she only wanted to think about the present and the future. Our future."

For the first time, Westerbury held himself completely still. Stubbornly still. Either he did not know or was determined not to reveal anything about Solange Vernet's past, leaving Martin to wonder if it had given him a motive to kill her. Martin wrote down "S V background" even as he was deciding that there must be many reasons for murder between two lovers that were more obvious. Martin drew several circles around his notation. Who Solange Vernet really was and where she came from were mysteries he could delve into later. He decided to move on.

"Did you and Mme Vernet marry?"

"No."

"You lived in a free union?"

"In a manner of speaking. We loved each other and wanted to stay together. We decided to come here so that each of us could escape social prejudice. Especially Solange. No one would take her seriously as an intellectual in Paris, because she ran a hat shop. Here, well, here we could start anew."

"But that takes money." A motive that pointed to premeditation.

"Ah, yes," Westerbury answered in a weary tone, as if this were the question he expected. "It is true, the money came from Solange."

"She sold her shop, then?"

"Yes."

"And she was the one who bought the apartment?"

The Englishman nodded. "The apartment is in her name. You can check. I would not steal from a woman."

Martin certainly would check. "Who arranged the purchase?"

"Picard, the notary. He has an office off the Cours."

Martin wrote down the name of his landlord.

"And—I'm sure you'll find this out—there was a will."

"And you—"

"Yes, yes, most of it goes to me." Westerbury pulled hard at his collar. Even the self-proclaimed genius knew this fact did not help his case. A shirt button popped out and bounced along the wooden floor, without his taking note of it.

"Then you did not make a great deal of money from your lecturing."

"Not yet, but when I write the book—"

Martin cut him short. He had learned enough about Westerbury's scientific theories for the time being. "Let's stick with the immediate past, shall we? When did you arrive in Aix?"

"Just last February." Westerbury's voice was almost inaudible. Martin could almost hear an "if only" forming in the Englishman's mind. If only they had not come here when they did. If only, then what? What fatal series of events would not have occurred?

"Are there any other members of the household? Children?"

"Only the maid, Arlette LaFarge."

"You hired her here?"

"No, she came with us from Paris. She had worked in the shop. You see, Solange was worried about leaving her, and—"

"I will be questioning her," Martin assured him and wrote down the name.

"You see," Westerbury explained, "this shows the kind of woman Solange was. She was helping Arlette escape from a brutal marriage. She was very, very kind."

Martin shook his head. Was Westerbury's praise for his lover a sign that he was trying to cover up his own murderous rage? Or was it an indication of his undying love? And had Solange Vernet felt the same way? That's the issue that Martin was about to probe.

"And your days?" Martin asked, still in an even voice. "How did you spend them?"

Westerbury shrugged. "I wrote my lectures. Tramped around the countryside, looking for the best sites for geological investigations. Worked on my book on the beneficence of nature."

"And Mme Vernet?"

"She managed the household. She read. She hoped to get involved in charity work. But her greatest passion was putting together our social circle, a salon to discuss the great questions of the day on a regular basis. You see, she was truly a Frenchwoman. She told me she would not be following me about, like Lady Lyell or some other Englishwomen, 'holding a basket.' But she was learning how to mark and classify my finds."

Solange Vernet and a pile of rocks. It seemed an unlikely image. But what of Solange Vernet, the *salonnière*—trying to create a little bit of Paris in the provinces? "I'm interested in your acquaintances in Aix," Martin said. "Did you succeed in putting together this circle?"

"We met every Thursday. But," Westerbury paused, "you probably know that. You were the young judge she invited, weren't you?"

For a moment their eyes locked. Then the Englishman gave him a lopsided grin. "Solange and I did not have any secrets."

Just as in the quarry, Martin felt somehow found out by the recollection of his chance encounter. Westerbury's attitude did not help. The Englishman's squinting expression indicated that he was trying to piece together what Solange Vernet had said about Martin. The fact that Joseph chose this moment to clear his throat only increased Martin's discomfort. He had to keep on the offensive.

"I know this may be painful, but I need to ask if you and Mme Vernet were having any difficulties."

"No," Westerbury replied, a bit too quickly.

"I mean," Martin decided to work his way up to specifics, "did you ever quarrel? What about religion, for example? You yourself said that Frenchwomen were funny about that, and we found a religious medal on the body."

Westerbury winced and then recovered by going on the attack. "I'd like that back. It was her favorite. In fact, I would like all of her 'effects' back."

Martin sighed, to signal that *his* patience was coming to an end. He had to make it clear that in his chambers, only he, the judge, had the right to be the aggressor. "I would like an answer to the question: did you quarrel about anything? And more especially, did you quarrel recently? Within the last week?"

Westerbury shook his head.

"Well, that is surprising, isn't it?"

"I don't understand."

"From what you said, Mme Vernet was a strong-willed woman. Independent. Yet a Catholic. You, however, are a promoter of science. And a man with no visible means of financial support. What was the basis of your relationship?"

The Englishman rose, put his two hands on the front of the desk, and leaned toward Martin. "We *loved* each other." Martin caught a whiff of alcohol on Westerbury's breath, and saw a faint sneer pass over the Englishman's pale face. Martin could felt his own face redden.

"Come now. This is a murder investigation. More to the point," Martin pronounced each word with great precision, "you are a suspect. You can either answer my questions or I can hold you in prison for the next forty-eight hours."

"Barbaric country," Westerbury muttered to no one in particular as he resumed his seat.

"If I decide you are the murderer, you will rot in your cell until the trial," Martin added. This was more brutish than he liked to be, but he did not like Westerbury's attitude. He seemed to think that Martin had been some kind of coward or hypocrite because he had not come to their salon.

"Look," said Westerbury, retreating a bit, "Solange was an independent woman. And tolerant. She could believe in me and science at the same time that she believed in the saints and the Virgin Mary. It gave her comfort to think of them watching over her. She knew I was not here to tear down religion. I'm a deist, not an atheist. It doesn't have to be like it is, here in France. Here, if you declare yourself a republican you feel it necessary to reject not only the Church but any semblance of religious feeling. And yet men of your party like your women brought up by nuns. So they'll obey you, I suppose. But whom do they obey in the end? Their anti-clerical husband, or the parish priest who has the power to save their souls? Solange and I were striving for middle ground where science and religion, and men and women, could truly meet."

Although he did not like being lectured to by a foreigner, Martin had no riposte for this. He knew from his own experience that what Westerbury was saying was not far off the mark. But how in the world did a foreigner and a Parisian hatmaker come to believe they could change things?

"As for money," the Englishman continued, "it really wasn't an issue. You don't fall in love with a milliner for her money."

Not unless you yourself are penniless, Martin thought. Then he asked, "What about other men?"

"Solange was faithful to me, I'm sure of it. We told each other everything."

Martin gave Westerbury time to go on, but the Englishman chose silence. He picked up his hat and ran his fingers around the brim, turning it slowly. All that could be heard was the scratching of Joseph's pen, and then the scrape of the clerk's chair along the wooden floor as he shifted his position. Given Westerbury's eagerness to expand on other topics, Martin was sure the Englishman was lying about this one.

"Even if what you say is true," he paused so that Westerbury could absorb his skepticism, "we will still need a list of all your acquaintances."

"Surely you don't believe that any of them would—"

"Please give their names and professions slowly so that my clerk can record them accurately."

Resigned, Westerbury began describing his circle quietly and mechanically. The only women who attended the salon were an aspiring artist and the wife of a law professor, who attended with her husband. The other men, a dozen writers and professors and a bookdealer, seemed respectable enough, and probably all republicans.

When Westerbury stopped, Martin laid down his pen and waited. Westerbury kept turning his hat slowly in his hands. Finally, Martin insisted that he did not believe the list was complete. When the Englishman shrugged, Martin pounced. "What about Cézanne?"

Despite Westerbury's best efforts, Martin detected a flinch. Even Old Joseph turned around, sensing a dramatic confrontation in the offing.

After glancing from Martin to his greffier, Westerbury began. "We knew Paul Cézanne, but he was not, precisely speaking, a member of the circle. If you knew him, you'd know he is a misanthrope, a bear, someone who. . . ." The Englishman groped for the right words. "Someone who is not really fit for the kind of world that Solange wanted to create. She liked laughter. She loved what you French call *esprit*. She thought that if we all took ourselves too seriously, we would never agree on anything. Cézanne, God knows, takes himself very seriously."

Martin wrote down and circled the artist's name several times. "Then why was he a friend?"

"There you go," said Westerbury, pointing his hat at Martin's pen. "There you go. Here's an example of something that Solange and I could disagree about without getting angry with each other. She thought he was a misunderstood genius. She felt sorry for him. She wanted to encourage him. She was that way, you know, generous. There was nothing to be jealous of. I would not have minded even if . . . even if she had agreed to sit for him."

"Quite generous of you," Martin mumbled and looked up in time to see Westerbury scowl. "And what," he continued, "do *you* think of Cézanne?"

"Frankly, I think he is a bore."

"Capable of murder?"

This question seemed to catch the Englishman off guard. One could almost read his thoughts: Should he try to save himself by accusing his rival? Or would that be admitting to his jealousy? Martin sat very still as he waited for a response, hoping against hope for some reaction. A rash accusation. Or a theory of the crime. Anything. Even Joseph's pen did not move. Finally, Martin added, "What would you say if I told you we found a piece of a canvas in the quarry and that it may have been painted by Cézanne?"

"Nothing." Westerbury was breathing hard. "I would say nothing."

"Are you sure?"

The Englishman only nodded. Once again he began to stare out the window, drifting away into a sea of private troubles.

Martin straightened his position in his chair as he frantically rehearsed in his mind what he needed to ask about the days immediately surrounding the murder. "Mr. Westerbury, where were you on August 17th and 18th?"

"Tramping about Mont Sainte-Victoire. Trying to decide whether it should become the cornerstone of my work. I camped there overnight." This came out in a monotone.

"Alone?"

"Quite."

Martin wrote down "no alibi" and gave Westerbury time to consider his vulnerability on this issue. Silence.

"And Mme Vernet? Where do you think she was?"

"At home. The only thing she had planned for the week was to follow the Procession on the Feast of the Assumption. Most of our circle was out of town. So she was going to take the time to read and to write." He hesitated. "Letters."

"Do you have any of these?" said Martin, alert. The letters might offer some clues about Solange Vernet and her past.

"No, they were sent."

Sent. Gone. "You don't know what these were about."

"No, I don't." The Englishman's eyes were fixed on the floor.

"Then, when was the last time you saw Mme Vernet?"

"We were supposed to sup together, late, when I returned from Sainte-Victoire. But Arlette said she had gotten a message—"

"A message?" Martin asked sharply.

Westerbury shook his head. "There's no hope there. I got so worried when Solange was still gone this morning that I asked Arlette to tell me everything that happened before Solange left. She only told me that Solange had read the note, dressed, and rushed out of the house. She didn't recognize the boy who brought it, either."

"Did the maid see the note? Would she recognize the handwriting?" Martin's excitement was mounting.

Westerbury looked up at Martin. "She doesn't read."

Taking up his pen again, Martin wrote, "Search for message in Vernet apartment and at the scene. Look for the messenger." Then he set it aside. "Do you think that the note summoned Mme Vernet to the quarry?"

Westerbury shrugged.

"Were you in the habit of going to the quarry?"

"I've taken my students there to hunt for fossils and to show them the strata formations," the Englishman said with a weary sigh, "to give them some idea about the age of the earth and its powers of regeneration."

"Women?"

"Yes, women."

Cartloads of corseted women wandering with baskets and pickaxes? What did this man think he was doing? "And Mme Vernet? Did she ever go there?"

Westerbury's "yes" was barely audible. He was still clinging to his hat, which now hung between his legs.

"When? Why?" Martin spoke in short jabs to penetrate the pall that was fast descending over his suspect.

"A few times. For picnics. She considered it a good healthy walk. We'd picnic under the trees and then I'd take her to the rocks. She always laughed about all the adventures I must have had there with 'my ladies.'" Each word dropped from Westerbury's lips more slowly and more quietly, until he burst out again. "*Oh God*," he gasped in English. "*Oh God*, my beloved in that quarry. Do you know if she was violated? If she struggled?"

Martin shook his head, painfully aware of the unread medical report on his desk. As the Englishman began to weep uncontrollably, Martin considered what to do with him. Sweat was tickling Martin under his beard and collar, as much from anxiety as from the heat. Never before had he felt his own lack of experience and imagination more keenly. He had run out of questions, and he had not come close to proving anything. At least he did know some things about the Englishman, and that he had two classic motives for murder: money and jealousy. And yet, without prompting or a struggle, Westerbury had revealed the existence of a possible witness, the little messenger. Would a guilty man have done that?

Martin could, as he had threatened, throw Westerbury into prison. But that was Albert Franc's world. A world where the inspector would feel free to beat a confession out of a foreigner without a family to stand by and protect him. That was not what Martin wanted. He wanted a valid confession and the real killer, who could easily be the artist who was the banker's son. Since the man sniveling before him hardly seemed a danger to anyone, Martin decided to demonstrate that France was every bit as civilized as England.

When Westerbury regained his composure, Martin asked, "What was Mme Vernet's parish?"

"Madeleine," Westerbury whispered.

"Then you will want to send a priest to arrange a burial. You may also want to bring some fresh clothes to the morgue."

The Englishman nodded.

"You may go now."

Dazed, Westerbury pushed himself up from the chair and put his hat on his head. "That's all?"

"No, I can assure you that this is only the beginning," Martin said, trying to sound cool and in command, while desperately hoping that he would do better in his next encounter with the Englishman. "Of course, you realize that if you leave town it will be taken as a sign of your guilt or complicity. And," he added, "I also expect that you will not threaten your maid in any way."

Westerbury backed slowly into the foyer. When he reached the door, he gave a little bow to Martin and Joseph before opening it and rushing out into the hallway.

Martin watched as the door swung shut. The next minute, Old Joseph was beside him, meekly offering his notes, pages and pages covered with spidery handwriting as wispy as the hairs on the old man's head. Martin took them with a sigh. It would take him all afternoon to decipher and analyze them.

"Would you like me to open the window, sir?" There was always a look of longing in the clerk's yellowing brown eyes, as if he wanted to prove that he was still useful.

"No, thank you, Joseph. I'd like you to go find Franc and tell him to have the Englishman followed. Then you can take the rest of the day off." When his clerk retreated and began to put away his things, Martin pushed out the window that overlooked the Palais square, letting in the voices of those going home for their midday meal. He watched until he saw the erect figure of Charles Westerbury emerge from the narrow street at the side of the courthouse, walking slowly and stiffly, as if he were putting his innocence and dignity on display for all to see.

3

WESTERBURY WAS, INDEED, CONSCIOUS OF the deliberateness of his movements. *Just one foot in front of the other, old boy,* he kept repeating to himself, *and soon you'll be out of sight.* Despite the wild pounding of his heart, he was not about to let them detect any signs of weakness. Especially not that brute of a detective. Nor that intolerable prig of a judge, always tugging at his neat little beard as if he fashioned himself to be some young Solomon. That clever glint in his eyes. Those little inquisitorial tricks up his sleeve. *Well, monsieur le juge, monsieur le petit juge, has a lot to learn before he can drag anything out of me.*

So concentrated was Westerbury on walking a straight line that he almost ran into a woman returning from the market with a recalcitrant child in tow. He bowed to apologize for hitting her basket, tipped his hat, and put on what he hoped was a winning smile. The woman's face was too blurred for him to know if she was one of his students. If not, who knew? For good measure, Westerbury patted the little brat on the head. *Life goes on. Must keep charming potential customers. Geology, anyone? Geology for the ladies?* Unfortunately, the woman drew her son away from him in a protective gesture and did not seem at all charmed. Westerbury knew then that he must look a sight.

As soon as the woman continued on her way, he made a sharp turn to the right, toward the apartment. Force of habit. He could not bear the thought of being surrounded by Solange's things. Nor did he want to listen to Arlette's wailing. He had to find a way to think things through, to wipe the image of Solange out of his mind.

Suspecting that he might still be under observation, Westerbury reversed his course with as much dignity as he could muster. When he got out his handkerchief to wipe the sweat from his face and dab at his eyes, he realized that he was still trembling. But he solemnly continued on, past the grand fountain in the center of the rectangle that divided the Palais square from the space in front of the Madeleine. This church, named for Jesus's whore, was where Solange had done her bit for charity. With luck, if the priests were not too hypocritical, they would allow her to be buried here as well. He'd let Arlette pick out a suitable dress and send her to the police with it. She'd like that. Arlette would light candles and keep the vigil. He would figure out how to survive until they probated the will.

But first he needed to find a drink. A strong one. Out of the way, where no one could see him.

When Westerbury turned into a side street out of sight of the courthouse, he picked up speed. Head up. Chin out. Like a ship parting the water. He cut past laundresses and porters carrying their loads, even a gentlewoman or two. It did not matter. They all passed just under his line of vision. He did not even bother to press himself against the buildings to let the carriages and wagons go by. He had a mission.

Finally, he reached the northern outskirts of the city. Just beyond what was left of the ramparts, he spotted a café, a workingman's establishment. It was the kind of place that he and Solange had avoided since their arrival in Aix. No one would know him there.

Once his eyes adjusted to the dark interior, he noted with relief that all of the tables were empty. The only inhabitant was a burly man in a dirty apron at the bar, busily wiping and setting up glasses for the afternoon clientele.

Westerbury laid his palms down upon the cool zinc counter and ordered an absinthe.

The barkeeper pushed a dish of sugar cubes and one of the glasses toward Westerbury, then reached under the bar for a spoon and a jug of water. Finally, he pulled down one of the brown bottles from a shelf behind him and poured out a few centimeters of green liquor. Westerbury took a sip. A small dose. But real. It burned a raw bitter path down his throat. "Good, very good," he nodded as he reached for the water and stirred some into the emerald fire. Then he downed the cool opalescent mixture in one long draught. "Another," he said, tapping his glass against the zinc.

The barman poured a second round of absinthe. It was a beautiful drink. And dangerous. Just one of the many bits of French wickedness to which he had introduced his lovely Solange. Westerbury ran his cooled hands across his burning eyes. He had never understood Solange's innocence. When he met her, she had seemed almost virginal. That had been part of the mystery, the enchantment. She was so beautiful and so innocent. Yet so French. Westerbury held up his glass to the light coming from the window. When he had first urged her to try it, he told her that absinthe, the green fairy, was the color of her eyes. "Hah." He covered his mouth to smother this bitter laugh. "I'm the green-eyed one, remember, *mon cher*? Me, me!" she had shouted during their last quarrel. "Let me play the jealous part. You are the foreigner that all the women love." Then she had pleaded with him, as if he were a child. "Listen to me. *Sois raisonable*. Please be reasonable!" He had never felt such rage before. And never had he been less reasonable.

He drank the second portion of absinthe in one undiluted gulp.

His coughing alerted the proprietor to his foolhardy transgression. Westerbury grabbed the jug and drank from it. The water dribbled down his neck. "Just a rough patch, old man," he explained in English, "just a rough patch." His companion lowered his arched eyebrows and shrugged, but he didn't take his eyes off his customer. Yes, Westerbury thought as he started to take some money from his pocket, what do the natives care as long as you pay the bills and don't break the pottery?

Westerbury lifted the brown bottle. There wasn't much left in it. "How much?" he asked.

Another shrug. "Four francs." Too much. "And—" the man pointed to the twice-emptied glass.

Before the barkeeper could finish his calculations, Westerbury slapped a ten-franc note on the counter. He had not come here expecting consolation from a stranger. Grabbing the bottle by its neck, Westerbury set out into the bright sunlight and continued up a hill, toward the mountain, away from the city.

This is where he would find his true consolation. From nature. If she could not help him at his time of greatest need, what good was she? Westerbury lurched as he climbed. He passed a few peasants and tinkers going to town. They made way for him, even though they had no idea who he was. Nor did they know the true history of the earth upon which they were treading. Besotted, priest-ridden lot.

When he reached the crest, Westerbury leaned his back against a great oak and let his body slide down the trunk so he could sit and observe. This is how he and Solange had first seen Mont Sainte-Victoire. They had hired a driver the day after arriving in town and asked him to find them the best view of the mountain. When they first caught sight of it, Westerbury had been so overcome by its shimmering white magnificence that he cried out. "Look, my love! Upon this rock I shall build my church!" Solange smiled and laid two gloved fingers upon his mouth, shaking her head. It was one of her signals, not to give offense to the driver with his blasphemy. Never to give offense. Not to Arlette. Not to anyone who was incapable of understanding. How very polite, how very French. Yet she had never been offended. She had always wanted to understand.

Westerbury took another gulp from the bottle. This is not why he was here: he was here to gain strength. To remember his purpose. To rid the world of ignorance and servile fear. Westerbury surveyed his surroundings. Sainte-Victoire, Holy Victory, indeed. The good Christians of Aix had named that great, beautiful mass of limestone after the triumphant slaughter of the barbarian hordes, whose pagan blood, they believed, still fertilized and colored their piece of the earth. They believed their God created the world in seven days. But Westerbury knew better. "No vestige of a beginning, no prospect of an end": that was what the great James Hutton, Lyell's teacher, said. How often had he repeated that to Solange, and to their initiates? "Your French geologists imagine that we are all dropping bit by bit into the ocean. But we English hold for perpetual renewal." "*Comment, mon cher?*" she would ask, right on cue. "How?" And he would explain: about the fiery center of the world. About the theories of vulcanists and plutonists. About the slow work of glaciers. About intrusion, upheaval, eruption. And, yes, about erosion. But only so that the earth could feed herself again in an endless cycle of renewal.

And Mont Sainte-Victoire, rising so incongruously, all by herself, was going to help him. Since that first day, he had explored her every facet, seen her every mood. He watched her changing colors from afar, searched for fossils on her highest reaches, picked at her lower regions for clues to her mysteries. She was his. Someday he would reveal how many millions of years it had taken to reach her full glorious height and what great subterranean forces had brought her there.

Westerbury drank more slowly. If he could just sit here for a while, watching the sun move over her face, he could regain his calm. He could think. In the noon light she shimmered white, silver, gray, blue. Just like—the memory invaded his consciousness with piercing clarity—just like Solange's body, above him, as they made love, the shafts of morning light streaming across her pale skin. He had told her, as he ran his hand up her back, that she was his mountain. Strong and pure and slowly rising to a spectacular peak, like Mont Sainte-Victoire.

"And what is this, *mon amour?*" She shook her hair and let it fall upon his shoulders, sheltering his face.

"Red and gold, pink and orange, like the strange Provençal soil," he answered. "You are the earth."

"And my eyes, *mon amour?*"

"Like the hidden, purest, primeval sea."

Then she would kiss him, cup his face in her hands, and ask, "And, *mon amour*, what are you?"

"I," he explained, "I am Pluto, the god of earth and fertility. I am all heat. I am coming to you and will make you rise with my molten liquids."

She would kiss him again. "*Mon sauvage,*" she would say, "Come here, *mon sauvage blond.*" And her eyes would close as he thrust upward. Sometimes she would whisper her invitation again and again, until, finally, he would gasp. And she would fall upon him. Gently now. All soft and warm. Hands around his face again. Eyes open, smiling, loving him.

"Oh God," he cried aloud, as he threw the bottle away. "Oh God," he covered his face with his hands. "How could I have been such a fool! What mere mortal deserved what we had? And I destroyed it.

"Help me now!" he shouted at the mountain. Help me now. But a mountain could not take back his words. Or his deeds. She had given him everything. Except for one thing. And that, in the end, had driven him mad. *Comment, mon amour, comment?* That *politesse*, that kindness.

What do you mean, *mon cher*? How would you like it? All, except for one thing. How he had longed to possess her completely. And when he found out about Cézanne, he had accused her. "What do you give him? Do you let him get on top?" That would be his eternal shame, the unkindest cut of all. Until the last knife thrust to her heart. Now nothing could be undone. Nothing. What a wretch he was. What a miserable, damnable wretch.

He was sobbing openly now. Solange was gone. There was no one to help him. Westerbury rose, using the tree trunk for support. This was no good. There was no forgetting. At least not today. He had things to do. He must talk to Arlette, explain the quarrel, and send her to the priest. And he must find Cézanne, the cause of it all.

4

"YOU LET HIM GO?" Franc shouted. No "sir" this time, only angry disbelief.

"I'm not sure that he is our man."

The inspector sank into the chair occupied six hours earlier by the sweating, fearful Westerbury. "Maybe we should find out where the Proc is hiding out and drag him here. Or get one of the other judges to help out."

The prosecutor was not due back for a week and a half and, as for another magistrate—"No," Martin said flatly. Definitely not that. To be pulled off his first important case? It would ruin him. No. Martin was going to solve the case, and solve it his way. With a reasoned, even-handed inquiry. At the very least, he needed to see what Cézanne had to say before charging the Englishman.

"I had Joseph put one of your men on Westerbury, thinking we could find out more that way than by having him rot in a cell."

"But by the time Old Joseph—"

"Yes," Martin put up his hand, "but he could not have gone far, and I did keep his identification card."

This precaution did not placate Franc, whose chest was still heaving with indignation. Martin decided to change the subject. "You searched the Vernet apartment?"

Franc shrugged. "This morning, while you were questioning our suspect. Nothing helpful, I'm afraid." He was beginning to retreat into a more appropriate attitude.

"Did you speak to the maid?"

"Tried to. She whimpered half the time, wailed the other half." Franc imitated a woman's high whining voice: "'Mme Solange, poor Mme Solange.'" He blew air out of his mouth in disgust. "Maybe after she gets over her hysteria—"

"Did she tell you that Mme Vernet received a note before going to the quarry?"

"No." Franc straightened up. "Who told you that?"

"Westerbury."

This small triumph was short-lived. "He could be lying."

"I don't think so," said Martin, standing his ground. "Did you look through any papers?"

"Yes. Bills, calling cards, that's about it."

"The purse?"

"Only a few coins."

"And the quarry?"

The inspector shook his head. "Me and the boys went over everything again. Found nothing. She was killed there, we know that. No trail of blood. But no knife either. And," Franc raised his eyebrows in amusement, "no other works of 'art.'"

"Very well," Martin said. In spite of the doubts that Franc had just aroused, he had to show who was in charge. "I've telegraphed Paris to see if they have anything on Westerbury and Vernet. Tomorrow I'll need to question the maid, and then Cézanne. If you or one of your boys could keep track of Westerbury. . . ." At least Franc refrained from delivering another reproach. "And" Martin reiterated, "let's not forget the note. Westerbury said that the message was delivered by a boy. We must find him. He may be a key—"

"If there really was a note, and if the killer did not get to him first. . . ."

"But if it was, as you say, a crime of passion, on the spur of the moment—" Martin stammered. He hadn't thought until that moment that an unknown child might be in danger.

"A murderer will do anything to cover his tracks."

And Martin had let Westerbury go. Cézanne was still out there. Martin's mouth ran dry. His mind raced. If the killer had argued with Solange Vernet in the quarry, if she had rebuffed him, surely she would be his only victim.

"Let's not get ahead of ourselves. I was only suggesting a possibility." Franc must have read the distress on Martin's face. "Like I said before, all my experience tells me it's a simple crime of passion. Nothing more. Committed by some weakling like your Englishman."

A possibility. A possibility that Martin needed to put out of his mind for the moment. He needed to stick to his plan. He fingered the medical report. At least Dr. Riquel's findings seemed to confirm the hypothesis that Solange Vernet had been killed in a moment of rage. She had also been raped.

"Did you tell Westerbury that Mme Vernet may have been violated?" Martin asked quietly. He was sure that Riquel had discussed the torn undergarments and traces of semen with Franc.

"No, I just question suspects to find out what they know. I don't give information unless I think it will get something out of them. As soon as he saw the body, he blubbered like a woman, and then he would not talk. Besides, who knows if it was really *rape*, considering the kind of woman she was?"

Martin had considered the kind of woman Solange Vernet had been and had come to different conclusions than his inspector. "Nevertheless, before you go home," Martin handed Franc a note, "could one of your men deliver this to Dr. Riquel? I am requesting that he not tell anyone about the rape. And I am asking the same from you. There is no reason why this has to be reported. It may only cause more panic, once the news of the murder gets out."

He had prepared this speech. The truth was that he did not want Solange Vernet to suffer this final public indignity unless absolutely necessary.

"If you say so." Franc paused for a moment, then said, "Sir, I was out of line—"

Martin held his hand up to signify that no apology was necessary.

"But," Franc continued, "this is the case that could make your career and mine. And, no matter what I said before, I'm sure we can do it. Together, before the Proc comes back."

"Yes, Franc, that's my hope too. But we have to be sure we have the right man."

The inspector hesitated before breaking the silence. "We'll find him," he said with quiet conviction, announcing an uneasy truce between them.

Franc had left the box of material evidence on Martin's desk. Martin did not dig deep to look at Solange Vernet's torn undergarments. That would have felt like another violation. Nor did he unfold the dress. He had already seen her blood. He only retrieved the medal that lay on top of the parasol. Wrapping the white cord around his hand, he took it over to the window to get a clearer look. It was the same one his mother wore, an emblem of the Virgin standing atop the world with the rays of the sun emanating from her hands. Under this image ran the familiar words "O Mary conceived without sin, pray for us who have recourse to thee." Had Solange called out to her Virgin for help in those last horrible moments? Or to God? Or had she just cried out in the pain and horror?

Martin clasped the medal hard in his hand, as if it could tell him what kind of woman Solange Vernet had really been. Had she been truly religious? Or a self-taught intellectual? Or, merely, a parvenu who had fashioned herself out of whole cloth, like one of the elegant hats she had made and sold to her wealthy customers? With a sigh, Martin dropped the medal into the evidence box and placed it in the wooden cabinet that stood against the wall across from his bookshelves. He closed the door, locked it, and carefully placed the key in his top drawer. He was done for the day. He had to find a way to forget for a while, to ignore the doubts that Franc had just aroused, about the boy and about Martin's ability to see through the lies and be tough enough to face down a killer. He needed a respite and longed to be among people for a time before returning to his solitary room.

So he headed to La Bonne Ménagère, a place where every evening bachelors gathered to enjoy the solid bourgeois fare, while they read the newspapers provided by the proprietors. When he walked in, Martin was relieved to see that at least here nothing had changed. Most of the diners were lost in their own thoughts, although a few acknowledged Martin's arrival with a silent nod. A top hat or bowler—and, for the older men, a walking stick and gloves—occupied the empty seats at the small tables. The couple who ran the restaurant never asked questions and never left their post, even in the most fearsome August heat. Most customers showed their appreciation by appearing several times a week. Although he could hardly afford it, Martin usually found comfort in the little restaurant's sedate atmosphere.

Tonight, however, he could not concentrate on the narrow, austere columns of yesterday's *Le Temps*. The case was stirring up his discontent. He was tired of being lonely and poor. He kept thinking about what "being among people" had meant only a few years ago in Paris, while he was studying at the Law Faculty.

It had been the only period in his life when he had given himself over to moments of pure frivolity and to previously unthinkable possibilities of pleasure. His fellow students, all richer and more sophisticated than he, had introduced him to the cafés of the Latin Quarter and to the *grisettes*, the working-class girls who vied to become their eating and drinking companions. Martin fell in love with one right after another, but had been too shy to do anything about it. Until Honorine. For almost a year, until he had to leave Paris, this pretty dressmaker's assistant had been "his" grisette. What an exotic creature she seemed, wearing bracelets that jangled on her plump little arms, showing her sharp teeth when she laughed, flirtatiously twisting her black curls around her fingers, and leaning over the table to show off her little round breasts. All this directed at him. She had been generous. So generous. An ever-willing listener and an unimaginably eager teacher. Martin closed his eyes and sipped the wine, remembering.

Before Honorine, his only experience with women had been a stilted courtship with his distant cousin Marthe DuPont. When Martin's mother had finally realized the calamitous state of the family finances, she had thrown herself on the mercy of the DuPonts, who sponsored Martin as a day student at the Jesuit high school and helped to finance his law school expenses. M. DuPont had even gotten Martin his first post as a prosecutor's assistant in Lille.

Early on, M. DuPont and Martin's mother had also decided that he would make a suitable match for the rich industrialist's eldest daughter. Marthe was a product of the fashionable Sacre Coeur boarding school, the perfect training ground for the perfect bourgeois wife. When he was younger, Martin's mother had forced him to go with her to tea on Wednesday afternoons, when the nuns opened the school to visitors. In the last few years, he had been thrown together with Marthe in the DuPonts' grandiose salon and dining room.

Raised in this environment, Marthe would never dream of revealing the flesh of her arms, wearing curls, or laughing at his feeble jokes. Indeed there had been little humor in their solemn, hushed conversations. And pleasure, never.

Martin stabbed at a piece of beef in the dark, thick stew. The only ornamentation that Marthe wore was a large, heavy medal announcing that she was, truly and officially, a Child of Mary. The medal was not hidden like Solange Vernet's, but on full display, a shield against a godless world and a challenge to any man who dared to think that a willing body lay beneath all that proper female armature. Marthe would be a good mother and a faithful wife and, God knows, as the daughter of Lille's richest textile manufacturer, she'd be a great match for a penniless magistrate. But would there be any pleasure, any true happiness, between them? Would Martin ever be able to talk with her about what was in his heart?

Martin took the last bite of the *boeuf bourguignon*. Westerbury and Solange had loved each other. That is what the Englishman had insisted. They loved and understood each other. They were making a new life together. They were capable of that, a new life. Of talking about science and religion. Of discussing all the great issues of the day. If everything the Englishman had said were true, he had been a very lucky man.

But what if Solange Vernet had changed her allegiance and had set her heart on Cézanne, the local banker's son? Or what if she had rebuffed the artist's advances? The key might be—Martin chewed slowly—the key might be finding out which man Solange Vernet really loved, and why.

Thursday, August 20

The Murder, *1868-70,* and The Woman Strangled, *1870-2,* are *bewildering in their expression of fury, their excess of emotion. . . . Even if the sources of their imagery were to be found, we would still have to account for Cézanne's interest in them. What we seek is the source of his own violence.*

—Sidney Geist, *Interpreting Cézanne*

5

CÉZANNE WOKE HER FROM A DEEP SLEEP. Even before she completely roused herself, Hortense Fiquet could hear the agitation in his movements—the search for the pitcher of water, the fumbling through the cupboards for a glass, the scrape of the chairs.

Hortense grabbed her robe and pushed back her hair. Because of the heat, the early morning hours were the only good ones for sleeping. She was very tired. She glanced at her thirteen-year-old son snoring in the bed next to hers before entering the other room in the house.

"Paul? Paul, dear, you're early." The endearment was meant to soothe, but she could see that Paul, already in one of his moods, was beyond appeasement. "Is something wrong?"

He shook his head, staring into space. His face belied his denial. He had taken off his cap and settled into the old sofa in the large rectangular living room that opened onto the kitchen. His kept his paint supplies and canvases there, tucked in the corner behind an armchair. Cézanne had chosen this house, halfway up the low hill that was all there was to Gardanne, for the light. She hated it, and everything else about the town.

"Would you like some coffee?"

A nod. He got up and took one of the three wooden chairs at the kitchen table.

Hortense lit the fire under the pot and reached into the cupboard for the sugar and milk. She stopped and looked for the hundredth time at the sorry assortment of cups and dishes they had gathered in Paris, in Marseilles, in Aix, in l'Estaque. They lived like nomads, like fugitives.

"Paul, did your father find out?"

"No, no, no." He pounded the table. "Nothing like that."

"Quiet, you'll wake the boy." It came out more like a hiss than a whisper.

"Then stop with this father nonsense. He's not to know. He wouldn't approve. And then—"

Then Paul would lose his inheritance. That was always the threat hanging over her head. If Paul lost his inheritance, they would never be able to marry. All the years of waiting would be wasted.

"Tell me what happened," Hortense said, joining Cézanne at the table. "You must have walked all this way in the dark. That can be dangerous." She reached for him, but his hand stayed clenched, resolutely refusing to meet hers.

"Don't worry, I waited for the sun to start. I even had time to post a note to Zola."

"About?"

"Nothing. At least this month we don't have to ask him for money."

"Then what? What is it?" She was used to his dark moods, his fierce, frowning eyes. This was different.

"The Englishman."

"Westerbury?"

"Yes." He looked at her. "Your famous professor Westerbury," he said.

Hortense ignored his sarcasm. She had borne enough of Paul's disdain when she told him she'd attended one of the geological lectures while they were still living in Aix. "I don't understand. You told me you stopped seeing them months ago."

"I didn't go to see them. *He* came to the Jas. Late last night. Shouting. Crazy. Tried to break the windows with stones. He even disturbed Papa."

Precious, never-to-be-disturbed Papa. Rich, stingy Papa. Sometimes Hortense dreamed of throttling "Papa" with her own hands to get it over with. But why had the Englishman come looking for Paul at his parents' home? Had Paul taken up with Solange Vernet again? Hortense got up and stirred the coffee into the boiling water. It always smelled burnt and stale here in this hovel. Not like in the cafés of Paris, where they had met. Hortense slapped the lid on the pot and poured the coffee into two chipped cups. When she turned again, Paul had his head in his hands. His bald forehead looked so vulnerable that she almost reached over to pat him, but stopped herself in time. If only they could be tender with each other again, everything would be more endurable. She sat down across from him and took a sip of the hot, dark liquid. She needed to know what had happened, even if they argued again. Anything was better than his silences.

"Tell me, before our son wakes up. What is this all about?"

"Westerbury says that I killed Solange. That I was the *real* murderer."

"What?" Killed Solange? Was it possible that the witch was dead? And that someone had murdered her?

"He kept shouting that I was responsible. That I should come out and face him like a man. I would have, except *Maman* begged me not to."

Paul looked up at her, tears in his eyes. It took all her strength not to slap him.

Hortense struggled to keep her voice even. "She's dead?"

"How would I know!" Cézanne's fist came down on the table, bouncing and clattering the cups. "How would I know? Do you think I killed her? Do you think I strangled a woman with my own hands?"

Hortense's eyes traveled from the scowling face to those strong hands, curled, ready for a fight. Paul had never struck her, but she had watched those hands tear up his canvases, break his paint brushes, rage against the fates, the furniture, even the walls of every place they had lived.

"I did not kill her!" He was shouting in her face, and she was shrinking from him. Why should she think he had? Why was he threatening her?

Cézanne stood up. "All I want is to paint. I don't want entanglements. Everyone trying to catch me in their webs, their little plots." His hands made furious little knots in front of her face as he said this. She shrank back further. What had gotten into him? Her throat was tightening, almost choking her, and her heart began to pound. "All I want is to be left alone!" he shouted, as he moved away from her. "Do you hear? No family! No women!"

"Papa!"

As soon as she heard the voice calling out from the bedroom, Hortense dropped her head into her hands and began to breathe more slowly. The boy. The boy would calm him.

Cézanne left her at the table as he went into the bedroom to greet his son.

6

AFTER ANOTHER NIGHT OF TOSSING AND TURNING, Martin woke up with a plan. If he pulled it off, he would finally begin to understand what kind of woman Solange Vernet really had been, and what had gone on between her and her lovers.

Martin was leaving the Picard house filled with a sense of purpose and direction, when the postman stopped him and handed him a letter. Martin recognized his mother's handwriting at once and, with a sigh, put the envelope in his pocket. He did not need to open it to know what the message would be. His failures as a son and suitor were old stories.

When he got to the courthouse, things did not improve. Old Joseph was waiting to deliver a most unwelcome message.

"M. Franc told me to tell you that they were not able to find Paul

Cézanne." Barely had Martin digested this piece of bad news when he heard shouts coming from somewhere inside the Palais.

"I believe that's the maid," Old Joseph explained in an unnecessary whisper. "M. Franc said he was going to get her right away."

Martin gave his frail clerk a weary pat on the back and walked out of his chambers in time to watch two gendarmes drag a woman by her arms and shoulders up the main staircase. Following this struggling trio, cap in hand, was Franc. "I won't go. I have nothing to say. Don't send me back. Let me go! Let me go!" The woman's cries echoed through the cavernous building. Her limbs kept hitting against the hard edges of the stairs, adding to her anguish. There was no easy way to stop this brutal procession midstream, so Martin did not even try. At the top of the stairs, the journey became easier for the police as they hurried down the hall with their burden between them and threw her on the hard wooden bench in front of Martin's office. She was still flailing, but her words had dissolved into sobs.

Franc caught Martin's eye. "Arlette LaFarge."

Martin stared at the small, sallow creature. A "true Parisian," as the inhabitants of the capital liked to say, meaning that she was an off-spring of the densely packed central quarters, raised without benefit of sunshine or fresh air. Her male relatives were a favored constituency of the Third Republic, the kind politicians called, with a mixture of affection and cynicism, the "little people." What an appropriate name, Martin thought, for men and women shrunken and bent by ceaseless labors in dank, dark shops. Because of his friend Merckx, Martin had known many such laborers in Lille. As a judge, he had become well acquainted with their counterparts in Aix. The "little people" never liked his chambers very much.

Martin leaned over to address the sobbing woman. "Mme LaFarge. Mme LaFarge."

She knelt down, clinging to his leg. "Don't send me back, sir. Please. He'll kill me. I know he will."

"Who will kill you?" Martin forced the woman off of him and back onto the bench.

"He beats me terribly."

"Who? M. Westerbury?" Martin was holding onto Arlette's shoulders trying to get her to look at him.

The name caught her attention. "Oh, no, sir. Not M. Westerbury. No. Never. My husband, Jacques, who's waiting for me in Paris." She broke into sobs again. "Mme Solange promised, she promised I'd never have to go back."

"The poor woman is terrified," Martin said to Franc.

The inspector shrugged. "She doesn't want to have to face a judge and tell the truth."

"Did anyone threaten her?"

"No, no," Franc seemed disgusted by the question. "We just told her she would have to tell us everything she knows. And that she would have to talk to you. And," he added, directing his words toward Arlette, who had flattened herself against the marble wall, "she has chosen to tell us nothing, except to give us a description of the messenger that would fit about a hundred street urchins in Aix alone."

Martin bent down to the woman. "Mme LaFarge, listen to me. Don't you want to find the person who killed your mistress?"

She nodded, her eyes wide and frightened.

"Then you must talk to me. It is the law. I will not hurt you. I will not send you back to Paris."

Her chest began to heave again. More sobs. And this was the woman who Martin had hoped would be his entrée into Solange Vernet's world.

Franc cleared his throat to catch Martin's attention and asked if they could speak in chambers. Martin was eager to speak to Franc as well, about why they hadn't been able to find Cézanne.

Before Martin could open his mouth, Franc began. He was quite agitated. "Don't be too easy on her, sir, I beg you. I just talked with

Riquel. She came to the morgue late yesterday afternoon while me and my men were off searching the quarry. Apparently the Englishman told her that she could have 'the honor' of dressing the corpse. If you don't mind my saying so, I think that Riquel played the fool. He left her alone with the body."

"How did that happen?" Not that Martin could see the harm.

"According to him, she begged to be left alone 'one last time' with her mistress. And she wanted to look at the clothes she was murdered in, to fold them nice and neat for her mistress." Franc's voice was laced with sarcasm. "She said that her mistress was a *lady*," practically spitting out the word, "and she wanted to treat her like one."

Martin could not fathom why his inspector found the maid's regard for her mistress so infuriating. If it was only because Solange Vernet had found a way to rise above her origins, then Franc, the ambitious, self-proclaimed man of the people, was a flaming hypocrite. And if it was something else, why should Franc care so deeply about whether or not the murdered woman had had lovers?

Franc took Martin's silence as leave to continue his ranting. "By the time I got back to bring the evidence box to you, the Vernet woman was dressed in a fancy white nightgown—as if she were some pure young thing—and every piece of clothing had been smoothed out just as nice as you please. I only got all the details of the 'final visit' this morning when I asked Riquel about her reactions."

After building up this head of steam, Franc suddenly stopped and waited for a response, making Martin feel like he was failing some sort of test.

"The note!" Franc finally exploded. "We haven't found it yet!"

Evidently Franc had come around to the view that it really did exist. Or was he just frustrated by his own failures of the morning? "Surely you had searched through the clothes," Martin said, trying to calm down his inspector.

"Yes, but don't you see? These women have their ways, their

secrets." Franc held up his two thick hands. "I couldn't search the way she could. They were hatmakers and dressmakers, remember? They know all the secret places where women hide things that they don't want us men to find. And think, what if Westerbury asked her to try to find it for him?"

What if? "Even if it were true, what do you propose to do about it? Strip her?" Not in his office. And not while he was in charge of the case.

"That might not be such a bad idea."

Martin did not want to quarrel with Franc. They needed each other. "Look," he said, "let's just think for a minute. Whose side would Arlette be on? Westerbury's or Vernet's? Surely she was not a love interest for Westerbury. How did she react around the body?"

"When she was done with her little game, she began to wail and keen. Riquel said that she threw herself on the corpse. He had trouble pulling her off. Then she kept holding onto Vernet's hand, kissing it over and over again."

Kissing those gray, swollen hands. Martin sucked in his breath. He hoped that the cool of the prison basement had slowed down Solange Vernet's decomposition, and that the ministrations of Dr. Riquel had quelled the smell of rot and excrement. Still, Arlette LaFarge must have loved her mistress very much. Or had something to feel guilty about.

"I'm not at all sure she would risk being sent back to Paris or to prison for helping Westerbury," Martin reasoned aloud in another attempt to try to steady his companion. "I'll question her carefully about the note."

Franc did not hide his skepticism very well. He was huffing and puffing like a bull in heat.

"I'm good at it too, you know. Questioning." It was demeaning to have to assert himself to his own inspector. Martin fully expected Franc to explode when he laid out his plan. But he forged ahead anyway. "Moreover, I'm thinking of sending the maid home and questioning her in the apartment."

"Back to the apartment!"

Martin held up his hand. "I'm *not* letting her off the hook. I've decided it would be a good idea for me to go there, to have my own look around. And she may feel more like talking, away from all this."

"But then she'll have even more time to make up some story," Franc protested. Their eyes met for a moment, and then a glimmer of approval lit up the inspector's face, blossoming into a smile. "Aha. So that's it. You're going to become a *real* investigating magistrate."

Or one bursting with unseemly ambition. Anyone who read the newspapers had heard of judges eager to make a mark by beating their prosecutors to crime scenes and breaking down the doors of suspects' houses. That wasn't Martin's style. He didn't want notoriety. Although from the look on his inspector's face, it seemed that Franc might prefer working with a judge who did. "While you're at it, you might as well consider going out to the Cézanne estate."

"What?" Did the inspector think that Martin should be out hunting for suspects?

"I think Old Joseph already told you." Franc began to talk very rapidly, as if to ward off any expression of Martin's displeasure. "I went out early this morning. The 'artist' wasn't around, and they had no idea when or if he will be. At least that's what the women claimed. But do you want to know who had been there?" A superior grin spread across Franc's grizzled face. "Our prime suspect, Westerbury. He was there last night, throwing stones at the windows and making a disturbance."

Martin sank into one of the wooden chairs facing his desk. On top of everything else, Westerbury was running amok. This case was slipping out of his control.

"Look, I'll take care of finding the Englishman. We can arrest him for disturbing the peace," Franc said. "You don't have to worry about that. And I assume you'll let me keep him in jail this time."

Still numb, Martin nodded his consent. Of course they'd hold Westerbury this time. The only real question was, why had he let the sniveling wretch go in the first place? To prove that French law was every bit as civilized as English? Martin scratched his beard in frustration. How stupid that seemed now. This was a murder case, not a patriotic civics lesson.

"And you, sir, you can deal with the Cézannes," Franc went on relentlessly. "That's a much more delicate situation. They're rich and have a lot of connections. On top of that, the women told me the old banker is sick. I don't think you want to be in a position of dragging any of them down here for questioning."

"First, before anything else," Martin said, pulling himself together enough to stop the flow of Franc's presumptions, "tell me what happened when you went to find Cézanne." Martin needed to drive home the point that he was not the only one making mistakes.

But the question did not even faze Franc. "It's a big place. It would have taken a dozen men to search it. And if he slipped out the back. . . ." He shrugged. "There are lots of ways he could have hidden or gotten away." The inspector seemed surprisingly unbothered by the artist's evasions. It was as if Franc were certain that they already knew who the murderer was.

"So you're not sure he wasn't there?"

"No, but the women insisted. You could go with one of my men this afternoon."

Martin rubbed his aching forehead. Not only might Cézanne have escaped, but he might have done so with the full complicity of his rich and influential family. Everyone in the courthouse would agree with Franc that Martin should tread lightly, that he should treat the Cézannes with more care and deference than a maid or a foreigner. Everyone except Martin. At least in this instance, Martin thought with a certain bitter irony, he would be treating the rich and influential family with the same courtesy that he planned to give the maid. Martin looked up at his inspector and agreed to visit the Cézannes.

"Good!" Franc's dark, bullish mood had completely evaporated. He was almost bouncing on his toes. "Frankly, sir, now that you've thought of it, I think sending the maid home and going there is a good idea. See how they lived, and tell me if you don't agree that there was something fishy going on."

Instead of reprimanding Franc for not rounding up Cézanne, Martin found himself oddly relieved at having gotten the inspector's approval. Franc, the man of experience, exuded righteous anger and confidence, while Martin was barely keeping his head above water. Without another word, he got up and went out into the hall where the maid and the gendarmes were sitting in a silent truce. He sent them all back to the Cours Mirabeau. Then he wrote out a warrant for Westerbury's arrest, which he handed to Franc, and ordered his clerk to go to search through the police and municipal records for anything he could find on Paul Cézanne.

Alone in his office, Martin sat for a moment, staring into space, before reaching in his pocket to pull out his mother's letter. He might as well read it, since the morning could not get much worse. He tore open the envelope and unfolded the sturdy cream-colored paper. Just as he expected, every line was calculated to make him cringe.

Lille
Feast of St. Helen

Dearest Son,

  How I do miss my only child! And how I pray every night that you will be safe. So does Marthe. I saw her in the street last week with her sisters and, I fear, I must scold you. She says that you have only written her twice since Christmas. The poor dear did not complain, of course, but surely it is time that you made your intentions clear once and for all. Being the oldest is becoming such a burden to her. She fears that none of her sisters will feel free to marry until she does.

  You know my feelings, dearest son. What a wonderful daughter she would make for me. And what a match for you! It's not only the money, it's the children. Coming from that large family, surely, she will give you many sons and daughters, and me, the greatest comfort for my old age, grandchildren.

But I not only scold. I bring news. As I write this Marthe is in Lourdes! She is taking three of her cases, a crippled boy, an old woman, and a poor, sick seamstress, on the famous white train from Paris. They are all hoping for a miracle. Marthe was so excited. I wish you could have seen her. She told me that more people than ever are going on the National Pilgrimage, and standing up for their faith. But, of course, you must know that. I am assuming they do have Catholic newspapers down there.

Marthe told me that she will ask our Holy Mother to protect you from the cholera. She did not say it, but I also think that she will be praying to get a marriage proposal soon. This would not be a miracle, just good sense and gratitude to a family that took us under their wing after your father died.

Enough preaching! My greatest wish is to see you again soon. Can't you find some time this summer to come and visit your poor mother? If not, write! Tell me that you are well and happy. You are my greatest, my only joy.

Your most loving Maman

Martin folded his mother's letter and put it back in the envelope. At home in his attic room, buried somewhere amidst the debris on his table, was a page, blank except for the date, "Feast of the Assumption." It had been his intention to describe the Virgin's procession to his mother and tell her that he had been left in charge of the Palais. But he could not do it. It would have been too hypocritical and duplicitous. It would comfort her to think that he still kept the holy calendar, but he did not. It would arouse her maternal pride to think that he was left in charge because he was important, but he was not. It would trouble her greatly to know that he had not yet decided to propose to Marthe, but he could not. At least not yet. He did not yet know what he was capable of, or what kind of man he would become.

Martin opened his drawer and took out a piece of official stationery. He uncovered his inkpot and dipped his pen. This time he could tell the truth.

20 August 1885

Dearest Maman, he began. *Thank you for your kind letter. I long to see you too, but I am very busy at the moment. A most important case has come up here, the murder of a woman. . . .* Martin wrote steadily, purposefully. When he finished, he was ready to think about what he would find in Solange Vernet's apartment.

7

An hour later Martin was winding his way to the Vernet apartment, hoping to catch a glimpse of a world that he had let pass him by. There was so much he wanted to know about Solange Vernet and her past. But even if he did not uncover all her secrets, he had every intention of finding out what had transpired in the days immediately proceeding her murder. The maid had witnessed a great deal, he was sure of it. All he had to do was to get her to tell him what she knew.

Solange Vernet had chosen to live on Aix's main thoroughfare, the wide, gracious Cours Mirabeau, which cut through the center of town, dividing the sleepy aristocratic quarters to the south from the rest of the city. Even before Martin turned the corner onto the boulevard, he heard the clatter of the wagons, carriages, and omnibuses that went constantly to and fro, past and around the three great fountains that marked the Cours's beginning, end and midpoint. The broad side-walks on the north side were home to spacious outdoor cafés, book stalls, and shops. Late in the morning, even in the middle of August, they were alive with the murmur of conversation, the shouts of waiters, and the clink of glasses and silverware.

Martin did not frequent the cafés. They reminded him too much of his carefree life as a student in Paris. Still, he considered the Cours the most beautiful place in all of Aix. He especially admired the tall plane trees that were planted in double rows on either side of the boulevard. Their sturdy blond trunks patched with silver-gray bark offered a muted, gentle contrast to Provence's garish red-orange earth and vivid blue skies. In the summer, their olive green leaves formed a shel-tering sun-dappled archway overhead. Today their branches swayed in the breeze, changing the patterns of light and shade along Martin's path. The Cours sparkled with possibility. It lifted Martin's spirits. He was escaping from the unhappy surprises of the morning, and he was setting out on an adventure. How many men get to walk upon—nay, have the very right and duty to embark upon—a path not taken?

Spotting the Vernet apartment was not hard. The two gendarmes posted outside the entrance were catching the curious glances of shop-pers. They saluted smartly as he approached, and Martin, putting on a solemn face, nodded in reply and headed up the stairs. He rang a bell fastened beside a heavy wooden door, which was polished to a soft mahogany sheen. Arlette LaFarge curtsied as he entered, took his hat, and led him into a large rectangular salon. She had calmed down since her morning's outbursts. Her black dress and the white cap and apron said a great deal about the airs that Solange Vernet had put on in Aix.

"I can prepare some tea. I think Mme Solange would have liked that," Arlette said, her lips quivering. She seemed to be clinging to form as if her life depended on it. What else did she have in a strange town without her mistress?

"Thank you, I would like that," Martin said, welcoming the opportunity to be left on his own. The salon had been the staging ground for Solange Vernet's and Westerbury's ambitions. The maid's absence gave him time to get a feel for the place without being watched.

Hands behind his back, Martin strolled slowly around the room, taking in the order and opulence of the arrangements. Chairs, divans, and side tables formed a large elongated oval around an empty space in the center of the room. In one corner stood a small grand piano. In front of a divan opposite the windows, a low mahogany table held glasses and a brandy snifter. The side tables held candelabras and gas lamps; books, cigar humidifiers, and settings for refreshments. Everything necessary to make the guests comfortable and, presumably, talkative.

Sunlight filled the room. The dark blue velvet drapes had been pulled back from the five high windows that faced onto the Cours, boldly exposing the salon to the indifferent aristocratic houses across the way. Solange Vernet had hoped to be the center of a "circle," the hostess to entertainments. If she really was a hatmaker of humble origins, what on earth had she been thinking?

The walls held four pretty, not particularly distinguished, landscapes and city scenes, one at the east end and three on the long wall in the middle. None hung on the west wall. Martin approached and looked closely. A small hole in the yellow-striped wallpaper indicated that a painting had been hanging there. One of Cézanne's? He took his notebook from his pocket and added "missing painting" to the list that he had made up in his office: "the message," "the boy," "arguments."

"Monsieur le juge, will you sit over here?" Arlette reappeared, placing a large tray with a teapot, two cups and a plate of little white, crustless triangles, on the table in front of the divan. It was all very English, making Martin wonder if the service reflected Westerbury's influence, or was yet another sign of Solange Vernet's aspirations.

"Sir, do you mind if I join you?" This was odd, a maid and a guest, but of course Martin agreed. After all, this was a strange household, and Arlette LaFarge looked as if she could use some sustenance.

Martin set his notebook and pencil beside him as she pulled up a chair. He scrutinized her as she began to pour the tea. There were few indications that this sallow creature had ever been pretty. Now her face, under the dark fringe of hair, was worn with care and her dark eyes red with crying, signs of grief and anxiety that would only make her more suspicious and timid. He needed to prod her gently.

"I'm glad to see that my men did not cause too much damage here."

The comment seemed to startle Arlette, who held the pot in midair for a moment before carefully setting it down, as if she were deciding whether he was one of "them,"or something nicer. She took a sip of tea, then smiled weakly. "No, sir, not here. Just opening drawers and looking all through the piano and under the cushions."

"But?"

"But . . . the bedrooms and M. Westerbury's study are a mess. They tore through everything. I can fix most everything except 'the collection.' They poured all his rocks and things on the floor. M. Westerbury was very upset."

"But he hasn't stayed here to put things right?"

Arlette shook her head. "He's been in and out. Restless. Unhappy. Yes, very unhappy," she added, as if she was deciding that the safest course was to depict Westerbury as the grieving lover.

"I'm sorry. I know this must be a difficult time. But I must ask you some questions. I'm sure we both agree that we want to find the man who murdered your mistress." Martin was watching her every reaction very carefully. He desperately needed to recruit Arlette to his side.

Her cup rattled ever so slightly in the saucer. She put it back on the tray.

"All you have to do is tell the truth when I ask you questions. You might even think of things I've left out. You loved your mistress. You can help me, can't you?" Martin gave her some time to think while he took a sip of the hot tea. It was good.

Finally, Arlette nodded her consent, and sat back, waiting. She was biting hard on her lower lip. Martin started off as gently as possible.

"First, how long did you know Mme Vernet? And how did you meet?"

"Five years ago. She took me in." Arlette said this with a steady voice. The past seemed to be a safer topic than the present.

"Took you in?"

"Yes. You see, she ran the hat shop she had inherited from her aunt, the Widow Charpentier. And Mme Solange took after her. Everyone in the neighborhood knew they could go to Aunt Marie—that's what we called the Widow Charpentier—if they were desperate. And Mme Solange was the same."

"Was Solange Vernet born in Paris, then?" This had been a small point of Westerbury's testimony, but Martin wanted to get a sense of how honest he had been.

"No . . . no. She and Aunt Marie always used to say they 'found each other again' when Mme Solange was about sixteen. She came to Paris from a village on the Seine."

"Do you know which?"

Arlette only shook her head, and fixed her eyes on the brightly colored Persian rug that covered the center of the floor.

"Please do eat something," he urged. "You must be very hungry and tired after what you went through this morning." As soon as he said this, he was afraid that his expressions of solicitude were coming off as false and manipulative, which to some degree they were.

But the maid reached for a sandwich and began eating. She was hungry. He also took one. Cucumber and butter.

"I understand that your husband beat you. Is that why you went to the hat shop?"

"He hit me a lot. For everything. He's not a bad man. Only . . . only," she swallowed hard, "poor, a drunkard. We never had enough money."

"Children?"

"No . . . maybe that would have helped . . . I don't know."

"And Mme Vernet? How could she help you?"

"She stood up to him. When he learned I was staying there and tried to get in, she told him he could not and that if he hit her, she would call the police. She shook a broom at him." The beautiful and graceful Solange Vernet with a broom, challenging a brute? It was Martin's turn to shake his head.

"Things got easier after M. Westerbury moved in. Then we weren't so afraid. It was good to have a man around."

"And he was never violent."

"No . . . never."

Martin noted the hesitation in her voice. "When did M. Westerbury move in?"

"About three years ago. They met at his lectures."

"So the household had three people? You, Mme Vernet, and Westerbury?"

"And five apprentices. Mme Solange did not want to leave Paris until they found a place. They were poor, like she was when she came. She was good and patient with them. Just as Aunt Marie had been with her."

"But even if the shop was quite successful, it could not have bought all this?" When Martin had questioned Westerbury, he had asked about the finances, but now he saw how right Franc had been. They had been living like kings.

"I don't know about that, sir," Arlette said. "I just keep the house." She began chewing on another soft triangle. "I think before M. Westerbury came, Mme Solange would have given everything she had when she died to charity or to a child that she took in, but he changed things."

Could this change have caused a breach in Arlette's admiration for her mistress, one that Martin could exploit to uncover Solange Vernet's secrets? "How did you feel about that?"

"About what, sir?"

"The change from . . ." Martin searched for the words which would not sound disapproving, "her change from being an Aunt Marie, a

benefactor for the neighborhood, to being a kind of society woman?"
A bluestocking, he thought to himself.

"That's not my place, sir. Besides," Arlette smiled for the first time,
"after they met, Mme Solange was so happy—he made her so happy.
How could that be bad? She was never bad."

Truly? Even though Solange Vernet had become someone's mistress, Arlette spoke of the dead woman as if she were some kind of
saint. Martin reached for another sandwich, this one filled with ham.
He bit into it as he searched for a way to get around the maid's loyalty.

"Let's talk about life in Aix then," he said. "You arrived?"

"In February."

"Did you know any of Mme Vernet's or Westerbury's new friends?"

Arlette took a few sips of tea and thought for a moment. "I saw
them when they came on Thursday evenings, but never outside of
that. Some of them left cards. The inspector took them."

Martin remembered a little table and umbrella stand outside the
door. More accoutrements of social ambition, having visiting days,
receiving calling cards.

"I don't suppose you know what went on during Mme Vernet's
Thursdays."

"Oh yes, sir. I did. Not that I understood. But see that?" She
pointed toward a narrow wooden chair near the door. "Mme Solange
couldn't make me come all the way in. But she hated the idea of *ringing*
for me. She said as long as I was going to serve things, I should be
allowed to listen, too."

This was more surprising than the maid serving herself tea. Had he
walked into a den of anarchists? Or just a trio of parvenus, plotting to
climb the social ladder?

"Where did Mme Vernet sit?"

"Over there." Arlette pointed to a green chair by the east window, a
place from which a gracious hostess could easily rise to greet newcomers, but not a chair from which one held forth.

"And M. Westerbury?" He followed her finger to a large brown chair with an ottoman, which took the central position at the western end of the salon, well suited to speechifying. "Who played the piano?"

"No one, yet. But Mme Solange was looking forward to having musical evenings."

"She didn't play?"

Arlette shook her head.

Westerbury had said Solange Vernet had taught herself to read and write. If she did not play an instrument or sing, it was indeed true that she had not had a formal education. "What did the others think of her?" Martin asked.

"Excuse me?"

That had come out crudely. "M. Westerbury told me who the guests were, and they came from a very different place in society than Mme Vernet. Did they hold that against her? Did they treat her well?"

"Oh yes, sir, yes. Everyone liked Mme Solange."

"But . . . did they know her background, that—"

"She didn't talk about that, sir, no. Mostly it was M. Westerbury who did the talking. He is very learned. He told them about all the great English geologists he had studied. He even helped my mistress with little things, like how she should act, what we should serve—"

"Like the tea?"

"Yes, sir, just like that, the tea and things, so, as he liked to say, 'we could offer something different.' He was sure we could get around 'social prejudice,' as he liked to say, if we showed how polite and learned we were."

Really? Did the maid also believe this? "And Paul Cézanne, the painter, where did he sit?"

Arlette chewed more slowly. Then she shrugged. "Anywhere. He only came a few times anyway." This show of nonchalance came off as just that—a show, an attempt to avoid a dangerous topic.

"I was noticing the paintings," Martin said. "That one," he pointed toward the west wall, "seems to be missing. Do you know where it is?"

"M. Westerbury took it down." The chewing had stopped.

"Why? Was it by Paul Cézanne?"

"Oh, I wouldn't know about that, sir." Her fingers pressed into the bread, squeezing out little bits of butter. Martin was quite sure she did indeed know about that.

"Was it new?"

Another shrug.

"Look here, Arlette. If you do not tell me the truth about everything, I will have to arrest you as an accomplice to murder. The murder of someone you claim to love. Someone who saved you."

"But I don't know who killed her." Arlette put her sandwich back on the tray.

"What you mean to say," he could sense that this was not the moment to let up, "what you really mean, is that you are not sure if Westerbury did it. Isn't that right?"

"No, no, no, no." Arlette shook her head. "No!"

"Are you afraid of him?"

"No!"

"We could protect you."

"No!"

Her denials came out in sobs, her face contorted. Did she suspect that the Englishman had killed her mistress? That she was living with a murderer?

"Then you must know that the only way to prove M. Westerbury's innocence is to tell me all you know. You understand that, don't you?"

Arlette nodded and took a handkerchief out of her apron pocket to blow her nose.

"Now, tell me about the picture on the wall. Was it a portrait?"

"No, only a mountain," her voice more hushed than ever.

"A mountain?"

"You know, the big mountain. Sainte-Victoire."

"Then how could it offend anyone?"

The maid sat very still. He set his tea cup down and leaned toward her.

"It was by Paul Cézanne, wasn't it?"

She shrugged again, without conviction.

"You had better tell me. I have ways of finding out, you know." Although he could not begin to imagine what those ways would be, especially since everyone kept lying.

Finally, she nodded. "Yes."

"Did they quarrel over the painting?"

"Yes . . . no . . . I don't know."

"But surely you do. Did Mme Vernet and Westerbury quarrel often?"

"No."

"But they did quarrel right before she died?"

The maid sat very still, hardly breathing. The great salon was silent, except for the muted sounds of the traffic echoing up from the Cours. Martin sipped his tea and waited, to no avail. "If you loved your Mme Solange, if you truly loved her, you must tell me the truth about what happened, or you could go to jail." He paused to let this sink in. "Did they quarrel about Cézanne? Or about something else?"

Arlette twisted the handkerchief in her lap. Martin kept his eyes fixed on her, giving her no escape.

Finally, she began to speak. "It happened right after we returned from the procession on the Virgin's feast. He had found the letters. Mme Solange should have destroyed them when she got them, but . . . but she told me that she needed them in case Cézanne returned, to help her figure out what to say to him. That's what she told me later, when it was over."

"M. Westerbury was very angry, then."

She nodded. "He kept shouting and shouting. Just like Jacques— my husband, Jacques." Her chest began to heave. "I ran into the

kitchen and covered my ears. I couldn't stand it. They had never quarreled before. Not like that."

"Did you hear anything of what they said?"

"At first I was too afraid. But they just got louder and louder. My
mistress had protected me. I couldn't just sit there and be a coward. If
he raised his hand to her, I had to help her. So I ran back. He had the
picture from the wall. He had it over his knee. He cracked it open and
tore up the canvas. Threw it into the fireplace. The letters were
already there. Torn up into little pieces. Mme Solange began laughing.
But not like I had ever heard her laugh before.

"She kept telling him that he was a fool. Men were fools. I remember
that. And I remember the last words she said before she ran to her room
and locked the door. '*Only two men could fight over a mountain.*'"

"What did she mean by that?"

"I don't know, sir."

"And Westerbury? What did he do?"

"He kept stoking the fire until everything was all burned up. Then
he shouted at me to have his things sent to the Hôtel de la Gare—
where we stayed when we first arrived in Aix. Finally, he left." The
maid sank back into her chair, as if relieved that the worst was over.

So at first Westerbury had merely taken out his rage on Cézanne's
homages to his lover, not on her person. In the two days between the
quarrel and the murder, had this rage simmered inside him and finally
boiled over? Or had Cézanne returned? Martin glanced at Arlette.

"Do you think Mme Vernet had any reason to fear Cézanne?"

The question seemed to surprise her.

"I don't think so. He always scared me a little. The two times he
came to the salon, he sat there all silent and gloomy, and then he'd
burst out with something, disagreeing with someone. He always
sounded angry. I think Solange felt sorry for him." Arlette paused for
a moment. "Around her he was always gentle as a lamb. I don't think
she was afraid of him. I don't think she was afraid of anything."

"Did Cézanne ever come here when M. Westerbury was not around?"

"Only a few times."

Only a few, spoken like a loyal servant.

"Did your mistress ever go to meet him somewhere else?"

"I don't know," she whispered.

"You don't? Really?"

She shook her head. "She never said anything to me."

And if she had, would Arlette tell? Martin was becoming more and more convinced that she would betray Westerbury, Cézanne, any man, rather than Solange Vernet, and would go to great lengths to protect her memory. Still, he was learning a great deal. He had verified the fact that Westerbury was jealous of Cézanne, and that the Englishman had been less than truthful about the last days of Solange Vernet's life.

"Now, let's return to what you do know. What happened after Westerbury left?"

"Mme Solange cried for hours and hours. I thought she would never stop. She kept saying things like 'I thought Charles was different' and 'What things we women have to suffer.' She had so many plans. She wanted to adopt a poor child. She had been so happy." The maid sniffled and wiped her dripping nose with her handkerchief. Martin pressed her to tell him more about the sequel to the quarrel.

That's when the little maid unwittingly rattled Martin to his very core. Mme Solange, she told him, had spent most of the next day and evening at her desk writing. On Sunday night she had asked Arlette to take a large envelope to the Hôtel de la Gare.

Martin could hardly believe his ears. "A letter? To Westerbury?"

Not to the post.

Arlette nodded.

That bastard. That lying bastard. Martin felt the blood rushing to his face. He put his head down and closed his eyes. Franc was right again. He should have let the Englishman rot in jail.

When Martin looked up, Arlette was staring at him, afraid.

"And M. Westerbury," he asked, suppressing a shout, "did you see him at the hotel?"

She shook her head, still staring. Frightened.

"Why not?" His head was pounding.

"He wasn't there. They said he was out. But they took the envelope for him."

"So you don't know what happened to the letter?" Martin could barely get the question out.

"No, no, sir. And I didn't see M. Westerbury again until . . . until right before the police came. When I told him Mme Solange had left the afternoon before, he got frantic. He was about to go searching for her when the police came to take him away."

"Was he drinking?" Martin remembered the strong scent of alcohol.

She kept shrinking away from Martin as she answered. "Yes, M. Westerbury was very upset. He poured something into his coffee."

"How was he before you told him Mme Vernet was missing?"

Had she been thinking about that herself? Did she have her own suspicions about Westerbury? Martin's ears were ringing. He wanted to shake her. Why didn't she just answer his questions? Finally she said, "Upset, I think. But, then, they had never quarreled before." He picked up his notebook. His hand was shaking. "Just a few more things," he said, as much to himself as to Arlette. He glanced down at his notes and saw the words "the boy" and "the message."

"Do you know why Mme Vernet decided to go to the quarry?"

Arlette stared at him as if he was trying to trick her. How many times had she already been asked that question? Finally she sighed and said, "She got a message to go."

"From whom?"

She shrugged.

"Who brought it?" he said more emphatically.

"A boy."

"Tell me about the boy. Did you know him? Can you describe him?"

Arlette told him little he did not already know. Her description of the boy was, as Franc had said, applicable to a hundred street urchins in Aix alone.

"And the message. Did you see it? What did it say?"

"I don't read."

"What did she say about the message?" he asked impatiently.

Arlette took a deep breath. "She said it said 'I love you. Meet me at the quarry.'"

"Was it signed?" And if it was, would she tell him?

"No," almost in a whisper, "I don't think so."

"Then why did she go?"

"At first she didn't know what to do. Then she thought that maybe he—M. Westerbury—was too humiliated to come back to the apartment. That maybe he had something to show her. Something he wanted her to be the first to see. Some surprise." Arlette stopped, her face in a grimace. "I think maybe he didn't want to come back here because of me. I don't think he likes me. I don't think he liked it that I was here when they quarreled." She could no longer hold back the tears.

"Why did she go alone?" Martin insisted.

Arlette wailed, "I don't know. I don't know. I asked if she wanted me to go with her. She told me, 'I have to do this. I have to do this alone. It's a place where we were happy together.'" By now, Arlette LaFarge's sobbing was so deep that it came out as a series of groans.

Why, Martin thought, why did Solange Vernet go? Did she really love and trust Westerbury that much? Even after their quarrel?

When Arlette finally quieted down, he asked her if she knew where the note was. The maid's eyes widened with fear as she shook her head. He was almost positive that she was lying.

"Did Westerbury ask you to find it for him?"

"No, sir, no. Truly. They tried to search me already. Don't—"

"If you know where it is, and you are not telling me—" Too late, Martin realized that he had been shaking his finger at her. He needed to be get control of himself.

"Don't, don't," she repeated as he withdrew his hand.

Don't what? Brutalize her? Bully her? Even if he wanted to, what good would it do? She had had a lifetime of facing up to men far more brutal than he. Perhaps it would be better, and certainly more just, if he got the information out of the real scoundrel, Professor Charles Westerbury.

Martin rose and slipped his notebook into his pocket. He stood, considering Arlette for a moment before he delivered his last admonition. "If you do find the note or the letter, you will bring them to me immediately. Or you will be in serious trouble."

Arlette nodded without meeting his eyes. Then she murmured, "She didn't have on her gloves."

"What?" he could barely hear her.

Arlette stared at the floor as she spoke. "You said you wanted me to help, to think of anything that was not right. When I went to the basement in the prison to fold her things, they didn't have her gloves." She was talking more to herself than to him. "That wasn't like her, not to wear her gloves. Mme Solange was a lady. I'm sure she didn't go out without her gloves."

Arlette's cataleptic declaration didn't strike Martin as particularly relevant, but it did catch him off guard, evoking unbidden images— the white-gloved finger pointing at Darwin's book, the gray swollen hands curled in anguished protest, the face distorted into a silent scream. It was good to remember these things, to remember that this case was more than a contest between him and Westerbury—or anyone else. No matter who Solange Vernet had been, she did not deserve what had happened to her.

Chastened for the moment, Martin found his own hat and headed down the stairs back to the Cours, leaving Arlette LaFarge in her chair to contemplate what she had and had not revealed.

8

WESTERBURY WAS IN THE QUARRY, trying to lay his hands on anything that could be used against him. He knew all too well how easy it would be to convict a foreigner and cut off his head in one fell swoop. If he was the great geologist who could pick up a rock and within minutes describe its million-year-old history, he thought as he frantically searched through the rubble, why in God's name, when it was a matter of life and death, could he not find anything now? His gaze fixed on the dark red stain beneath the quarried archway. His Solange. His lady of secret sorrows. And secret sins. How he longed for a drink! But he knew that the only way to survive was to remain sober. Logical. That's what it had come to. No flights of fancy. No acts of genius. Think and see. What pieces of himself had he left behind here? Were there any more traces of Cézanne?

After another quarter hour, Westerbury sat down on a boulder and swatted at a bug that had crawled up from his collar. The insects with their incessant buzzing and stinging were the only signs of life in the hellhole of mutilated sandstone. He wiped the sweat from his face with a handkerchief and took a flask from his pack. The warm water did little to quench his thirst. Frustrated, he almost threw the flask away, but thought the better of it. *Sois raisonable.* Be reasonable. If only he had listened to her. He must keep searching. Or flee. *Sauve qui peut!* Wasn't that another one of their favorite expressions? Run for your life!

But where to? Surely they were watching the train station. Even if he got away, where could he go? Without Solange, he already felt hollow. Every doubt that he had ever had about himself, his bastard birth, his lack of station and education, kept gnawing at him. What could he do without the confidence she gave him, the admiration that shone in her eyes—and, of course, the money? If he fled, he would not be "the famous Professor Westerbury." He'd be a man on the run. He would be nothing.

No, Solange was right as always: he needed to act *reasonably*, without the kind of foolishness that had possessed him at the Jas in his drunken fury. He had to lie low, going about his business while crying for justice like a righteous soul. If he managed to stay out of jail, he would eventually confront the bastard, the great artist, the self-professed seer who saw *nothing*.

Westerbury scoured the blazing orange boulders one last time before limping up toward the Bibémus road. The pebbles were cutting into the soles of his boots. How weary he was. At least he had gotten to the maid before they did, imploring her to find the note for him. But there was so much more they could get out of her. She had heard the quarrel. She knew about the letter. Why hadn't he gotten rid of Arlette in Paris? They certainly had not needed that sad little creature in their new life. Now she could ruin him. All she cared about was Solange.

Arlette LaFarge could not possibly understand what Charles Westerbury was suffering.

He staggered on. The letter would forever be a knife wound in his heart, tearing at him, humiliating him. No one must ever see it, even if it cost him his life. If only he had destroyed it instead of burying it at the foot of the mountain. Somehow he had known, even then, that he was burying their love there, forever.

9

MARTIN RETURNED TO HIS CHAMBERS in a gloomy mood. He had been deceived. He doubted that the maid had told him everything she knew, and he was absolutely certain that Westerbury had lied to him. Not only was the note beckoning Solange Vernet to the quarry missing, but so was a letter that she had spent hours writing just before she died. A letter that Westerbury had kept hidden from him. A letter that had become Solange Vernet's last testament.

Martin needed some good news, and Old Joseph did not provide it; quite to the contrary. The greffier's report only gave Martin a compelling reason to confront the Cézannes immediately, for it revealed that Paul Cézanne was in the habit of evading authorities and getting away with it.

In 1870 the artist had fled Aix to avoid military service during the

Prussian War. When the gendarmes searched the family estate for the deserter, his parents claimed they did not know where he was. It turned out, Joseph noted in the margins of the copied police report, that Cézanne spent the war just twenty-five kilometers to the south, in a village on the Mediterranean called l'Estaque. Cézanne's lack of patriotism apparently had not turned the Aix establishment against the family. In 1871, after the French defeat, his father Louis-Auguste got elected to the new Republican municipal council, despite the fact that he was seventy-two at the time and had not even offered himself up as a candidate. Then the city records show that Cézanne *père* nominated his son for an arts commission. This had probably been a way to provide Paul Cézanne with a salary, for, according to Joseph, the census consistently listed him as an "artist" or "painter." Nothing had come of the proposal for a commission and, as far as Martin knew, nothing had come of the art either.

Even so, the Cézannes were a formidable family, and he was unlikely to find the son without their help. The father had gone from haberdasher to banker in rapid order, and owned a town house as well as the eighteenth-century noble estate, the so-called Jas de Bouffan. Striving to be helpful as always, Joseph had translated the Provençal as the "Habitation of the Little Puffs of Wind." Martin set the report aside and pulled at his cravat. He hoped, on this endlessly still, hot afternoon, that the Jas would live up to its name.

Martin decided to go alone. There was no reason to put up a sign of force when he could not possibly round up enough men to prevent an escape or smoke Cézanne out of a hiding place. Instead, Martin thought ruefully, he would have to rely on his youthful charm. Older women seemed to take to him. He brought out all their maternal and match-making instincts. For once, this might work to his advantage.

Before leaving for the Jas, Martin searched through the material evidence in his cabinet. Just as Arlette LaFarge had said, there were no gloves. Why? The scrap of canvas found at the quarry offered one answer. If her gloves had been stained with paint, there would have been a motive to get rid of them. All the more reason to haul in Cézanne. Martin stared at the painting fragment, fixing it in his mind. He would be looking for a match at the Jas.

It took less than an hour to get there, walking due west of town past neat, fragrant, freshly scythed wheatfields. When he reached his destination, Martin took a moment to scrutinize the Cézanne estate through the tall iron fence that separated it from its neighbors. The Jas de Bouffan was not a welcoming sight. Its gardens, in stunning contrast to the well-tended farms he had just passed, were a jumble of neglect, overgrown and desiccated. Even the three-story mansion beyond them looked a little off-kilter. Half of the top floor seemed to have an upward tilt. Before pushing open the heavy barred gate, Martin slapped the dust off his coat and pants and retied his cravat. He wanted be presentable, even if the Jas was not.

As he made his way up the driveway, Martin noted that the Cézanne property extended well to the west and back of the house. Presumably, Louis-Auguste was one of the richest men in Aix, yet he had let his holdings fall into a deplorable state. The orange stucco on the house was chipped and peeling, as was the dark green paint on the shutters. The whole place seemed closed off, hardly inhabited. Yet Martin knew the Cézanne family was there. He moistened his lips with his tongue and took a few deep breaths before pounding the knocker against the thick wooden door.

A woman wearing a crimson dress and white apron answered the door. She was a country girl, younger, bigger, and healthier than Arlette. Martin tipped his hat, introduced himself, and was left standing in the hallway while the maid went upstairs to find "the mistress."

Finally, a tall middle-aged woman descended and invited him into the large, darkened salon behind the wooden doors on his left. "You've come to hear about our complaint. Good," she said, as she pointed to an easy chair.

Already he was on the wrong footing. He had expected an older woman, and he certainly had not come with the intention of appeasing the household.

"You are Mme Cézanne?" He hoped not.

"No. Mademoiselle. Marie Cézanne. But I do most of the managing around here for my mother and father."

"Ahh." He forced a smile. She looked for all the world like an older version of Marthe DuPont. Straight back, dark hair piled at the neck, plain navy blue dress, a cross protecting her bosom. "I've come about a number of matters, but I will also need to speak to your mother."

"I don't see why—"

"Murder is a very serious business."

That brought her up short.

"I don't see what we could possibly have to say about murder."

"Please, I will need to speak with everyone who witnessed the disturbance and—"

"So she's really dead then," Marie Cézanne said, ignoring his last words. "That's why that man was shouting and carrying on last night." Without waiting for him to respond, she left the room, closing the double doors behind her.

While he waited, Martin grew increasingly anxious that someone was warning Cézanne about his presence. Martin finally got up and, feeling a little foolish, pressed his ear to the door. Hearing footsteps and female voices, he made a quick retreat. This time an old woman entered with Marie and the maid.

Mme Cézanne, a shorter, plumper version of her daughter, was more cordial and forthcoming. "So, a serious business, monsieur le juge. I hope you understand that causing a disturbance is serious too, especially since Papa is so ill. And, as we told your officer, Paul is not here." She smiled as if she had just told him all he needed to know. "It's hot. Would you like something to drink?"

"Water would be fine."

"Jeanne, water for everyone," she announced, as if this were an act of singular largess.

"And so. . . ." She and her daughter sat before him, in two straight chairs on either side of a small round table. Their hands lay folded on their laps as they waited for him to start.

What Martin desperately wanted to know was whether or not Paul Cézanne was in the house or on the grounds. If they had plans to protect him, as they had done during the war, they were not likely to tell Martin anything until he got them on his side. He cleared his throat and took out his notebook.

"I'm sorry about what happened. I'm sure the inspector also expressed—"

"Not really," Marie said, righteously.

"Do you know who the intruder was?"

"Why, Mr. Westerbury, of course." Marie again.

"How did you know that?"

There was a pause, then both spoke at once. "Paul—" said the mother; "I—" began Marie. They stopped, glanced at each other, and fell silent.

"Paul *told* you it was Charles Westerbury?" Martin asked, turning to Mme Cézanne.

She looked down and nodded, realizing her error.

"Then Paul must have been here at the time."

Another nod.

"Was Paul here when my inspector arrived?"

"Oh no, no. He took off early this morning and he hasn't come back." She said this with great conviction.

"Do you know where he went?"

"No." This was Marie.

"How can that be?" he said to the sister.

She shrugged. "He goes off and paints all over. He takes provisions, he carries his paints and easel on his back, and just goes."

"When will he return?"

"Sometimes he's gone for days." This was the mother's contribution to their story.

"If he is here or if you know where he is—"

"We don't." Marie again.

Martin sighed. Paul Cézanne could be anywhere. In the very next room, hiding in a cupboard. Or behind a tree. Or even, as they alleged, off painting. As long as they were united against him, he had little chance. He need to change course, and quickly. "Then what were you going to say before?" he asked Marie. "Did you know Westerbury?"

She glanced at her mother. "I knew of him."

"I mean, had you ever met him?"

Marie sat up tall, defiant. "I went to one of his lectures."

"Only one?"

"I didn't find it that interesting."

"Really, I've found Westerbury to be quite a talker."

"Yes, and a godless charlatan."

"Really? Westerbury told me—"

"My confessor told *me* that the lectures were a campaign of irreligion. There is no need to teach women about new, unproven so-called 'science.' And Paul knows that Westerbury is a charlatan. Paul has known Fortuné Marion for years. Fortuné teaches geology at Marseilles. They used to paint and hunt fossils together. We don't need some foreigner to come in and exploit our environs." Having delivered herself of her priest's and brother's opinions, she sat back, arms folded, daring Martin to continue the discussion, any discussion. He should have known he would get nowhere with the sister.

The water arrived just in time. Martin accepted a glass from the tray presented by the maid and took a long swallow. He wrote down, "who attended Westerbury's lectures?" if only because writing gave him something to do that looked serious and official. Marie Cézanne's little speech and the uncomfortable silence that followed were all too reminiscent of those long pauses at the DuPont table, when Marthe, her sisters, her parents, and his own dear mother waited in vain for his assent to one of M. DuPont's reactionary declarations about church and state. Martin took another slow draught to fill the time as he thought up some way to win over the mother. Only then did he become aware that the walls of the salon were covered with paintings.

"May I?" he stood up.

"Oh, yes." Mme Cézanne rose. "Marie, pull the curtains so that M. Martin can see Paul's work. We close them," she explained, "to keep out the sun in the heat. We sometimes forget all this is here. He did them so long ago."

The movement of the heavy drapes coughed up swirls of glittering dust as the bright sunlight streaming through the tall windows illuminated the walls of the salon. Martin took his time circling the room. He was looking for a match with the quarry fragment. And trying to figure out something to say that would please the mother. The strange amalgam of crude works painted on the walls did not make this an easy task. There were allegorical pictures, portraits, illustrations of religious themes, and even a naked male torso. Oddest of all were the five pictures in the alcove, which could be lit up by gas lamps. Four of them were festive depictions of ill-proportioned women in various postures and dress. The fifth, in the center, was a portrait of a man reading the newspaper.

"That's the four seasons. They're the earliest, copied from magazines," said Mme Cézanne, who had stuck to Martin's side. "And that," she pointed to a darker panel that divided representations of spring and summer from winter and fall, "that's Papa." Martin approached to take a closer look at the father's portrait. At this point, the artist seemed to have reduced his palette to two or three colors. Strangest of all, Martin discovered when he bent slightly and squinted hard at the bottom of the four seasons, someone had signed each of the panels with the name of the great painter Ingres.

"That was a joke." Marie had crept up behind them.

"Ahh." Martin smiled at the mother. "These are all done directly on the wall, then, making this a lovely eighteenth-century drawing room, with frescoes." This was a lame compliment, but the mother did not seem to mind.

"No, I don't think so," Mme Cézanne answered, pursing her lips. "More like practice, trying things out. Papa even got a little upset when Paul did the nude, because of our daughters. But art is art," she added brightly.

Indeed. The only problem was that none came even close to matching the piece of canvas that Franc had found in the quarry. And none could be construed as having anything to do with Solange Vernet.

"Are there more?"

"Oh, yes, dozens and dozens. Paul has gotten better and better," the mother assured him.

"Are they here?"

"Paul doesn't like anyone to disturb his things." Marie was still hovering behind, ever alert.

"I would like very much to see them."

"Oh, he's very insistent on that. Even we—"

"Yes, even we," echoed the mother, "dare not touch anything."

The other paintings were in the house somewhere. But how was he going to get to see them without a full-scale confrontation? "Perhaps later," Martin murmured, heading back to his chair.

"I don't think so," Marie's voice rang out behind him.

"Please," he took up his notebook again. "I have a few more questions." He could probe what they knew about Cézanne's love affairs before he tried to see the paintings again.

The sister stood stock-still at the end of the room until her mother bade her over. "Come, Marie. Let's help out the young judge. Get this over with." The mother sat down and folded her hands in her lap again. Marie complied, but remained standing by her mother's side.

"You know of Charles Westerbury then," Martin began. "Had Paul ever talked to you about a woman named Solange Vernet?"

"No!" Even Marie must have realized that this came out too sharply. "No," she repeated, more quietly.

"Did he ever tell you," Martin continued evenly, "that he had taken part in their—that is, Westerbury's and Vernet's—circle?"

Mme Cézanne shook her head slowly and thoughtfully, as if she were seriously striving to answer the question. Marie's gestures of denial were more vigorous. And much less convincing. Martin surmised that she must be Paul's confidante.

"Mlle Cézanne, did your brother ever talk about Westerbury or Vernet?"

"I told you, he didn't know them. Not as far as I know, anyway."

"Then why would he have such strong opinions about Westerbury?"

"I told him about the lecture."

The old maid *was* quick on her feet.

"Well, we *do* know that he attended at least a few of their Thursday evenings. And it is quite possible that he was carrying on an affair with Solange Vernet."

The mother gasped. Marie's mouth froze into a grim line.

"Is she the one who was murdered?" Mme Cézanne inquired. Whatever secrets the brother had told the sister about the affair had not been shared with the mother.

"Yes," he said, "strangled and stabbed to death in the Bibémus quarry."

Mme Cézanne covered her mouth with one hand while grasping her daughter's hand with the other. Marie was calmer. "When?" she asked.

Martin ignored the question. He wanted answers first. "Can you tell me where Paul was each day and night from last Sunday evening until this morning?"

"Of course we can't. That's four days. He's a grown man with work to do." Marie was stroking her mother's hand, taking charge.

"How about last Monday? Was he here? Do you know where he went to paint?"

"I told you we don't—"

"What if I told you that we found a piece of a canvas in the quarry not far from the body?"

"Oh my!" Mme Cézanne stood up and turned away from him.

"How do you know it was Paul's?"

Martin looked straight at the sister. "That's one of the things I am here to find out." Then he got up and approached the mother. "Do you know anything you should be telling me?" he said to her back.

She whirled around. "No, really. No. I just can't believe that Paul would even know people who could do something like this."

"He didn't." Marie repeated the lie through clenched teeth.

"Ah yes, but he did."

"You're hateful." Martin could have sworn that she was about to stamp her feet.

"And," he moved to capitalize on the mother's shock, "there may be others in danger. There was a boy who brought a message to Mme Vernet, the message that lured her into the quarry. The boy has not been found."

"This is ridiculous!" Marie Cézanne crossed her arms.

"Can you tell me," he persisted in ignoring the sister, "anything about your son's whereabouts on Monday and Tuesday?"

"No," the mother was shaking her head, peering into his face, as if pleading with him to believe her. "No. It was just as always. Painting here, painting there. Always working."

"And there was nothing different about his behavior?"

"No, no." Her head kept shaking.

"And of course you believe that your son is incapable of murder."

"Of course."

"Then you must help me prove him innocent."

"There's nothing I can—"

"Yes, there is. You can show me your son's paintings. Now. Who knows? I may find that he had nothing to do with the quarry canvas." Martin's entire body was taut with tension. He had to see the paintings. He had to know once and for all whether Paul Cézanne was the author of the quarry fragment.

"Mother, he has no right."

"But you know," he said to Marie, "that I do. And if I cannot look at them here, then I will send the gendarmes to bring them all back to the courthouse."

"No!" The mother put up her hand.

"Mother!"

She laid her hand on her daughter's arm. "Who knows what more commotion would do to Papa. We can't have the police tramping about. And we know Paul did not do anything to that woman."

Marie broke away again from her mother and turned her back on both of them.

"You may come up as long as you keep very quiet," Mme Cézanne told Martin. "Papa is ill."

"Of course." He was breathing again and intent on showing this mother that he was a nice, respectful young man worthy of her confidence. There was so much more that he wanted to get out of her.

"All right, then," she put her finger to her mouth as a signal to him before opening the door onto the hall.

He followed the mother up the stairs, past a room where he caught a glimpse of the maid talking to her bedridden master. When they reached the third floor, Mme Cézanne led him into one of its two rooms. "That," she said, pointing to the left, "is Paul's bedroom, and this," she swung open the door, "is his studio."

Martin's heart sank. It would take him hours to get through everything. The room was a jumble of bottles, paints, brushes, vases, bowls, tools, and bizarre objects standing in disarray on tables and shelves.

Rags, spotted with paint, lay on the wooden floor. Innumerable canvases pinned to wooden frames were stacked up against the walls, while others lay curled up in the corners. On the easel in the middle of the room was a half-painted still life, which immediately identified the sour smell that had announced itself when they opened the door—rotting apples.

"Oh dear." Mme Cézanne rushed to the table behind the easel and picked up a bowl of decaying fruit. "I wish Paul would let Jeanne come up here more often." She set the bowl out in the hall and returned. "Let's open the windows. I don't think there is enough wind to blow anything about, do you?"

As Martin helped her yank open the windows, he discovered why the house had seemed askew from the outside. The windows had been enlarged to bring more sunlight into the studio.

"I like the smell of apples," he said. "It reminds me of my mother making cider in the fall." Martin's hope that this would be a winning remark was rewarded.

She smiled. "You're from the north." His accent had given him away again.

"Lille."

"A long way to come to start your career."

"Yes."

She smiled again and took a seat on a stool. She was not entirely unsympathetic, but she was not about to leave him alone in her son's studio.

Martin waded in. He hadn't thought, until he saw the disarray, that he might find a murder weapon. But after examining the painter's knives, he knew that none of them were long or sharp enough to have harmed Solange Vernet. He could see Mme Cézanne's relief when he put them aside and gave her a quick reassuring smile. Then he picked up a skull, the most ghoulish of the objects sitting on the shelves. Mme Cézanne explained that her son liked to draw it because of the way the light and shadow hit its curves. Martin put the human head back on the shelf and began the daunting task of going through the paintings.

According to Mme Cézanne, the most recent works were standing in stacks against the walls. Martin could see in these still lifes and landscapes a vibrancy that he had not discerned in the scrap found by Franc. What connected these paintings to the fragment was their geometrical aspect, the way that the small straight strokes became little blocks of color, which, laid side by side, actually produced a recognizable shape. When Martin uncovered a picture of Mont Sainte-Victoire, he sucked in his breath. Solange Vernet's words echoed in his mind. "Only two men could fight over a mountain." Was this an earlier version of the painting that had hung in her salon? It really didn't matter. The artist's unique style had already given him away. There was no doubt in Martin's mind that Cézanne had painted the quarry canvas.

"Do you need to see more?" Mme Cézanne's question made Martin realize that he must have been standing still for quite some time, holding the depiction of the mountain before him.

"Yes." He gathered his thoughts. "Any portraits?"

The mother made a gesture toward a pile of rolled canvases in the corner. She positioned herself more comfortably on the stool and began fanning her face with a little flowered fan she had pulled from her pocket. The sun pouring in through the enlarged windows made the room damnably hot.

The canvases displayed a hodgepodge of styles and subjects— bathers, fruit, flowers, portraits, landscapes, houses, allegories. Martin paused during his rapid survey to ask Mme Cézanne to identify some of the sitters. The first was a self-portrait, showing Paul Cézanne in one of the hats made in the shop his father had once owned. The artist wore a full dark brown beard and mustache that matched the strands of unkempt hair falling beneath the black bowler. His nose was large and slightly hooked. Most remarkable of all were the ebony eyes, which stared out warily at the world. A more recent self-portrait revealed the baldness that Cézanne had covered with his father's haberdashery.

Then Martin unrolled a series of portraits that seemed to be laid on with a trowel. According to Mme Cézanne, these were "early works," depicting her brother Dominique, a bailiff at the courthouse. Martin did not recognize him from the pictures and was getting discouraged. He was going further and further back in time, away from the possibility of seeing anything that had to do with Solange Vernet. Just as he decided that he had to make one final push before he melted, he began to unroll, one right after another, lurid scenes of eroticism and violence.

Martin's mounting interest drew Mme Cézanne to him. "Oh, those," she said. "They were from his studies in Paris, twenty years ago."

Ignoring her comment, Martin scrutinized each picture with growing fascination. What kind of a man could have produced them? The figures were too crude to be recognizable as individual people. But many of the women in them had golden-red hair. One small canvas that struck Martin as particularly vulgar depicted a naked woman with her legs spread apart, suspended on a bed above a legion of adoring men. She was almost faceless and not particularly attractive. Yet the men, who came from all walks of life—including musicians, wrestlers, a soldier, even a bishop, identified by his miter —seemed to be worshiping her. At the bottom, in the very center, was a man seen from the back. His profession was not identified by his attire, but the man's baldness was fringed by the same ring of dark hair that circled Cézanne's head in his self-portraits. The only thing Martin could discern about this unidentified figure was that he could not keep his eyes off the woman who was so lewdly revealing herself. Is this how Cézanne saw Solange Vernet in her salon? Embarrassed, Martin tried to move the painting away from Mme Cézanne's insistent eyes, but she was right behind him.

"Some were just illustrations, you know, from other paintings or from stories or plays," she explained. "Paul doesn't do this kind of thing any more."

Martin said nothing as he rolled up this canvas and set it aside to take with him. At the very least, it was evidence of a troubled mind.

The next two canvases were even more disturbing—murder scenes. Both victims were women with golden-red hair. In the first, the homicidal instrument was a knife; in the second, strangulation. In each, there were two accomplices. In the knifing, a strong woman held the victim down while a man aimed his weapon straight at her heart.

"See here," Mme Cézanne's finger pointed to the background of the second picture. "Doesn't that look like curtains in a stage play?" Or an archway cut out of a quarry, Martin thought. There was no doubt about the strangled woman's anguish. Her head hung toward the viewer, hair falling in all directions, just as Solange Vernet's hair had been in the quarry, in fiery disarray. The only signs of life were her outstretched arms. Her eyes were open. Had she been pleading with Cézanne for mercy? Was she pleading with Martin now for justice?

He stood up straight with the lewd scene and the graphic portrayal of the strangulation in his hands. "I'll have to take these with me," he said, as casually as possible. "Can I roll them together?"

"You know they may be quite valuable some day. I am not sure I can let—"

"Madame," he wished he could soften the blow, "I am sure that your son painted the fragment we found in the quarry."

"But these are old pictures. I've told you. Can't you tell how much better Paul has gotten?"

"Yes, yes, of course." He tried to assure her. "But I want Paul himself to tell me about these." *To tell me whether they are evidence of a murder or only the product of a disturbed mind.* These were thoughts he would not dream of expressing to the poor mother.

Martin stood there like a fool for a few minutes, gingerly holding the paintings. He did not want to barge out. He still needed the mother's help.

"Here, let me," Mme Cézanne finally said as she took the canvases away from him, rolled them together, and tied them with a string. She was frowning during the entire operation. Martin was no longer a nice young judge.

Mme Cézanne thrust the two rolled paintings into his hand.

"One more thing." Martin took a deep breath. *The most important thing.* "You need to tell me where your son is."

She shook her head. "I don't—"

"If I have to, I will question everyone in the house, including the maid and your husband." Martin could see from her face that he had hit the mark.

"My son did not do anything."

"Madame—"

"Is this what you call justice? Allowing a family to be bothered and bullied? Accusing them?"

"This is a murder case. Others may be in danger." Martin said the words slowly and distinctly, hoping that this would persuade her.

There was a moment of silence, then she relented.

"Please be quiet coming down the stairs. I will explain everything when we get back to the salon." Behind closed doors, out of the hearing of the father.

In the salon, Mme Cézanne revealed a secret that was far beyond anything Martin had imagined. Cézanne had a mistress who had borne him a son thirteen years before. According to the proud grandmother, Paul Jr. was a beautiful, strapping boy, but his grandfather had never been told that a grandson existed. Louis-Auguste believed that a man should be able to support a wife before marriage, and so Paul and his mistress, Hortense Fiquet, were waiting for the right moment to inform the patriarch of their relationship. Then, and only then, would they marry. This summer Paul had settled his family in Gardanne, about ten kilometers away. That is where he went almost every day to work. After the Westerbury disturbance, Mme Cézanne explained, he had told Marie that he would be staying with Hortense and Paul Jr. until things quieted down. He did not want Papa to be disturbed, and he needed peace to do his work.

Martin left the Jas with a sense of relief. He had managed to bypass the bulldog of a sister and gotten Mme Cézanne to talk. Best of all, he believed the old woman. Finally, someone was telling him the truth! The most urgent question in Martin's mind, as he headed back to town with the two rolled canvases in tow, was whether he should organize an expedition to Gardanne that evening, or wait until the morning. That was the first thing he intended to take up with Franc when he got back to the courthouse.

10

FRANC WAS IN A TRIUMPHANT MOOD. He'd been waiting for Martin, to tell him that they had caught Westerbury "drowning in his sorrows" in a bar just outside the ramparts. When the inspector heard about what had happened at the Jas, he was even more buoyant, praising Martin for making Mme Cézanne "come clean" and for confiscating two pieces of the artist's "decadent works."

"Good work, sir, good work," Franc said, putting on his cap, getting ready to leave.

"But there is still so much more to do." The rolled canvases lay on Martin's desk, requiring a more thoughtful analysis than "decadent." Then there was a unopened telegram from Paris, the missing boy, the unfinished search for the artist, and Martin's notes to go over. So many things that warranted discussion here and now.

"Monsieur le juge," Franc said, as a crooked grin spread across his grizzled face, "I beg you, rest on your laurels. Enough for today. The Vernet woman will be dead forever."

"Let's at least see what Paris has to say." Martin picked up the telegram from the *police judiciare*, hoping to recapture his inspector's attention.

"Okay," Franc swiped off his cap and sat down impatiently in the chair. He folded his arms and kept shaking his head as Martin read the report, which, indeed, did not tell them much that they did not already know or suspect.

The Parisian police had kept a sharp eye on Westerbury, because he was a foreigner who lectured in public, and, depending on one's beliefs, promoted science or flirted with blasphemy. Yet he had never committed a blatant enough offense against public morality to warrant arrest or expulsion. As for Solange, "born Sophie Vernet in 1850 in the Seine-Maritime Department," she had arrived in Paris around 1868, and apprenticed at the Widow Charpentier's millinery. The tax rolls indicated that Mme Charpentier had been on the brink of financial ruin. But after Vernet took up residence, the shop not only survived, but it expanded, becoming a hat emporium attracting a quality clientele. This reversal of fortune elicited the special scrutiny of the police; however, no criminal activity was discovered. Vernet herself had called upon the gendarmes on two separate occasions to deal with disturbances caused by Jacques LaFarge. She paid her taxes regularly and on time, making her a singularly law-abiding shop owner, and left Paris a wealthy woman.

"You see, Franc, you were right about the money," Martin said after he finished. "And it's not only a question of how Solange Vernet brought so much money to Aix, but how she and her aunt managed to transform a failing shop into a huge success."

"You're going around in circles. You need to take your mind off all this."

"You don't think the money could be part of the motive?"

"Sure I do. But so could jealousy. Or godlessness. We're not sure yet. Murder investigations take time."

"Picard will be back any day now. I'll see what he thinks," Martin said more to himself than to his companion, who had already risen to his feet and put his cap back on his head.

"When the notary comes back you can ask him all about the money, *and,* in the meantime, my men will search for the boy through the night. We've already agreed to take off for Gardanne first thing tomorrow. So for now, my—" Franc stumbled over the words that were about to come out of his mouth. Was he about to say "my boy"? "For now," Franc repeated, "I know exactly what will take your mind off all this. How about a nice dinner served by a pretty girl?"

"I don't think—"

"Is an inspector too lowly a companion for a little dinner?"

"Of course not." Martin bristled at the implication that he shared the social prejudices of his well-born colleagues.

"Well, then? We can talk about the case. *Again. If you insist.* And you, you can get something good into that stomach of yours."

Martin brushed a damp strand of hair from his forehead. What could be the harm? Franc was determined to leave, and Martin was starving. The last thing he had eaten were two little tea sandwiches served to him by Arlette LaFarge. And the last thing he wanted to do was to have another solitary meal surrounded by the staid, contented souls of La Bonne Ménagère. With a nod, Martin gave in.

"Good!"

The twinkle in the inspector's eyes should have been a signal to Martin that Franc had scored yet another victory.

Once they got outside the courthouse, Franc led Martin at a breathless pace down the rue Rifle Rafle, the aptly named street abutting the prison, toward the university. A new restaurant, Franc explained as they galloped along, was the kind of thing you noticed when you kept an eagle eye over the town. The Choffruts had just come from Arles with the idea of opening a place for homesick students from their town. The food was good and cheap, and, Franc added as he stopped and gestured toward Chez l'Arlésienne, he and Martin had the chance to become favored regulars before the onslaught of law and literature students in the fall.

When Franc swung the door open, a bell tinkled overhead, announcing their arrival. As soon as they stepped inside, they were enveloped in the tantalizing aroma of tomatoes and garlic. In a glance Martin saw that Chez l'Arlésienne was the kind of good, humble eatery that he and his fellow law students had cherished in Paris. It was small, holding only ten or twelve tables. The two longest were already occupied by workmen.

"M. Franc, M. Franc." A short, stout middle-aged woman came out of the kitchen to greet them. She was attired in traditional Arlésienne style, a lace fichu wrapped around her shoulders and fastened at the waist over a printed dress and her head crowned with a knot of gray hair circled by a wide black ribbon. Franc introduced her as Henriette Choffrut.

"Come in, come in. So this is the judge. He does look like a nice young man." Before Martin had a chance to react to the fact that he had obviously been expected, Henriette Choffrut was leading them to a small table in a cool corner. She told them that she would send her niece, Clarie, over right away.

Martin gave Franc a murderous look as they sat down, but the inspector ignored him. Franc was in his element, happily surveying the surroundings and sniffing the inviting smells, while Martin kept his head low, determined to get away as soon as possible.

"Tonight daube or aioli." Martin glanced up. Clarie was a surprise. Dressed like her aunt, except that her hair was bound by virginal white, she was taller than most southerners, and slender. But it was her eyes, sparkling with some secret amusement, that really caught his attention. They were dark brown, almond-shaped, and very large. Above them, her black eyebrows were drawn in an arch of curiosity. Not quite as gay and mocking as Solange Vernet's green eyes had been, but almost as bold. Her aquiline nose gave her oval face more length than it needed, but it also led one quite naturally to her red lips, pressed together in a long, bemused smile. Head tilted toward him, hands on hips, she gazed at Martin with an air of expectation.

He began to trace the red and white checks on the stiff cotton tablecloth with his finger.

"Daube? Or aioli?"

"Aioli—I should explain to him, he's from the north, you know—" Franc intervened.

"*I do know*," she said with a sigh and turned to Martin. "It's cold fish and vegetables with a sauce. Very good on a hot night."

"Good, yes, good." Martin was avoiding her eyes.

"Good choice. Me too," Franc chimed in. "And some of that tapenade with your good bread and white wine."

"Two aiolis," Clarie called to the kitchen and left their table.

Martin glared at Franc. Match-making was the last thing he would have expected from someone so deeply embedded in the virile camaraderie of police work.

Franc met Martin's stare with a wink. "Quite a gypsy, isn't she? Those dark eyes. Those gold earrings. She's their niece, but she's half Italian. Falchetti. Clarie Falchetti."

Realizing that any sign of anger or embarrassment would only encourage his companion, Martin decided to do his best to show neither. Just as he was fitting on this mask of indifference, the bread, the tapenade and a jug of wine were slapped on the table. Clarie had returned. And Franc could not keep his mouth shut.

"I was about to tell the young judge over here that you are thinking about going to that brand-new school near Paris so that you can teach high school. Imagine a young woman like you around all those over-grown brats. Doesn't seem right."

"Better the brats than men with big paws," she said, as she removed Franc's hand from the top of her skirt.

"Now don't take offense. We were just wondering why a beautiful girl like you would want to teach a bunch of brats instead of bringing up a stable of your own."

"We?"she looked at Martin, who was trying to signal his innocence by shaking his head. Her lips parted in a big smile, as if to say she understood. Then she took off to serve another table.

"I think we had better change the subject," Martin said, as Franc poured the wine and began to slather the black paste on their bread.

"Try this." Franc handed him a piece. "Anchovies and black olives all mashed up together."

Martin bit into the rich mixture, which was salty, but good. He reached for the wine and drank, a little too quickly. It was sour, and he almost had a coughing fit. Martin closed his eyes. *Slow down, relax*, he told himself. After all, he had succeeded in communicating his inno-cence to the girl. And he'd have no trouble getting Franc to go on about any number of safe topics. His inspector was, after all, a great talker.

And, indeed, Franc held forth through most of the meal, while Martin listened and observed. He watched the laborers laughing together as they gulped down their food. He noted how often Mme Choffrut kept making the rounds, clucking like a mother hen, making sure that everything was in order and everyone was satisfied. He saw Clarie, strong yet graceful, carrying trays back and forth, fobbing off the attention of forward customers. As they ate their way through a pile of cold whitefish, carrots, potatoes, and green beans, Martin heard all about Franc's heroic role in the annals of Aixois crime and how much he was looking forward to solving his greatest case yet, *their* case, with its special cast of characters: the foreigner, the artist, and the loose woman trying to force herself into high society.

As the evening wore on, Martin was finding himself more at ease and increasingly amused by Franc's yen for the dramatic.

"You know, my hero is Vidocq."

"Vidocq?" Martin put his carrot back on his plate, and lifted his glass to his lips to cover his smile. Anyone interested in crime knew of the brawler, petty thief, convict, and escape artist who had served both the Emperor Napoleon and the monarchy. Vidocq's methods for infiltrating the underworld had left an indelible mark on the way the police operated in Paris.

"I would have thought you fashioned yourself more after Javert," Martin said, referring to the police inspector whose relentless pursuit of Jean Valjean was the subject of Hugo's great novel. "He was more on the up-and-up, righteous and persistent, like you." Vidocq had been brought down because his ever-expanding corps of agents and informers turned out to be every bit as unsavory as the lawbreakers they were pursuing.

"No," Franc shook his head and wiped a bit of the garlic mayonnaise from his shiny black mustache with his checkered napkin. "I like someone who is real, who really lived, who really changed things. He's been my hero ever since I read his autobiography. But you know, sir," Franc leaned forward, "this does not mean that I would ever dream of breaking the law. It's just that you have to understand how criminals think. Talk to prostitutes in their own language. Pay a beggar who might have something to tell you. Sometimes even look like one of them. And if necessary, get tough. That's what I'm going to do tomorrow after we bring back Cézanne, if they haven't found the boy yet."

As Franc kept talking, Martin was trying to recapture a memory. "Vautrin! That's it. That's what I remember best about Vidocq."

"Sir?"

"Balzac befriended Vidocq, admired him, I think, but made him seem rather despicable as the notorious Vautrin, no?"

"I wouldn't know, sir. I'm not a novel-reader. Too much dirt, too much fantasy."

"Ahh." Martin sipped on the strong sour wine. How had Balzac described Vautrin? A spy, a wearer of wigs, a master of disguises. Even Satanic. Vautrin's unmasking in *Père Goriot* had sent chills down Martin's spine when he was a boy. And Franc? That could explain the hair dye and the bluster. Martin once again covered up his amusement by holding his glass up to his lips. It had to be difficult to maintain one's image as a Vidocq in this backwater town.

"Coffee?" It was Mme Choffrut. Clarie was clearing off the tables vacated by the laborers, who had consumed their meals at a hard and fast pace.

"Two please." Franc's expansive mood continued, "and—"

"I'll bring the pear tarts too," she said in a high lilting voice as she headed back toward the kitchen.

Franc sat back and patted his stomach. "How do you like the food?" he asked Martin.

"Very much." No reason not to show his enthusiasm for the moment. Martin knew that he would never have the nerve to come back to a place where he had been the object of such obvious interest.

When Mme Choffrut brought the coffees to the table, she was accompanied by the cook, who was carrying the tarts and wearing an apron covered with the colors of the evening's offerings. She introduced him to Martin as her husband, Michel. He was not much taller than his wife, almost as wide and just as cheerful. As Martin watched Mme Choffrut while he ate, he had thought of his mother in those happy days when his father was still alive, managing everything and everybody who came into their clock shop. As the Choffruts began to tell the story of their move to Aix, Martin was reminded of the way his parents had seemed to be part of a single being, always touching each other, agreeing with each other, finishing each other's sentences. He was not surprised to learn that the Choffruts were childless—and that they had found an outlet for their excess of affection in their only niece.

"The only girl of seven boys. The only child of Giuseppe. He married Henriette's sister after her husband died—"

"Yes, he took over my brother-in-law's smith shop and the burden of all those boys!"

"They only had one kid together, Clarie, many years later—"

"And then last year my sister—" she drew her handkerchief to her mouth.

"Died—and you know that Henriette could not bear to pass her house, so we decided to start over again."

"That saint of a man!" Henriette Choffrut was back to the subject of Giuseppe Falchetti. "When his only girl, his little *benjamine*, said she wanted to go to that new school in Paris, he agreed."

"But only as long as she tried out being away from home for a while, to see if both of them could stand it."

"That's why she's here. An experiment, he said." By this time the weight of it all—her sister's death, Giuseppe's goodness, and Clarie's independence—brought tears rolling down Henriette Choffrut's cheeks and required the comfort of one of Michel's strong arms. It even drew in Clarie, who could hardly have escaped hearing everything. She gave her aunt a hug and kiss.

"Papa will be fine. It's only a few years. And besides," she said to Martin with an apologetic smile, "everyone does not need to hear the whole sad story." She steered her aunt back to the kitchen. Michel also withdrew with a smile and shrug.

Martin finished the meal with mixed emotions. For some reason, it pleased him to see Clarie's affectionate response to her aunt's tears. It made her seem more warm and womanly. But the entire scene also evoked bittersweet memories. His own mother had always found many reasons for tears, and his father had often enlisted Martin's support in comforting her with hugs and kisses. Their little circle of affection had been broken only by death. As the years stretched out, Martin found it harder and harder to open his heart to his mother's woes. Perhaps this was because he suspected that if she really knew what he was becoming—an agnostic, a republican, a man of reason—*he* would become the major source of all her sorrows. Clarie Falchetti was leaving her father to attend an experimental school; he had left his mother and her beliefs far behind him. Were children always destined to disappoint their parents?

Martin was brought out of his reveries by the business at hand. The Choffruts were refusing to take any money. He joined the fray, insisting on paying the bill, but they resolutely rebuffed his offers. "When you come back and bring your friends, you can pay then," Mme Choffrut said as she gave him a motherly pat. "And this old fellow," Michel slapped Franc on the back, "he's promised to bring us many customers and to keep an eye on our place all year." Franc was beaming. He seemed to have no trouble accepting the generosity of these newcomers to Aix. Martin had to wonder how many other shop-keepers and restaurateurs felt beholden to the inspector.

In any case, the Choffruts did not seem to mind. They accompanied Martin and Franc to the door and shook their hands warmly and vig-orously. As Martin was leaving, he caught a glimpse of Clarie Falchetti, busying herself, ignoring their departure. He felt an unex-pected twinge of regret as he realized that he might never see her again, for he did not want to be any more entangled with Franc or his plots than he had to be.

Friday, August 21

Ni Dieu Ni Maître
(Neither God Nor Master)
 —Masthead of a revolutionary socialist newspaper 1880–81

11

THE GREAT SAINT-SAUVEUR CATHEDRAL BELLS were tolling six o'clock as he strode through the square. The morning was fresh and so, for once, was Martin. He was beginning to think that going to Chez l'Arlésienne with Franc last night had been a good idea. It had provided pleasant distractions, like his inspector's braggadocio, good food, and a pretty Arlésienne girl. Martin even suspected that he had imbibed some of Franc's optimism. If all went well today, they'd catch the artist. Then Martin thought, with a little bravado of his own, he might just be able to look him in the eye and see if he was a killer.

This good mood carried Martin only to the back entrance of the courthouse, where Jacques, one of the younger gendarmes, waited with a note. Martin unfolded the piece of paper slowly, and his zeal congealed into a hard lump in his chest. "We have found the boy.

Come to the morgue. Franc." Though his mouth had suddenly run dry, Martin managed to thank the officer and cross the narrow street to the prison. By the time he reached the door, he barely had the strength to open it. He stood for a moment, his hand pushed hard against it, as frenzied questions whirled about in his mind. Could he have prevented the death of the child? Had Westerbury murdered the little messenger after Martin released him? Or, had the artist managed to find and kill the boy on his way out of town? Clinging to the railing with a clammy hand, Martin made his descent into the basement where Riquel set up his operations. Franc was there, talking to the doctor, who had on his blood-stained working apron.

"Do you want to have a look?" Riquel turned to him. "We just found him, and I haven't had time to clean him up."

Coming from Riquel, the science professor who reveled in his part-time police work, this was a warning. But Martin needed to see the disastrous consequences of his own failings. He nodded, and Riquel uncovered the body. It was worse than he imagined. Insects had left black liquid holes where the boy's eyes, nose and mouth had been. The body was bloated beyond all recognition. The smell was over-whelming. Martin's stomach lurched. He went to a corner and vomited, without forethought, and without shame.

The convulsions shook his entire body again and again. He was wracked with guilt, for the boy, for Solange Vernet, for his own stupidities, and for the little bits of vain ambition that had begun to move him. If the same man who killed Solange Vernet had murdered the boy—and how could it not be so?—he was up against a monster. How was he going to reason this out? What good were his paltry untested talents to him or to anyone else, dead or alive? By the time Martin's heaving shuddered to a halt, he was hanging on to the cold stone walls for support. He forced himself to stand up and wiped off his mouth with his handkerchief.

"I'm sorry."

"Oh, we're used to that in here." Riquel barely glanced up from his own calm examination of the body, before covering it again with the sheet. "Franc, get one of the prison guards to bring a mop."

Martin avoided meeting the inspector's eyes as he started up the stairs. They both knew that Franc would never show such weakness.

"When?" Martin asked Riquel.

"Probably about the same time as the woman, give a day this way or that."

"Before? After?"

"I can't be sure."

Martin sucked in air through his mouth, as he covered his nose with his hand.

Riquel put a hand on Martin's shoulder. "I don't think this happened after you released Westerbury."

Franc and the professor had obviously covered that territory before Martin arrived. *If only that were true.* Career be damned. The courthouse be damned. The ridicule they would all heap on him be damned. How could he continue to be a judge, knowing that he had abetted the killing of a child?

"We don't know who it is?" Martin dropped his arm and kept his voice as steady as possible.

Riquel shook his head. "Not until someone reports him missing."

Martin took one last look at the white mound that had once been a boy. Controlling his trembling, he shook hands with Dr. Riquel and went up the stairs, out into the fresh air.

Martin headed up the narrow cobblestoned street that divided the prison from the courthouse, to the fountain on the square. He stumbled a bit over the three low steps that led to the spouting water. When he reached his destination, he dipped in his hands, splashed his face and swiped at his frock coat, cleaning himself off. All too soon Martin heard a wagon and men on horseback clatter to a halt behind him. The search party to Gardanne was ready. Martin gritted his teeth and closed his eyes before turning to face them. He hoped to God that they would not ask him whether he was all right.

The rest of the morning went by in a daze, as Martin fought hard to keep the images of grotesque, bloated, dead bodies out of his thoughts. Sitting with Franc on the driver's seat of a horse-drawn wagon, he tried to concentrate on what lay ahead in Gardanne. Franc had enlisted four mounted gendarmes to go with them. He had the sense not to be solicitous, but he made it clear that he was not a man to be defeated by another murder. He encouraged the horses cheerfully and directed the few remarks he felt compelled to make to the men in uniform on either side of the wagon. The horses pulled them through a forest, over the river Arc, and onto an unshaded plain. Off to the east, a long line of limestone hills dogged their path, their rugged faces looking like chalk-white death masks, staring at Martin, mocking him. What in the world was he doing in this place?

12

HORTENSE HEARD THE COMMOTION AND RAN to the window. The gendarmes were slowly making their way up the narrow stone street. They looked like overgrown Napoleons with their horizontal hats and military dress, only these Napoleons wore black uniforms with white braiding and carried rifles slung over their shoulders. Agents of death, she thought, or, at least, messengers of disaster. Behind them she saw two other men, one broad-shouldered and stocky in a jacket and cap; the other younger, more slender, more formally dressed. They were knocking on doors, asking directions. They were coming for Paul, she was sure of it. Soon, all the nosy heads would be popping out of windows, watching and talking about them. She had little time to figure out how to protect Cézanne.

Paul Jr. was on the sofa, reading. "Quick, son. Go find Papa. Tell him that some people from Aix are looking for him." She did not want to alarm the boy by telling him the police were after his father.

"Oh, Maman, I was just—"

"Now!"

Her thirteen-year-old, her darling, started for the door. "No, wait." She grabbed one of his arms. "Climb out the back window, I think he is painting up by the church."

"Maman, that's silly," he whined.

"Do as I say!" She had startled him. Hortense rarely raised her voice to her son. To emphasize her point she gave him a little shove toward the bedroom door. Let Paul decide if he wants to hide or not. At least this way he would have a chance.

Hortense heard the knock. Already! She licked her fingers to moisten them in order to smooth down her hair, then searched frantically in her bun for a pin to hold the loose strands. Wiping her hands on her skirt, she went to the door.

"We are looking for Paul Cézanne," said one of the gendarmes.

"He's not here."

The burly middle-aged man pushed himself in front of the soldier. "Where is he?" He was practically at her chest, sweating, his mustache almost touching her forehead. Hortense stepped back.

"He's out painting somewhere. I'm not sure."

"Not sure?"

She didn't like this man. He was not polite. "He paints in different places. Why do you want him? What is this about?" She could stand her ground even against a brute.

"It is about a murder. Your lover is a suspect." *Lover!* He was an exceedingly rude man. Paul was certainly more than her lover.

"Sorry, I can't help you."

"Well, then, we will look for him. In the meantime, we will be searching your house." He tipped his cap and smiled. "Jean, François," he called out, "with me." He waved two of the men up the hill. If Paul were up there by the church, it would not take them long to find him.

That left her with two gendarmes and a young gentleman. He took off his top hat and introduced himself as Bernard Martin, examining magistrate at the court of Aix.

"May I?" he pointed his hat toward the entrance.

She moved back to let them in. Her heart was pounding. She had to stay calm. She had to figure out the right thing to say.

"The knife, the gloves, any letters. That's all. Don't make a mess of things." The judge gave orders in a low voice. Then he shifted his attention to her.

"May we sit? I need to ask you a few questions."

"Yes, of course. Would you like some coffee? Water?" Hortense could barely talk, but she was going to show them that hers was a civilized household.

"No, thank you," he answered. "We stopped at the well at the bottom of the hill." At least he was more polite than the other man.

Hortense poured herself a glass. Her mouth was going dry. Besides, if she got stuck she could sip on the water until she had a good answer.

"The table's fine," he said, before she asked where he would like to sit. "I can take notes more easily."

Yes, she thought, as she pulled out a chair and sat down. The table would be fine. If her hands started shaking, she would have a place to hide them.

Hortense watched as Martin removed a pencil and a small notebook from his pocket. He seemed weary and overburdened. He was very young to be a judge, almost too young to wear that hat and sport that beard. His light brown hair was matted against his forehead, which glistened with sweat. He was almost good-looking. When he turned a little gray he would have more distinction. He would have a position in life. He had, despite the expression on his face, much to look forward to.

"And now," he said, after turning to a clean page, "Madame?—"

She almost said "Cézanne," answering too quickly. Was this a trick? Paul always told her she talked too fast and said too much. She had to be careful and make a show of being utterly honest. "I am Hortense Fiquet, born in the town of Saligney in the Jura in 1850."

He had dated the page and was writing this down.

"Then you are not married?"

"Engaged."

"But you have a son."

"Yes, Paul. Born in 1872."

"Where is he?"

"With his father."

"Painting?"

"No, watching." Even though Paul hated anyone to watch him work.

"Then you have been together a long time."

"Yes, we met in Paris in 1869. I was. . . ." If she told him she was a model, would he think she was a common, loose woman? She took a sip of the water. He waited, pencil poised. "I came to Paris when I was nineteen, and worked as a model for only a little while until I met Paul. We have been together ever since. Now I model only for him." The judge had nice gray-blue eyes, but he was making her nervous, never taking them off her. She could hear the sounds of the men opening drawers, going through her things in the bedroom.

"May I ask why you haven't married?"

She thought this might be coming. Hortense drew herself up. "Paul is waiting to get his father's permission." This did not seem to surprise the judge. Had he been to the Jas already? "As soon as Paul is established, we are sure his father will agree. We expect that to be any day now. His paintings are becoming better and better known. He has many of them with a dealer in Paris, who shows them constantly." This was only half true. "Father" Tanguy had not sold a painting in months, and Paul still owed him for paints and supplies.

He wrote none of this down, just watched as she talked. Did he see her as a rejected woman? How much did he know about Paul and that witch Solange?

"Mme Fiquet, I must ask you some difficult questions."

She would soon find out. She folded her hands in front of her, ready for battle.

"Did you know about Cézanne's relationship with Solange Vernet?"

Without any hesitation, she answered. "No, actually I don't believe there was a relationship."

"Then you knew Mme Vernet?"

"No." Paul had certainly never bothered to introduce them.

"Did you know a Charles Westerbury?"

Since he probably had some way to check on this, she admitted that she had been to one of his lectures.

"Not the whole course, then?"

She shook her head.

"Why?"

She shrugged. Marie had been so horrified, and Paul so scornful. Yet he had gotten involved with their circle. The judge was maddening. He kept staring at her, waiting. One of the gendarmes had just come into the living room across from them.

"Please don't disturb the paintings!" she said as she rose. Paul would be furious.

Martin turned in his chair. "I'll look through the paintings later. Leave them be. You can wait outside when you are done." He settled in again. "You were telling me why you did not complete the course with M. Westerbury." Now the gendarme was upending the cushions and searching behind the books. Hortense sat down again.

"Paul told me they were a sham, that he knew more about the geology of this place than the Englishman ever would."

"Yet we know that Paul went to their salon."

Hortense sat back, motionless. Paul had taught her how to do that during those endless, long sittings. He'd shown her how to remain expressionless, to hide what she was thinking and feeling.

"Did you know?" the judge persisted. "Did he talk about them?"

"Not really. I am sure they were not that important to him. He was probably seeking some stimulation, which can be very hard to find in Aix. You must know that yourself. You're not from here." This seemed clear from his accent. Martin did not respond. "You have to understand," Hortense continued, bravely, "Paul is an important artist, interested in science, painting, literature, the whole gamut."

The judge was drawing circles on the paper.

"You've been to Paris, of course?"

He nodded. The other gendarme, the bigger one, was moving about behind her, going through the kitchen drawers. He laid all their knives out on the table, one by one.

"Why is he doing that?" She could hear her own voice rise to a high pitch. "Those have never left my kitchen."

Martin fingered the knives and pushed them aside. "Put them back," he said quietly. "Sorry," he said to Hortense. "Please go on."

"Well," she swallowed hard and tried to concentrate on what she needed to say, "if you have been to Paris, then you must have heard of the impressionist group. About Manet." Everyone had heard of Manet. "Paul is a friend of Manet. When we lived in Paris, we used to meet with him and others at the Café Guerbois practically every night. I don't know if you have heard of Monet or Pissarro, but Paul is very good friends with them too. We've just visited Monet's new place at Giverny this summer."

Although the judge had written down "Manet," he did not seem moved. Maybe he did not know much about the art world. She had to make him understand that she and Paul were not merely provincials. They couldn't just take Paul off to prison and throw away the key, even if he had been crazy enough to commit a crime of passion. She had to use the last trump card.

"And of course his best friend is Zola."

This time Martin looked up, impressed. After all, Émile Zola was France's most famous writer.

"Oh, yes, they grew up together in Aix," she assured him.

"Zola" went down on the note pad.

"They were schoolmates. Zola always said that Paul was his protector because Zola's family was so poor. His father built the town dam near the Bibémus road. But after he died, the town ignored the family. Zola had to go to Paris with his mother to make his way right after he left school. But he and Paul kept in touch. They correspond constantly. We've stayed at his house at Médan many times." Or at least Paul had. He usually avoided taking her, so that he could have Zola all to himself. "It's a magnificent place. Filled with antiques and books and art, including several of Paul's paintings. We were just there in July. We're all very good friends," she added for emphasis. She knew she was talking too much, but she just couldn't help herself. She had finally gotten the young judge's attention.

"The only reason Paul is in Provence is because he believes that he will create his greatest works in this landscape. We would be welcomed in Paris, at Médan, any time. As for Gardanne, Paul thought his son and I might like a little break from Aix while he explores different landscapes. Here, let me show you." She got up, ready to go into the living room.

"Just a moment, please, then we can look at the paintings."

Hortense was relieved that the judge had finally said something, but dismayed that he was beginning to scrutinize her meager living quarters. She chewed on her lip as she waited for him to say more.

"How often does Cézanne come to Gardanne?" he finally asked.

"Every day."

"Even on Sunday? Last Monday?"

"Every single day and . . . let's see . . . ," Hortense paused, as if she were trying to make sure that what she said was correct. "Last Sunday and Monday. Oh yes, right after the Feast of the Assumption. Paul was here. He had seen the procession in Aix so often, we decided to picnic and then he stayed the night." Hortense wished she knew exactly when that witch had been murdered. "I think he only went back on Tuesday to see his sick father." There, she had done it. And he was writing it down.

But then he did the most disconcerting thing. He began to leaf backward through his notes, notes he had taken elsewhere. Where? Whom had he spoken to? Hortense's heart started pounding again. If she was going to save Paul, she had to be more careful.

"All right, then." He closed his notebook and got up with a grim little smile. A smile of obligatory politeness. Or pity. Perhaps he stopped questioning people who lied to him. She could feel hot tears coming to her eyes as he went through the pile of papers and gloves that the gendarmes had placed before him on the table. When he handed them back to her, with a quiet thank-you, she went quickly into the bedroom, relieved to be out his sight, while she put her things away.

By the time she was done, the judge was already searching through the paintings stacked against the living room wall. She caught him staring at a portrait of her sitting in a chair. How she hated the way she looked, blank and unrecognizable. She never understood why it took Paul so long to produce so little. No feeling, no character. "Sit like an apple," he would tell her. "Be still." And for what?

She took a breath, clasped her hands together and reentered the room. "Paul says," she needed to explain, somehow, that Paul painted her that way for a reason, "Paul says that he is interested in the whole canvas, not just the subject. With the portraits, sometimes he will start in the middle, just like he starts a still life or landscape, and then he builds outward. That's why, in his art, a face has no more significance than the chair or the wallpaper." Sometimes she wondered if she was any more significant to Paul than apples or the wallpaper. Still, she needed to rattle on, and try to set things right. To show the judge that Paul painted that way on purpose, not because he could not do better. "It's the whole canvas that's important. The whole thing. That's his new idea."

Just then, they heard a commotion in the street. She ran to the window. The gendarmes had Paul by the arms. He was shouting at them to let him go. His hair was sticking out in all directions, his bald head beaming in the sun. When he saw her, he yelled, "Get in touch with Maxim."

"Yes, dear, of course," she called out, as he passed below. She closed the shutters. If he wanted her to find his brother-in-law Maxim, then he knew he needed a lawyer. And she knew what she had to do.

"How are you taking Paul back?" she asked the judge.

"In a wagon. It's down the hill." He was pocketing his notebook.

"Take me and my son, please. We need to be with Paul."

"I don't think it will be very comfortable. And it might be disturbing for your son to see his father—"

Just then Paul Jr. flung open the door. "Maman, Maman, they are taking Papa. The gendarmes are taking Papa away." Hortense was relieved to see he looked more excited than scared.

"Please!" There was nothing she could do in Gardanne. In Aix she'd make sure that Maxim was notified. She'd even send a telegram to Zola. And she'd escape this godforsaken town.

"I am not sure that you and your son—" Did the judge really care about what her son might feel?

She'd beg on her knees if she had to. Grab on to Martin, and not let him out of the door. First, though, she'd play the part of a concerned and affectionate mother. Hortense took hold of her son's shoulders and turned him around to face the judge. "Don't you want to go back to Aix with Papa and ride with the gendarmes?"

Paul Jr. looked back and forth between the judge and her. It was beginning to dawn on him that something serious was happening.

"We'd feel isolated here, wouldn't we, son? We'd worry about Papa," she continued, smoothing down her son's straight brown hair.

He nodded his head slowly. "I'd like to go with my father, sir."

Martin stared at her son as if he knew him from somewhere, or was trying to recognize someone else in him. Hortense couldn't tell which, and she couldn't have cared less. What was important is that Paul Junior's plea seemed to do the trick.

"All right, then," the judge relented, "but you must hurry."

"You stay here with the judge," she told her son, "and I'll be right back." She flew to the bedroom and began tossing some clothes and hats into two cloth sacks. They would stay in the family house on the rue Matheron, where Paul had never dared to let them stay before. How could he refuse her now? It was he who was causing all the trouble. He needed her. He needed her help. She'd be the one to get in touch with Maxim, contact the Jas and, yes, telegraph Zola.

13

IT WAS GOOD TO BE ON HORSEBACK, away from Franc's incessant talking. Martin was not a skilled rider, but the gendarme's horse was well-trained, and guiding it along the uneven paths between Gardanne and Aix gave him something besides the dead boy to think about. So did the inhabitants of the wagon. Franc was none too pleased that Martin had allowed the woman and her son to come along, and ordered François, the biggest and most experienced of his men, to sit with them. Martin, in turn, had insisted that Cézanne did not need to be tied up. With four men on horses, there was no possibility of escape. And, just as Martin predicted, the presence of his family calmed down the artist, whose cries of protest had alerted the entire town to his arrest.

At times, Cézanne, who was wearing a gray cap hastily provided by Hortense Fiquet, sat silently, watching the receding road. Other times, he chatted with his son, who insisted on sitting next to him. Martin overheard Zola's name as they were crossing the Arc. The artist was pointing to a particular spot near the river with one arm while he held on to his son's shoulder with the other. He seemed to be recounting a story from his own childhood. Martin drew closer, but could not hear what they were saying. The woman had told him that Cézanne and Zola were the best of friends. If that were true, and the famous author decided to get involved, he would be a formidable adversary.

Martin was struck by the artist's seeming nonchalance. He could not tell whether Cézanne was trying to demonstrate his innocence, or just putting on a brave face for his son. The artist had no such tender concern for Hortense Fiquet. Their conversation before getting into the wagon had been loud enough for all to hear, an argument about whether or not they should stay in the family apartment. Evidently, Cézanne would have to go to the Jas and beg for the key, and he did not want to do that. Once the journey was under way, the two of them never exchanged a word. She sat with the bags beside François, across from her son and lover, staring at the road before them. Paul Cézanne seemed to dote on his son, but this was clearly not a happy family.

Were there happy families? Martin stroked the neck of the gentle, snorting chestnut horse. If there were happy families, then how did they hold on to their happiness when fate could intervene so cruelly? Dead fathers, dead children. The child lying in the morgue had been small, much smaller than Cézanne's husky boy, and probably younger, too. The dead boy might not have had a father who doted on him, who took care of him, who had made sure that he was fed and clothed and sheltered. If he had, he would not have been so willing to hire himself out to strangers. The dead boy would never know the joys and sorrows of manhood. Or the inevitable failures and self-doubts that Martin knew all too well. He looked again at Cézanne talking to his son, holding him close. Could this man have really killed the boy?

As soon as they entered the square in front of the Palais, Martin saw a carriage parked at the main entrance. His hands tightened around the reins. This was not a good sign.

Without pausing to investigate, Franc skillfully maneuvered their little entourage down the narrow street that led to the back of the courthouse and the front of the prison. They passed through in single file as the horses' hooves slowed to a mournful, drumming cadence. Martin could not keep his eyes off the low yellow building that held the dead body of the little messenger. A reminder, as if he needed one, gripped at his stomach: this investigation, and these deaths, were his responsibility. This is what it meant to be a judge. A real judge with murders on his hands.

In oblivious high spirits, Franc jumped off the wagon and ran over to Martin. "Your little visit yesterday must have tipped off the Cézanne clan," he said under his breath. "We'll see if they got out the troops." He, too, suspected that the artist's relatives or lawyers had arrived.

So did Cézanne, who began to scuffle with the gendarmes as they tried to get him off the wagon. He lurched backward until he had caught the attention of Hortense Fiquet. "Go to the Hôtel de la Gare. I'll meet you there. Quick. Papa could be here." Once he had spit out this vital message to his mistress, Cézanne was noticeably calmer, but leaned pitifully toward his son, dragging the men along with him.

"Let him go," Martin ordered. "Let him say good-bye to the boy."

Franc threw up his hands in exasperation. He nodded to the men, seconding Martin's command, but could not hold back a protest. "What are you doing? We have him where we want him. If his family is here, we have a chance to humiliate him. Crush him. Wring everything he knows out of him." Franc held up a thick clenched fist.

"Whatever he did, it's not the boy's fault." Martin said, and, ignoring Franc, turned to stroke the warm, panting creature that had carried him from Gardanne. If only he had the animal's steadiness and strength. He heard the inspector's heavy footsteps as he impatiently headed toward the door. Martin took a deep breath and handed the reins to one of the gendarmes. For good or ill, now was the time for him to take full command. He could no longer depend upon Franc, even with all his experience. He could rely on no one but himself, his training, and his reason to see that no more boys would be hurt and no more decaying bodies found.

Franc waved the prisoner and two guards inside, where they stood in silence until Martin caught up to them. When they got to the main floor, the faithful Old Joseph was waiting to give Martin and Franc a report. "The whole family has been here for an hour," he said in a low voice, "the mother, the father, the sisters, and the son-in-law, who is the lawyer Maxim Conil. They came pounding at the great door, demanding to get in. I finally got someone to unlock it. The father can't walk much, so we couldn't exactly insist that he go around the back." The clerk looked around and added in a confidential whisper, "He barely made it up the stairs."

Heads had already appeared at the railing above them. Martin recognized Marie, who was with another, rounder woman and, most fashionably dressed of all, a male, undoubtedly the lawyer, Maxim Conil. One of the sisters saw Cézanne in tow and cried out, "Paul!" Martin and Franc stepped aside to let the grim-faced artist and his guards pass.

"I don't suppose you want me to sit in and listen to the testimony," Franc said. "He could be dangerous, you know."

"No." As much as he knew it would displease his inspector, he had no intention of letting him, or anyone else, intervene. "Sit with the family. Watch their reactions. We'll compare notes afterward."

This time Franc did not even bother to argue. He must have seen a new determination in Martin's face.

At the top of the stairs, Marie had already grabbed her brother and was hugging him and crying. Martin hurried past, only to be confronted by the dandy. "Maxim Conil, attorney. I will be representing

Paul Cézanne and attending any interviews. He is a member of an important and established family in Aix—"

As Martin put up his hand to halt this little speech, the white-haired old man sitting on the bench leaned forward and, with two hands on his cane, launched himself into a standing position. "That's right, Maxim, you earn your keep," he said before he fell back again and began muttering through his walrus mustache. "For once, let someone, anyone, earn their keep around here."

"As you know," the lawyer continued intrepidly, "I have a right, if you allow me, to be in the room with my client."

"Yes, yes." Martin could see that Conil would try his patience, but he did not want to argue about the rights of counsel in front of the entire family. He would allow Conil to stay only so long as he did not interfere.

Having made his point, the lawyer stepped aside, while Martin went over to the bench. "Monsieur, Madame Cézanne, I will be speaking with Paul in my office, along with his attorney. M. Franc, my inspector, will stay out here with you. If you have any questions, I'm sure he can help you."

Before they had time to respond, Martin went through the door to his chambers, which was being held open by Old Joseph. Once the suspect and the lawyer followed, the clerk closed the door behind them, effectively blocking out the family. Martin took off his coat and hung it up. He loosened his cravat and opened the window. He hoped there might be some exchanges between Cézanne and his brother-in-law during these deliberately slow actions, but they barely looked at each other. Cézanne sat in one of the two chairs opposite Martin, his hat still on his head. He stared up at the ceiling. Conil remained standing, impatiently tapping his foot.

"We need to know what this is about," he said.

"You must know what this is about," Martin murmured, "or you wouldn't all be here."

"We do not. We fear Paul will be falsely accused of some heinous crime and we are here to protect him."

"Very well. I am investigating a murder, the murder of Solange Vernet." This they knew. No one yet knew about the boy.

"What could Paul possibly have to do with that?" Conil *was* annoying.

"That is what we are here to find out." Martin looked squarely at Cézanne, but the artist refused to meet his eyes, or those of his brother-in-law.

"First you should see this." Conil slapped a document on Martin's desk. "This is an affidavit, signed by M. Louis-Auguste Cézanne and myself, guaranteeing the presence of Paul Cézanne in Aix for necessary interviews and proceedings. He can reside at the family town house, rue Matheron, 14. M. Louis-Auguste has put up the Jas and the apartment as a guarantee of his son's presence." Martin pushed the document to the side of the desk without reading it. Clearly, the family was trying to save themselves from the embarrassment of an imprisonment.

"I will take this under consideration."

"No reason to consider, we have given you ample guarantee."

"It's not yours to give," growled Cézanne, coming to life.

"Oh?" This could be interesting.

"As Maxim well knows, most of the property is already divided between my sisters and me—"

"However," the lawyer smoothly intervened, "Marie and Rose, my wife, and I, have agreed, as you will see," he said pointing to the signatures, "and surely Paul will want to guarantee—"

"It does not matter, my father controls everything anyway." Cézanne said, and turned his head away, disengaging himself from the talk about money.

Doling out the property before death was a tried-and-true strategy for evading the inheritance tax. Martin was not surprised to hear that the old banker had found a way to protect the family fortune while still holding on to the purse strings. He had his son over a barrel.

"In any case," Conil continued, undeterred by his brother-in-law's lack of tact and good sense, "this is a solid guarantee of my client's continuous presence in Aix and its environs as long as you need him as a material witness." Getting no reaction from Martin, he took a seat and folded his gloved hands over the silver head of his walking stick

"Well, then," Martin began as he perused the documents Old Joseph had gathered and demonstrably ignored what Conil had laid before him, "I think we have the most basic information. Paul Cézanne, born Aix, 1839, et cetera. So let's talk about the more immediate past." The sweat prickled down Martin's neck and through his beard, yet the artist did not remove his cap or jacket. Martin could not decide whether his immobility signaled resignation or stubborn resistance. "M. Cézanne, where were you on the day and the night of Monday, August 17th?"

"At the Jas, painting, or in Gardanne," he said with a shrug. "I can't remember. I go practically every day and come back at night. It depends on what I am working on."

Martin was stunned. Cézanne did not seem to grasp the significance of this question. Hortense Fiquet had, and evidently had lied for him.

"If this is about Solange Vernet, I know nothing about it," the artist added, as if this were enough to end the discussion.

"That is for me to decide." Martin paused to let it sink in that he intended to exert all of his state-sanctioned authority. "When did you last see her?"

"Before we left to go north to stay with my friends, Renoir and Zola. You can check on that. That was most of June and July."

"You did not *see* her at all this summer?"

"I *saw* her about a week ago, but she refused to *see* me." Cézanne emphasized his words with bitterness.

"Where did you see her? Why did she refuse to see you?"

"On the street, the Cours, by her apartment. I don't know. She wouldn't let me in; she said she did not want to see me any more."

Were those tears in his eyes? Was he a lamb with the roar of a lion? His voice had gotten softer, less aggressive, and Martin had hardly begun.

"Why?"

"*I don't know why!*" Cézanne exploded. The roar had returned. He was breathing hard.

"Had she communicated with you in any way? Had she written you letters?" If what Cézanne said was true, then why would Westerbury have been so jealous?

"Never!" the artist crossed his arms, striving to seem indifferent, despite the contrary evidence in his eyes and voice.

"Had *you* written her letters?"

"A few."

"And what were these about?"

"You know." The shrug was an attempt to be dismissive.

"No, I don't." Martin did know that whatever the artist did write had angered the Englishman enough for him to tear up the letters, crack apart one of Cézanne's paintings, and throw the whole lot into a fire built on one of the hottest nights in the middle of August.

"Tell me what was in those letters," Martin insisted again.

The brother-in-law was bouncing in his chair, waiting to jump in, although both he and Martin knew there was nothing to object to in any of these questions. The scratching of Old Joseph's pen had stopped, and he turned his head slightly. Martin did not move, willing to let the silence go on indefinitely. The artist was stubborn, but evidently guileless. Martin could wait him out.

The lawyer, however, could not keep quiet. "May I talk with my client for a bit? I know nothing about this."

"*May* you let him leave the room?" Cézanne retorted. "Not everyone needs to know my business."

Excellent. Martin would love to carry on without the lawyer. "M. Conil, I think M. Cézanne wishes to talk with me alone."

"Paul, this is not very smart."

"Go."

"You don't want to be alone with an examining magistrate if you can help it."

"Go!" louder this time.

"It seems," Martin interjected, "that your brother-in-law does not want you in the room. That is his right." Martin got more pleasure than he should have out of this small victory. He had, in this very short time, developed a visceral dislike for the lawyer.

Defeated, Conil sighed and put on his hat. "I'll be outside with the family," he told Martin, and took his leave.

Martin started again. "I know these are difficult questions."

The artist said nothing.

"But you must answer them. This is a murder case. You wouldn't want your son to see you in jail, would you?" Martin said nothing about the rest of the family. They were Cézanne's particular burden to bear, with their overweening protectiveness of him and his utter dependence on them. At what age? Martin glanced at his notes. At the age of forty-six. Martin was not going to bludgeon him with these facts. At least, not yet. "As I said," he repeated, "you would not want your son—"

"All right, all right. What do you want?"

"For you to answer my questions."

"Your *difficult* questions. Isn't that what you said? Difficult?" The artist rose, and began pacing in the small space in front of Martin's desk. "What could you know about what it's like to be entangled by a wife you never intended to marry, and a family that's in your business every minute of the day? You're too young. You've probably been on the straight-and-narrow all your life. Me? I couldn't stand law school. I couldn't be a banker. Everyone laughs at me. No one understands, no one *sees* what I'm trying to do. Then finally you meet the one person, the only one you can talk to, be with, who can look at the world and see what you see, and. . . ." The outburst stopped almost as abruptly as it had begun. Cézanne gave Martin a disconsolate look. "Is she really dead?"

"You must know that," Martin said quietly, hoping that Cézanne would keep on talking.

"How would I? How could I?" Cézanne sat down and swiped his hat off his head. "How would I know that? It must have been him. Westerbury. With his shoddy ideas and shady background. He must have been jealous. Jealous of us."

From everything Martin had just seen and heard, this seemed unlikely.

"Did you give Charles Westerbury reason to be jealous?"

"No!"

"No?"

"I only kissed her once. She only allowed me that one time. I thought then that she would—" Cézanne stopped.

"Would what?"

"I don't know. Leave him. Love me." His blinking eyes darted around the room. He really did not seem to know.

"Well, what did you tell her in the letters?"

Cézanne stiffened.

"What did you tell her in the letters?" Martin repeated, slowly and loudly.

A moment passed before he began. "Just that I loved her. I could not help myself. I saw her, and I loved her. From that first moment, the very first time out on the Cours. Then, when we talked, I loved her more. Just the way she looked at me. As if she knew my very soul. I thought I couldn't live without her. But now. . . ." He bent down to put his head in his hands.

What must it be like to see someone once and love her so passionately, so irrationally? To believe, even for a moment, that a woman as beautiful, as extraordinary as Solange Vernet loved you? Martin did not know. It was true that he had never strayed from the "straight-and-narrow." Perhaps he did not understand love. Martin realized that he had been holding his pen so tightly that his fingers were cramping. He loosened his grip. He had been pouncing, without attempting to understand.

"M. Cézanne, I need to know what it is that you and Mme Vernet had in common. Why did you think—"

"Why did I think she loved me? Is that what you are about to say? Why *shouldn't* she love me?" Cézanne gave Martin a fierce look, but the question hung in the air as if the answer were all too obvious. A failed artist. A man more afraid of his old, sick father than of a murder charge. A father who could not fully claim his own son. Cézanne wiped his eyes and nose with the back of his hand, gave out a little sigh, and sat back.

"I wasn't implying anything about your relationship. I am just trying to understand."

"It was my art that attracted her. She saw what I was trying to do."

"And that was?"

"To create something new, but as old as the world itself, if you only took the time to think it through and see it."

That was it? A way of seeing the world that was old and new at the same time? Martin thought back to the pictures he had seen at the Jas and in Gardanne. Some, those that apparently had been painted years ago, like *The Four Seasons* on the salon wall and the murder scenes, just seemed crude. Yet others, the most recent works, *were* different. The quarry fragment, the mountain, the apples and flowers, the portraits of Hortense Fiquet. Different enough to embarrass Hortense, who had tried to make the best of it by bragging about her lover's Parisian friends.

Cézanne had once again composed himself into a picture of defiant nonchalance, eyes wandering, arms crossed. But Martin knew exactly how to break through this show of indifference.

"M. Cézanne, this seeing the world in a new way, wasn't that what Westerbury was trying to do?" When the suspect did not react, Martin continued, "Mr. Westerbury told me—"

"Hah! Him? Him?!" The artist's voice rose with each utterance.

"Yes, him. He was studying the environs and trying to find out—"

"Studying? Oh yes, studying. Being able to say a few phrases that anyone could have gotten out of reading a couple of books. 'The mountain was thrust up untold millions of years ago.' Or 'What we are walking on is the sediment of an ancient lake.' Or 'The forces of nature have sent the folds of the mountain this way and that, hiding the inner core of its most ancient elements.'" Cézanne's Provençal drawl made bad work of Westerbury's English accent.

"Yes, but certainly books are a part of it." Martin had got him going again. But he was not understanding what Solange Vernet had seen in the artist.

"Books? *Use your eyes*! I've been gathering fossils around here with friends ever since I was a boy. I know the ages of the mountain, the quarry, the river. And I know them where it counts. Here," he pointed to his forehead, "and here," he thumped at his heart. "We don't need some foreign charlatan to come here and tell us what to see." Cézanne was almost panting. The mere thought of Westerbury roused his fury.

"It's not something you can get out of a book," the artist continued. "It's reflection. You don't need to make stupid, arrogant claims about religion and science. All you need to do is to see, to think, to understand, and then to try to show it to others."

"And you explained all this to Mme Vernet?"

Cézanne nodded.

Which is to say that the artist had explained very little. Except that he was against everything that Westerbury stood for. Surely Cézanne had not talked to Solange Vernet in the same way. Or why would she have bothered to spend any time with him? Remembering his encounter with Hortense Fiquet, Martin decided upon another tack.

"Did Mme Vernet know about the work of other artists? Did you discuss them with her?"

"You mean my old friends, the painters that everyone is talking about?"

"Yes."

"Of course we did."

"And you told her your work is different because—?"

"Because," Cézanne said impatiently, "they're still trying to capture 'the moment.' *I* am not interested in reproducing an *impression*. I don't want to paint the surface or the weather or a mood. Or the time of day. I want to do something with permanence." The artist leaned forward, one finger pointing at the floorboards. "I want to show the world as it really is. I want to get at the structures beneath everything."

Martin nodded encouragingly.

"What excited her was that I could see the harmony in all this, in the true motifs, the shapes and colors, that hold everything together. The motifs that have built up over millions of years. Like the mountain. I told her that I know more about the mountain than Westerbury will ever know. That some day I will show its whole history, the way the past vibrates in every stone, in one painting."

He paused. Martin had stopped nodding.

Cézanne leaned forward and peered into Martin's face. "I can see you don't get it."

Obviously, Solange Vernet had reacted in a more pleasing manner. Had this been because of a certain natural politesse on her part, or had she only been play-acting, toying with the artist as she probably had been toying with Martin in the bookstore?

"You don't understand," Cézanne confirmed, and once again crossed his arms and turned his head toward the side of the room. Here was a man accustomed to the world's skepticism.

"And she, Mme Vernet, comprehended all this?"

"She said she did."

"And she disappointed you?"

Cézanne did not answer. Disappointment did not come close to describing what he was feeling. Rejection, humiliation, and grief were written all over his face. It was clear to Martin that despite all the proud theorizing, Westerbury and Cézanne were not fighting over the mountain. Or the quarry. They were fighting over Solange Vernet. But what would have made Solange Vernet shift her attention and affections from one man to another?

"M. Cézanne, how much do you think Mme Vernet knew about your family?"

Cézanne's shrug was barely visible.

"Did she know how wealthy your father is?"

Another shrug.

Martin raised his voice to show his impatience. "Did you ever talk about your family and its standing in town?"

"No." A quiet shake of the head.

"You're sure?"

"Yes." Less audible still.

"And Mme Fiquet. Did Solange Vernet know about your relation-ship with her? And your son?"

"Yes."

"Then how could you possibly expect—?"

"I don't know what I expected!" Cézanne glared at him. "I told you. I couldn't help myself."

The man had been thoroughly humiliated, but Martin was becoming irritated with his blockheadedness and naïveté. Why enter into an adventure of this kind with no thought of the consequences?

"It was never about the money. Mine or hers," Cézanne volun-teered. "It was," he said, looking straight at Martin with his dark, wary eyes, "it was about love, and art."

Love and art, love and science, how pure all their motives were! If only the murder victims were around to give their side of the story.

"Very well, then." This was going nowhere. Martin pushed his chair toward the open window, hoping to catch a breeze. Poor Old Joseph, stuck in the airless alcove, sat in discreet stillness, waiting for Martin to get at something useful.

"M. Cézanne, when was the last time you wrote to Solange Vernet?"

"In July."

"Not more recently?"

"No."

"Not even a note?"

"No!"

"Why not?"

"She didn't answer my letters, any of them."

"How could she? Wouldn't your family find out?"

"I had arranged for her to send them to Médan."

To Zola's grand estate. Martin was astounded. This had been quite an intrigue, at least on Cézanne's part. "You did not send her a note right after the Virgin's feast?" he asked.

"No, no, no. What could I say? I had decided to give up."

"You did not, then, give a note to a little boy to deliver, a boy who has been found murdered?"

The artist's eyes widened, his mouth fell open.

"Good God, no. A boy? A boy, killed? Good God." He shook his head back and forth. "Who would do that?"

"Not Westerbury, then?" Martin decided to take the true measure of Cézanne's hatred of the Englishman.

"A boy?" Martin had managed to stun Cézanne out of his own little world of jealousy and unrequited love. "A boy? No. But then, who?"

"Why not you?"

"Me? I have a son."

That was what Martin had been thinking. But he was not about to let the suspect off the hook." What about your violent art?" He had been waiting for the right moment to spring this on Cézanne.

"Violent?" The artist gave Martin an astonished look and put his hand to his heart like some peasant declaring his own honesty. "Violent?"

Could he really have forgotten his own depictions of murder? "M. Cézanne, we found a piece of your canvas in the quarry where Solange Vernet was killed. I have also gone to the Jas and found two pictures of a woman being killed. A woman with golden-red hair. I have one of them right here." Martin pointed to the cabinet beside his desk. "I also brought back a leering, lascivious painting of men worshiping at the altar of someone who resembles Solange Vernet, a *nude* Solange Vernet." "Resembles" was a generous interpretation; the woman in the painting did have Solange Vernet's golden-red hair, undone, hanging loosely on her shoulders.

The artist responded to Martin's parries with unexpected deliberation. "Sometimes I get upset and tear up what I am doing. I think I've done that in the quarry, but no. I am not violent, no. That's myself I'm angry at, because I can't do what I see here," he pointed to his head.

"And the murdered women in your pictures? Do I need to show one of them to you?"

"No. I should have torn those up too. That was so long ago. I had nightmares when I was young. Maybe it was all those serial novels I was reading in the newspapers. I put the bad dreams on canvas. I . . ." the artist was swallowing hard. He was beginning to realize that his own work might be used against him. "I don't paint like that any more. That's not me now."

"It's not you, then, or Mme Fiquet?" It had just occurred to Martin that there were two tormenters in each of the murder pictures. And one of them could have been a woman.

"Hortense?" This really stunned Cézanne. "Hortense? That's madness. You can't blame her for any of this."

"Where was she at the beginning of the week?"

"She's been at the apartment in Gardanne since our return at the end of July. We went there so I could work without . . . without thinking about other things. She could not have left without my knowing. No." He looked up at the ceiling, tears glistening in his eyes. "A boy? Solange? No. I could never. . . ."

"Yet these are pictures of great violence, and they have a certain erotic charge. And Solange Vernet was raped before she was murdered." Martin's words were heated, provoked by an unexpected anger at what had happened to her.

"No!" Cézanne seemed just as shocked.

"You didn't have fantasies about her, fantasies that she would not let you fulfill in any other way? You did not think of her all the time? You yourself said—"

"No . . . that cannot be. That cannot be." The artist shrank away from Martin's charges. "I would never harm a woman or a boy, I . . . I only shout sometimes. I get upset. But I would never, I couldn't have . . . no. I can barely remember painting those pictures. I was young, foolish. I did not know then what I had to do."

"Then how can you explain their resemblance to Solange Vernet?"

"I can't!" Cézanne was more and more agitated. "It never occurred to me that she looked like any of them. I can't explain any of this. Rape. Murder. A boy. How could anyone think. . . . This is impossible. . . . I could not hurt her. I'm so shy with women. Everyone knows that. This is complete madness."

From everything he had seen and heard, Martin had no doubt that the artist was shy with women, perhaps even pathologically so. He pulled his damp collar farther away from his neck. He had miscalculated. He thought bringing up the boy, the rape, and the pictures all at once would jar Cézanne, force him to speak, either to back up his accusations against Westerbury, or to give himself away. Instead, the accumulation of horrors had sent him into a spiral of denials. Denials Martin was not likely to shake until he had more evidence against him.

"One last question for now," Martin concluded. "When was the last time you were in the quarry?"

Cézanne gave a listless shrug. Sometime after they returned from their vacation on the Seine. A week or two ago, he mumbled. He could not remember. He kept shaking his head, his protests growing less and less audible.

"So what you are telling me is that you don't know where you were on the afternoon and evening of August 17. That your violent paintings had nothing to do with Solange Vernet. You claim that you had nothing to do with the murders, and you have no idea who did." Martin wanted to impress upon Cézanne all the gaping holes in his testimony.

"Right, right, right." Cézanne kept shaking his head.

"Well, I will be questioning your"—*mistress? wife?*—"Mme Fiquet again. For now, let me talk with my inspector before I decide what I will do with you." Martin got up and stepped around his desk. He looked down at the artist. "If we decide to let you go, you must not say a word to anyone about the rape or about the boy. We do not want to start a general panic."

Cézanne met his gaze. "Who would I want to tell about all this? Who *could* I tell?" Finally he said, "You have my word."

"And you realize that if you leave Aix this time, you could bankrupt your entire family."

The artist shook his head. "I'll stay here until you catch him. Don't worry." He appeared to be thoroughly beaten down.

Joseph's chair scraped against the wooden floor. Martin had no doubt his clerk was relieved the interview was over. He had been struggling mightily to keep up with the artist's outbursts. Martin left his chambers, still not sure what he was going to do next. Perhaps he was being naïve, but he believed Cézanne was telling the truth, if only because he did not even attempt to cover his tracks. Yet he had an explosive temper. And the scrap of canvas from the quarry, the violent pictures, and the missing gloves, which might well be stained with tell-tale paint, made him a prime suspect.

This is what Martin told Franc as they huddled in the corridor out of the hearing of the family. The most compelling reason to hold Cézanne would be if they considered him to be dangerous. But to whom? They already had Westerbury in jail, and they'd send word to Arlette LaFarge not to let the artist into the Vernet apartment. Either because Westerbury was his favorite suspect, or because he did not want to tangle with a rich, important family, Franc was uncharacteristically amenable to the least drastic course of action. He promised to have one of his men keep an eye on Cézanne and agreed to release him.

Martin watched the artist pause at the door of his chambers, contemplating the familial gauntlet. The mother and father were still huddled together on the bench. Across from them, standing by the railing, the two sisters and brother-in-law waited anxiously. Finally, Paul Cézanne put on his cap and went to his father, offering his arm. As he helped the old man to his feet, Conil stepped toward them. Martin heard Cézanne grumble, "We'll talk later." When the lawyer opened his mouth to say something, Cézanne repeated, "Later!" He pushed past his brother-in-law and, with his father leaning on him, led the silent procession down the stairs to their privileged exit through the main door. Cézanne held his head up high, just as Westerbury had done. Despite himself, Martin felt a little sorry for him, as he had for the Englishman.

"Humph." That was Franc's reaction, as he stepped back into Martin's office. He had no soft-hearted concern for the weak. And he was undoubtedly right. One should not waste pity on murder suspects.

They agreed that Martin should spend the afternoon writing orders to get as many members of Solange Vernet's salon as possible into his chambers the next day, and that Franc should continue to question Westerbury about the letter, the note, the weapon, and the gloves. Martin hoped that Franc would not be brutal, but he no longer gave a damn about the Englishman who had proved himself to be an accomplished liar.

Before Franc left, Martin turned down the inspector's invitation to join him at Chez l'Arlésienne for dinner. Instead, he sent Joseph out for sandwiches. Official work, at his desk, always put Martin on an even keel. It kept fatigue and discouragement at bay. Later he would go over again and again in his mind all that had transpired in the last few days. He would try to understand how the rage and pain in one throbbing human heart had led to two murders. What Martin had no way of knowing is how much his own heart would be tested that night.

14

"IT'S ME, BROTHER."

The only one who called Martin "brother" was his old schoolmate, Jean-Jacques Merckx.

"Jean-Jacques?"

A shadow emerged from the corner. "Yes, Jean-Jacques," he answered in a tone heavy with sarcasm. He had caught the fear and hesitation in Martin's voice.

What else could Merckx expect? He had been Martin's best friend, the only other scholarship student at Xavier. But ever since leaving school, his reappearances had brought trouble, demands that Martin could not possibly fulfill, yet could not refuse—demands for money, for help, for support and approval of his radical political activities. What would he want this time?

"Let me have a look at you." As Martin reached for the oil lamp on his table, Merckx edged away, toppling the chair and falling onto the bed.

"Not by the window, and close the door."

After securing the latch and righting the chair, Martin held the light over his friend, who sat on the bed with his back against the wall. Merckx looked worse than ever. Thinner and dirtier. Even in childhood, his watery blue eyes had been rimmed with dark circles. Now they sank back into his head, duller and more distant. There was a smell, too, of sweat and desperation and, when Merckx began to snicker, an odor of sickness and neglect.

He noticed Martin cringe. "A bad conscience always smells bad, don't you think, Brother Bernard? And I am, as always, condemned to be your conscience." His voice was as harsh and hectoring as ever.

"What do you want?" Martin asked, the anger rising in him.

"I need help."

Martin put the lamp on the table and sat down. This could be disastrous. His heart began to pound.

"I thought you were in the army." He barely got the words out.

"I am . . . or was."

Merckx never asked for anything directly. He always wanted Martin to pull it out of him, to prove his friendship. Martin hated this game, but knew it was necessary. Every other boy at Xavier had ridiculed Merckx because of his ill-fitting clothes, his dirty corn-yellow hair, and his Flemish accent. Most of all, they had scorned him because he was the sickly progeny of the workers their own parents employed and exploited. They had given Martin a hard time too. But at least his relatives were "respectable." So were his demeanor and attitudes—too respectable, according to Merckx, who never hesitated to point out the hypocrisies of the rich and pious.

Merckx coughed, as if to signal that it was Martin's turn to speak.

"Are you on leave?" Hope against hope.

"Don't you wish, monsieur le juge."

Martin could hardly breathe. "You have deserted, then?" That was it. A lawbreaker, a traitor, in his own room. Martin rose above his companion, fists clenched. "What have you done?" He couldn't take the pleading out of his voice, even though it might bring down a shower of scorn. Merckx knew that as an officer of the court it was his duty to report a desertion. Why had Merckx come *here*?

"That's why I need help." Merckx had dropped the mocking tone. He knew full well what he was asking.

"But you told me you could get through your service. You said you'd be among men like yourself. Peasants. Workers. People you could talk to." Martin was glad he had not turned the lamp up high. Tears of frustration rushed to his eyes.

Merckx spit on the floor. "With the officers on my neck all the time! You don't know what it's like. You got exempted because you were in law school and because you were mommy's only son. But believe me, they're no different from the Jesuits. Except they don't only rap you on the knuckles when you're insubordinate. Oh no. The great Republican army throws you in solitary. Or makes you stand at attention for hours at a time in the sun until you fall down, so they can kick you back up again. Until you can't take it any more." His voice rose with emotion.

Martin put his hand to his mouth to signal quiet. The window was wide open.

"How did you find me?"

"I went to the Palais. I asked around. Everyone seems to know the young judge."

Martin sank down into the chair again. It was worse than he had feared.

"Don't worry, I was careful."

Martin stared out his window at the darkening sky. Merckx, careful? Merckx, who made it a point to insult Martin's "bourgeois" friends, even his mother? Thank God the Proc and the other judges were out of town. He desperately wanted to know who Merckx had spoken to. If Martin were lucky, it might have been Old Joseph, who barely remembered his own name, and who had a certain loyalty to his "young judge." But it more likely had been one of the gendarmes, whose loyalties were only to Franc.

"I told you I was careful. No reason to worry. I told you."

Martin got up and ran his hands through his hair. Merckx had an uncanny ability to read his mind. Had he become that predictable, that bourgeois? He had always helped Merckx before. But this? Asking him to abet desertion? This. Martin started to pace.

"Tell me what you want."

"Right now, the rest of your wine, while you consider whether or not you will step off your pedestal and come to the aid of an old friend."

Martin handed Merckx a half-empty bottle from his table and continued to circle the small space in front of the bed. What *he* really wanted was for Merckx to disappear, that he not be forced to make a choice between the law and his friend.

Making choices and taking risks had always been a part of their friendship, from the very beginning when Merckx forced Martin into his one true act of moral and physical courage. It had happened about a year after his father's death, and it had bound them together forever. Jean-Jacques had once again challenged Father Campion's lessons in morality. Called in front of the class for the usual punishment of three strokes, he refused to apologize. Perhaps worse, he refused to cry out. The rod came down on his hands again and again. Martin winced at the memory. He thought he had heard bones crack. And still Merckx stood there, silent, tears trailing white streaks down his perpetually dirty face.

"Stop! Stop!" Martin had shouted. And when Father Campion persisted, he had run to the front of the room and grabbed the priest's arm. "Stop!"

This had earned Martin his first punishment of six strokes. He had tried to stay as silent as Merckx, and kept telling himself that he had done right, that he had brought the priest to his senses by diverting him away from the poor, incorrigible boy. Afterwards, as his mother tenderly salved his hands, she admonished him to listen to his superiors. He always wondered what his father would have said to him. Martin smiled to himself. What would Franc have said? Would he have given him a lecture on watching out for oneself, or admired Martin's audacity?

Merckx had said nothing, and he certainly had never thanked Martin. He would never recognize anyone else in that class as being as courageous as he. But he had befriended Martin and shown him an entirely new world: a world where whole families cooked, slept, and propagated in a single room in tottering wooden buildings; a world where merit was measured not by wealth, education, or piety, but by loyalty and solidarity—and by a distrust of the rich. What a different view Merckx had given him of the DuPonts. Merckx taught him that his benefactors made the money that funded their "charities" by exploiting women and children. His mother and sisters worked fourteen hours a day on DuPont's loud, clanking, dusty looms, which never stopped for any reason. What Martin remembered most vividly is that in Merckx's world everyone coughed. The women wheezed out the brown detritus of the woolen mills, while the men spat out the coal-black dirt of the mines. And Merckx himself, it seemed, had been born coughing. That's why they let him go to school. They had ceded their weakest child to the bourgeoisie and the Church, in the hope that he might somehow survive.

Now Merckx sat on Martin's bed, doubled over, his hacking cough worse than ever. What did Martin really owe Merckx? His sense of justice? His vocation? If that were so, he had certainly never been able to live up to his friend's standards. Merckx denounced him for going to law school, mocked his choice of the magistrature, and, during their last angry encounter in Paris, even berated him for "exploiting" a working-class girl, the ever-willing Honorine. If he hadn't been so frightened, Martin might have enjoyed the irony of his situation. Maybe Merckx *had* become his conscience, a confessor more fearsome than anything the Church had ever produced.

And maybe Merckx was the only thing keeping him from the complacency of a slow, predictable climb up the ladder in the civil service. Maybe Merckx was his one true friend.

As he watched Merckx struggling to sit upright on the bed, Martin knew that he would never give him up. Merckx was everything, everyone that Martin hoped to protect in his chambers: the poor, the suffering, those who struggled merely to survive. Like Arlette, Martin thought, and like the boy he had seen this morning, who had unwittingly sacrificed his life for a pittance.

As their eyes met, Martin spoke. "I can't keep you here. The landlord and his family are returning tomorrow. If you decide to go back, I can help you."

"I can't. Don't you understand? They'll send me to Devil's Island this time."

They both knew what that meant. More beatings, and a slow, rotting death in the hot sun thousands of miles away from everything Merckx had ever known. There was really nothing else for Martin to do. He asked, "What do you need?"

"Not much, just enough to keep on going."

"But where? You are in no condition—"

"I've made it this far. When I get there, they'll take care of me."

"Who?"

"My *real* brothers."

Martin ignored the intended insult. If he were going to help Merckx, if he were going to keep them both out of trouble, he had to keep a cool head.

"Where are you going, Jean-Jacques? Who are these people?"

"If I can make it to Italy, I have contacts there who will help me get to Switzerland. I can stay with one of the Swiss workers in the movement, or with other exiles, Russians, Poles, Italians. Some are even training to be doctors so they can go back to their countries and serve the poor while they talk sense into them. Maybe I'll do that, become a doctor. You'd like that, Bernard, wouldn't you? You always told me to make something of myself. I'll get a new identity card, sneak back in, and help my people."

Without knowing it, Martin had begun to shake his head in disbelief. He could not imagine Merckx living long enough to become a doctor. He could not even imagine how Merckx would complete his dangerous journey.

"All right. So I won't become a doctor. Maybe I'll just sneak back in and bomb your Palais."

"Stop it! Stop this talk." Of course Merckx would never demonstrate any sentimentality, even at the thought of his own demise. Only Martin was weak enough to do that. "You need to get away. All right. Maybe you can make a new life. Good. But I don't need to hear about your crazy anarchist plots."

"Or what? You'll turn me in?"

"What do you need?" Martin punctuated each word. This was not a game.

Merckx shrugged. "I have nothing, as always. I'm hungry, as always. I get cold at night, and I need something to lay my head on. And, yes, Bernard, I want to get away from here as much as you want to get rid of me. If you can't help, I'll just leave now."

"No." Martin held up his hand. If Merckx had to go begging, both of them were doomed. "Stay back there." He pointed toward the wall behind Merckx and turned the lamp higher. He shuttered the window, then opened the drawer of his table and pulled out the box that held the money he intended to send to his mother. He laid it on his table. It was enough to buy Merckx food and lodging for a week, if he was careful. Martin looked around. He had a bottle of wine on his book-shelf, but little else to offer his friend. He went to the armoire and took out his student jacket and a pair of boots.

"Do you have something to carry these in?"

"Yes, my sack."

"Good. But you still need food."

"Yes, I ate the piece of bread——" Merckx began coughing again.

"But you'll need something for tomorrow."

"Even tonight, brother." Merckx smiled that old smile of com-plicity, reminiscent of the secret jokes they used to share against the rich and well-larded.

"Yes, even tonight," Martin echoed dryly. After all that had been said and implied, it was too late to fall back into old times, even if Merckx had suddenly become willing to do so. Besides, Martin had to act quickly. Where could he get food? Only restaurants would be open. He could not carry away a meal. Then he saw Clarie Falchetti in his mind's eye. She was a bold girl. She would help a starving judge who, in the anxiety of solving an important case, had forgotten to eat his supper.

Martin peeked through the white lace curtains into Chez l'Arlési-enne to make sure that Franc was gone. The place was almost empty; the last customers were already pulling away from their table. The bell announcing his entrance jangled his nerves, but he pushed himself for-ward, toward the center of the restaurant. When Mme Choffrut spotted him, she clasped her hands together in delight and invited him to a table.

Martin demurred. "I know it is late. I wouldn't impose upon you to serve a meal at this time. I was just wondering. . . ." Suddenly his story seemed quite feeble.

"Are you hungry?" she smiled.

"I do need something. . . ."

"And you'd like to see Clarie!" She almost clapped her hands.

He had been counting on her desire to get Clarie and him together, but, confronted with her enthusiasm, felt ashamed of himself. Why was deceit so easy in his chambers and so difficult here?

"Clarie! Clarie!" Mme Choffrut called, then made a show of going into the kitchen to leave them alone.

As soon as Clarie saw Martin, she stopped and stood with her hands on her hips and her lips pursed in a questioning, lopsided grin. He had meant to play the role of the absent-minded, hungry judge, but he could not play the fool in front of this straightforward girl. He moved to the table that was farthest from the kitchen and sat down.

When Clarie joined him, Martin explained that he had an unexpected visitor, an old school friend, who was in dire straits. They needed food for the night, but no one should know about the friend. This was the reason he had to carry something away. Martin took some francs out of his pocket and laid them on the table. "Anything portable." He was taking a risk, but he somehow knew he could trust her with his secret. Before answering, Clarie stared at him, considering his request. Then she nodded and touched his arm. "I'll think of something. And someday you will have to tell me more, yes?"

Martin nodded, "Yes," although he could not imagine telling anyone he was abetting a deserter.

When Clarie returned from the kitchen, she handed him two loaves of bread and some pears and cheese wrapped in an old newspaper. Martin rose to receive them. Clarie took money from the table, counted out some for the Choffruts, and thrust the rest into the pocket of Martin's coat.

"There, that's fair."

"Thank you." Martin saw Mme Choffrut watching them from the kitchen, so he said no more.

Clarie walked him to the door and, as the bell chimed, he turned to thank her again. Her only response was a look of concern.

Saturday, August 22

Up until now, science like law, made exclusively by men, has too often considered woman as an absolutely passive being, without instincts or passions or her own interests; as a purely plastic material capable of taking any form without resistance; a being without the inner resources to react against the education she receives or against the discipline to which she submits as part of law, custom or opinion. Woman is not made like this.
—Clémence Royer, "On the Birthrate," 1874

15

HORTENSE FIQUET CLOSED HER EYES and for one marvelous moment let the clink of silver and glass, the smell of hot, strong coffee, and the murmur of *real* conversation transport her to Paris, to the old days at the Café Guerbois, where sometimes she had been permitted to sit at the edge of the table listening to the arguments and laughter of enthusiastic young writers and painters. Now they were older, famous—her eyes shot open—unlike *her* artist. Instead, here she was with Marie Cézanne, who, as usual, was going on and on about something. Hortense sighed. Here she was, once again making it possible for the two Cézanne women to see Paul Jr. in the anonymity of a crowded café, far from the Jas and Papa. Here she was in Aix with everyone expecting her to eat humble pie. This time she would show them.

"Well, now," Mme Cézanne interrupted her daughter as she put her hands on the table and pushed back her chair, "don't you think that it's time for a treat? Let's see if there are any new shops on the Cours." She was looking straight at Paul Jr., smiling. Then she nodded to Hortense and Marie, still smiling, eager as always to absent herself from the serious conversation that would ensue as soon as the boy was safely out of hearing.

Yes, time to get started. Hortense glanced with distaste at the melting remains of the extravagant dessert that Mme Cézanne had insisted upon ordering for her grandson. His spoon stood straight up at its center, signaling his final surrender. Dribs of chocolate and strawberry ice cream ran down his chin.

"Wipe your mouth, son. And this time—books, eh?" This was the first building block in Hortense's case for indispensability, the fact that she was and always had been a devoted mother to the beloved grandson.

"Or paints?" the proud grandmother suggested, always trying to push Paul Jr. into his father's footsteps. As if they were going to lead somewhere.

"Oh, Grandma," the kid groaned.

"Run along, darling," Hortense forced a smile, "and listen to your grandmother." Accommodating, too. How could they wish for a better wife for Paul?

Her son ran his napkin over his mouth and sprang up to help Mme Cézanne out of her seat. He knew she'd get him anything he wanted. After all, given the fact that she could not bring him into the family house, invite him to a holiday dinner, or even introduce him to his own grandfather, what recourse did she have except to buy his love?

Hortense watched her son take the old woman's hand as they threaded their way toward the front of the cavernous café. He genuinely cared for his grandmother. In any case, Paul's mother was not the problem. Hortense turned to Marie, who sat against the mirrored wall. She was not the problem either. Although Marie Cézanne thoroughly believed in the sanctity of marriage, the real problem was that she and her mother refused to show any backbone against the old man. After all, the boy *was* thirteen years old. Hortense shifted her head slightly to catch an image of herself and pat back her hair.

Marie, all business, placed the key to the Cézannes' town apartment on the table. "Paul told us we needed to bring this to you," resentful that someone else should have access to the family property. She always acted so superior, despite the fact that she had never had a man, any man. "And," Marie reached in her purse and took out some bills, "this should tide you over for a while," as if Hortense Fiquet were some courtesan, instead of a member of their family in everything but name.

Hortense couldn't let this get to her. She had to find out what they knew and what they had said. She leaned toward Marie. "We need to talk before they get back. That judge came to the Jas, didn't he?"

Marie nodded, bending forward so that they could keep their voices low.

"I need to know what you told the judge. We need to get our story straight."

"We told him the truth," Marie said with a pious sniff.

Just then a waiter, in a white cotton jacket, appeared to clear the dishes. Hortense reached to retrieve the money and put it in her purse. "Another coffee, please." Once that was delivered, he would leave them alone for a while. "Marie?" Cézanne's sister shook her head. She was probably adding up the bill in her head, oblivious to how one should behave in any place more worldly than her provincial charity circles.

"Just one, then." Hortense smiled at the waiter. She had enough *savoir faire* to know that one did not linger at a table without eating or drinking something. As soon as he left, Hortense continued. "I mean, what did you tell him about where Paul was when that witch was killed?"

"I told you. We told him the truth. We said we didn't know. We're never sure where Paul is, except when he's up in the attic or painting at the back of the Jas."

God, she was dense! "Do you know *when* Solange Vernet was killed?"

"Sometime after the Virgin's feast. I'm quite sure of it, but it doesn't matter. Paul didn't do it." How could she be so sure? Besides, didn't she read the newspapers? Didn't she know how important an alibi was?

"When he came out to Gardanne, I told the judge that Paul had spent the entire time with us."

Marie raised her eyebrows. Then she began to finger her empty cup. "I don't really think that was necessary. "

Of course not. The Cézannes would not deign to show any gratitude even if she had lain down in front of a roaring train for them. "Really?" Hortense paused to emphasize her disagreement. "I got the impression that Paul was a major suspect."

"And," Marie countered, "I got the impression that they already had the major suspect in prison, the Englishman."

Hortense shook her head in disbelief. Didn't they know how easy it was for the authorities to jail a foreigner for as long as they wanted? That didn't mean they wouldn't go after Paul. *She* had watched him being dragged down the streets of Gardanne. *She* had been forced to sit still answering questions while two hulking gendarmes went through their things. She had seen that young judge taking all those notes and checking up on every little detail. At least Hortense had kept her head and known what to do. Apparently Paul's mother and sister had not.

"Nevertheless," she had to give Marie a dose of realism, "I fear that Paul is still a suspect. How long did they question him at the courthouse?"

Marie shrugged her shoulders and stared straight ahead. Hortense was beginning to get an inkling that Marie's nonchalance was just another way of shutting her out. Or maybe they'd had an easier time at the Jas. That wouldn't surprise her. They lived in a grand estate, not some hovel in the middle of nowhere. Their house bespoke money and influence, no matter how miserly they were about keeping it up. Hortense had seen the judge, and she had been under his microscope. She did not think he'd easily be dissuaded from his mission.

"Didn't that judge make you nervous? You should have seen the gendarmes he brought with him. They were all over the apartment. He even went through Paul's paintings one by one, as if they were going to tell him something."

"He did that in Gardanne?" She had finally piqued Marie's interest. "Did he take any of them with him? Did he say anything?"

Hortense sat back. It was her turn to shrug. "What was there to take? Pictures showing Gardanne from the top, Gardanne from the bottom, and Gardanne from the middle. And some apples. And me."

This time Marie pulled Hortense toward her. "None of the quarry?"

Hortense shook her head. "Why the quarry?"

"That's where she was killed!" Marie hissed. Just then, the reappearance of the waiter made them both jump a little. Hortense recovered enough to thank him and communicate that they would be sitting there for a while, continuing their nice little conversation. When he left, she leaned toward Marie again.

"What difference does that make?"

Marie's eyes darted around, making sure they would not be overheard as she mumbled, "They found a piece of one of Paul's canvases there."

Oh God. Hortense covered her gasp with her hand. She felt the morning's coffee lurch up from her stomach. It was worse than she thought. How stupid of Paul. How often had she told him not to tear up his work, if only to preserve the canvas, if only to save them a few sous? And what if he had taken Solange Vernet there, and in a rage—

"Of course," Marie continued, "I told him it could be anyone's, but it was pretty clear it was Paul's work."

Paul's work, as unmistakable as it was unprofitable. Hortense stared out toward the front of the café. Everything was a blur. Voices buzzed around her like annoying insects. She looked at Marie. Was there more? It was her duty to tell her everything.

"Did he find a picture of the quarry at the Jas?"

"No, but. . . ." Marie still holding back on her.

"But what?" She gripped Marie's arm. "What?"

"He seemed to be interested in a number of paintings and even took two with him. Old ones. Yet he seemed to think they were important."

"Which ones?"

"Mother said that he kept looking at paintings that seemed violent and," Marie paused and whispered, "lascivious."

"What did he take with him?" It took some effort to keep her voice down.

"A woman being strangled and a naked woman being worshiped by a group of men. And," Marie lowered her voice even more, "all of the women had hair the same color as Solange Vernet's."

Hortense closed her eyes against the din and tried to conjure up the images.

"Of course, Mother told him that Paul did those long ago, when he was very young, when he was trying to find his style. But still they could use these as proof."

Of what? Marie did not even try to say. Of Paul's temper? Of the fact that he had been so bewitched that he had become insanely jealous?

"Do you know which paintings I'm talking about?" Marie's face was close to hers. Hortense saw her yellowing teeth and caught an unpleasant whiff of pungent cheese from the midday meal.

She pulled away to think. She swallowed hard and willed her stomach to be still. She knew all of Paul's paintings. They were always packing or unpacking them, getting them ready for sale or moving them back to a studio. "Yes." She could picture them. "Some of them he did before we met. I think he said they were inspired by those horrid serial novels in the newspapers."

The "horrid" was for Marie's benefit. Hortense rather enjoyed the serials; she even admired some of the paintings. At least they told a story. She had especially liked the large canvas he gave to Zola, depicting a naked man, tall, strong, and muscular, with skin so dark it was almost red, carrying a fainting white-skinned woman into a woods. A woman with dark brown hair like her own. It still gave her a *frisson* of sensuality to think of it. Hortense had always assumed that she was the woman in that painting. But, as for the rest—she closed her eyes again, trying to remember. The woman on the cloud, the many failed versions of the temptation of Saint Anthony, and the clumsy rendition of two nudes in bed during an afternoon lover's tryst—all the women had golden-red hair. Why had she not realized that before? Her throat was constricting, choking her. She had known for a long time that Solange Vernet had touched something deeper in Paul than she ever had. But she had never considered that he had known her—or someone very like her—in another life. In the life before theirs. A first, incomparable love. A buried, reignited love. How dare he?

"Your coffee is getting cold."

Hortense realized she had been clutching the cup. She took a sip. Marie was staring at her. Despite what she was feeling, she had to stick to her plan. She *was* the only one. The family owed her. She had given the best years of her life to Paul Cézanne. Even if he were in terrible trouble, even if he had killed Solange Vernet in a jealous rage, she, Hortense Fiquet, needed to get something out of all those years, all her devotion, all her waiting.

"So you think," she could not resist a little jab at Marie, "that they will see Paul as some obsessed, crazed murderer?"

"Of course not!" Marie almost rose in horror. "Of course he didn't do it."

"Then why was he mixed up with her?" Hortense could no longer hold in her anger, and spoke too loudly. She took in a breath and looked around. No one seemed to have noticed. She glanced back at Marie. "Well?"

Marie had the nerve to look away, uninterested. Of course she did not deign to answer that question. She would not say anything against Paul, the beloved brother, the beloved son. A grown man who never really had to worry about tomorrow, because in the end he knew that Papa would rescue him. Until now. This time, money and his family's influence might not be enough. This time, Paul had gotten himself in too deep.

"You know," Hortense announced, "I'm going to help Paul get out of this."

"Really?" said Marie, laying her hand on Hortense's arm, as if to rein her in. "Don't do anything foolish." By which she meant, of course, don't show yourself in public. "If worse comes to worst," Marie continued, "Rose's husband—"

"Maxim!" Hortense almost snorted. "You would trust that little dandy to defend Paul's life?"

Marie glared at her. Hortense took a slow sip from her coffee. She wanted to make Marie suffer a little. "I don't know if Paul told you, but after all these years Zola had finally consented to come to Aix this summer. Then his wife got sick and made a big fuss about the cholera." Neither she nor Paul had been all that surprised that the condescending, hypochondriacal Alexandrine had refused to come. Zola's account of Aix was not a very attractive one. "Zola wrote us to apologize. He's taking her to a spa. It's really not that far from here. So, I sent him a telegram yesterday, asking him to come as soon as possible. I told him it was a matter of life or death." She paused. "Please don't mention this to Paul," she added, as if she were taking Marie into her confidence. "I don't want to disappoint him if Zola can't come."

"Zola? That's ridiculous!" Marie objected. The Cézannes did not approve of what Paul's childhood friend had become, a writer of scandalous novels. "He's not a lawyer. Maxim——"

"You're right about that. Of course." Hortense did not need to hear a catalogue of the supposed virtues of Paul's ne'er-do-well brother-in-law. "But Zola does know more about crime and murder than any small-town lawyer ever would. He's made a thorough study of them. And," she looked straight at Marie, trumping her at last, "you must know that by now he is one of the most influential men in France."

16

THE WORDS OF SIBYLLINE BEAUREGARD droned over Martin. He was
exhausted. He could not even call up the strength to drive away the fly
that had landed on his hand. At this hour, in this heat, he was grateful
that most of the habitués of the Vernet salon were still out of town.
Mlle Beauregard was the fourth and last useless interrogation of the
day. At least all that effort had yielded one positive result. As the day
wore on, he was worrying less and less about Merckx. No gendarme
had appeared with him in tow. No reports from Franc of a deserter in
the jurisdiction. Merckx, whom he had spirited out of the house at
dawn, must be far away by now.

Martin ached for his bed, which he had ceded to Merckx the night
before. He longed for a good meal. He would have preferred to be
almost anywhere but here, with his head pounding, listening to a

detailed account of the Life and Work of Sibylline Beauregard. Martin flicked his wrist and sent the fly on his way. He tugged at his damp beard, willing himself to stay alert. Twenty more minutes of concentrated effort, and he could finally go. He gave what he hoped was an encouraging nod to assure the witness that he was still paying attention.

Martin had been observing Mlle Beauregard for well over an hour. It was obvious that she made a career of her singularity. The yachting dress, cravat, and boater were distressingly à la mode, but at least they matched. The tightly coiled black curls that fringed her round little face harkened back to a more romantic era, as did the three long white feathers that hung quite incongruously from her straw hat. The feathers bobbed in rhythm to the torrent that issued from her mouth, a mobile organ lined in red, offset by a sharply pointed nose and close-set, piercing black eyes.

Mlle Beauregard's greatest claim to being thoroughly modern was the cigarette she held between two fingers of her ungloved, paint-stained right hand. When she paused to think, she took long draws from its holder. If she was making a point, she waved it about like a torch. Under other circumstances, Martin could well imagine her using it as a beacon of female emancipation, the Declaration of the Rights of Woman and Citizen 1885. Today, knowingly or not, she had declared something quite different: her love for Charles Westerbury.

She described Westerbury as a brilliant orator whose words had thrilled all the ladies who attended his lectures. Even she had sat in rapt silence as the Englishman unveiled the true history of the earth. In the salon, reserved for the favored few, he was different. He stood behind the circle of chairs, letting Solange elicit the opinions of her guests, only to come forward when it was necessary to correct some intellectual error or add depth to the debate between science and religion, which, of course, he insisted should never have been a debate at all. Science and religion were not opposites, but complements, a sign of the advance of humankind and the benevolence of the Creator of All Things.

When Martin probed Mlle Beauregard's opinion of the victim, she described Solange Vernet as uneducated but intelligent; gracious, beautiful, and charming. Despite this, Martin noted, the witness did not show that much dismay about Solange Vernet's death. Did she hope to become Westerbury's next mistress? Or had Westerbury already taken advantage of her all-too-obvious affections? Martin doubted that.

His big mistake of the afternoon had been to ask the witness about Cézanne. The question evoked a bitter diatribe. Paul Cézanne had come late to the circle, very late, having attended only two or three sessions, and had brought with him all the advantages of his sex. Trained in art institutes, heir to a fortune, connections in Paris. How could she, the daughter of a poor widowed literature professor—who had, by the way, had the foresight to name his only child after the ancient prophetesses, the Sibyls—how could she compete for the right to make an artistic contribution to Westerbury's great work? How could she even speak when Cézanne glowered at her so? Who would take her seriously as the "artist of the Aix landscape" when a man, the scion of a wealthy family, laid claim to the same title?

Solange Vernet and Westerbury had been the sun and moon of a shining new world, the only place Sibylline Beauregard felt welcomed and accepted. Cézanne had threatened that world. Did she think him capable of destroying it?

"Mlle Beauregard," Martin jumped in while she took a long pull from her cigarette, "were you aware that Solange Vernet and Paul Cézanne were lovers?"

The impossible happened. Sibylline Beauregard was speechless. The silence was broken by a familiar sound, the movement of Old Joseph's chair as he turned to survey the scene. Would Martin have to order his greffier not to look around every time he asked that question?

The noise did not disturb the witness, who sat across from Martin, holding her cigarette aloft between two fingers. "No," she roused herself, "no, how is that possible?"

What was going through her head? That she had missed the opportunity to console Westerbury?

"No," she shook her head again. "No, it is just not possible."

"Why not?"

"He was a beast. So uncivilized, despite all that education, all that travel. A beast."

"Was he violent?"

"I don't know. But he was rude. Very. He could only talk in outbursts."

"But how did he act toward Solange Vernet?"

She sucked on the holder, and blew out a long stream of smoke.

"Now that you bring it up, he was extremely polite to her—and to the maid. He seemed afraid of the men. Or angry with them, I couldn't tell. And with me, of course. Because I was a rival. Now that you bring it up," she repeated slowly, "I really never knew why he was there."

Martin waited. He had given her the reason. But when she spoke again, it was not about Solange Vernet or Cézanne, but about Westerbury.

"Oh, poor Charles, poor, poor Charles. Did he know? What he must be going through! Do you know where he is? I must go to him. What he must be suffering."

"Are there any indications that he knew what was going on?"

"How would I know? Oh, Charles, he couldn't have—"

"What? Killed her?"

"I didn't say that!" Sibylline Beauregard cried in indignation. "Never say I said that!"

"Certainly jealousy is a motive for murder."

"No! No! It can't be. He would give his life for her! Because of her weakness!"

Surely the witness had gotten it backward. It was quite likely that

Solange Vernet had given her life for Westerbury. Because of *his* weakness. And his rage.

"What about his work, his great work?" Mlle Beauregard pleaded, "No! He must finish it."

"Very well." Martin rose. He had had enough. "You've been very helpful. Thank you. I think you can go now."

"No. He didn't kill her. You can't believe I meant to imply. . . . Where is he? Who is with him?" She stood up as if she was about to run to rescue Westerbury, wherever he might be.

"Please sit down, Mlle Beauregard."

She backed down onto the edge of the chair, her hand holding the cigarette over her heart, her face lifted in horror.

"He's not. . . . He didn't—"

"He's in jail. I am thinking of charging him with Solange Vernet's murder."

"He's alive, then, and well." She sank back in relief. There was still some hope that her dream might come true. "Surely, you are not going to keep him in that awful place long? When are you going to let him go?"

"When the time comes. And when I know more."

"You can't—"

"Mlle Beauregard, thank you again. I'm going to ask my clerk to escort you out." Martin had to get rid of her. He was so tired. Fortunately, Joseph had heard Martin's dismissal and rose to the occasion. If slowly. The hunched old man even offered his arm as he led the witness out of Martin's chambers.

Martin slumped back in his chair. Tomorrow was Sunday, a day of rest. Rest! If only he could forget all those bloated dead bodies. And his own guilt and fear. A tapping at the door interrupted his thoughts. *What now!* "Come in!"

"I was waiting for your greffier to return. But I can see that they're still talking, so I took the liberty. . . ."

It was Picard. Had his landlord rushed to the courthouse because he had seen evidence of an intruder? Had Merckx been insane enough to come back for something? If so, Martin hoped to God that the long-winded notary would get to the point and let him know quickly that he was done for.

"M. Picard," Martin stood and motioned toward a chair in an attempt to appear calm and cordial. "Please. Come in. Sit down."

René Picard was a portly middle-aged man, with a mustache that rose up in a curl to the left and right of his nose, and a penchant for strong cologne. He had taken the time after arriving home from the country to put on his dark blue pinstriped suit and top hat. Picard sat down, crossed his legs, which bulged like fat sausages in his pants, and began wagging his finger at Martin.

"You've been holding out on me."

Martin's mouth went dry. "I don't understand."

"Well," Picard said with a mischievous smile on his face, "as soon as I settled the ladies in, I went to the Cours, to see if there was anything that needed my immediate attention. And then I began to hear rumors. First, about one of my clients, a certain Solange Vernet."

Martin sat down and folded his hands, trying to look interested. Maybe, just maybe, this was not about Merckx.

"After that," Picard continued, "I could not resist going to my friend, the editor. And, I'm pleased to tell you, my boy, that by tomorrow morning when our one liberal weekly comes out, you'll be quite well known around all these parts. A murder! Your first big investigation!"

Martin kept his face a blank, all the while suppressing a groan. Already in the press. At least they had managed to keep the news of the boy from getting out.

"My girls will be thrilled. And so will Mme Picard. She always knew you would go places. That's why she'd never forgive me if I didn't invite you for dinner tomorrow. At one o'clock sharp."

Martin, who had been working hard to hide his anxieties, now had to scramble to cover his dismay. Marguerite Picard had made it clear that she thought he would be an exemplary suitor for at least one of her two older daughters. He had already suffered through two family dinners, during which M. Picard held forth at one end of the table while Mme Picard, whenever she got a word in, questioned Martin in detail about his future prospects. Martin, of course, had responded as briefly and discreetly as possible. Still, his answers seemed to have provided endless amusement for the three Picard daughters, who said little but communicated with each other by rolling their eyes and making faces. He had no idea what the daughters thought of him. And he didn't know what he was more afraid of: that they found him a singularly boring guest, or that one of them might actually find him attractive.

Picard was never deterred by hesitation. "Food fresh from the country. Of course you'll come."

"I—"

"No, no, we won't take no for an answer. It's the summer. It's Sunday. We've been neglecting you, scurrying out of town at the first sign of the cholera. I told Mme Picard we had no worries in Aix."

"Thank you." If he accepted immediately, maybe Picard would go away.

"Good! And now," Picard said, recrossing his legs. "I am at your disposal. What do you need to know about the Vernet estate?"

"Allow me to go outside and get my greffier," Martin rose, still a little shaky from the scare that Picard's unexpected appearance had provoked, and started to go around his desk toward the door.

"No need, my boy." Picard had caught him by the sleeve of his jacket as he went by. "I'm in no hurry. We can just sit and chat."

That was exactly what Martin did not want to do. The story was out. He'd want to think about what he was going to say to curious people, like Picard, as well as what he needed to ask the notary about his clients.

"M. Picard," Martin assured his landlord, "your deposition is going to be crucial. I want to make sure we have it all down." That said, Martin pulled away. He knew that Picard would enjoy spending the next few moments contemplating the important role he'd be playing in a delicious scandal.

Martin made his way into the cool cavernous hallway, and closed the door behind him. Holding the knob in his two hands, he leaned back on the heavy door and waited until his breathing slowed. Then he hurried down the stairs to rescue Old Joseph from Sibylline Beauregard, who was still holding forth at the back entrance of the Palais.

There were few surprises in what Picard had to say. But the notary did draw out every suspicious possibility. All the money was hers, from the sale of her shop. Solange Vernet's estate, which had gone mostly toward the purchase of the Cours apartment, would, except for an allowance to one Arlette LaFarge, go to Charles Westerbury, unless, "and this is the interesting part, unless she *adopted* a child before her death. Adopted." The notary gave Martin a knowing look. "What could that mean? Surely she was young enough to still hope for a child of her own. Or. . . ." He shrugged, and then Picard did Martin the favor of waving his finger to make his point. "Something you can look into. What if Westerbury did not want to share his fortune, or have to take care of a child? What if he did not have the potency, the capability of giving her one himself?" Satisfied with his incisive reasoning, Picard relaxed into his seat, waiting.

Indeed, what if? Martin was sure that Westerbury had mentioned nothing about adoption. But had Arlette? He'd have to go back through his notes.

"Do you think that Westerbury and Solange Vernet could have continued living at the same level of expenditure for very long?"

The notary shook his head. "I don't see how, unless he really did begin to earn some money."

"All right, then." Martin got up. "You've been very, very helpful."
Although, of course, not nearly as helpful as Picard thought he had
been.

"And we can continue this discussion tomorrow, at one," Picard
said, as he rose to offer a farewell handshake.

Martin forced a smile. Rest would not come easily during the
waning days of August.

Sunday, August 23

Our wives and our daughters are raised, governed by our enemies. Enemies of the modern spirit, of liberty and of the future. It would serve no purpose to cite such and such a preacher or such and such a sermon. One voice to speak of liberty, fifty thousand to speak against it.

—Jules Michelet, *The Priest, Woman and the Family*, 1845

17

IT WAS THE ITCHING THAT WOULD finally do him in. And the heat. And the stench. And the tragic absurdity of his fate. Westerbury scratched at his beard, trying to pry loose the lice and their eggs. He began pacing again, back and forth, back and forth, the length and width of his tiny cell. How long would they keep him here? How long must he endure the waiting, not knowing, not being able to talk to another living soul? His steps quickened, and, with them, the infernal pounding in his chest. He could feel his teeth grinding against each other. He pulled at his hair in a mad attempt to rid himself of the vermin and vent his frustrations. He wanted to shout and pound on the thick iron door, demanding to be let go. But that would be useless, and it would show them that they were winning. He could not let them win.

Calm down, calm down, he told himself. *Weaker men than you, and certainly men with less intelligence, without philosophy, have survived such confinement, and survived it for years.* Stoicism—the philosophy of Marcus Aurelius—is what he must aspire to. Wisdom, Justice, Fortitude, Temperance. Wasn't that it? To practice them would lead to tranquility and make him a worthy follower of the greatest of all Romans. But, Westerbury paused mid-thought, at least Aurelius had a great country estate to run to when the battles, plots, and conspiracies became too much to bear. In this foreign land, Westerbury had only his wits.

He sat back on the thick board suspended by two chains. This piece of wood, covered by an inch of matted vermin-infested straw, and one thin woolen cloth, was his bed, his chair, and his table. They allowed him no books, no pen, and no paper. Not even a chamber pot. Westerbury glanced toward the filthy hole in the corner, where the odor of his own urine and feces mingled with that of other unfortunates who had occupied the cell before him. Barbarous race. Barbarous, sewerless, lawless, insalubrious, arrogant race. Why bother to even think about being treated like an educated man when they can't even treat you like a human being?

Westerbury felt the tears building again. Sniffling, he watched the dust glisten and dance in the streams of light that flowed from the tiny square window high in his cell. It was almost noon on Sunday. The daily meals and the changing light were the only way he kept track of time. By his count, he had been here for three days and three nights. The wardens came only two times each endless day, slid open the slot in the big iron door, ladled water into his cup and pushed a bowl of mush toward him. The first time it happened, not knowing the routine, he had let his meager provisions fall on the stone floor. He learned quickly to have his cup ready, and to shovel in his food with the battered spoon. The guards left the opening ajar while they made their rounds. Westerbury found himself looking forward to those few isolated moments, when he did not feel completely alone. He eagerly listened for the rattling of the food cart, the insults of the guards, and the cacophony of defiance and despair that the other prisoners shouted from their cells as they cursed their jailers, their food, and their rotten luck.

If he had been a lesser man, Westerbury would have joined them, or at least cheered them on. But they were common criminals, thugs, and petty thieves. Not like him. They had done nothing to better their condition. They had never aspired to higher knowledge or a higher calling. Besides, he was innocent. Innocent of murder, at least. But, he buried his head in his hands as he suppressed a moan, not innocent of weakness, of not loving enough, nor of having let his poor, dear girl fall into the hands of a killer. Westerbury pulled himself up. Why play the stoic when her murder might go unavenged? Why stay here and suffer when he could be finding the monster and killing him with his own bare hands? A cleansing anger drove him to his feet. His sobs turned to rage, and he began pounding on the iron door with his fists. "I want to talk to Franc! I'll give him what he wants!"

Miraculously, the slot slid open. Mealtime. "Wait, wait." Westerbury grabbed his cup. He could not bear to lose his portion of the precious water. "Wait!" he shouted. He got back in time to push the tin cup under the ladle and to face the guard. "Tell Franc I will give him the note. Tell Franc I want to speak to the judge, but before I do, I will tell him where the note is. Tell him that I am ready to tell everything."

The guard thrust a tin bowl through the slot. This time the substance was brown. Westerbury scooped it up. "Tell him."

"Don't worry. As soon as he comes in for duty tomorrow." The opening was so small that Westerbury only saw half of the warden's face. The mouth had widened into a crooked grin. "He'll be glad to hear it. He knew you'd break."

18

SHOUTS AND LAUGHTER DREW MARTIN TO his window. The day was bright and sunny. It was a day that should have made almost anyone as gay and carefree as the three Picard girls. Protected by oversized white aprons that covered the plaids and stripes of their Sunday best, they were picking pears from the tree which dominated the little walled garden behind the house. The youngest, perched precariously on a ladder, was ignoring the warnings of her two older sisters as she reached into the high branches. Having the best view of Martin's window, she caught a glimpse of him before he moved out of sight. She gasped, pointed toward his attic room, covered her mouth with her free hand, and set off another gale of laughter.

"M. Martin, we are getting pears to eat with your cheese!" she shouted, much to the chagrin of those below.

"Amélie, leave M. Martin alone. I am sure that he is studying or thinking about serious matters."

Martin was not sure which of the older sisters had delivered this admonition, but he returned to the window, in the hope that no one had noticed his furtiveness, and gave what he hoped looked like a cheerful wave to all three of them. They seemed excited about the prospect of having dinner with him, while all he wanted to do was get through it as briefly and as gracefully as possible.

Martin stepped back into the darkness and sat down at his table to make one more attempt to comprehend the words dancing on the page before him. He had been going over his outline of the case for hours, but he could not vanquish the anxieties that had haunted him throughout the night and kept circling through his mind: he was incapable of finding the murderer of Solange Vernet and the boy. He might be persecuting an innocent man. The murderer might kill again because of Martin's incompetence. There were so many holes. The identity of the boy. The missing letter. The note. The gloves. The source of Solange Vernet's wealth, and so much more about her past that he did not know, so many details that did not make any sense.

Worse, he could not get Merckx out of his mind. What if he had not escaped? The gendarmes would find Merckx and discover that Martin had abetted a deserter. Martin might go to prison. All his hopes, as well as his mother's, would end in shame and ignominy. *Good God*! Martin covered his face with his hands. *How did I get myself into this?*

The irony was that his most dangerous mistake was the one he would do all over again. Had it not been just to help his oldest friend, an exploited man of the people, escape from certain, torturous death?

Martin tugged at his beard and ran his fingers through his hair. *No more*! No more thinking. He had to prepare himself. The Picard dinner would be good place to start practicing concealment, something he would have to become an expert at.

He shoved his notes into the drawer, pushed his books against the wall on the shelf above his bed, and smoothed out the covers, in an attempt to hide every part of himself in case his landlord decided to come and fetch him. He left his copy of *Le Courrier d'Aix* in plain view. Having been forewarned by Picard, Martin had gotten up early to buy the local newspaper. The article had given a fairly accurate account of Solange Vernet's murder and her circle, until it concluded with an unjustified polemic aimed straight at him. Martin picked up the newspaper and read the last paragraph again.

No one knows why Vernet went to the quarry where she met her tragic end. Unfortunately, the murderer struck just at a time when our prosecutor, Serge Lasserre, and many of the more seasoned magistrates are out of town enjoying the final week of the holidays. Thus it has been left to a young northerner, Bernard Martin, to carry out the investigation. So far, according to our sources, he has questioned only Westerbury himself. In our minds, he is a most unlikely suspect, but the forces of reaction, in the person of the church-going Martin, may want to take this opportunity to persecute the new ideas and their purveyors. We are hoping that the investigation will widen once the prosecutor returns to town. We cannot rest easy with a murderer in our midst.

Church-going? Martin thrust the paper aside. Had someone spotted him at the procession? Or did they label him as a believer simply because he had chosen to arrest a so-called promoter of science and progress? It didn't matter. It was beginning. It was inevitable. This case would bring pressures from the left as well as the right.

As if on cue, he heard a knock. Martin took the three steps required to reach the door and opened it to find his landlord, smiling smugly, as if he were about to rub his hands together in delight and anticipation. Without being asked, Picard stepped into the room and walked over to Martin's table.

"Ah, I see you have already read the *Courrier*. Well, I have something even more interesting downstairs. Can you join me for a talk before dinner?"

"Certainly. Give me a minute and I'll be right down."

They stood looking at one another, until Picard realized that he was supposed to leave.

"Yes, monsieur le juge, yes. I can hardly wait."

As soon as Picard left, Martin dipped his hands in his washbasin and poured the water over his face in a vain attempt to wash away his weariness. As he wiped his face and hands with the towel hanging by his basin and tied his cravat, Martin rehearsed the system that he had devised for remembering the names of each of Picard's brown-haired daughters. The eldest was Lucie, about twenty years old. The most *lucide*, reasonable and sensible of the lot. Bernadette, perhaps nineteen or so, had been named for the peasant girl who claimed to have seen the Virgin Mary at Lourdes. Undoubtedly this had been *Madame* Picard's choice. Bernadette seemed to be the most *pious* of the sisters. The youngest was easy, eleven-year-old Amélie, *amiable*, as her name implied. She was plump and giggly, and so obviously the apple of her father's eye. Martin smiled. Even he found her free-spiritedness amusing. The bustling matron, Mme Picard, was Marguerite, Martin recounted as he walked down the stairs. The cook was Hélène, the more-traveled cousin of Louïso, who was proud of the fact that she had once worked in a restaurant in Lyon. And M. Picard, if he once again insisted upon the intimacy of using their Christian names, was René. Martin was as ready as he'd ever be.

Apparently, so were the Picards. As soon as the door opened, Martin caught a whiff of the smoky scent of frying *lardons*, thick bits of bacon, coming from the kitchen at the other end of the hall. The hallway itself was overheated with cooking preparations and an over-abundance of humanity. All three daughters were lined up to eye Martin as his landlord let him in. After the obligatory greetings, Picard shooed his daughters away. "Girls, girls, let the judge in the door. And do run along. Leave us men alone for a few minutes."

"I thought that men only wanted to be alone to smoke *after* dinner." Amélie was precocious—and emboldened because she knew she could never make her father angry.

"Today, my precious, we will talk *before*. Go on, now. Help your mother!" Picard gave Amélie a little pat on her well-covered behind, and sent his daughters off in a rustle of taffeta.

"Sorry," Picard apologized, "they're all a-twitter because of the murder."

Just as Martin feared. Nonetheless, he managed a smile.

"Let's go in here." Picard led him into the parlor. "I have something to show you that you will find very interesting."

Once Picard closed the door, the room was cooler and blessedly insulated from the smells that had set off sudden hunger pangs. Martin held his hand over his growling stomach. Oblivious to his plight, Picard led him to a small round table that held a decanter, two aperitif glasses, and a folded newspaper, which he thrust into Martin's hands.

"Have you seen this?"

Martin read the masthead, *La Croix de Provence*, with a sinking heart. "No, but I have seen the northern version, *La Croix de Lille*." It was his mother's favorite newspaper, and during his last visit had been the starting point of religious and political discussions at the DuPont table.

"Well, then you know that it is run by the Assumptionists, the same priests that run all those sick people down to Lourdes." Picard lowered his voice. "I had to make sure to bring this home with me last night or they would have never let me in the house. It's got all the latest news on the National Pilgrimage. How many trainloads they managed to get down there. How many miracles, complete with heart-rending descriptions of every single cure." He rolled his eyes to demonstrate what hogwash he thought it all was. "Women, you know."

Martin certainly did know. If all had gone well, Marthe DuPont would be arriving home with her "poor sick ones" this very day. But why did Picard, presumably a liberal, bring the reactionary clerical paper into his home?

The notary grabbed the paper back and opened it up. "That's not the most interesting thing in it. Not for us. They've got wind of you all over the region, my boy. Here." He pointed to an article titled "The Hand of God" and left the Catholic newspaper in Martin's unwilling hands. "Read it! And I'll pour us some nice British port. You may need it."

Martin settled slowly into the armchair while he began. The article was much less accurate than the one carried in the *Courrier*, and much more chilling.

The hand of God reached deep into the Bibémus quarry during the feast of the Virgin. While the pious women of Aix gathered to pay homage to Our Blessed Mother, a retired hatmaker, Solange Vernet, was being strangled in an isolated and deadly spot far from the holy celebration. Is it not striking that on the day marking the miracle of the Assumption of the Virgin Mary's body into heaven, a worldly woman infested with ungodly ideas should be cast down into the deepest hole of our environs, prefiguring her descent into hell?

This was the tone Martin remembered so well from his last visit to Lille: righteous, arrogant, and wrong.

As is well known in Aix, the article continued, *"Madame" Vernet was the paramour of George Westerbury, an Englishman who propagated the heresies of English science, spreading blasphemous lies about the origins of the world. These sinners even hosted a weekly "salon" to discuss their heretical ideas, in imitation of our foolish aristocratic ancestors, who opened their homes to the likes of Voltaire and Rousseau, and unwittingly brought Revolution and destruction on themselves. Fortunately the noblewomen of France have repented these sins and denounced the errors of the 18th century. True French noblewomen now bravely uphold Catholic and monarchical values against the braying of republicans and socialists. But Solange Vernet was no noblewoman. She was a Parisian import of inde-terminate origin, who enticed the so-called "men of ideas" into her web, where she ensnared them in the deadly sin of overweening pride in their own weak intellects. Worse, Westerbury and his paramour were not content to limit their evil deeds to men of weak morals and intellectual pretensions. They rented a hall so that this* soi-disant *professor could give public lec-tures, propagating the lie that the earth is millions of years old. They offered "courses for ladies" in a shameless attempt to capture the souls of the wives, mothers, and daughters of Aix.*

We do not know what drove Solange Vernet to the quarry, where no decent woman would wander alone. Was she searching for some proof of Westerbury's blasphemies? Or was she going there to commit a sin of the flesh, so heinous and so secret that she had to hide it even from her lover? Let us not be ensnared into the trap of committing sins of the imagination. God Our Father sees all, knows all, and judges all. And He decided that this woman's sins would not go unanswered on a day meant to celebrate the Most Immaculate of all Women.

Martin could feel his jaw clench, and his fingers tightened around the paper. Everything he was reading was to be expected. Yet it still felt like a violation. The next paragraph almost made him cry out.

We are proud to report, too, that despite the pleadings of Solange Vernet's maid and the request of our Republican judiciary, the brothers of the Madeleine Church refused to bury the woman's body in holy ground. The rest lies in the hands of the godless Republican courts. Most of the agents of the impious government are now away, indulging in their leisures. Only the young, inexperienced Parisian Bernard Martin remains to pursue the case. Is his soul pure enough to see through the lies and decep-tions of Westerbury and the other "men of science"?

The article left the question hanging, but did not leave a doubt about the last violation of Solange Vernet's poor body. They had buried her in a potter's field. And the boy? Where did they bury him?

Why hadn't anyone told Martin, especially Franc, who would have known about this final insult? It took all of Martin's efforts not to squash the paper in his hands and throw it on the floor. Franc probably had not told him because he was a pious hypocrite who judged Solange Vernet every bit as harshly as the reactionary priesthood.

Picard was staring at him, waiting for some reaction.

"Your whole family has read this?" Even as he said this, Martin knew that there was little hope that they had not.

Picard lifted his glass and shrugged his shoulders. "If they didn't read it here, I'm sure the priests would read it to them next Sunday, word for word. This is going to be big. Huge, in fact. It's not often that we have a murderer on the loose in Aix."

"Right," Martin mumbled as he took his glass and sipped. "Right." The port tasted sickly sweet. Martin really did not want to drink before he had something in his stomach. He set the glass down.

"This could make your career, my boy. You know that, don't you?"

"Yes, of course, but that's not why—" Martin was not at all surprised to hear his landlord echoing Franc's crass words.

"Of course not! I wasn't at all implying that that was why you would try to do the right thing. And," Picard raised his fist in enthusiasm, "to stand up to these black-cassocked bullies in the bargain. Such scandal!" Picard shook his head. "Quite lurid. Had I read the local section before my eldest got ahold of it, I might have snipped it out, just for your sake today. Sorry. You can't imagine what ideas are running around in their heads." Picard tapped Martin's knee with the refolded paper. "Just wanted to prepare you."

Picard did not look at all sorry. He looked like a man anticipating an entertaining meal.

"I can't really say anything about the case." This would have to be Martin's most effective defense.

"Oh, yes, yes, I know, but before they come in to get us, can you tell me if Solange Vernet was violated?"

Just then a breathless Amélie opened the door. "Dinner's ready. And it's Hélène's special salad, so you have to come at once!"

"*Salade Lyonnaise?*" Picard's eyes gleamed with pleasure as he looked upon his excited little daughter.

"Yes, sir," the girl said brightly, then turned and ran off.

Picard rose and winked at Martin. "You know, in this house, the real boss is Hélène. So we'd better go. But before we do, can you tell me if she was——"

Martin shook his head. He had no intention of telling René Picard that Solange Vernet had been raped.

The first course went smoothly. As soon as they were seated in the airy sun-filled dining room, the Picard elders at either end of the table, and Martin beside Lucie and directly across from Bernadette, Hélène took over. She circled around them, placing a steaming poached egg on top of their individual bowls of vinegary mixed greens and *lardons*. "Eat before the eggs get cold," she commanded, as she flew out of the room and closed the door.

"Eggs laid just yesterday," was the only remark Picard allowed himself before digging in. Mme Picard tried to maintain a dignified posture, but the girls, who had been suffering through the torture of the inviting aromas for hours, pressed their forks into the slightly cooked yolks with undisguised relish, smearing the yellow contents all over the salad and dipping their bread to catch the runoff. Martin hesitated, and then followed suit. He had never seen a hot egg planted on a salad before, but the results were wonderful, especially since the creative urgency of mixing, stirring, dipping, and stuffing their mouths kept the girls well occupied.

"Ahh." Picard pushed his bowl forward. "One of Hélène's specialties. But only a preview of her skills. Next, duck with olives. Duck fresh from the country."

"And old olives from last year!" Amélie loved teasing her father as much as he loved teasing her.

"Amélie!" The mother nodded her head toward Martin, signaling that they had a guest, and good manners were expected.

Bernadette wiped her mouth with her napkin and shot her sister a look across the table. Martin was not sure which member of their family the older girls were passing judgment on. Before anything else was said, Hélène set a large, steaming tureen in front of Picard. "At last, I can turn off the oven. Your cheese and pears are on the side-board. Call me when you need dessert." She waddled away with a huge sigh, fanning herself with a towel.

"Dessert, and not before," remarked Lucie, having her own fun. Then she bent toward Martin as she explained, "Our cook hates to use the oven in the heat."

"Hélène or no Hélène," Picard declared, "surely we need to put forth some effort when we have such a special guest." All eyes once again fell on Martin. He cleared his throat and tried to act as if Picard's distribution of the stew were all he had on his mind. When everyone had a full plate in front of them, they began the intricate work of cutting the flesh away from the bone. This took some effort, but not enough to discourage conversation.

Mme Picard was the first to speak. "Before the investigation, M. Martin, did you know Solange Vernet?"

The dark stew was delicious, much more earthy than anything he would have gotten at his mother's table. The food and wine were putting Martin in a better mood. He realized that to be sociable he would have to say a little. "Not really," he said, then put a piece of duck into his mouth, chewing slowly to discourage other questions.

"Well, I did." Forks almost dropped as the three daughters turned to their mother. "Mother!" exclaimed Bernadette, "you never told—"

"There was no reason to," said Mme Picard as she popped an olive into her mouth and smiled at her husband. The plain brown hen was enjoying her chance to trump the peacock at the other end of the table.

"How? Where?" Lucie leaned past Martin to get a better look at her mother.

"At two of our charity meetings."

"At the church?" Bernadette asked, surprised. Although Martin kept his silence, he was every bit as interested in the answers as the Picard girls.

"Yes. You see, your father is not the only person in this household who gets to meet interesting people. She came and wanted to help out, although I must say she did not have a proper idea of what a ladies' organization does. She asked if we helped poor abandoned girls and babies and little children, as if we went directly to their homes to feed them and change their diapers. We told her about our yearly fair and the annual charity ball, and how this provides money for the sisters, who are in a much better position than we are to go directly to the poor. After two meetings, she seemed to lose interest, and I must say, *although we invite everyone in*," she emphasized to Martin and Picard as if she knew that men would wrongly accuse her of small-mindedness, "most of us were not that interested in having her, either."

"So you've both seen her," Amélie said, looking from her mother to her father, "and maybe you too." She had caught the ambiguity in Martin's answer about whether he "knew" Solange Vernet. "I mean," she suddenly blushed, "did you see her before she died?"

"Amélie, please." Bernadette nudged her little sister. "Let's not talk about corpses at the table."

"I just wanted to know if she was beautiful or intelligent."

Oh yes, Martin thought, *she was all that and more*. How much more? Had she really thought the upper-class women of Aix would welcome her into pious circles? Perhaps, unlike them, she was willing to go into hovels to feed and care for the poor. Clearly Solange Vernet had had no understanding of how well-brought-up women like Mme Picard and Marthe DuPont performed their "charities."

"Well," Picard was not one to lose an opportunity to be the center of attention, "I think some people might have found her attractive. She certainly was fashionable. In a Parisian sort of way, of course. And, yes, I would say she was intelligent—"

"What did you think, M. Martin?" Mme Picard asked, interrupting her husband before he got going.

"Excuse me?"

"I know that if I were a different kind of woman, I might have been jealous of René's dealings with her. Despite his hemming and hawing just now, he did tell me that he thought she was quite beautiful."

"Yes, yes." Martin kept his head down, as he fished around in his stew. "But I only really saw her once, before. We both happened to be at the counter of a bookstore and I heard the man say her name."

"What did she get?" Amélie seemed very excited by this notion. "I mean, what book?"

Martin looked at her and smiled. "I really don't know." At least that was truthful. After all, Solange Vernet had insisted he take the translation of Darwin with the preface by Clémence Royer.

"Probably some impious book," Bernadette sniffed. "Father Grevier mentioned her and M. Westerbury in a sermon just before we left for the country. Actually he didn't call them by name, but he said there were outsiders who had come to town trying to propagate the lie that the world is millions of years old, when, he said, everyone knows that Adam and Eve could not have lived more than four thousand years ago."

"Really." The word slipped out before Martin could stop it. In truth, he was torn between wanting her to go on, so that they would ignore him, and wanting her to shut up.

"Yes, of course. Don't you agree?"

"I haven't made any study of science." Martin was trying to be noncommital, but, as soon as he said it, he realized that his answer had come out as either a challenge or an evasion.

"What about the Bible?"

"Bernadette!" Mme Picard obviously thought her daughter had

gone too far. Picard, on the other hand, pulled back from the table to get a better view of the fray.

"Well, I think she got what she deserved." Bernadette glared at Martin.

Well said, Martin thought, *you and all the pious women of Aix.*

"Dear, that is not a very Christian attitude." The mother moved in to quell the flames.

"And when, my dearest, have Christians ever been Christian?"

"René!"

"Here we go again!" Amélie interjected with impish delight. This was obviously an old and familiar argument, but, as far as Martin could tell, the mutual affection of the Picards was older and deeper still. Their exchange reminded him how his own father had tried to tease his mother out of some of her opinions, although his father would have never displayed the notary's pomposity.

"Still," Bernadette was not about to give up the floor, "I want to know what M. Martin thinks. Do you think she deserved what she got?"

This was an easy question to parry. "No one deserves to be murdered."

"Well, she went to the quarry by herself, she lived in sin, she was a hypocrite who acted like she was religious when she really wasn't."

A red heat was rising from Martin's neck to his forehead. He did not know why, but he was sure that Solange Vernet had practiced more true virtue in her short life than Bernadette Picard would in a hundred years.

"M. Martin, are you all right?" Lucie's hand fell gently on his wrist. He realized that he was clutching his fork and glaring at Bernadette. He gave his head a shake. How gauche and unreasonable to be angry with a young girl, just because she was expressing conventional opinions. "I'm sorry, I was just thinking."

"About her?"

"Solange Vernet? Yes."

"It must have been horrible to see her afterward," Lucie said as she pulled her hand away.

"Yes." It had been horrible, and he hoped that the girl's sympathetic intervention would end the conversation.

"Do you think he did it? Did you talk to him? Do you think he is a murderer?" Amélie's eyes were large and excited.

"M. Westerbury?" Martin had regained his composure. The child was asking the obvious question, innocent of prejudice and judgment.

"Yes, yes. M. Westerbury. The lecturer. The Englishman. Did he do it?"

"I'm sorry, but I cannot speak of any specifics of the investigation at this point."

Even this vague, innocuous answer seemed to thrill little Amélie, if only because it sounded so official. She was speaking with the investigating judge who was going to catch the man who had committed the most heinous crime in all of Aix. *If only*, Martin thought, *if only and soon.*

"I know you should not speak ill of the dead, but," although Bernadette sounded somewhat chastened, she was not to be dissuaded, "I just wondered what you thought of her when she was living. The kind of life she was leading. The lies she propagated. After all, like Maman said, she didn't even know how to act like a lady. Where did she get all that money?"

"Well, I can probably say more about that than our young judge." Picard had given up the stage for far too long. "The money was hers, not his, and I believe that she *earned* it."

"Earned it?" This took Mme Picard aback. "A woman earned a fortune?"

"Well, you know that I don't like to talk about my clients' business, but since she is dead, I can tell you that she was a very successful milliner in Paris. In a poor neighborhood, but obviously she attracted a rich clientele."

"A hatmaker? What kind of family did she come from?"

Picard looked at Martin, who shrugged, noncommital. He could have recited another official-sounding, meaningless piety about the "ongoing investigation," but he didn't bother. The truth was that he did not know. And he should.

"I'm sure M. Martin, being a man of the world," the notary declared, "does not find it all that shocking that a woman made her own way. And when he finds out how, I'm sure we'll all know about it. It will be in the papers. And if we are polite, perhaps M. Martin will grace our table again."

"*La Croix* said that she was a woman of 'indeterminate origin,' whatever that means," Bernadette sniffed. "I can just imagine."

"Girls, girls, enough." In Mme Picard's circles, it was a mother's first duty to keep her daughters from such imaginings. "Your father's right. Let's engage our guest in more pleasant conversation. Lucie, would you bring the pears and cheese from the sideboard and call Hélène to ask her to clear?" Now that Mme Picard had had the fun of springing the surprise of her brief encounter with Solange Vernet on her family, she was pulling them back to proper form.

Martin hoped that the rustle of Lucie's movement covered his sigh of relief. The rest of the meal continued in a more pleasant vein. The fruit was ripe and delicious, and so was the cheese. They conversed about the Picard country home, the coming theater season in Aix, and the differences between the food of the north and the south.

Despite the fact that the family banter released Martin from having to strain to find things to say, he grew more and more uneasy as the afternoon wore on. Bernadette's remarks had roused unexpected anger in him. What right did she, a thoroughly conventional and inexperienced girl, with a privileged place in the smug society of Aix, have to look down upon Solange Vernet, who had worked hard to make something of herself? By all accounts, Solange Vernet had always treated others with graciousness and compassion. Cézanne had loved her deeply. Westerbury said that she was a remarkable woman. Because of the boy, because of Merckx, and because of his own fear of exposure, Martin had been neglecting in his own mind the first victim to whom he owed justice. He realized that he urgently needed to do more than clear up this or that detail of her life. He longed to know her. Who was she really? Where had she come from? What had she hoped for? Only Westerbury could begin to answer these questions.

Monday, August 24

Until Darwin, what was stressed by his present adherents was precisely the harmonious co-operative working of organic nature, how the plant kingdom supplies animals with nourishment and oxygen, and animals supply plants with manure, ammonia, and carbonic acids. Hardly was Darwin recognized before the same people saw everywhere nothing but struggle.

—Friedrich Engels, *Dialectics of Nature*, 1872-82

19

THE NEWS SHOULD HAVE BEEN GOOD, but it could not have been worse. Martin was at the back door of the courthouse ordering a gendarme to fetch Old Joseph, when Franc interrupted them.

"I just spoke with the Englishman. He said he'd tell you everything you need to know. But he insists that you come to him, in his cell, alone."

"That's odd. I was planning on interrogating him in chambers—all day if necessary," Martin said with an ironic grin. Franc did not return his smile. Was his intrepid inspector upset that Martin might be the one to break the case?

"He says he won't talk there. Only in the cell."

Martin thought for moment, then shrugged. If Westerbury was really going to tell the truth, then Martin was ready to meet him anywhere.

"I—" Martin was about to agree when he realized that Franc was scrutinizing him, watching his every reaction.

Franc took hold of Martin's arm. "Before you do anything else this morning, you need to come downstairs to identify a body."

The blow struck Martin hard in the chest. Another murder victim? Or, was it the unthinkable: they had found Merckx.

"He was wearing your jacket."

If his life had not depended on his staying on his feet, Martin might have fainted. His ears began to ring. He could not move, he could not breathe, he could not speak. It was as if he were drowning. Merckx. Or maybe—this was a crazy hope, he knew, but it was his only hope—maybe it was someone else, someone who had waylaid Merckx or taken the jacket from under his head while he was sleeping in the woods. Maybe it was a poacher, a prankster, or a common thief. But every rational bone in his being told him there was no hope.

"Sir?"

"I'm just confused about how someone could have gotten my jacket." A feeble lie if there ever was one. "Did you find any identification on him?"

"Only a passport, obviously false. I suspect he was a deserter."

By now the fear had coalesced in Martin's chest, weighing him down. Soon he would be gasping for air. But he had to breathe, move his legs, and think. Most of all, at this moment, he had to show a willingness to go the morgue.

Suddenly he felt Franc's heavy hand on his shoulder. "Come on now. Remember, we are a team. We're in this together." This gesture only told Martin that his fright was all too evident. It did not tell him whether Franc intended to be an accuser or a friend. Nor did it tell him how much Franc knew or suspected. And if Franc knew or suspected anything, how could Martin ever be sure that his ambitious, ever-vigilant inspector would keep his silence?

Afraid that any of the questions whirling around in his head might tumble out, Martin said nothing. He nodded his assent, pulled away from Franc, and crossed the street to the prison. As he descended into the basement, he kept reminding himself not to hang on to the railing for support. Franc was two steps behind him.

Dr. Riquel was waiting by the covered corpse. Despite a numbing sensation in his chest and limbs, which made it almost impossible for him to walk toward the table, Martin somehow did just that. He took a place opposite Riquel, who said his good-mornings and began to peel the sheet from the body. The first thing Martin saw was the corn-yellow hair, then the pallid thin face. Martin's knees would have buckled under him if he had not been holding on to the edge of the cool iron slab.

"How?"

"Shot by two of my men," Franc answered from behind. "We heard there was a deserter in the district, Jean-Jacques Merckx, and that he was an anarchist and a traitor."

And my oldest and best friend. My impossible, demanding, and persistent conscience. Martin could not stop the tears, so there was no use denying that he knew the dead man.

"Was he running away? Did he say anything before he died?" *Did he mention me? Did you have to shoot him?*

"We tried to get him to stop, but he kept running."

This could not be. Any normal man could outrun the sickly Merckx. Martin looked down at the body. Four bullet holes had pierced Merckx's emaciated frame.

Martin swiped at the tears that were running down his cheeks, and forced himself to stop sniveling. Then he pulled the sheet up over his friend's face. "I can confirm that this is Jean-Jacques Merckx, born in Lille, about twenty-six years ago." He managed to say this in a steady voice, devoid of feeling. He was getting used to dead bodies. "Merckx was a boyhood friend. But," his heart began to race as he formulated another lie, "I have not seen him since Paris. He must have found out my address, gone there while I was away, and taken things. I've been so busy, I must not have noticed what was missing from my room." He hastened to add, since they had probably found Martin's paltry savings on Merckx's body, "Nor have I had occasion to look in my money box. I assume there's nothing left."

"You hadn't seen him—?" Franc sounded unconvinced by Martin's flimsy fabrications.

"No." The denial would have come out like a shout if Martin had had the strength. Instead, it was merely a rasp.

"Apparently he had been asking about you near the courthouse. You were in luck, sir, if you did not cross paths."

Franc's "if" hung in the air. Martin glanced across the corpse at Riquel, who showed no signs of caring one way or the other. "What are you going to do with the body?" Martin asked quietly.

"I'll take a photograph." Riquel was businesslike as usual. "We'll send it to the army and bury him here in the common grave."

With Solange Vernet. Martin had meant to make sure that she would be treated with respect. He had failed her. At least Merckx would not care about being buried in sacred ground. Quite the opposite. A violent and anonymous end was the only one he had ever wished for.

Merckx's cold gray hand lay exposed on the table. Martin touched the fingers and said in his heart what he could not say aloud. *Good-bye, dear Jean-Jacques. May you find more peace in death than you ever did in life.* Martin pushed his friend's hand back under the sheet while he considered his next move. He had to get away without revealing anything else. He had to find a place to recover his forces.

Martin turned to Franc. "I assume there is no hurry in going to see Westerbury?"

The inspector shook his head warily, never taking his eyes from Martin's face.

"Well, then, I'm going to let him rot in his cell a little longer. Let's make sure he knows who's in charge. I'll be back this afternoon to decide when and where I am going to interrogate him." Having delivered this bit of unlikely bravado, Martin turned to the professor to shake hands. "Riquel, thanks as always for your service." Giving a final nod to Franc, Martin headed up the stairs, leaving his companions to decide for themselves how much of a coward and liar he really was.

Walking a straight line had never been more difficult. Or more necessary. Anyone could be watching. Franc, a gendarme, even a reporter. Martin passed a café but knew he would not be able to stomach a coffee, or even give the order for one. Habit took him along the narrow streets that led past the Saint-Sauveur Cathedral. He decided to slip inside. It was the one place where no one would bother him, and where he could easily see if someone were following. If they were, he thought with bitter irony, at least they would not accuse him of being a godless anarchist.

After he closed the wooden door, Martin slid to his left to watch the entrance. Save for a few old women in widow's weeds, no one else came in. The burning wax and the incense, which still lingered from the morning mass, filled the air with the comforting odors of innocence and childhood. What he saw before him was just as familiar. Two nuns glided from altar to altar, dusting and replacing votive candles. Worshipers were scattered throughout the cathedral, fingering their rosaries or hanging their heads over folded hands. Wrapped in their private sorrows and supplications, they took no notice of Martin.

The paintings, statues, and tapestries were all obscured in the vast darkness, but Martin did not have to see the huge crucifix over the central altar to feel its presence. How many visible wounds were there on Jesus's body? Seven? He should know. Every Good Friday the priests and his mother had recited His sufferings in precise and mortifying detail. Merckx had received four mortal wounds. At least someone in Christ's entourage had tried to chop off the ear of a persecutor. Martin had done nothing. And he would probably not be able to do anything to avenge his friend's murder. He closed his eyes and swallowed hard. Before the cock crowed the Passover night into the day of death, Peter had denied Christ three times. Martin had just denied his oldest, dearest friend at least that many times in less than half an hour.

He stumbled away from the main part of the cathedral into the ancient baptistry, the only part of the church that he liked because of its simple, classic dignity. The rotunda, once part of a pagan temple, was over a thousand years old. Its eight great columns surrounded a square that contained the round recess into which early Christians had stepped to receive the water of baptism. They had entered between the two black columns representing darkness, been washed of their sins, and then left by another, lighter path, spiritually renewed. Now all the marble columns were pockmarked and darkened by age and neglect. Martin stepped behind one of them and began to cry. In an effort to muffle his sobs, he pressed his face against the marble column and clung to it in a cold embrace.

He had no idea how long it took for him to come to his senses. What would Merckx have said if he could see him now? Martin thought bitterly as he spread out his handkerchief and wiped his face and dripping nose. Certainly he would have mocked the fact that Martin's mind had so easily turned to old religious myths. Martin sighed as he stared up toward the light that came from the opening in the cupola above the rotunda. Merckx would have preferred to be compared to the anti-Christ rather than the Christ. He would have asked Martin why he wasn't thinking about Liberty, Equality, and Fraternity instead of religion. Neither God nor Master, remember? That was Merckx's motto. If you know what justice is, not bourgeois justice, but real justice for the poor, the weak, and the sick, then to hell with the state. No need to be honest with them. Do not think of St. Peter, do not think of having to become a martyr for me. Go on. At the very least, be a man.

Be a man. Martin walked through the columns of the baptistry and retraced his steps to the back of the cathedral. He took a seat. Merckx's hectoring voice would stay with him for a long time, perhaps for the rest of his life. Martin had always hated his friend's mocking cynicism, so often directed at him. This time it could work for Martin, as a reprieve rather than punishment. Merckx would not want him to confess. Merckx would not care if Martin called him a sneak or a thief. Merckx would want him to think of the final cause, the end that justified the means. For Martin, that end was justice for Solange Vernet and the boy. After the Proc got back, if Franc knew something about his meeting with Merckx, the inspector could turn him in at any time. Martin leaned back and closed his eyes. In the meantime, he would honor Merckx's memory by fighting on and not giving up.

20

AS THE BURLY GUARD SWUNG OPEN the thick iron door that led to the jail cells, Martin was stricken by the kind of dread that only an accused man might feel. This could be his fate. His only chance was to get Westerbury to tell the truth, before the Proc returned. Then he would prove that he was a real judge. A judge capable of solving a murder. And a judge who was incapable of treason.

Martin took a deep breath to calm himself. A mistake, for with that breath he imbibed the stale, putrid odor of prison life. Then there was the noise. As soon as the prisoners guessed who he might be, a chorus of complaints and shouts erupted all around him. Some of the prisoners were housed six to a cell. These men rose up as soon as they saw him and began to call out. "Is that a judge?" "Hey, judge, let me out, I'm the innocent one, Pierre!" "No, not that bastard, me, Jacques. I'm not a thief!" "Tell them to feed us real food in here." "Judge! Judge!"

Martin and his guard gave no signs of hearing these taunts as they walked to the end of the hall where the dangerous prisoners were held, one to a cell, behind thick windowless doors. The guard stopped at one, chose a large key hanging from a chain on his belt, and unlocked it.

"Do you want me to stay, sir?"

"No, wait outside. The prisoner made it clear he wanted to talk to me alone."

"You're right," Martin's protector said, as he opened the door and jerked his head contemptuously toward the bed. "I don't think this one could hurt a fly. Not any more."

When Martin stepped inside, the guard closed the iron door behind him with a clang. Westerbury was sitting on the bed, his back against the stone wall. He looked awful. His beard was matted into tangled clumps. His hair hung down in dirty strings. His sagging face had aged ten years, and all the dapperness had gone out of him. And the smell. Martin had managed not to vomit out his pain and fear in front of Franc and Riquel, but he was not sure how long he would last here. He began to breathe through his mouth.

Taking note of this, Westerbury roused himself enough to smirk, and pointed toward the hole in the floor. "Welcome to a French prison, monsieur le juge." A bad start, if Westerbury was trying to garner any sympathy, but Martin did not take the bait. He was going to make this as short as possible. All he wanted was to get the Englishman's confession and get out. He took a small notebook out of his pocket.

Westerbury stood up. "Would you like a seat?" His arm swept toward the bed in a mock gentlemanly gesture. "I warn you, you might catch some lice. But that would be instructive. Insects are so much more clever than us human beings. They're millions of years older, and they will outlast us by millions more, I am sure."

"I'll stand." Obviously, the sight of Martin had brought out what life was left in the Englishman. "You wanted to talk. I'm here. I am eager to hear your confession." Martin did not want to think about what it would be like spending years, even weeks, in a place like this.

"Confession? Confession? Did your *inspector* tell you that?" Westerbury circled around Martin. "That's what he tried to knock out of me. See this?" He approached and lifted up his grimy shirt. His chest and stomach were colored with purple, black, and yellow blotches. "And this?" He held up his wrists, where ropes had been tightened around them. "But I only gave him one little piece of evidence before I asked him to get you."

"What was that?" Martin was determined not to react to Westerbury's goading. Or to his pain.

"The note."

Despite Martin's efforts, Westerbury saw that he did not know.

"Just as I thought. That bastard wants to frame me. Take my word for it. That's why I will talk to you only if you swear that you will never reveal what I am going to tell you."

"I cannot make that promise." The Englishman must know—or must be made to know—that there were laws and procedures. And then, of course, there was the absolute necessity of keeping Franc on his side. Martin was not about to be fooled by Westerbury again.

"Well, then." Westerbury returned to his bed and sat down, arms folded.

They were at an impasse. Martin felt the desperation rising in his chest. He had to keep Westerbury talking. "You might as well tell me what was in the note, and how you got it. I'll find out soon enough anyway."

"I need your promise. I will lead you to where the letter is if you let me out and tell no one else what is in it."

Martin's heart leapt. The letter! The letter that Solange Vernet had spent hours writing right before her death. It could be the key piece of evidence. Yet how could he get it without making promises that he could not keep? He needed to proceed with caution, take it step by step.

"What did the note say?" Martin asked again.

Westerbury stared at him for another long moment, then turned his eyes up to the ceiling. "It said, 'I love you more than ever. Please meet me at the quarry.' Signed with a 'C.'"

A C for Charles. Or for Cézanne. "In French or English?" Martin asked.

"French."

"Handwritten?"

"Printed, in block letters. The kind I used in my posters. And, as you know, and I know, from talking to Arlette, my poor, dear Solange thought it was from me."

The Englishman looked as if he were about to burst into tears.

"Where was the note?"

Westerbury gave a wave of the hand. "Tucked inside the sleeve of Solange's dress. Arlette retrieved it for me."

Just as Franc had suspected. At least this was honest. "And where is it now?"

"Ask your inspector."

Of course he would ask Franc. "I will. We didn't have time to talk about you this morning. There was another case." It was humiliating to have to lie to cover up Franc's insubordination.

Westerbury let out a snort. "If it was another murder, then you can be sure the killer is still out there, and it isn't me."

Martin ignored this remark, as he tried to remember the sequence of the morning's events. There was no reason for Franc not to tell him about the note. He certainly had had time to mention it to him during their encounter. Did Franc think that finding Merckx had given him that much power? Despite the heat, Martin felt a chill rising in him, the icy fear that he had been caught, and was doomed.

"So will you promise?" The Englishman seemed to sense that he had momentarily gained the upper hand.

"I told you, I cannot—"

Before Martin got these words out, Westerbury was on his feet and shouting at him.

"Why can't you? You told me that you have the authority. Well then, use it. Forget the rules for once. Look what your rules have done to me. Is this fair?" Seeing he was getting no reaction, he lowered his voice. "Listen to me, listen to me just this once. As a man listening to another man. Not as a judge prosecuting some foreign charlatan." Westerbury paused until Martin looked him in the eye. "I know that's what you think I am. I know. I don't care about that. But I don't deserve to rot in some foreign prison and die for something I didn't do. What I did, what I deserve to suffer for, I will suffer for all my life. If you have ever loved anyone you will know why I can't allow the world to see what I have done."

The world! As if the world cared about Charles Westerbury. "If you want to be free, you must tell me about any evidence you have access to," Martin insisted.

Westerbury stretched out his arms before Martin. "Please! Please, I beg you! Let me out and I'll take you to it. Just let me go. We can get there before it is too dark."

"Before I release you, I will have to see the evidence myself. If it exonerates you—"

"At least," Westerbury kept pleading, "at least don't tell anyone about what is in it unless you absolutely have to. If that is the price I have to pay for freedom, I will pay it. But if you can keep it from others, I promise you, I will take this letter, wrap it in thorns, and wear it against my heart for the rest of my life."

Martin stepped back until he felt the cool iron door behind him. He was disgusted by Westerbury's extravagant supplications. Yet hadn't Martin spent much of the morning seeking expiation for his own failings? If Westerbury was a lesser man than he, it was only by degrees. They were both cowards. And both likely to be condemned. Martin wanted to shout at Westerbury to stop begging. Instead he kept his voice low. "You don't have to beg like that." At least Martin had kept his anguish to himself.

Westerbury stepped back. "You're right. You're right. It's not you that I should be on my knees to. It's her. Solange, my dear, sweet Solange. You're right. But I can't. She's gone. He murdered her. She's gone. And I can never ask her forgiveness. I can never make her happy again. Or see her smile. Or—"

"Please." This was getting nowhere.

"Oh, you don't want to hear this? Well, monsieur le juge, it is crucial to your case to know something about what went on between us. And between her and," he practically spit out the name, "Paul Cézanne. This is life, my boy."

Martin did not respond. If he had not desperately needed the Englishman's help, he would not have stood for the insulting insinuation that he was callow, not as much of a man as Westerbury.

"And if you want to understand anything about the letter, you have to *feel*," the Englishman continued. "You have to imagine how beautiful Solange was at sixteen. And how vulnerable. How good. How curious. How ready to make something of herself. You have to understand that, and then you will know the depths of what I have done. And what he did. You have to understand the mystery of her."

"Then tell me about it," Martin said quietly. He stood motionless, hardly breathing, willing the suspect to keep on going. "Tell me about her." *Her mystery.*

Westerbury sat down again on the filthy bed and stared at the floor. "She came to one of my lectures. That's how I met her. Intelligent, but unschooled. Assured, but humble. And so unaware of her beauty. So completely unaware. She was a mature woman, but strangely virginal. When she came up to me after my lecture, she told me that she had never done anything like this before. Never asked a question at a lecture. Her hands were trembling ever so slightly, and she spoke almost in a whisper. Yet she had walked up to the lectern with a proud carriage, as would befit a woman of independence and means. I could not take my eyes off her. I used every trick in the book to make her keep talking. I assured her that her questions were quite appropriate. I proclaimed that she was my favorite kind of pupil, a neophyte. I told her, not in so many words but in everything else I did, in the way I ignored everyone else, that she was worth more than all the educated literati in the room. I found out who she was, and I determined that I would see her again in her world, a place where she would be more comfortable.

"I thought, you see, that she was embarrassed only because she was surrounded by men and women of a different class. More educated. I was such a fool. I had no idea. . . ." He paused to wipe his nose and cheeks with his dirty sleeve before going on. "I became her teacher, a teacher thoroughly enthralled with his student. I improved her writing, taught her a bit of English, and, of course, the lovemaking. I thought I was her Pygmalion, she my Galatea brought to life by Aphrodite, who looked down on us with unwarranted favor. I was a fool! I thought I was creating her, when she had really created herself. And yet she let me act the teacher. The great man. She did everything I asked. She learned to express herself with more confidence. To offer tea. To sit among the rich and learned. She became a wonderful lover, full of innocence and abandon all at once. Except—" Westerbury looked up at Martin and stopped. "I'm not sure I can do this."

"What is it you want?" Martin prodded as gently as he could, although his whole body was taut, bound by a fierce amalgam of tension and hope.

"If you promise that you won't tell anyone what is in the letter, I'll tell you where it is. And when you find Solange's gloves and see that they are covered with Cézanne's paint, you'll know that he killed her." Westerbury's laid back against the stone wall, waiting.

The Englishman had lied before. So in return for something Martin would give almost anything to have, he offered the prisoner only conditional hope. "Let us understand what we can and cannot do." Martin drew himself up and spoke in the calm, authoritative voice of a magistrate of the Third Republic of France. "I cannot release you until I see the evidence. I will, since it is so important to you, keep the contents of the letter to myself unless it is absolutely necessary to reveal them. If the letter exonerates you, I will let you go on the condition that you will not leave Aix."

This promise might upset Franc. However, Martin reasoned, the fact that his inspector had not told him about the recovered note gave him the right to find this crucial piece of evidence on his own.

Realizing that he had driven the best bargain possible, Westerbury wearily beckoned Martin to him. Then, in a low voice, he told him where to find the letter.

Tuesday, August 25

Between 1871 and 1940, a Frenchman charged with a felony crime "against property" was, by a large margin, likely to have committed grand larceny. If charged with a felony crime "against persons," he was, again by a large margin, likely to have molested a girl fifteen years or younger.... Statistics for so-called "sex crimes" are believed to be understated because of the embarrassment involved in contacting the police. Even with this caveat, girl molestation accounted for 32.21 percent of the felonies against persons....

Benjamin Martin, *Crime and Criminal Justice under the Third Republic*

21

GO OUT OF THE CITY TOWARD the mountain. Not the road to Vauvenargues, but the road to the south, below the Cours, the road to Le Tholonet. Start out early and take a hat. The sun will be merciless. There is an inn at Le Tholonet at the side of the road. If you have no way to carry water with you, drink what you can there before going on, for you will have to walk at least another hour before reaching the village of St. Antonin. You do this by continuing on the same road. After a while, it zigzags upward until you reach a high plateau. The village is at the top of your climb. Go to the café, it is the only one, and tell Mme Calin that you are a student of mine and you need to borrow her spade. You won't be far away. As you leave the village, you will enter a meadow. The sheer face of the mountain will be rising to your left. Walk about half a kilometer. If you take the time to explore the meadow, you may find a sea shell, proof that the mountain *began as a coral reef rising from an ancient sea, a primeval sea as pure as her soul and green as her eyes.* Westerbury stopped. His grandiloquence had plunged him into dangerous territory, catching him off guard. He composed himself, before continuing. *Look to the right for two solitary pines intertwining their branches like lovers. I wrapped the letter in a cloth sack and buried it under their arch. I suppose I hoped that one day I would take Solange on this walk. That one day we would resurrect our love together, embrace under the pines, and forgive everything that had gone on before.* Again Westerbury had to fight back tears. His last words were spoken mostly to himself, almost beyond Martin's hearing. *I don't know what I hoped for, or why I buried the letter, except I could not bear to destroy it, and I was filled with shame.*

The unrelenting sun was not the only reason to set out early. Martin needed to avoid detection, and he hoped for solitude, some escape from the ghosts inhabiting his attic room. He wove his way through back streets, watching at every corner for Franc or one of his men. Once he reached the outskirts of Aix, he walked with more purpose. Toward the letter. Toward a piece of evidence that might save him and explain everything.

The stony white road to Le Tholonet cut through a tall forest. Martin knew that the quarry where Solange Vernet had been murdered lay somewhere deep in the woods to his left. If he scoured them, would he find the place where Merckx had been shot? Would he see his friend's blood or some evidence of his own paltry belongings? These questions kept pestering Martin. It was depressing to realize that the unfamiliar road was every bit as haunted as Aix.

The pallid face of the mountain came into view before Martin reached the inn at Le Tholonet. He made a hurried stop, then continued on. It was only as he walked up the slow incline leading out of the town that he discovered that Mont Sainte-Victoire was not the single peak one observed from Aix, but a great wall of limestone rising to three peaks, reaching far to the east. The wall shone white under the burning sun, and closed in on him as he climbed toward St. Antonin. There was no wind. Not even a breeze. His only companions were the cicadas, screeching at him from their hiding places.

By the time Martin reached St. Antonin, his shirt was heavy with sweat, but his spirits had lifted. So far everything Westerbury had told him was true. He found the café without any trouble, and drained two glasses of water before telling Mme Calin that he had been sent by Westerbury. It was easy to persuade her to lend him her spade. As she told him, she had done this often for the English geologist, who did not like to carry everything from the city. The professor was a good customer and a charming man, she said. What was Martin looking for? He hesitated. Proof of the world's origins, he told her. This seemed plausible, and he hoped that this would not offend her. She patted his hand and told him he was just like his teacher.

But he was not like Westerbury at all. He did not have time to ponder the origins of the world, or look for the ancient sea shells still lingering in the meadow. His only thought was to measure his steps for half a kilometer until he could scan the horizon for two trees "intertwining their branches like lovers." Even though he caught sight of them right on target, a twinge of doubt assaulted him as he dragged the spade through the still meadow toward the pines. What if the letter wasn't there? What if someone had discovered it before him?

Martin quickened his pace. As soon as he reached the trees he began probing the ground for newly turned earth. He found the spot almost immediately. The digging did not take long. Westerbury had either been too hopeful or too distressed to really bury the letter. Martin grabbed at the sack, turning it round and round until he found the opening. The pages tumbled out of the envelope. He gathered them together and sat down under the pines, holding the letter to his chest. *This was it.* The pages stuck to his moist fingers as he tried to wipe away the dirt and the few tiny insects that had penetrated the sack.

That's when he caught a slight whiff of lavender, the scent he remembered from his encounter with Solange Vernet in the bookstore. Martin smoothed the delicate purple-tinged pages out on his knees and closed his eyes. *Tell me, please tell me, Solange, who killed you.* He wiped the sweat off his brow with his sleeve and dried his hands on his trousers before he began to read.

The handwriting was surprisingly childlike, as if composed in a schoolroom. At first it was neat and precise, but it grew more erratic as, Martin presumed, weariness and emotion had overtaken the writer. He went over the letter again and again until he made out every word, even the few that had been smeared by sweat or blotched by tears.

My Dearest Charles,

You must read this before we can meet again. You must understand why I became so upset with you, and why I was so deeply hurt by your accusations. At last you must know everything.

You accused me of having an affair with Cézanne. Indeed, dear Charles, nothing could be further from the truth. You accuse me of betraying you. Of betraying us. But isn't that the same thing? Didn't you always tell me that in our hearts we were one? Worse, you accuse me of granting him the one favor that I have not granted you. How could you? That is why I had to send you away. I was too angry with you. And too ashamed for both of us.

Now that I am a little calmer, I realize that I must share the blame for your wild accusations, because I have not told you everything. I am weak, Charles, not like you. I cannot conquer the world. Yes, we have both known poverty, and yes, as you said, I have, unlike you, kept part of my past a secret. This was not because I wanted to be mysterious or alluring, as you seem to think. It is because the past shames me. Despite your love, despite all you have done for me, I cannot overcome it. Not completely. Especially not after seeing Cézanne on the Cours the first time. I cry as I write this. When you know everything, you may not even want me.

The first time I saw Cézanne was not in Aix. It was in Bennecourt, almost twenty years ago. I was sixteen. I don't know how old he was. I had been sent to live with my aunt, to work on her farm. When summer came, the inn needed extra help, and my aunt offered my services so that I could help to pay for my upkeep. For weeks at a time young artists came to stay at the inn. Sometimes they brought their wives and lovers, but usually not. I even saw Zola then, before he was famous. I was fascinated by them. I had only a few years of schooling before my mother died. Despite my ignorance I wanted to hear them talk and laugh, to see their paintings, and to know what they were reading to each other. Oh Charles, it was all so new to me, the world of art and the mind. I listened as I cleaned the pots and the dishes in the kitchen. My aunt said I was too pretty to serve the men.

I have never told you about my aunt, my father's sister. She was an ugly, cruel woman. I could not wait to get away from her. But I could not figure out how to do it. We women are different from you men. We cannot just set out in the world. It is full of dangers for us. This I know, Charles, I know this in the depths of my being. I hesitate before telling you the worst part.

Solange Vernet had scratched out a number of lines at this point.

I was curious. I'll admit that. I wanted to know everything about these men, these vacationers from Paris. And when the other servants told me that they went to the river in the moonlight to swim together, I had to see it. How foolish we are at that age. I knew nothing. I had never seen a man naked. At least my father had kept me from that. I had only seen my little brothers. But that was not why I wanted to see them. I think I wanted to see their joy, to know what freedom and happiness looked like.

The second time I went to watch them, my aunt and her lover caught me. They had been looking for me because they wanted to make sure that I brought them the week's wages. My aunt's lover called me a whore and decided to teach me a lesson. He was so big and blond—a brute of a man. He grabbed me by my arm and hair, and dragged me into the woods. My aunt even held me down as he lifted my skirt and took me again and again. He covered my mouth so that no one could hear my cries. I was frantic. I thought I would die. My eyes went round and round looking for help. And then one of the artists appeared through the bushes on his way back to the inn. It was Cézanne. I will never forget his dark eyes staring at me. He stood still, watching me. And he did nothing. Nothing. I will never forgive him for that.

And, dear Charles, do you want to know the irony? Cézanne did not even recognize me when we first met in Aix. He still does not recognize me. It was you who kept telling me that I was a desirable woman. It was you who gave me the courage to pursue a plan of revenge once I understood that I meant nothing to him that horrible night so long ago. I decided that I would mean something, everything. I decided to seduce him so that later I could reject him with as much cruelty as possible. When I found out that he was still trying to make his name in art, I decided that once he had fallen in love with me, I would ridicule him both as an artist and as a man. That's why I laughed when you accused me of making love to him. I almost slapped his face the first time he tried to kiss me.

I owe so much to you, dear Charles. My happiness. My belief that I am a woman worthy of being loved. And because of you, I could not carry out my plan. Why be cruel to someone who is obviously so unhappy? Why take vengeance on another human being when you have everything you want, everything you always wanted, except of course a child. I could not carry out my plan. It was beneath us. Now I am hoping he will grow discouraged and go away.

There was another hiatus and row of scratching out before she began again.

I said I would tell you everything. For my shame does not end with one night in the woods. My aunt's lover was the village constable. His name was Alain Duprès. You should have seen how he strutted around, catching the poor poachers and starving little pickpockets. So righteous, so exacting in his punishments. He even wore his saber, the emblem of his paltry office, to mass on Sunday to show how important he was. But he was just as poor as the rest of us. This is why he was pursuing my aunt, to inherit her pitiful piece of land. I grew more and more sure that he didn't love her. For soon after that night, he took me aside, and told me that I had become his second mistress. He warned me that if I ever told anyone about our "lovemaking" he would give me a beating that would scar me for life. Lovemaking! Oh, Charles, you wondered why you were my first lover. It was because you were so different from all the men I knew. You can't imagine how much I risked when I surrendered to you. That is why I cried that first night. I was so afraid that I would feel the shame and humiliation again.

Yes, Charles, Alain Duprès was the man on top, the only one. I never knew when he would meet me on the road as I was heading home from work, and force me to come to his cabin. This went on for two long, cold seasons, until the next spring. Sometimes I felt that he would crush my very being.

This is why I was so horrified when you accused me of letting Cézanne "mount me." You cannot imagine how cruel your accusation was.

I wrote my father, begging him to let me come home, promising him I would do all the housework, care for the children, and hire myself out to anyone who wanted me. But I did not tell him why. I was too ashamed. And then I found out that I was with child. I knew the signs. I had seen my poor mother go through it again and again, until it finally killed her. At first I refused to believe it. I thought of throwing myself into the river. I was desperate. If my aunt knew, she would have thrown me out. My father would have never taken me back. I talked to one of the servants. She told me there were women in Paris called angel makers. If I could get to Paris, they would spot me as soon as I got off the train. She was sure I looked that desperate. I never told her who the father was. I was too afraid. She probably thought it was one of the guests, one of the artists, but those young men hardly knew I existed.

At least, Charles, I managed to garner a little courage. This is what saved me. One night, when I knew my aunt and her lover were together at the farm, I went into his cabin looking for money. I wanted just enough to get to Paris. He owed me that much. But—perhaps God or the Virgin was with me—what I found was a bag full of gold coins. I put one in my pocket, and stuffed the rest into my sack. They would take me to Paris, they would allow me to pay for a place to stay until I found work. I had no idea how much money was there. I could not believe my luck. I don't know what got into me then, but I wanted to tell Duprès that I had gotten back at him a little. I wanted him to know that at least one person knew what a hypocrite he was. So I left him a note. I could not write very much in those days, so I remember it well. It said "I know who you are. Sophie." And then I stole into the night, walking as fast as I could to the station, and waited there for the train.

When I arrived in Paris, I was made to pay very dearly for my sins. The angel makers did find me before I even left the station. I went with three of them to a hovel on the outskirts of Paris where I saw other girls, some younger than me, waiting their turn. I do hope my child became an angel. I nearly became one of the eternally damned. All I remember was pain and blood, blood that seemed to flow for days. One of the angel makers was very kind. When I finally came to my senses, she held my hand tenderly as she told me that I would be barren. She was also the one who found the money. The Virgin smiled on me again, for she did not steal it or divide it with the others. She kept it for me. She had a plan.

At first, when she told me about it, I became very frightened. Was I to be robbed? Left destitute, and alone in this vast city? She looked into my eyes, while she held my hands, trying to gain my trust. She told me that she did not care how I had gotten all the money. If I had robbed the man who had done this to me, so much the better. She needed to know if I had a family to return to. She was sure I could not make my way on my own.

I told her that I had no family, that I had been rejected by them and was afraid of them. Thankfully, she did not question me further. She had much experience with girls like me, who had gotten into trouble and wanted only to escape. She then told me that she knew where I could find work if I loaned the money to someone. I was still very frightened. What did I know about these things? I felt so alone.

She explained that she had a sister who had a shop that was in debt. This sister, she said, was the kindest woman in the world. Everyone who knew her called her Aunt Marie because she helped everyone. And now she needed help. This sister, like me, was barren. She had always longed for a daughter.

When I met Aunt Marie I felt, for the first time in months, that maybe I was not among the damned. She was so kind. I gladly helped her. What could money have done for me? She gave me everything, her love, her home, her livelihood. She was more of a mother to me than my own mother had been. This, my dear Charles, is the real secret of my success. This is how I became a rich woman. Aunt Marie and her sister Berthe became my family. Berthe bribed the other angel makers to tell anyone who had asked that they had never seen me. I don't even know if anyone ever came looking for me.

The last paragraph was written in a more deliberate hand, the letters large and neat.

There. Now you know everything. I don't know what I want from you. I can imagine you reading this, rushing to the apartment, and going down on your knees asking for my forgiveness. If you still want me, that is, now that you know that I am not the pure angel you thought I was, and that I killed my only child. What you feel is your affair. What I can tell you is that I can't see you here, not now, while the walls still echo with your terrible words. Give me a little time, time to think, to pray, to walk out in your beloved nature before you respond.
Solange

Martin dropped his arms to his sides and fell back against the tree. Poor Solange. The mystery of her past had turned out to be a sordid tale, like so many others. And yet she had risen above it to make something of herself. Martin sighed. Poor Westerbury. The fool had every reason to be ashamed. Their argument had been his fault. Whether or not he had intended to be cruel, he had been so. Horribly cruel. Martin did not understand everything that had gone on between them, but he knew this: Westerbury should have run to Solange Vernet and fallen on his knees, despite her wishes. She was worth everything, every risk. Despite their terrible quarrel, she had continued to shore up the Englishman's fragile pride, confirming his best image of himself. He could have saved her. No wonder he was so tormented.

Martin folded the pages and put them back into the envelope. Solange Vernet loved Westerbury, needed him. She knew his weaknesses, his rashness, and yet she still forgave him enough to set off to the quarry as soon as she thought he had declared his love anew. Unless, Martin sat up alert, unless she thought the author had been Cézanne. No, Martin hunched back again. No, this was not possible. Her letter rang with truth. Westerbury was the love of her life. And as insane as it was, Martin felt a kind of envy for that pitiful example of manhood.

Would anyone ever love Martin enough to forgive him for who he was? For all the things he was not? Westerbury and Solange had risked so much to be together. He had told her everything about himself, and she had taken the chance that he would be kind and interesting, and honest enough not to be after her fortune. Martin had never ventured and lost in love. He had never risked his heart. When had he become so cautious? When his father died? When he began to hide his new beliefs from his mother? When he stopped arguing with Merckx, allowing his friend to follow a path that had become more and more destructive? He should have sent him back to the army. Or, better, he should have chosen to risk everything by really helping his oldest friend to escape. Martin's half-measures had been as fatal as Westerbury's hesitations. But at least the Englishman had loved and been loved in return.

A gray cicada wriggled its way out of the bark of the tree behind Martin, brushing against his cheek. Although the insects were everywhere, he had not been aware of their nagging rasps for a long time. He had to move on. What difference did it make who he was, or what he could become, unless he managed to get out of this mess? Regret would get him nowhere. Martin got up and dusted himself off, before starting across the meadow. Think! That's what he was good at. Reasoning things out. What had the letter told him?

That Cézanne was a more likely suspect than Westerbury. That the Englishman was almost certainly innocent. The letter had given him no motive for murder. Quite the opposite. And Cézanne? Why hadn't he helped the poor girl all those many years ago? Undoubtedly, had Westerbury come across the violation of an innocent young girl in the woods, he would have played the gallant and thrown himself into the fray. Perhaps that is why Solange Vernet loved him. She knew he would have tried to save her.

But the painter had not, and Martin wondered whether Cézanne's inaction still haunted him. What if he had finally recognized her? And, what if she had accused him of cowardice, mortifying him until he couldn't stand it any more? Or, more likely, he had tricked her into coming to the quarry in order to press his cause, and she had finally, scornfully—and fatally—rejected him. Martin had every intention of pushing Cézanne to the limit, until he knew the answer to these questions.

22

HORTENSE ARRIVED ON THE PLATFORM A full twenty minutes before the train was due and took her place by a post with a good view of the incoming tracks. She wanted to be sure that she would have Zola to herself for as long as possible. She needed to tell him her side of the story, and to find out what he knew about Cézanne's dealings with Solange Vernet and Charles Westerbury. She'd have to keep him away from Paul, Paul Jr., and who knows who else. There would be no peace if any of Zola's many admirers found out that he was in town.

The tiny station possessed only four tracks, two for passengers and, across the way, two for the freight trains that rumbled through much more frequently. At least there was an overhang on her side to protect her from the sun. Hortense patted the hair around her ears and repinned her hat. She wanted to look her best. She did not want Émile's pity; she wanted his help.

She didn't mind the wait. What else was there to do in Aix except wait? Wait until Paul told his father about them. Wait until the old goat died and they got their share of the estate. Wait until they could all—finally!—return to Paris.

At least there was some life at the station. Women and children were coming out on the platform, excited about a day trip to Marseilles or a loved one's arrival. Vendors in blue workman's smocks were maneuvering their baskets of fruits and drink into place in order to sell refreshments through the open windows of the train during its stop. A few middle-aged men, probably on their way to cut a deal in the port city, stood by checking their watches. The hawkers and businessmen waited in stoic silence, while the mothers talked to their children, telling them to stay back and stay quiet. Hortense peered around the post looking for her own son and smiled. He was the liveliest of the lot, inspecting the wares and luggage that lay about, and scanning the crowd for boys his own age. Every few minutes, he ran out to look down the tracks. He loved watching the trains come in. It probably reminded him that there were other places in the world.

Hortense reached in her purse and unfolded the telegram. The message was uncharacteristically terse. "Arriving on the 10:00 from Lyon. Zola." Émile could have said even less. There was only one daily train to and from the north every day. One connection to everything she had ever known. Hortense wondered if he had also contacted Paul. Would Zola have complained about her meddling too?

She crossed her arms and turned her back to anyone who might be watching her. She was not in a mood to be pleasant, not after the row they had had last night. She waited until their son had gone to bed to show Paul Zola's telegram. Paul never came home before dinner, anyway. He spent his days at the Jas, painting. Apparently, now it was the chestnut trees. Hortense sighed. She wished he'd paint something that actually sold. He just went along doing what he wanted to do, not caring about what was happening to her or their son, not giving one thought to the possibility that he might be thrown in prison, which is precisely what she was trying to prevent. But instead of showing gratitude, he accused her of interfering in his affairs.

Paul even told her that the murder of Solange Vernet was none of her business. "Do you really think I could be a murderer?" he had shouted. "Can you really believe that?" She had finally answered, "No, of course not," although she did not know what to think. There had been a kind of madness in his pursuit of Solange Vernet. An irrationality that went beyond Paul's usual doubts and temper tantrums. How was she to know whether he had done it? He never told her anything. He probably said more about what was going on in his head in any one letter to Zola than he revealed to her in a year.

And it wasn't as if she had tried to keep Zola's arrival a secret. She just did not want to mention it until she was sure Zola would come, because she didn't want to get Paul's hopes up. After all, she had told Marie about the telegram, and *she* could have told Paul if she had wanted to. Evidently, though, brother and sister were not talking much these days either. Or Marie did not want to admit that the only one who knew what needed to be done was Paul's mistress, the taken-for-granted Hortense Fiquet.

Hortense managed a smile and a wave for Paul Jr. as he signaled her from the north end of the platform. He'd stay put for a while, so that he could be the first to spot the train. All she had told the boy was that Cézanne's friend was coming for a visit. Even at his age, he knew who Zola was, although he hadn't seen him for years. She had warned him not to shout out a greeting. They needed to keep the great Zola all to themselves.

Hortense crossed her arms again. What had really gotten to her, the night before, was that Paul seemed more upset about "involving Émile" than the possibility that she might think he was a murderer.

What did her opinion matter? Or her feelings? When she realized that he cared more about what Zola thought than she did, Hortense had been ready to give Paul as good as she got. Until she saw the look in his eyes. It had always been there, that look of being hurt when he was angry. Hurt that his work never turned out on canvas exactly the way he saw it in his head, that no one recognized what he was doing. These days, she saw the hurt more and more often.

She opened her purse and took out a handkerchief to wipe her eyes. She couldn't be crying when Zola arrived. She had to be strong and alert and ask all the right questions if she wanted to find out the truth. Paul must have told Zola something. Just last month, when they were up north, Paul had spent two whole weeks circling Zola's grand estate like a dog in heat, waiting to get in. It had been just like him not to check first and find out that Médan was filled with guests. Instead, he settled the three of them across the river with the excuse that he was painting the landscape. When Zola finally admitted him, he had gone alone. And he never told her about anything they had discussed.

Hortense put her handkerchief back and stared out toward the tracks. After the visit, Paul had, for the first time, made fun of his friend, saying his belly was growing even faster than his wealth and fame. The way Paul described it, Zola received him in his huge study like some kind of pasha, dressed in a pure silk smoking jacket, surrounded by expensive antiques and books, offering only the best cigars and wines. Maybe that was the real source of his upset: Paul could no longer stand it that his childhood friend was so much more successful than he was. Or maybe he was afraid that if Zola knew too much about the murder, he would include it in one of his novels. But how was she to know unless he said something to her?

"Maman, it's coming."

Hortense peered toward the north and saw the gray wisps of smoke. She pulled at her gloves and patted her hair again. As the locomotive

chugged and hissed its way into the station, those standing on the platform backed away to escape the noise and the smoke. When the train
finally came to a halt, Hortense spotted Zola almost at once. It was just
like him to be standing in the vestibule, legs apart, hands behind his
back, absorbing every detail. Although he was a relatively short man,
he always managed to seem larger than life. Yes, he had grown fatter,
just as Paul said, and he was decked out in an expensive travel suit and
bowler. Still, seeing him for the first time in years brought tears to her
eyes. Much was the same: the high forehead, the stubby nose, and the
ever-attentive, almost feminine eyes. This was the famous oft-carica-
tured Zola. But this was also Émile, growing older like the rest of
them, his short bristly beard flecked with gray, his eyes undoubtedly a
little dimmer behind the famous pince-nez. This was Émile, who had
rescued them again and again, paying off bills when Paul Jr. had been
deathly ill, giving them loans he knew would never be repaid, encouraging Paul's work, and urging him to return to Paris. Émile, the
friend. Perhaps even Émile, the savior.

Hortense waved and moved toward Zola as he jumped off the train.
She grabbed his arm and steered him through the bustle toward a relatively quiet corner of the platform.

"Hortense," he put down his luggage, lifted her gloved hand to his
lips, and kissed it in greeting. Then he turned to see Paul Jr., who had
come up behind them. Zola took hold of her son's shoulders and held
him at arm's length, admiring him. "Look at this strapping boy. My,
my, how you have grown. So handsome, too. Just like your Papa said."

Paul Jr. smiled, bouncing up and down on his toes. The famous Zola!

"Alexandrine did not come with you?" Hortense asked, only out of
politeness. She doubted that Zola's wife had any interest in a rescue
mission. Alexandrine had always treated her and Paul like interlopers.

"No, no. As I told Paul in July, I was hoping to finally come down
here this summer, to refresh my memories about the place—and to
spend some time with all of you, of course—but Alexandrine," he

pursed his lips and shook his head, "her health. And when she heard about the cholera scare, that was it. We decided to go to Mont Dore instead. Better for her, you know."

How nice to have a solicitous husband who took your complaints seriously. And God knows, Alexandrine was always complaining. "Let's go." Hortense linked her arm in Zola's and began maneuvering him through the station. Her son picked up Zola's bag and followed closely behind. "Should we hire a carriage, or walk?" she asked. "It's not very far."

"Walk. Definitely." Zola responded enthusiastically. "I've only got today and tomorrow morning. I should get a good look at the town. I'm doing another Plassans novel."

"What's Plassans?" the question came from behind them.

"M. Zola's name for Aix." Hortense whispered to her son. "Shhhhhhh."

"That's right." Zola patted her on the arm and then turned back toward Paul Jr. "Shhhhhh. Let's not let anyone know I'm in town. We'll take the back streets. I don't want to pass any booksellers. Although," he confided to Hortense, "they may not even recognize me in this place."

False modesty. Even so, she was surprised that they were moving so easily past the other passengers, when Zola came to a full stop, staring ahead of him. Her eyes followed his. There stood Paul in his cap, wrinkled pants, and worn-out jacket. That morning he had sworn he was returning to the Jas and would have no part of "this business." She should have known that he would not be able to resist seeing Émile. The two men stood stock-still for a moment. Then they stepped forward and hugged each other. When Paul leaned back to look at Émile, she saw tears in his eyes. "At last I've got you back here," he said.

"Yes," Émile nodded, "at last." And then they hugged each other again.

"Well, we must make the most of it. Did you bring some tramping clothes?"

Hortense's heart sank. Would the two of them be at it again, and leave her out as usual? "But Émile," she interrupted, "we don't have much time."

Émile slapped Paul on the back and shrugged. "Neither, my dear, do we. Wouldn't it be possible to say all we have to say at supper? Or," he glanced at the boy, "afterwards?" As she began shaking her head, Émile took her hand. "I promise I will find out everything I can while we are visiting the old haunts."

Hortense shot Paul an angry look. After everything he had said last night! It was bad enough that Émile announced he was only staying the day. She had to get him into the courthouse to show the judge once and for all how important their connections were.

"Come on, Hortense," Paul stepped forward and put his finger under her chin, directing her eyes toward his. "Émile has not been back here for years, and he doesn't have much time." How, Hortense wondered, did he know that? Émile must have sent a longer message to the Jas. Before she could say anything, Paul had turned toward his old friend. "I've hired us a donkey cart. We'll go to the river, tramp around, and be in town by supper. And I'll tell you everything that's been going on," he looked back toward Hortense, "I promise."

Hortense found Cézanne's drawling Provençal accent, which seemed to grow stronger with each passing day, especially irritating when he was attempting to mollify her. Even though she was bursting with things to say, she was speechless with fury.

"Can I come too?" Paul Jr. finally piped in.

"No, young man, no. This afternoon is for your father and his old friend. But, as soon as I get somewhere I can change, I think I've got something in that pack for you." Émile pointed to the bag by the boy's side.

"Well," said Hortense, "since the daily train doesn't leave until noon, at least you'll have time."

"Time for—"

She tilted her head toward the boy.

"Yes, yes," Émile coughed. "I'll find the time to do what needs to be done."

"Excuse me, could you be—" a young man who had been selling oranges was standing before Émile, cap in hand. The station was rapidly emptying out around them.

"Zola? Yes." Émile stretched out his hand. He never ignored a working man.

"Thank you," the young man said as he shyly reached for Zola's hand. "My family read parts of *Germinal* in the papers. My father was a miner near Gardanne. You told the truth. That's what it's like for us. Thank you, sir."

"Thank *you*." Émile reacted in a way that was meant to be modest and gracious, although Hortense, having observed this scene before, knew that deep down Zola had great pride in what he had accomplished.

"Come, come." Paul clapped his friend on the back. "We must be going! Get you out of town." He smiled at the orange seller in mock apology as he led Zola away. The man stood back, still in awe. With his arm on Zola's shoulder, Paul led him out of the station. Gesticulating with his other hand, he probably was detailing the plans for their outing. It was so irritating to watch the two of them carry on. No wonder Paul did not dare look back at her. He knew she had every reason to be angry with him.

Hortense was left to trail the two men to the donkey cart. She'd have to find some way to amuse her disappointed son, to shop and cook their dinner. She was left to stew all day, and to figure out what the great Zola could do to help them.

23

MARTIN WENT BACK TO HIS ROOM to change for the courthouse. He had to hurry, before Franc began to ask questions. He slung his vest over the chair, unbuttoned his shirt, and wiped his face, chest, and neck with the towel hanging by his basin. He pulled his frock coat, top hat, and cravat from the armoire and threw them on the bed. How ridiculous these expensive clothes looked, flung about in his shabby little room. Ridiculous and utterly necessary. These, Martin thought as he slipped on the jacket, are the signs of my rank, my coat of arms, my only protection. He needed to look every bit a judge if he were going to prevail in the inevitable confrontation with his inspector.

After yanking his cravat into place, he was almost ready. Only the most important task remained: concealing Solange Vernet's letter. He carefully stuffed the delicate envelope into the inside pocket of his frock coat and ran his hand over its front, smoothing away the bulge.

When he got to the Palais, he was not surprised to meet Franc halfway up the grand staircase.

"Where have you been, sir?"

Martin detected an accusatory tone in Franc's voice. "On a wild-goose chase," he answered as he leaned against the polished wooden railing, in a pose of equanimity.

"Sir?"

"Our prisoner, in his ravings yesterday, mentioned a hidden letter. Something Mme Vernet wrote just before she died. I went looking for it. It didn't say much that was relevant to our case."

"Why didn't you tell me about it? I could have sent one of the boys."

"I wanted to see it myself first." Martin kept his voice even, and goaded himself to keep looking Franc in the eye, searching for any sign that the inspector knew more about Merckx's visit to Aix than he was saying.

"So what's in the letter? Can I see it?" Franc moved a step closer to Martin.

"All it said was that she loved Westerbury and planned to break off with Cézanne." This was, of course, far from all that had been revealed. Who, Martin wondered, was playing the more deceitful role—him or his inspector?

"A whore, just like I thought she was. Still, I should read it. Maybe I'd see something else in it." Franc was as aggressive as ever.

Martin shook his head, acting out the scene that he had imagined all the way to the Palais. "Westerbury told me where to find the letter only on the condition that I would not show it to anyone until absolutely necessary. I have to keep that pledge, at least for the time being, if I am going to get anything out of the Englishman the next time we talk." Martin expected his inspector to complain about this agreement, but he was not about to give in. It was less a matter of the Englishman's sensibilities than his own. For he realized at that moment that *he* did not want Franc poring over Solange Vernet's confessions. Not yet. Perhaps not ever. If he hadn't caught himself, his hand would have gone up to his chest in a protective gesture. Instead, he gave his frock coat a little tug while he watched Franc trying to contain his impatience.

Martin broke the silence first. "I understand you found the note."

"Yes, I left it on your desk."

When? Martin wondered. But he did not ask. Not when he was about to stir up a hornet's nest. "I'd like to see Westerbury right away. I need to clear a few things up."

"And then?" Franc's terseness spoke louder than his words ever had.

"I'll need to see Cézanne, first thing in the morning."

"Why? You're not thinking of letting the Englishman go again, are you?"

"I'll decide after I talk to him. In any case, you can keep someone on him."

Franc clapped his hand to the side of his leg in exasperation. "Don't you understand? You've got your man. This case should be easy."

"I want to make sure I have the *right* man."

"Look," Franc pointed up toward Martin's chambers. "When you see that note, you'll see it's in the Englishman's hand." *The hand that anyone could have copied from Westerbury's posters.*

"You've got him! Unless there was something in that letter—"

"Only as I told you. She was going to break it off with the artist. That makes him the more likely suspect." Martin still did not understand why Franc so adamantly preferred the charlatan geologist to the failed artist as a suspect. Unless it was because a foreigner would be so much easier to prosecute. "Let me talk to the Englishman again," Martin continued, "and I'll decide what to do with him."

Franc's mouth and mustache hardened into a straight, grim line.

"Westerbury?" Martin's heart began to pound, but he kept his voice calm.

Still, Franc did not move.

"I think," Martin was trying desperately to maintain the upper hand, "that you have to trust me to know what to do with the suspects. At this critical point in the case, it is best if we each concentrate on our own jobs."

"I have been doing *my* job."

"I know you have. But what about the boy?"

"What about the boy?" This came out almost as a growl, as if Franc were making a monumental effort to keep his emotions under control.

"Do we have any idea who the boy was? Do we know what part of town he was from? Hasn't anyone come to you about a missing child?" These questions were so obvious that, despite his own efforts to remain calm, Martin's voice kept rising. "Surely, if we know who he was and where he was from, we might be able to track down an important witness, someone who saw him getting paid to take a message." *Someone who saw the real murdering rapist.*

"And you probably think that there is some poor, sobbing mother out there looking for him?"

"Yes, that too."

"Well, I doubt it. I've spent enough time around beggars and whores to know that they don't give a damn. They're probably relieved not to have another mouth to feed."

"Even so." Martin bit his tongue, although he was confounded by Franc's callous, nonchalant attitude. Not only was the boy's identity crucial to the entire investigation, but the poor child himself had been the victim of a heinous crime. These were things a police inspector should care about.

Neither man had moved during the last few moments. They were still perched on the same two steps of the great staircase, as if poised for battle. "Even so," Franc finally conceded, "so me and one of my men get to spend another night searching among the riffraff."

"It might be important," Martin said quietly. He had no intention of escalating their conflict. He just did not want to be the first to back down.

After another uncomfortable silence, Franc said, "I'll get the Englishman." With a bitter glance toward Martin, he started down the stairs.

Martin waited until the inspector reached the main floor before asking about Merckx.

"Franc?" The name reverberated throughout the empty atrium.

"Yes." Franc turned to look up at him.

"Yesterday I was so taken aback to see my old friend on the table that I didn't ask you about the circumstances. Were you there when he was shot?"

"Yes, sir. We don't take deserters lightly."

Martin had to swallow hard before getting the next question out. "Did you order the shooting?"

"What else could I do? Let him escape?"

"No, I suppose not." Whether in the line of duty or not, Franc had killed Jean-Jacques.

"And his body?"

"Buried. You identified him. We took a photograph to send to the army. We had to get rid of all three of them as soon as possible. Riquel's worried about the cholera."

Just like that. Merckx, Solange Vernet, and the boy. Banished. Buried in unmarked ground.

"Do you know where, in case someone comes forward for the boy?"

"Yes." Even in the shadows of the great hall, Martin could see the inspector pursing his lips as if irritated by the excessive delicacy of his superior. "Just in case."

"Very well." There was nothing more to say. Martin had made Westerbury powerless to bury his lover by throwing him in prison. Arlette, the devoted maid, had been born, and would forever remain, powerless. So all three bodies lay in a potter's field. It wasn't right. Not for Solange Vernet, with her medal and her saints. Nor for the boy. If his parents came forward, if Westerbury desired it, they could mark their graves later. Martin would do all in his power—if he still had any—to help them.

The inspector was still waiting. "Thank you, Franc. I will see you in a moment." Then Martin headed up the stairs. When he reached his floor, he saw that the door to his chambers was open, and remembered that Franc said he had left the note on his desk. When and how had he gotten in?

"Oh, M. Martin, I heard your footsteps." Old Joseph stepped out to greet him.

Martin pushed past his clerk to get to his desk. The quarry message sat folded on top of one of Martin's notebooks. The message read, "I love you more than ever. Please meet me at the quarry. C." Just as Westerbury had said, in printed block letters.

"M. Franc brought that in, sir."

"When?"

"About two hours ago."

"You let him in?"

"I. . . ." Joseph's chin, with its few wispy white hairs, began to tremble.

Would the greffier of a more experienced, better connected judge have opened his office to an inspector? Martin doubted it.

"I wanted to open your office to give you some air when you came in. And I didn't know when you were going to get here. I . . . I didn't think. . . ."

"That's right, you did not think." Martin knew it was useless and cruel to be angry with the quivering old man, but he couldn't help himself.

"Sir, I'm so sorry, so sorry. But M. Franc told me to. He assured me it would be all right."

"Did he do anything while he was in the office?"

"No, sir. Just left that piece of paper. And sat on your chair, staring out at the square, waiting for you." Joseph was wringing his hands, as he backed away from Martin. "I was here the whole time. Nothing happened. Why should it?"

Why should it indeed? Martin looked at his chair. It had been rather presumptuous of his inspector to take over his chambers. What had Franc been thinking while he was sitting there? That he had Martin over a barrel? That the case was his and his alone? Martin wished to God that he knew what game Franc was playing. And who was helping him. Martin turned his attention back to his clerk. He had observed him talking his way through his timidity on innumerable occasions. He could only imagine what Joseph might have blurted out to Franc. Martin sighed. He needed to state the obvious. "We must be extremely cautious, you know. This is a murder. Two murders. We may be accusing a member of an important family. We must make sure the evidence and our notes are protected at all times. You understand that?"

Joseph nodded meekly.

"And you must not talk to anyone, even Franc, about what has happened in our interrogations. I am planning to give all my findings over to the Proc as soon as he returns. It is very important that no information get out. This is a very delicate matter."

The old relic was staring straight at the floor. He might as well have just come out and said it. He had been talking to Franc.

"Even if you have already—"

"Oh no, sir!"

"Even if you've been discussing the case with Franc or others," Martin continued, "from now on, especially because I will be bringing Cézanne in again, we have to be particularly careful. And, above all, I don't want anyone in this office unless I am here." Martin hoped this little scolding would be enough to protect the letter. He didn't really give a damn about the artist and his family.

"Yes, sir, yes." Joseph shuffled back a few more steps.

"Good." Martin picked up the quarry message. "I need you to copy this into your report," he said as he handed it to the clerk, "then I want you to write an order for Westerbury's release."

Joseph's watery yellowed eyes opened with surprise, but he didn't say anything. He did not dare. He took the quarry message and maneuvered himself around Martin to get to his desk in the alcove.

As soon as his clerk's back was to him, Martin unlocked the cabinet and took out the box containing the material evidence. He picked up Solange Vernet's green and white striped dress. After a quick glance toward the alcove to make sure Joseph was occupied, Martin pulled the letter from his frock coat and folded it into the heavy, thick cotton. Then he quietly shut the cabinet door.

Martin did not have to wait long before Franc knocked on the door and pushed the sorry Englishman into his office. "Still not talking, at least to me," Franc said, as he gave Westerbury a final shove into one of the chairs in front of Martin's desk.

"We'll see about that." Martin did not look at Westerbury, although he could feel the Englishman eying him, wanting to know if he had found the letter. First, Martin had to get rid of his inspector, who, after a cursory exchange, left the office shaking his head in exasperation.

"*Did you find it?*" Westerbury exploded in English. He was not a man accustomed to isolation and deprivation.

"Mr. Westerbury, we will conduct the interrogation in French," Martin murmured. For all he knew, his talkative clerk had picked up a smattering of English somewhere. He raised his voice to ask Joseph if he had the order ready.

"Yes sir, yes." The clerk rose and brought the document authorizing the release of the Englishman to Martin's desk.

"*What's that?*" Westerbury cried out, again in English, as he stood up. Did he imagine that Martin was ordering the construction of a guillotine? He must truly be at his wits' end.

"Mr. Westerbury, if you do not sit down, I will have to call a gendarme," Martin said as he wrote his signature.

Westerbury resumed his seat, nervously rubbing his thighs. His beard and hair were a matted mess. His clothes, stiffened by days and nights of fearful sweat, no longer conformed to his body. He looked and smelled like a wretch who had been begging on street corners for weeks on end.

"Joseph," Martin gave the paper back to his clerk, "please take this down to the prison immediately and retrieve any of Mr. Westerbury's things that they may be holding there. Then wait outside on the bench with them. I'll call you when I need you."

"Yes, sir." The clerk did not even blink. Martin's lecture had had its effect.

Martin waited until he heard the door close before he addressed the Englishman. "That was an order for your release."

"*Thank God!*" Then in French, "So you found it. And you know. You know that Cézanne killed her."

"I know no such thing."

"Who else could it be?" Westerbury was on his feet again. "It wasn't some vagabond hiding in the quarry. Someone sent her that note. And someone wanted to implicate me."

"All this is true." Martin looked steadily at the Englishman. "Sit down."

"So what are you going to do about it?" Westerbury said, as he fell back into his chair.

Martin could not believe that the Englishman thought he had any right to make demands.

"That's actually none of your business. Indeed, the entire investigation is not your business. It is mine. And if I hear that you are going around making trouble, you will be right back in your cell."

"Oh," Westerbury waved his hand, "here we go again. Monsieur le juge, so smart, so in charge. But what have you done? Where would you be without me?"

When Martin did not respond, the Englishman continued, "Did you *read* it? Did you actually *read* it? Do you understand what I have been going through?"

"What the woman you claimed to love went through. That is what this case is about. Not about what you went through." Martin delivered this pronouncement loudly and distinctly. It was meant to be hurtful, and it struck the mark.

"I know, I know. My poor dear girl."

"You betrayed her," Martin said more softly. "You should have gone to her."

Westerbury's head yanked up and down in emphatic agreement. "I know. I know." He ran a dirty sleeve across his face. "Do you think I will ever forgive myself? I should have seen it. I should have known there was something she was not telling me. I told her everything about myself. She knew about my doubts. She knew what an egotist I could be. What an ass, sometimes." He looked up at Martin. "She thought me kind, you know. Very kind. That's what she always said. Of course it was easy for me to be kind to Solange. I adored her."

Of course. This much had become clear to Martin.

"You know it wasn't the money. Ever. It was *her*. A woman of mind, of substance, of spirit. Someone willing to go against the tide, to find her own way. She was stronger than me, always. More steady. She risked everything for me, poor fool that I am. And I was so unworthy. In the end, I was not man enough for her."

Westerbury could not stop talking. And this time Martin had no desire to stop him.

"You know, I did ask her questions about her past. But whenever I got too close, she would laugh and tell me it wasn't interesting, or wasn't important. I should have listened better. I should have seen. I should have known. How can you tell when you really know a person, when you really see them?"

The question, coming from Westerbury who, by his own repeated declarations, had experienced deep and passionate love, was of course rhetorical. It made him stop short, as if remembering all the accusations of callowness that he had made against Martin.

"I hope some day you will know what this is like," the Englishman continued quietly. "Not only the pain, but also the happiness."

This sudden solicitude was unexpected. This time it was Westerbury who had hit the mark. Martin realized that he did long for the happiness and the passion. Even the pain.

A silence fell between them. Westerbury was the first to recover. "May I have the letter back?"

"It is evidence."

"Do you need to tell anyone?"

"Yes." There was no reason to lie. "I need to use it in my interrogation of Cézanne. I assume that you will tell no one else about its existence for your own reasons, and for the good of the investigation."

"Of course," Westerbury murmured, "of course." He knew he had no right to ask for the letter. Not any more.

"Do you have anything more to say?" Martin asked him. "Anything else that can help me?"

Westerbury shook his head.

"Then," Martin picked up his pen again, "you may go. M. Gilbert will be waiting outside with your things."

Westerbury got up from his seat and looked around, almost in disbelief. "I'm free to—"

"Yes. As long as you stay in the city limits and cause no trouble. This is very important. Otherwise, I will have no choice—"

"I understand." Westerbury stood, straightened himself up, and by habit looked for the hat that wasn't there. He was flustered only for a second. He retreated with a parting nod to Martin that was almost a salute. Or even a gentleman's valediction, as if the secrets they shared had created a bond between them.

"Sir?"

Lost in his contemplation of the very beautiful, very dead Solange Vernet, Martin had almost forgotten about his clerk.

"I gave M. Westerbury all of his things," Joseph said as he timidly reentered the office.

"Good." Martin forced himself out of his trance.

"Do you need me any more today, sir?"

"No, no. Let's all go home and rest. But I want you in by nine tomorrow because I will be interrogating Cézanne again."

Martin watched as the old man began to put away his things. He had no idea whether his clerk had a home. He knew that he did not, not a real one in any case. And that, not having eaten all day, he was starving. And that it was too early to expect anyone to be serving dinner. Unless. Martin wiped off his pen as he thought it through. Unless . . . the early hour could work to his advantage. If he put in an appearance at Chez l'Arlésienne well before dinner, he'd be sure to avoid Franc. And he might even have a chance to talk to a girl who, like Solange Vernet, was "willing to go against the tide."

24

WESTERBURY COULD NOT HAVE IMAGINED HOW happy he would be to see her. Arlette greeted him with tears of joy and threw herself into his arms. Before he knew it, he was holding the pitiful little creature tight to his chest, patting her head and comforting her.

"Now, now," he said as he held her away from him, "they let me go. The judge believes I am innocent. It is going to be better."

"Did they find the murderer?" Her eyes glistened with anticipation and hope.

"No, my dear. Not yet. Although you and I both know—"

"Oh, my God." She backed away from him. "I wish they would find him! Poor Solange." She covered her face with her hands and began to sob in earnest.

The tears were contagious. Westerbury led her into the salon and sat her down. "Arlette, we are alone, you and I. She is gone. I know. That is the worse part. Our Solange is gone. But," he tried to compose himself, "we must go on. We must do the best we can. She would want that, you know."

"I'm so glad you are back, sir." Arlette reached for Westerbury's arm. "I've been so afraid."

"No reason to worry. They'll catch him. And you're not letting anyone in, are you?"

Arlette shook her head vehemently.

"Well, then, nothing to fear."

"What will we do?" Her expression was so childish and trusting. And stupid.

"We will survive," he said, emphatically. "And," he got up, "the first thing I need to survive is—"

"Oh, M. Westerbury. I forgot all about *you*." Arlette jumped to her feet. "Are you hungry? What do you need?"

Westerbury smiled, feeling the old gallantry coming back. "It is I who have forgotten about you, my dear. I embraced you smelling worse than a fishmonger."

"Oh," she smiled, "don't worry about that. When Jacques worked at the tannery he was much worse."

Manners were wasted on a woman who did not hesitate to compare you to a drunkard who had spent his days in the blood and detritus of dead animals. Yet Westerbury had to be kind to her. At this point, she was all he had.

"The first order of business is a bath, then if there is any food—"

"Oh, yes, sir, I've gone to the bakery every day, hoping you would return. And I have put up cheeses and hams and tea and—"

"All right, all right." He gave her a gracious smile. "I can see you have taken care of everything."

"I'll get the water right away." Eager to serve, Arlette set off for the kitchen, where she dragged out the iron tub and four big buckets. She laid out a little table of bread, cheese, and wine, then went down to the Cours to fetch water from the one of the fountains. After she heated it on the stove, she began pouring it over Westerbury. He lay back, hands on the sides of the tub, feeling each delicious bucketful bringing more relief than the last. When the water was all gone, Arlette stood up, with her hands behind her hips, stretching her back. Fringes of black hair were sticking to her forehead and cheeks. Arlette had been toting a heavy load, but she did not complain. Instead, she smiled at him, before leaving to fetch his clothes.

For once he sympathized with the maid. When he was a boy, one of his duties had been to heat and carry the water for Reverend Westerbury's weekly bath. The kindly old parson had been much too modest to let Charles's mother near him when he was bathing. He had even been too modest to take off his underclothes in front of his godson. So every Saturday night, until his death, Reverend Westerbury had dipped into the tub half-clothed and sighed with pleasure as Charles scrubbed his back through his undershirt. When the parson retired for the night, it had been Charles's turn to wash in the cold, gray water before putting away the tub. How innocent his godfather had been. How English.

Westerbury had probably told this story to Solange during their first night together. He remembered that he had tried to make light of his past, because he had been so embarrassed by having to reveal his threadbare shirt and underclothes. He had never cared about the opinions of the other women, for they had been either prospective benefactresses, whom he hoped to charm into supporting a starving genius, or just as poor as he was. But Solange was different. So he confessed everything from the start. That he had been born a bastard in a dank Liverpool hospital, that he had been hounded out of England by debts, that he lived hand to mouth in Paris, tutoring and lecturing for whatever fees he could get. And that he had dreams.

The past had not troubled her, and the future had captivated her.

Not only that he would write a book reconciling religion and science, but that he would address it to women as well as men. The truth was that he had not really thought about how his work might liberate the female sex until he was lying beside Solange, living with her, loving her. She was the one who made him realize that he could do something original and necessary. Reconcile men and women, as well as heaven and earth. And they were going to do it together.

Arlette did not say a word as she put a towel and clean clothes on the chair beside the tub. She must have seen the sadness on his face, the sadness that would never leave him now that Solange was gone.

"Just a few minutes more, Arlette," Westerbury said as he closed his eyes and lowered himself into the water. It was time to consider his situation. He had promised the judge that he would not interfere, would not *act* to bring Solange's murderer to justice. Perhaps he should lie low for a while and figure out how he was going to survive. But, if they did not jail Solange's killer soon, wouldn't it be his duty to track him down? At the very least, they could not stop him from thinking, going over everything again and again until he proved that Cézanne had done it. Oddly, it was something the maid had said earlier that week that had become one of his obsessions in prison.

He opened his eyes. She was still there, busying herself at the stove. "Arlette," he asked, "are you sure that Solange was wearing gloves when she set out for the quarry?"

"Oh, yes, sir. And I looked everywhere for them at the prison, but did not find them."

He closed his eyes again. The gloves had to be part of the answer.

25

MARTIN TAPPED AT THE DOOR LIGHTLY. In the short walk from the courthouse, he'd lost some of his resolve. Why would she want to talk to him, or listen to the little he could tell her about his adventures of the last few days? Martin was about to walk away when he saw a hand reach out and pull back one of the lace curtains. It was Clarie Falchetti. He was caught. She swung open the door with a smile, setting off the tinkle of bells that alerted her aunt and uncle to his arrival.

"Oh, monsieur le juge, how nice to see you," Mme Choffrut said, brushing the flour off her hands onto a big white apron, as she walked toward Martin and her niece.

"I'm sorry to disturb you. Again, I've come at the wrong time." He sounded so befuddled.

"Henriette, let's leave them alone, " Michel Choffrut called from the kitchen. "Clarie can pour the judge a glass of wine while he is waiting to taste the bouillabaisse. Come, come," he said, waving his wife back into the kitchen.

"You, come this way," Clarie commanded. She grabbed one of the clay *pichets* of wine from the sideboard as she walked toward a table in the corner, as far away from the kitchen as possible. Following her, Martin caught a glimpse of shapely ankles under her swinging skirt. He lifted his glance upward, trying to squelch an unwanted warmth infusing his body. Fortunately, as soon as they got to the table, Clarie started talking. "I have a little time. I've set the tables. And they don't let me get near the stove." She sat down, poured a glass of wine, and waited for Martin to settle in. "I'm glad you came," she whispered as she pushed the glass toward him. "I've been worried about you."

He was surprised and flattered by her concern. "Really, there was nothing to worry about."

She shook her head. "I'm not so sure." Her large brown eyes were shining with sympathy. And seeing right through him. "A few nights after I last saw you, Franc and his men came in here, bragging about how they had 'bagged' a deserter. I was afraid it might be the friend you told me about."

"Bagged." That's how they talked about Jean-Jacques, as if he were an animal. Martin took a swallow of wine to cover up his chagrin.

Clarie leaned a bit closer to him. "If it was your friend, I am sure you had a good reason to help him."

Martin clutched his glass. He was not sure how he had envisioned their conversation, but this certainly was not it. Unless he started talking, said something, this beautiful, intelligent girl would think him a complete dolt. And a traitor. He glanced toward the kitchen door, which was closed, and he knew at once that this glance had given him away.

"You don't have to tell me if you don't want to. And don't worry, I haven't said anything to anyone, if that is what you are thinking."

"Oh no!" Martin was in no position to expect anything from her. "If I did such a thing I certainly would not want to implicate you."

"I'm not implicated," she said calmly. "I did nothing. I gave you food. You were hungry."

This story was too generous. If she was going to protect him, part of him wanted to tell her the truth, especially since she seemed to have guessed it already. Perhaps if he explained, she would understand and take his side. But he had no right to drag her in.

"We'll leave it at that then," she said, sitting back in her chair.

But he did not want Clarie to move away either. "He was sick, very sick. And they were going to send him to Devil's Island or New Caledonia. He was my oldest and dearest friend." Martin could feel his entire face shrink into a grimace. Embarrassed by a sudden flood of emotions, he put his head down.

Clarie laid her fingers on his. "Don't worry. I won't tell. I just recited for you what I know. That is my story. Have you told anyone else?"

Martin shook his head, not daring to look at her.

"These last few days must have been terrible for you, with Franc's bragging."

Clarie's sympathy threatened to breach the dam holding back Martin's grief and remorse. He squeezed his eyes closed.

"Here," she reached in her apron and pulled out a napkin. "Take this. We should talk about something else before they come back."

This time they both looked toward the kitchen door, behind which they could hear the reassuring sound of her aunt and uncle talking above the hissing and slamming of pots and pans.

"I'm sorry." Martin laid the napkin down as a sign that he had regained his composure.

"It must be difficult for you to be so far away from everything you have known."

"What about you?" he asked, in a voice he wished were steadier. "Aren't you doing the same? Leaving your family to go north?"

"Yes. Maybe that's why I'm so curious about you. I can see your loneliness."

It was disappointing to think that her interest in him was motivated by pity. Yet Martin had no right to expect more than the help she had already given him. "It will be different for you," he reassured her. "You're going to school. You'll have companions. Just like I had when I went to Paris. That's where you're going, isn't it?"

"No, just south of Paris, to Sèvres. The school's in an old ceramic factory. But it's supposed to be very nice. I don't think they'll let us gad about in the city the way you men do."

Clarie did not say this with bitterness. The amusement had returned to her eyes. Her lips were pursed into that wonderful long, crooked smile. How much better it was to be thought of as a carefree student than as a law-breaking judge. If only for the moment.

"I was not one of your biggest 'gadders.'"

When she burst out laughing, the solemn spell seemed almost broken. "I'm not surprised. You are very serious. Anyone can tell that. And," she said, pointedly, "a very morally upright man. I know that. Really, I do."

This reference to their secret threatened to darken the mood again, until Clarie continued.

"I bet you half-agree with your inspector that young women should not be teaching in secondary school."

"Oh, no!" He objected, even though he knew she was teasing him. She had a way of being honest and playful at the same time. He was not sure how he felt about that.

"No?" she arched her eyebrows.

"Well," he entered into the game, "maybe I would have—"

"Would have?"

"Yes." He sat back and took her in. Franc had called her a gypsy. Marthe DuPont had half-jokingly cautioned him not to fall in love with a dark-eyed Arlésienne. Clarie Falchetti was very attractive, and she was getting him to say all sorts of things. "Maybe I would have even a few weeks ago." he explained. "But this case has changed my thinking somewhat."

"Yes?" Clarie drew the word out in expectation. Of course she was interested in the case. Wasn't everybody?

"The victim. Solange Vernet. I've learned more about her. She was a remarkable woman, in many ways. She came from a poor family, but she found a way to make something of herself and not be at all unwomanly. In fact, she was very gracious and beautiful."

"And how would you know that?" She was very direct, this one.

"From witnesses." This was only a little lie. "And," he might as well confess it now, "I met her once briefly in a bookstore."

"Oh." Clarie sat straight up, waiting.

"We were both looking for a book on science."

"That's right. Her husband—"

"Lover—" The word did not seem to embarrass her. He liked that.

"Right, her lover was a geologist, a lecturer. If I hadn't already passed my exams, I might have gone to hear him."

"You took exams in science?"

"In everything. Is that so surprising?"

"Oh, no, of course not." Although he was surprised, a little.

"I didn't do so well the first time." She cast her eyes down for an instant, as if embarrassed. "I've not had much schooling. Only the nuns. Poor Papa, had to take me to Nîmes twice to take the tests, and when I passed them we had to go up to Paris for an oral examination in front of a panel of professors." Clarie put her hand on her hip and tilted her head before she added, "Imagine that."

He hardly could, but he was not about to admit it.

"I know what you are thinking. All this to learn how to teach girls."

Martin barely managed to stop himself from saying "oh, no" again. Clarie was full of surprises. Much happier surprises than anything else he had encountered in the last few days.

"So when you graduate you will be a civil servant?"

"Just like you."

"A republican."

"Of course."

"No religion?"

"Do you think we women need it?"

"Oh, no." There he had said it again. She must think him an idiot.

"But?"

"Not but. I was going to mention another thing that has come up in this case. The reconciliation of science and religion. That's what Charles Westerbury, the lecturer, said he was working toward. And he particularly wanted to teach this to women."

"Good!"

Would the beautiful, sensible Clarie Falchetti have become a disciple of Westerbury, like the wretched little Sibylline Beauregard? This was a terrible thought.

"Don't you think it is good?" she pressed.

"Surely it is one of the great controversies of the day." How priggish that sounded. And the arch of her eyebrows signaled that she had not missed the lecturing tone.

"Here's what I mean," Martin hastened to explain himself. "The Church has fought so hard against science, against the acceptance of transmutation, and against the Republic—"

"And against socialism?"

She was truly surprising. He was not sure that he had ever heard a woman of his acquaintance utter that word.

Clarie did not wait for his response. "Yes, I know about socialism. My father is the biggest Red in Arles."

"Your father?" Martin took another sip of wine. It was beginning to be difficult to take it all in. "Does this mean that there was no religion in your home?" Or that the wife and husband were at odds, as they were in so many families?

Clarie interrupted his thoughts. "There was plenty of religion in my home. There was my mother, who had no political ideas, except that she loved my father. And my father, well, he believes that his God wants justice for the workers." She smiled. "He even goes to mass once or twice a year. And he loves the processions. He says it's because he is Italian. He helps carry the statue of the Virgin and the crucifix sometimes."

"Isn't that a little odd, though. A socialist who believes—" She had described him as not just any socialist, but a "red."

Clarie shrugged her shoulders. "When his friends object, he tells them that he is big enough to believe in the workers and God at the same time. And that his God is even bigger."

"And you? Your studying science?"

"My father may be only a blacksmith, but he is the smartest, most generous person I know." Her eyes were flashing as she rose to the defense of Giuseppe Falchetti. "He is big enough to let me at least try to be what I want to be. Maybe he spoiled me—" she said with increasing vehemence.

"As my father did me. I was his only child." Martin so much wanted her to know that he understood how she felt.

"Was?" she asked softly, having been stopped in her tracks.

"He died when I was thirteen. He was a clockmaker."

They fell silent for a moment and contemplated each other. Like him, Clarie had come from a humble background. She, too, had lost a parent and was striking out on a new path to work for the Third Republic. It was strange to have these things in common with a woman.

"When you get through with your schooling, will you teach in Arles?" he asked, finally.

"We don't know. It's just like you. Wherever they send us. Maybe by that time, if I'm assigned too far away, Papa will come live with me. I don't want him to be alone when he is old."

Clarie's father had given his daughter his generous soul. She was quite remarkable.

They were both startled by the arrival of Henriette Choffrut, balancing a pile of dishes. "Here we are," she said, cheerfully.

"Let me help you." Clarie leapt up to take the load from her aunt's arms.

"Have you ever eaten bouillabaisse before, monsieur?" the older woman asked.

"Of course." He had to make Clarie understand that he was not so lonely and pitiful that he knew nothing of southern life.

"Good, then you can let us know what you think of this."

While Clarie was setting down a large bowl of steaming broth, a dish of fish, and his own bowl with two toasted pieces of bread in it, Mme Choffrut placed a small clay jar on the table. "This is the rouille. It's a bit hot, so just start with a little on top." When she straightened up, Martin asked if she and her husband could join him. Although what he really hoped was that Clarie would stay at the table with him, alone.

"No, no. Tonight you are our taster." Mme Choffrut gave him a pat on the shoulder. "You have to let us know if we need to add something."

He shook his head. He surely could not do that. Then Clarie explained that they only had their supper after all the customers left. "Whatever is left over, and whatever we cannot use the next day."

Martin stared down at the pungently fragrant reddish broth and pieces of white fish. Would he be consigned to eat alone or, worse, suffer through the meal as Henriette Choffrut stood there watching him, waiting for his approval after every bite?

Clarie came to the rescue. Getting up from her seat, she asked her aunt if she could keep "the judge" company while she sat at the table and wrote out the day's menus on the slates.

This arrangement, which assured Martin and her niece more time alone together, sent Mme Choffrut happily back to the kitchen. Clarie soon returned with the two black slates and a piece of chalk, and started writing as Martin ate.

"If we don't get a big crowd tonight, tomorrow we will undoubtedly serve a fish purée for lunch. We'll use it up one way or another," she murmured as she wrote out the description and price of the bouillabaisse.

"Do you mind all this, the restaurant business?" Martin asked between bites. He was desperately hungry and the garlicky tomato broth was flowing through every vein in his body, enlivening him.

"It's terribly hard work. For them, I mean. For me, it's only being nice to the customers, most of which is easy. Except for certain ones." She paused to give him a look.

"You mean like Franc."

She nodded. "Yes."

"Why don't you like him?" This was not surprising, considering Franc's behavior toward her.

Clarie glanced toward the kitchen before she answered. "I don't like the way he takes over. He came in here, assuring my aunt and uncle that he'd watch over the place like he watches over the entire neighborhood. All with the hint that if they were not nice to him, he might not be nice to them. They're so good, they hardly noticed. And so he comes in whenever he wants, and pays only when he feels like it. They've risked everything to start this new place. They work so hard. They count every penny. It's not fair. I don't like it when someone treats them that way."

Martin found Clarie's passionate objection to injustice charming. And he certainly did not disagree with her assessment of his inspector, who was crude, used his position to his advantage, and upheld the law as he saw fit. Yet, despite knowing all these things about Franc, he had no sure way of dealing with him.

Clarie got up again. "Let me go check the desserts, just to be sure. And you had better eat up. Who knows who will show up in a few minutes."

Martin watched regretfully as she hurried to the kitchen to talk with her aunt and uncle. He had only a little more time to savor his meal and Clarie's company.

Wednesday, August 26

Not the power to remember, but its very opposite, the power to forget, is a necessary condition of our existence.

—Sholem Asch, *The Nazarene*

26

WHEN MARTIN CAME OUT OF THE Picard house, Franc was waiting for him, leaning against the wall to the left of the door, his cap firmly on his head, his arms crossed. Martin's heart almost stopped.

"Sir."

"Sir"—a good sign. Surely Franc was not going to arrest someone in the same moment that he was referring to him as "sir."

"Franc, you gave me a fright. What are you doing standing there?" Martin pulled at his frock coat, trying to recover his composure.

"I didn't mean to startle you. I didn't want to disturb you, so I decided to wait for you to come out. I know you're off to the Palais, and I thought you deserved a warning."

About what? Martin sucked in a breath.

"You'll never guess who the Cézannes have got down here to help them out," Franc said. "They're pulling out all the guns."

The warning was about Cézanne, not about him. Martin coughed to cover up his relief, then asked Franc to tell him.

"Zola!"

"Zola, the writer?"

"Who else?"

"Zola is down here?"

"Yes, the master of pornography has decided to make an appearance in his home town to help out his old friend." Franc shook his head in disgust.

"And do you know what he is planning to do exactly?"

"See *you*! Talk to *you*! Convince you that his friend didn't do it. At least, that is what Cézanne's mistress told one of my men when we tried to find the artist yesterday. She guaranteed that *both* of them would be at the Palais today. Ten o'clock sharp."

Émile Zola in his chambers, cajoling him, convincing him? In Aix? Amazing.

"And I can't help you, sir. You know I can't deal with intellectuals. Especially intellectuals who write dirty books. I know you've been educated, and maybe you have a different attitude. Have you read any of that filth?"

"Yes." Martin could not help smiling. It felt good to be back on the old footing, being a witness to his inspector's pious, and undoubtedly hypocritical, opinions. "I've read several. You might even appreciate the last one, *Germinal*," he added, only to tease Franc a little. "It was serialized in many of the penny presses. It's about laboring men, northerners like yourself."

"I don't need to know more about him. He's all yours. I'm sure you are smart enough not to let him change your mind about anything."

Martin was not so sure. Matching wits with the greatest living writer in France was a daunting prospect. But this was not a discussion they should be having outside the windows of the Picard house. Martin took Franc by the elbow and led him to the other side of the narrow street.

"The landlords," he explained in a whisper before asking the inspector if he had managed to find out anything about the boy.

Franc shrugged. "Me and François asked around all the obvious places, for the third time, last night. Finally we got an old toothless whore to say she thought that a runaway calling himself Pierre had come to town a few weeks ago and disappeared around the time of the Vernet murder. He came begging, asking for odd jobs, and ended up running errands for the 'ladies of the night.'"

"He did not say where he was from? Had no friends his own age? Anyone who might have seen—"

"I'm still working on it. Listen. Let me handle my job. It looks like you're going to have your hands full too."

"Right. Zola. Well, I guess I'd better get over there." Martin tried to sound jaunty. "I'll need to prepare even more now."

"Yes. In the meantime, I'll just concentrate on fulfilling *my* duties."

Franc's resentful tone brought Martin back down to earth. They were not on the "same old footing." Something had changed between them, and most likely it had to do with Merckx. Martin held out his hand. He could not tell if Franc hesitated before he took it. "Thank you for the warning," Martin said. "We'll talk later."

Franc tipped his cap and set off, leaving Martin to wonder what Zola could say that would prove his friend the artist was neither a coward nor a murderer.

Waiting for the bells of the Madeleine Church to toll ten times was like waiting for the clock to strike the hour of his orals in front of the final examining committee. Martin had done everything he knew how to prepare, yet there really was no way for him to be fully ready. When the ringing sounded through his half-opened window, he was tempted to go out in the hall to see if Zola had arrived, but forced himself to stay put. He did not want to start off by appearing too eager. As he went over the questions again in his mind, Martin nervously repositioned his pen, his ink, and his notebook on his desk. Finally, he heard Old Joseph's timid knocking.

"Come in."

"The gendarme has brought up M. Cézanne and a M. Zola. M. Zola requests to speak to you first, because he must catch a train."

"Show him in, please."

"Shall I stay to take notes?"

"Please."

Martin watched his clerk leave. "*A M. Zola?*" What world was the old man living in? At least his antiquated greffier would not be nervous. Martin stood up in front of his desk and gave his damp hands a quick wipe on his trousers.

When Zola followed Joseph into the room, the author held out his hand and introduced himself, although there was no mistaking the pince-nez, the close, wiry mustache and beard, and the girth. It was as if he had walked out of a satirical magazine.

"Bernard Martin," Martin said, as they shook hands. Zola's grip was firm and dry. Before Martin had time to say more, Zola flipped his bowler onto one of the two chairs in front of the desk and walked around it to look out the window.

"You have a fine view of the square. Is there a market here any more?"

"Most Thursdays."

"And they sell good things? Anchovies, olives, earthy things?" Zola scrutinized Martin. "Do you like those things?"

"Of course."

"You're not from here?"

"No, Lille."

"Via Paris?"

"Yes." Zola was sizing him up.

"Everyone comes via Paris. I was born there," Zola said as he once again stared out the window, "and the people of Aix never forgave me for it. When my father died, after he had built them the best dam in all of France, the leaders of the town refused to help my mother and me. Earthy things, combined with petit bourgeois avarice under the thumb of snobbish passé aristocrats. You like it here?"

It was hard to know what to answer, so Martin remained silent.

"But, of course," Zola worked his way around Martin toward one of the wooden witness chairs. "I am not here to interrogate you, am I? You need to know about my friend."

"Yes." Martin knew that once he got started he would do fine. It was clear that Zola liked to hold forth. He watched as the writer settled in, putting down his heavy walking stick, undoing the only button on his jacket that had been fastened, and, with some effort, crossing his legs. It seemed a paltry thing not to recognize who he was, and what he meant to men like Martin.

"M. Zola, I must tell you how much I admired *Germinal*."

The writer's face burst into a smile. "Ah, then you are my kind of republican." Zola took off his pince-nez and held it in his two chubby hands. "My latest project—well, I have two actually—but the one I'm worried about, is getting *Germinal* on the stage. I may have trouble with the censors. You know there are some government officials—including some in the police—who do not like me. It's because I tell the truth."

"Yes, I can see that." Any support of the workers aroused controversy, Martin knew this only too well. "And your other project?" Martin felt it only polite to ask.

"Another in my Rougon-Macquart series, about an artist. A man who cannot create the masterpiece that he has in his mind, his problems with women, the influence of heredity and the environment, et cetera, et cetera, et cetera."

"Oh?" Could it be about Cézanne?

Zola paused, as if he were reading Martin's thoughts, and then continued more slowly. "The main character is a composite of all the artists I know, of course. And I know many. As you may recall, I've defended much of the new art in my journalistic pieces."

Martin did not know anything about Zola's role in the art world. Was the writer's talk of a "composite artist" a way of covering the tracks he had inadvertently traced? The phrase "problems with women" had certainly caught Martin's attention.

"M. Zola, I don't want to keep you. I understand that you have to catch a train at—"

"Noon."

"Noon, yes. Then may I ask why you wanted to see me?"

"To offer my services, of course."

"In what way?" Zola was so nonchalant, so sure of himself. It was obvious that Martin would have to hear the writer out before he got to the questions that he was desperate to ask.

"I thought you and I could share information. If I had the opportunity to peruse your notes, for example, maybe I'd see something in them that you don't. I've done a lot of investigating. Not police work, of course. But for my novels. My whole career is dedicated to describing what makes men do what they do."

The request to see Martin's notes was presumptuous. "I'm sorry. No one can see my notes until I pass them on to the prosecutor," Martin said, hoping that Joseph, who was writing away so quietly in the alcove, would also get the point. "But I see no reason why we cannot talk over some aspects of the case."

"All right, then." Even Zola knew that he was not likely to get away with this audacious ploy. So he tried another. "The most important thing is this: Cézanne is innocent."

Martin was surprised, he had expected Zola to lead up to this assertion with some proof. "How do you know?"

"He is psychologically incapable of hurting anyone. He is a very sensitive man. Very loyal. In fact, in some ways much more sensitive than I. I always expected that he would have surpassed me by now because of this."

"I've heard quite differently. I've heard that he has a very bad temper.

That he throws things and tears up his canvases." For the first time since Zola had entered the room, Martin felt he was gaining some control.

"Oh, that." Zola waved his pince-nez. "That's frustration with himself, his work. He keeps trying to paint what's up here," the author pointed to his head, "and it doesn't come out quite that way. He sees something that he can't quite commit to the canvas. All artists go through this. In fact, I do almost every morning when I sit down at my desk to write."

"And, may I ask, what happens to your frustrated artist—the one in your novel—at the end?"

"Oh, it's sad. He commits suicide."

Anger and frustration turned against himself instead of against another human being.

"And 'the problems with women'?"

"Oh, dear," Zola sighed and sat back in the chair. "As soon as I said it, I knew I should not have brought it up. I'm always too eager to talk about my work. And you, you're good. That's what Hortense and Paul told me. A pouncer, like any examining magistrate worth his salt should be. Well, then let me tell you why Cézanne could not have killed Solange Vernet."

Martin waited through the dramatic pause.

"He could not have killed her because he loved her. She was the love of his life."

Surely the great portrayer of human passions knew how easily love could turn to hate. "You know that because?" Martin could hardly believe that he was challenging the great Zola.

"When we met in July, she was all that he could talk about. She understood him. She understood what he was trying to do. Hortense and all the other women had always been a burden to him. He told me that Solange Vernet could be his muse."

Muse? Like the woman with her legs spread for the assorted men in Cézanne's obscene painting?

"I understand that you received some letters for Cézanne in July," said Martin, trying to move Zola from pious generalities to specifics.

"Actually, I did not. They did not come. I'm sure it was a great disappointment to him."

"Then this love of his life may have been on the verge of rejecting him, and what would that mean to a sensitive soul given to temper tantrums?" asked Martin, pushing himself to keep pressing the famous writer.

"Not murder." Zola's face was grim. "Besides, I am his best friend. And I can tell you that in all confidence."

"How?" The author, the legendary investigator, still had not offered any evidence.

"I asked him. I was quite upset by Hortense's telegram. That's why I came. So I had to ask. We were standing on the banks of the Arc yesterday, where we had dreamed our boyhood dreams together. For us, for our friendship, this place is almost sacred. He swore to me there, *swore to me,* that he did not do it. Cézanne is not capable of lying. Everything shows in his face."

Zola's word. That should be enough to convince a novice judge in this backwater provincial, petit-bourgeois, aristocratic-ridden town.

Martin got up, in part to relieve the tension caused by what he was about to do. In exchange for eliciting information about the artist's past, he was going to have to reveal Solange Vernet's secret. The only question was, how to begin. "Let me show you a few things," Martin said to Zola, who had taken out his watch to check the time. "Perhaps you can help me with them." He reached into his cabinet for the two small canvases that he had taken from the Jas de Bouffan.

"Did you know," he said, as he unrolled the first of them, "that Solange Vernet had golden-red hair?"

"Yes." Zola placed his pince-nez on his nose and rose to examine the pictures.

"This one," Martin held down the small painting of the worshiped woman on his desk, "is this what you would consider a 'muse'?"

Zola smiled broadly. "I remember this. It was a kind of a joke. I love the bishop standing there, being one of the 'inspired.'" The author removed his glasses. "I'm afraid that Cézanne has grown much more pious since then. He would not do anything so iconoclastic these days. In any case, my impression is that Cézanne had a much different relationship to his Solange. I doubt if he even saw a bare shoulder. At least not from what he told me."

"And this." Martin rolled out the depiction of the young woman being strangled. Zola peered at it and nodded.

"They are very early. They have nothing to do with what Cézanne is painting now. He could not have known her then."

"When do you think these were painted?"

Zola shrugged. "The late sixties. I own one from that period. A striking painting of a muscular man, almost red in appearance, carrying away a woman whose skin is so white it's almost luminous. With dark hair, let me add. White-skinned with dark hair. Both nude, in the middle of a forbiddingly dark canvas. I call it 'The Abduction.' Cézanne gave it to me almost twenty years ago. He was very obsessed by the human drama then. Now he does not seem to be at all interested in showing human passions. Quite the contrary."

Martin rolled up the canvases and set them aside. "You say he was obsessed by the human drama in that period," he said quietly. "Would that include rape and murder?"

"Well, as much as any of us." Zola pursed his lips. "Even before my work, although my critics would not admit it, there was a lot of violence in the theater and serial novels."

"Would you say that Cézanne was obsessed by violence during those years?"

"Obsessed? No."

If Zola was here to prove Cézanne's innocence, he was unlikely to have answered that question in the affirmative.

"Do you have anything else to show me? Any current paintings of Cézanne's?"

Martin shook his head. He did have the quarry fragment, but that would only be a diversion. "What about his relationships with women?" he persisted.

Zola sat down again. "At that time, we were both very shy with women."

"Would you characterize Cézanne as being afraid of them? Of having 'problems with women'?"

Zola hesitated before answering. Martin guessed he was not thinking about whether Cézanne did have a fear of women, but, rather, what he should say about it.

"Shyness, yes. Fear may be too strong. Besides, you certainly cannot base any of these assumptions on what a man paints. I write about depravity and murder, but I would never engage in them." Zola was trying hard to close the door he himself had opened with the description of his new novel.

"Then you do not think it unusual that a young man, as Cézanne was in those days, would paint pictures of women that show them to be either overwhelmingly powerful or cruelly overpowered?"

"No."

Having said his piece, Zola put his pince-nez in his breast pocket and took hold of his walking stick, preparing to leave.

"I realize you are in something of a hurry," Martin said. "But I think there is one more thing you can help me with. We must keep it between ourselves. I need to be able to question Cézanne without his being aware of it."

Zola arched his eyebrows, his curiosity piqued. "You mean something you are going to confront him with after I leave?"

"Confront may be too strong. But I do not want to taint his testimony."

"Yes, then. Yes." Zola sat back again, ready to listen. "We won't have time to do anything but say good-bye anyway."

"This goes back to those early days that we were just talking about. I understand that when you were young men, you spent part of a summer or two in town on the Seine called Bennecourt."

Zola nodded.

"Did you hear about a rape of a young woman at that time?"

Zola shook his head. "Surely you do not think that Cézanne—"

"No, no, nothing like that. What I think may have happened is that Cézanne witnessed such a crime."

Zola shrugged. "He never said anything to me."

"What if he had?"

"What if he had what? You yourself know that all of us have 'witnessed' that kind of thing. It's common. Particularly among the lower classes."

Martin was taken aback by the great writer's response, which was meant to protect his friend. Nevertheless, what Zola said was true. It was a fact, recited by droning law professors, that the abuse of young women was by far the most commonly committed and least prosecuted crime in all of France. The implication of these statistics had been that new judges were not to waste too much time on these cases. That was before Martin knew Solange Vernet's story.

"I am talking not just about abuse, but an obvious rape, by two individuals on a helpless young woman. Do you think that witnessing such a crime could have unbalanced your friend enough to cause the kind of obsession that I see in these paintings?" Martin knew he was not on solid ground in claiming to "see" anything in the paintings, but he wanted to push Zola.

"If that were so, I think I would have known about it."

"And if he could have helped her and he did not, wouldn't he have been too ashamed to tell you? To tell anyone?" The words came out sharp and heated. The thought of one of these privileged young men not coming to the aid of the helpless sixteen-year-old Sophie Vernet had suddenly got Martin's blood up.

"I don't know," Zola responded, unperturbed. "None of this seems likely. Cézanne is a man of such simple passion and tenderness. So much tenderness, in fact, that he often acts the crude peasant in society in order to protect himself. I can't imagine him harming someone or watching while someone else did so."

"You mean to say that Cézanne comes off much rougher around the edges than he really is?"

"Indeed. Like all of us, he is a man of classical learning."

"I see." No wonder the artist despised Westerbury and his pretensions so much. No wonder Westerbury hated the man who had been given all the opportunities that he did not have.

"In any case," Zola asked, rather aggressively, "what does what happened in the sixties have to do with this murder?"

"Did you know that Solange Vernet was a servant in Bennecourt in 1866 or 1867? Do you think Cézanne knew?" Martin pressed on. "Do you think he knows she was the victim of this rape?"

"No." Zola's mouth formed a perfect O on the inside of his beard and mustache as he communicated his surprise. "No." His mind was obviously at work. "So you think there is a connection."

Martin nodded. Just then, Joseph, who had been diligently recording the interview in his alcove, turned around. How many other people would know about Bennecourt before the day was up? Martin glared at his clerk, who returned to his notes without making a sound.

Zola pressed down with both hands on his walking stick, considering. "A connection?"

Martin moved to capitalize on his interest. "M. Zola, can you think of anything that happened during those years in Bennecourt, anything at all, which would help us to find Solange Vernet's murderer?"

"And the murderer of the boy."

Martin caught his breath. Cézanne had told Zola about that, although he had been instructed not to tell anyone. If they were truly the oldest of friends, having only a few hours in which to trade confidences, Martin did not find this damning. "And the boy," he conceded.

Zola got up and began pacing, tapping his walking stick with each step. "There is something. Not the rape of a servant. That is too common. It would not have made the newspapers. But something that I read about at the time that happened during the off-season at Bennecourt or in Gloton, the village across the river. In the early spring, I think. A murder, perhaps? I can't quite remember. As you say, it was almost twenty years ago." He paused and turned to Martin. "Do you think that Solange Vernet could have taken part in some heinous crime?"

"No," Martin said quickly. That is not at all what he was thinking.

"I do know this," the writer continued, "whatever it was, was not resolved. I brought my mother and wife to Gloton to get them away from Paris during the Commune uprising and, having a lot of time on my hands, I asked around." He pressed his fingers to his forehead as if trying to squeeze the memory out of his brain. Evidently to no avail. "I even thought of making it an episode in Rougon-Macquart." He looked up at Martin. "No, no. I can't remember."

There was no telling whether a second crime committed near Bennecourt would have any bearing on the Vernet murder. In his desperation, Martin was not above grasping at straws.

"You understand that so far there are only two suspects in the case."

"And Cézanne is one of them."

Martin nodded.

"Then I must do what I can. I cannot let Paul be dragged through the mud, falsely accused."

This made Martin bristle. False accusations were not his style. And whatever Cézanne found himself mired in was not the fault of the judiciary.

Zola must have noticed Martin's irritation. He offered a conciliatory smile before adding, "I know you have your job to do. And I wish you luck. Let us agree that we are both men who seek justice."

"Yes." The fact that Zola was treating him as a kind of equal gave Martin a flush of pleasure. His embarrassment at being so easily flattered flustered him even more. Zola began pacing again.

"This is what I can do. I am taking the train to Paris—it's too hard to get back from here to the spa, where my wife is staying, anyway. Easier to go through Paris. I keep my old files there, the ones I use for research on my novels. I'll have some time. A day. I'll look through them. And if I find the articles, I will telegram the essential information to you immediately."

"Thank you." If only he would follow through. If only there would be some new piece of evidence.

"Should I send the telegram to your home or to the Palais?"

"My home." Martin did not want anyone else to read the information before he did. He tore off a piece of paper, quickly wrote down his name and the Picard address, and handed the note to Zola, who folded it and put it in the breast pocket that held his pince-nez.

"Very well." Zola held out his hand. Martin took it eagerly. He was relieved that he had gotten through the interview with a modicum of dignity, and that the great man had not fallen below his expectations. Martin would be the last person in the world to condemn Zola for his loyalty to Cézanne. He knew only too well the lengths to which friendship and loyalty could make a man go.

He ushered Zola out of his chambers and watched as he and Cézanne hugged and kissed each other good-bye. Their parting was full of emotion, as if they were saying farewell for the last time. They were an odd pair. The one rich and confident, the other shabby and vulnerable, despite the gruff exterior. Martin wondered, as he prepared to do battle with the artist, if Zola's efforts to save his friend would be as futile as his own efforts to save Merckx had been.

27

THE THUMP OF ZOLA'S WALKING STICK sounded a slow, hollow retreat down the marble hall. Cézanne waited until his friend reached the staircase, then he turned to Martin and, without a word, pushed past him into his chambers. The artist took a seat, cap in hand, eyes fixed on the floor, looking for all the world like a schoolboy resigned to a scolding from his headmaster. But Martin was not a schoolmaster. He was a judge who only felt mounting scorn for the suspect and his puerile demeanor. At best, the artist was a man with a son and common-law wife, who had tried to insert himself between another woman and her longtime lover. At worst, he was a liar, driven by his own demons to kill. And most certainly he was a coward. Martin hoped that once he had driven home to Cézanne that there was a connection between his youthful cowardice and his absurd infatuation with Solange Vernet, the artist would break down and tell him everything.

Martin peered down on Cézanne. "Did Zola say anything to you about our conversation?"

"Only to be brave," was the mumbled reply.

Only to be brave. How solicitous of the artist's presumably delicate feelings, Martin thought as he went back to desk. He nodded to Joseph, signaling that the interrogation was about to begin. "M. Cézanne, I need you to tell me more about your relationship with Solange Vernet."

Cézanne lifted his head. "But I've told you everything. What more do you need to know?"

"How did you meet?"

"I told you. I saw her on the Cours. Buying something or other at one of the stands."

"And you approached her?"

"No, no," the artist shook his head. "I wouldn't do that."

"Then how did you *meet?*" The man was such a blockhead.

"Almost by accident. I didn't plan it. In a café."

"How? When?" Martin punched out the questions.

"One afternoon in March. She was having tea. And for some reason, she decided to speak to me."

"For some reason? You never found that strange, or asked yourself why?"

Cézanne shifted nervously in his chair. Obviously he had never asked himself why. "She knew I was an artist. She was interested in my art."

"Really?"

"Yes, really." Cézanne huffed defensively.

"Did she ever talk to you about having seen you before that day?"

"No, why should she?" The suspect's eyes were wide with puzzlement, and the very first signs of fear. None too soon for Martin's taste.

"And had you ever seen her before she came to Aix?"

"No."

"You're certain."

"Yes!"

Martin folded his hands behind his back and went to the window, pretending that he was contemplating the next question. After giving the artist time to swelter, Martin faced him again. "Your friend Zola writes a great deal about hereditary forces and irrational passions. Do you believe that men are driven to do terrible things for reasons they themselves don't even recognize?"

The only response was a shrug. Cézanne was shrinking against the wall as if it was the only way he could keep his balance. Martin had thrown him totally off kilter.

"You don't know. Well, then, what about yourself? Would you say that you were obsessed with Solange Vernet?"

Cézanne only stared up at Martin, not answering. There was a drop of sweat hanging at the end of his nose, which he did not bother to wipe off. The room was very still. Even Old Joseph had stopped writing. Martin took off the coat that he had left on for his interview with Zola, pulled his cravat loose, and undid the top button on his shirt.

Still no answer. Martin sat down, leaning back in his chair. "Well, I suppose you would not admit that outright, would you, although everything you did shows signs of an irrational obsession—involving Zola in your intrigues, going unannounced to the Vernet apartment, writing unanswered letters. And, of course, these." Martin pointed to the two rolled canvases on his desk. "Explain these. Who is the woman in these pictures?"

"I don't know what you mean. I've already told you—"

"Told me what? That you don't paint that way any more? Maybe there's a reason for that, too." Martin's voice rose. "Maybe once you at last found again the true, living subject of your obsessions—or, as you told me last time, your *nightmares*—you did not need to try to paint her over and over as a victim or as a whore. You could make the real woman into anything you wanted her to be. Who is this woman?" Martin pounded his fist on the desk.

"I don't know. No one. I painted those years ago."

"Ah, yes. Years ago." Martin glanced at his Joseph's back to make sure he was taking down every word. "Years ago. Yes, and you didn't know why then—bad novels and worse dreams—those were the reasons, right?"

Cézanne just sat there, staring at Martin, waiting for the next blow to fall.

"You also told me 'you saw Solange Vernet and you loved her,' but you 'didn't know why.' Right?"

Cézanne swallowed hard and nodded.

"Well, I think I can tell you why. What if I told you that Solange Vernet had been your obsession for almost two decades? What if I told you that you knew her years ago?"

"But," Cézanne shook his head, "I did not."

"Yes, yes, you did." Martin stood up and unrolled the smaller of the two canvases on the desk. "Look at this! Look at this!" he shouted.

The artist put his cap on the chair next to him and obediently shuffled to his feet. He peered down at the girl being strangled, crying out for help.

"Are you telling me that you don't remember when you first saw her? Or maybe you saw her many times before, and you just watched while they raped her."

"I don't know what you are talking about."

"Really?"

The artist's only answer was an expression of confused disbelief.

"Bennecourt. Two decades ago, when Solange Vernet was a servant called Sophie. A girl of only sixteen, who was brutally raped before your very eyes."

Cézanne retreated, falling into the chair. Joseph was frozen into a position, not making a move or a sound. At least he did not turn around this time. Martin stared at Cézanne, waiting for a response. The artist began running his hands through the hair on the side of his head. "I don't know what you are talking about."

"You don't remember seeing this scene with your own eyes?"

"No!" Cézanne's denial cracked through the air.

"She remembered you." Martin said quietly. "She remembered you," he repeated. "Your eyes. The way you stared at her."

"How would you know that? She's dead. She could not tell you. Did Westerbury make up this lie?" Cézanne cried out in his own defense.

"Sometimes," Martin said, keeping his tone measured, "sometimes the dead can speak for themselves. Solange Vernet explained everything in a letter to her lover the day before she died. She told him how much she hated you, because she would never forget the way you just stood there and stared while she screamed for help. Maybe the reason she is dead, is that you killed her to keep her from telling the world what a coward you were."

"I swear, he made up the whole thing."

"I've read the letter."

There was a silence, then Cézanne whispered, "No, that cannot be."

"Were you not there in Bennecourt during that summer?"

Cézanne began to rub his forehead with his fist.

"Answer me! Were you not in Bennecourt in the summer of 1866 before you painted this picture?"

"Yes, yes. I was there. But I didn't know any Sophie."

"And you did not see a rape?"

"No, no. I would not have. . . . I could not have. . . ."

"Look at this. She is pleading with you. And when she saw you in that café, she recognized you. She said she would never forget your eyes staring at her, refusing to help, getting I don't know what pleasure out of merely watching—"

"No, no. That's not true. This is all a torment to me. Pleasure? The only thing I remember is that I used to have nightmares. Lots of them. I painted them. Those," he pointed toward the paintings on Martin's desk. "Those were the nightmares. I read silly novels in Paris. I was lonely. I never would have . . . never. . . . It cannot be. I would never just watch—"

"Why else would she have accused you?" Martin shouted in frustration. Could it be that Cézanne really did not remember the rape? Martin let the canvas go and watched as it turned itself inward, once more obscuring the plight of the young Sophie Vernet. He pushed it aside and sat down. "Did you and Mme Vernet ever quarrel? Did she throw her memory of your cowardice in your face?"

"Never!" Cézanne was breathing hard.

"And when she told you how much she hated you, how much she had always hated you, did you imitate her lover's handwriting and lure her into the quarry?"

"No! No, I told you!" He clutched his hair in his hands, covering his ears.

"Maybe you only got her there to plead your case one last time. Or maybe you had always intended to kill her."

"No!"

"Then whom am I to believe?" Martin said. "An artist, who presumably sees everything and claims he did not see what was right before his very eyes, or the tear-stained last testimony of a murdered woman?"

After a moment of quiet, Cézanne mutely lifted his arm toward the rolled paintings as if he could not express what he was feeling. Then he let it drop. "You're sure? She said this?"

"You really have no memory of this scene as it was played out in the woods near the Seine nineteen years ago?"

"Only the nightmares." Cézanne was mumbling. "That's all I can remember. Years of them. Years. Everything I did then was either in imitation of someone else or something that came from inside my head. From my fantasies. I was just learning. Nature had not yet captured me."

That was it? Nature had not yet captured him? Martin was beginning to believe that Cézanne did not remember. That he had been so drunk, or self-centered, or overwrought that he had wiped the crime against Solange Vernet from his memory. Even if this were so, this amnesia certainly did not prove his innocence. Martin glared at the suspect. "M. Cézanne, you do not seem to be grasping the gravity of what I have just told you. It gives you a motive for murder. Did Solange Vernet confront you with your cowardice? Did she tell you about her true feelings?"

"That she hated me? No, never." The artist's body was limp, his voice barely audible. "Never. She hated me. Because I was a coward." He was talking to himself more than to Martin. "I loved her so much. I thought she loved me. She was always so beautiful, so gracious with me." He looked up at Martin. "Are you sure it was me? Did she say she hated me?"

He was pitiful. "Should I read you her words? Will that help your *memory?*" Martin said as he got up to open the door to his cabinet.

Cézanne held up his hand and shook his head. Martin caught his breath in relief. He had gotten carried away, and forgotten that the letter was hidden among Solange's clothes. He did not want to go fishing for it in front of the suspect and Joseph. As he closed the door, he caught a glimpse of the forlorn white and green striped dress folded neatly in a box and saw before him the image of the older Solange, of the woman that Sophie had become. He shut the door and held his hand against it, as if his physical force could hold back these images.

"M. Cézanne," he said quietly. "Did you ever see Mme Vernet without her gloves?"

"Do you mean . . . did I see her . . . unclothed?"

"No," Martin retorted sharply. "I asked about her gloves. When she went out."

Cézanne shook his head. "I don't think so."

"When we found the body, she was not wearing them. Did Mme Fiquet tell you we were looking for them in Gardanne?"

"No, no." His head was still shaking in confused denial.

Too confused. Too complacent for Martin's taste. He let go of the door to his cabinet and sat down. "We think," he said through clenched teeth, "we believe, that they might be covered with paint and blood. Your paint. Solange Vernet's blood."

"I've told you." The artist was rocking back and forth in the chair. "I've told you. I have not been near her for months."

"M. Cézanne, if you denied seeing Mme Vernet being raped as a girl, and we know that you did see this heinous crime, how can we believe you when you say that you did not kill her?"

"I did not. I could not. This is impossible."

"Maybe you did it in your sleep. In your dreams." Martin hoped his sarcasm would smite the artist.

"No, no. I sleep either in Gardanne or at the Jas. Ask anyone."

Said in all innocence. Where Cézanne slept, of course, did not matter. Solange Vernet's rendevous with death must have taken place in the late afternoon or evening. Martin stared at the artist. Had he been so obsessed that he could commit a murder in his waking hours and not know it? Only an alienist could answer that question. If Martin were dealing with some kind of madman, he was well over his head.

But Cézanne did not look mad or crazy. He looked sad, broken down. Martin took one more stab at provoking him. "You know now, don't you, that you had run across Solange Vernet when you were young and strong, and you chose not help a poor girl—"

"Yes. Yes!" Cézanne obviously did not want to hear him say it again. "What do you want me to do, tear out my eyes? Tell the whole world what a coward I am? That I am blind! What do you want me to do? All I know is that if she said it, it must be so."

If she said it, it must be so. The poor bastard was still in love with her. In love with the fantasy of his own making. In love with a corpse. Martin sighed. It all seemed so hopeless. It would be so much easier if he did not believe Cézanne. Incapable of lying, isn't that what Zola had claimed? Westerbury's words also rang out with the same egotistical, passionate truth. *I aspire to greatness! I loved her! That's enough to prove my innocence!* These two were more alike than either of them was willing to admit. To decide between them, Martin needed evidence. The gloves, the knife, the boy, more witnesses. Something!

Cézanne was staring at him. Martin rose to his feet.

"You may go."

"Huh?"

"I cannot prove whether or not you killed her. Yet. Do not leave town."

"Well, I didn't do it," the artist said as he picked up his cap and, with furtive glances at Martin and Joseph, got up to leave. "I didn't."

"And," Martin said, needing to pound in one more time that Cézanne had betrayed Solange Vernet when she most needed him, "I cannot put you on trial for having witnessed a crime twenty years ago, even though we all know now that you did."

Cézanne paused for just an instant before his escape. Martin hoped that he was considering who "all" might be, and that he realized that their number included his most hated rival, the man Solange Vernet really loved, Charles Westerbury.

As soon as Cézanne was fully out of his chambers, Martin opened the window all the way, hoping to air out the sadness and disgust that were weighing in on him. There was barely a breeze. But there were the reassuring sounds of life two stories below. Men carting their loads, women off to do the daily shopping, a priest with a heavy wooden rosary hanging from his waist. All of them going about their normal lives, at peace with their thoughts, be they of heaven or the next meal. None of them weighed down by the burden of knowing that they may have caused the death of a boy, and of a friend. None of them a complete failure in everything.

"Sir?"

Joseph was becoming more and more irritating, but at least this time his intrusion saved Martin from a useless descent into self-pity.

"Sir? Is there anything that you need me for?"

"Yes." Martin wanted neither solicitude nor advice, so he had to keep the his clerk occupied. "Keep checking to see if anyone else on the witness list has reappeared and make the appointments."

"Yes, sir."

Martin did not turn around, but he was sure that Old Joseph had bowed his head ever so slightly, accepting his orders. "When you're done here, I'll do the locking up."

"All right, sir."

With slow, gentle steps, the little man retreated into the alcove to begin working through the list. It was unlikely that any of the remaining salon participants would return to town before the Proc. And when the prosecutor did come back, it was very likely that he would take the case away from Martin. Or worse, prosecute *him*— depending on what Franc knew or was willing to tell about Merckx. There was a chance that Zola's telegram—if he actually sent it— would reveal something. In the meantime, Martin had to do the one thing he was good at, think through everything again and again, per-severing even though he knew that his hopes were hanging on a very thin thread.

28

HORTENSE WAITED FOR HIS RETURN ALL day and all night. She finally got Paul Jr. to bed by telling him that his father and Zola had decided to spend more time together, exploring old haunts. She knew this could not be true. Émile had made it quite clear that he had important affairs to see to. Besides, whether Paul or Émile were aware of it yet, it was obvious to her that something had changed between them. The extravagant gaiety of the night before—the praise for her dinner, the retelling of schoolboy jokes for Paul Jr.'s benefit, the toasts to old friends and teachers—seemed forced to her. She needed to know what they had really talked about and what Paul had thought of the visit. Had he finally come to terms with the fact that Émile had passed him and everything else in Aix by? Is that why he was wandering about, hiding from her?

Had he betrayed them again by sleeping at the Jas? Or was he in jail? Hortense got up from the sofa to peer at the clock over the fire-place. Two o'clock. She sat down again and stared at the worn Persian rug that covered the floor of the salon. Why was she even worrying about how Paul felt about Émile? What would it matter if he were to go on trial for murder? Why hadn't one of them come and told her what had happened with the judge? Why hadn't she heard something from somebody? Anything! Didn't they know it was her future too? And her son's? If Paul did not return by dawn, she would start wandering the streets herself. She'd look in all the cafés. She'd go to the prison. If she had to, she'd demand to see the judge and plead her case. And if all else failed, she would do the thing that she had been forbidden to do for so many years: she would go to the Jas.

Just then, Hortense heard a key in the door lock, and Cézanne came stumbling into the family's apartment, more disheveled than ever.

"Where have you been? I've been insane with worry!" Hortense cried as she got up to meet him.

"Walking."

"Walking? Since when?"

"I'm not sure. Since I saw the judge."

"Have you been drinking?"

"No," he stepped forward and kissed her on the cheek. "But that's a good idea, dear Hortense. Let's sit down and have a glass."

She held him away from her and took a good look at him. He didn't smell of drink, but his eyes were reddened and dull. With fatigue? Defeat? What had happened?

She followed him into the kitchen. Were they really going to talk, like two adults who actually cared for each other? Or would they begin shouting again?

Her fingers were trembling as she switched on the gas light and uncorked one of the bottles of red wine that they had opened the night before. She poured two glasses and set them on the table, where Paul had already slumped down, his head in his arms. She'd have to be careful. When they were young and in love, she had been so good at gauging his moods. She'd happily chatter away when he wanted to be silent, and instinctively knew when he was ready to tell her what was in his heart, pouring out all his hopes and dreams in great torrents of words and gestures. That had been so long ago.

"Paul?" she touched his arm.

He reached for the glass and took a long drink. Too long. He was not a drinker. He began to sputter and cough. Hortense got up and poured him water from the faucet.

"Thank you. Thank you. I've been such a fool," he pronounced between gulps. "Such a fool. I went after a wisp of a dream, not knowing it was my worst nightmare. I didn't see what was right in front of me."

"You mean—" Was he talking about her and their son?

"Everything! Everything! You know"—there were tears in his eyes from his coughing spell—"I pride myself on being able to see what others don't, below the surface, deep into things. And yet I have been blind to everything."

"Like Paul Jr. and me."

He gave her a look of incomprehension, then he nodded. "Yes, like you and our son."

She wished he sounded more convinced, and convincing. "And Émile?"

"What about Émile?"

She thought for a moment about how to put it. "Did you see something about Émile too?"

"Hah, Émile," he gave a bitter laugh. "Émile. The big man." Paul sniffed in, swallowed, then said, "I still love him like a brother, you know. I always will." Of that she had no doubt. Even during their best years she had suspected that Paul loved Zola more than her. "But," he went on, "sometimes I feel that he is looking at me under glass, like one of the specimens in his novels, wondering why I haven't. . . ."

Paul took another gulp of wine without finishing his sentence. He did not have to. Why he hadn't stayed in Paris, and made something of himself, fulfilled their boyhood dreams. When Paul was courting her, Émile had told her more than once about how he and Paul were going to conquer France together. Paul, who had always protected him when they were in school, was supposed to take the lead. Stories told long ago, Hortense thought. Stories that would never come true. It was best that she change the subject.

She took a sip of wine, not because she really wanted to drink, but because she wanted so much for this to be like a real conversation, going from one thing to another, until they got to the heart of the matter. "Did he talk to the judge?"

"Yes," Paul said quietly.

"Do you know what he said?"

He shrugged.

"Surely he helped you."

"Surely? Surely? How can you be so sure? Maybe this would be the best drama of all. Seeing his friend on trial."

"Oh, Paul, really. He said he would help." Besides, she was the one who had asked him to come.

Paul stared down at his glass. "Maybe there was nothing he could do to help."

"What do you mean?" She sat straight up, alert.

"Nothing."

"Paul," she pleaded. "Tell me. What happened?"

"Nothing. . . . Nothing that concerns you."

"Paul, it all concerns me. And your son."

"Come on, now. Drink something. Relax. It's going to be all right."

She must have looked every bit as anxious and exhausted as she felt. But she was not giving in.

"Why didn't you come back after you saw the judge?"

"I had to think."

"About what?" Émile? The murder? "What?" She repeated. She wanted to shake him.

He reached over and folded her hand in his. "I didn't murder anyone. You know that. Westerbury did it. Or some other fool." With his other hand, he tipped Hortense's face up toward his, and smiled a little. "Don't worry. It wasn't this fool."

If he hadn't added that tender little joke, the dam inside her would not have burst. Before Hortense could stop herself she began to cry in great compulsive sobs that shook her entire body. When she finally managed to steady herself, he was holding on to her hand, even tighter. She wiped her face with her sleeve, and looked down at his fingers entwined with hers. How she loved his hands. They were the most frightening, expressive, strong, and gentle part of him. How she longed to feel them again, moving up and down her body, forming her into an object of desire. It was an ache she had almost forgotten. Still, she pulled away and reached in her pocket for a handkerchief to blow her nose. She had to know more.

"Paul, I know you didn't kill her." Although, how could she really be sure? In the last few months he had stalked Solange Vernet like a starving animal tracking his prey. Maybe he had finally cornered her in the quarry and. . . . No! That was impossible. Hortense sucked in a breath and continued, "But innocent men are sometimes accused. That's why I have to know. What did the judge say?"

Paul slumped back in his seat. "He said I was obsessed by her. That's why he believes I might have killed her. Obsession."

Seduction was more like it, Hortense thought, remembering all of Solange Vernet's Parisian airs. "He talked to Émile before he talked to you?" Hortense asked.

Paul nodded.

"And he still thought that you were—"

"Obsessed. But I'm not any more."

This was hardly a concession, since the witch was dead. Hortense felt the coldness creeping up on her again, clutching at her heart. Sometimes she thought she would never forgive him for everything his foolishness had gotten them into, for his weakness, his self-centeredness—

"Hortense," he said, "I'm sorry for all I have put you through. For the last few months I've been living in a fantasy without even knowing it. A terrible fantasy of a callow, selfish, blind young man. I've learned a great deal about myself today. Too much. But it is over."

He seemed so contrite. Still, Hortense was growing more and more annoyed. She had no idea what he was talking about. "What? What fantasy? What happened?"

Paul thought for a moment before responding. "Hortense, what I have always loved about you is that you have stuck by my side. You have never humiliated me. Or even wanted to."

Obviously Paul did not realize the depth of her anger. Hortense nodded, waiting.

"Apparently," he continued, "I had met Solange Vernet before."

In spite of her best efforts, Hortense gasped. Was it as she had feared? Had Solange posed for Paul? Was she a long-lost love?

"But," he continued, giving her hand a tug to get her attention, "I did not realize that I had known her. I only saw her maybe two or three times. It was only by chance that she recognized me and invited me into her circle. And then—"

"And then!" Hortense burst out. "How could you have been so weak, so childish?"

"That, my dear, is the question. How could I have been so weak? So cowardly."

"Well?"

"I don't know. I've thought about it all day. And I still don't know. When I saw her those many years ago—"

"Does that matter? Were you lovers back then?"

"No, nothing like that. She was a servant in the inn at Bennecourt even before I took you there."

"A servant? Why did she remember you?"

"I . . . ," he stopped and bit his lip. "I didn't help her when she needed me."

"That's it? That's all? And then years later, she went after you?"

"I should have helped."

"Oh, Paul," she said, making an effort to demonstrate her concern, "sometimes you are too tender-hearted. Too ready to give pity. I know that. Sometimes you feel things too deeply." Not all the time, Hortense thought bitterly, not when it came to her.

Paul had closed his eyes. He was grimacing as if he were in pain. "Someone was hurting her, and I didn't. . . ."

His hesitations were beginning to drive Hortense mad. "Paul," she whispered hoarsely, "all I really want to know is if you were lovers these last few months."

The question seemed to have startled him. Paul stared at her for a moment. Then he shook his head. "No."

Hortense stopped herself before she asked whose decision that had been. Paul had just said he loved her because she did not try to humiliate him, and Hortense already knew the answer, that Solange Vernet had refused him.

"Perhaps all you need to know," he said this with patience and kindness, as if he really cared about her, "all you need to believe is that Solange Vernet was the last mistake of my youth. I must not be a dreamer any longer, but a grown man. A man with only three important things in his life, you, our son, and my art. I know now what I am supposed to do. I'm on the right path. I will never let myself be deterred again. I promise you."

Their fingers were touching, but she could not reach for him or even look at him. She doubted that he would have given up on Solange Vernet if she were still alive. Could he ever really give up being a child? Chasing after dreams? Raging in despair because he was not Émile or Monet? Why should she believe him?

He took hold of her hand again. "And I promise, before the year is up, I will tell my father about us. And we will marry if you will still have me."

She almost pulled away again. If she would still have him? What choice did she have? She had given him *her* youth. Who else would have her?

"Hortense?"

"What?" This came out sharply, almost breaking the mood.

"Will you still have me?" He almost sounded humble, like this was what he really wanted, like this was what she really deserved.

"Yes," she swallowed hard. "Yes, of course."

"As soon as possible?"

She could barely get the words out. "As soon as possible." Her heart was pounding. If nothing else went wrong, it they didn't drag him off to the guillotine, she would be Mme Cézanne with an inheritance and a future. It was terrible to feel no joy after waiting for so long.

"Good!" Just as oblivious to her feelings as ever, he got up to retrieve the bottle and pour more wine for both of them.

She forced herself to smile when they clinked glasses. There was nothing romantic about the moment. The marriage was an arrangement, necessary for her and for their son. Then it would not matter whether Paul ever became successful or not. At least they'd all have bread in their mouths.

After they had managed to consume the wine, they got up and walked toward the bedroom. Would they lie on their bed, as they had for months, two separate islands of thwarted hopes and desires? She was not sure she was ready to make love with him. And she was not sure that he was ready to, either.

Thursday, August 27

Hydrangeas were especially popular in the late nineteenth century, and they flourished in the Midi. The French word for this plant is hortensia, *which occasioned the charming verbal-visual pun that makes this page so winning, giving it something of the quality of a valentine.*

—Joseph J. Rischel, *Cézanne*

29

WESTERBURY SAT IN THE SUN-FILLED SALON, enjoying his morning tea. Although he had no way to pay her, Arlette was still keeping up appearances. This morning she had discreetly waited for him to rise and wash up, then promptly delivered a tray with all the right accoutrements: napkin, steaming pot of tea, pitcher of warmed milk, slices of fresh bread, and a bit of jam and butter. No reason to discourage the service, Westerbury thought with a sigh. After all, what choice did she have? Like him, Arlette was stuck in Aix until things were settled. The real problem was how many more mornings would she be able to go to the baker, the grocer, and the butcher. That's why he had to see Picard as soon as possible. Westerbury took a long, last sip, before pushing the tray away. Of course, the notary might refuse to probate the will until the judge indicted the killer. Just one of the reasons why it made no sense for him to try to get on with his life until he—or someone else—had avenged Solange's murder.

He certainly could not concentrate on his work. Westerbury had spent most of the previous day trying to deal with the chaos the police had created during their search. He managed to put his fossils and rocks back in order, but he had not had the heart to touch the pile of papers that Arlette had stacked on his desk. How long would it take before he built up the courage to go through them? What if he had nothing new to say? What if wiser men had said it all before, and said it better than he ever could? Westerbury got up from the armchair. No. He could not let all his old fears paralyze him. He had to do something.

Westerbury brushed the crumbs off his pants and approached the tall windows that faced the Cours. He didn't have to lean out very far to see that they had posted a gendarme at the front door. Going to the Jas would be too dangerous, but he could use the servants' entrance and make his way to the rue Matheron. Solange had told him about the Cézannes' apartment on one of their last good nights. The idiot had actually once proposed that he and Solange meet there. Westerbury clutched at the heavy velvet curtain. If only he had believed in her laughter and smiling eyes when she scoffed at the very idea.

"M. Westerbury. Are you through with your breakfast things?"

Good God! She certainly had a way of creeping up on you. Soon Arlette would be filling the room with her mournful sighs.

"M. Westerbury?"

"Yes, dear." He turned to Arlette and forced a smile. "Could you bring me the cap and jacket I use for my explorations?" Best to look as inconspicious as possible while he was on the hunt.

After his successful escape from the building, Westerbury took a circuitous route to the north end of the city, criss-crossing his way toward the rue Matheron. Every few blocks, he stepped inside a doorway to see if he was being followed. When he was sure there was no one behind him, he started up again. He did not know the address, but he did know what most of the Cézannes looked like. He had "met" the mother and sister at the Jas the night before his arrest, and he once had seen the mistress, *en famille* so to speak. All three women were horrors. Then there was the boy, who had fully inherited his parents' utter lack of grace. If none of them appeared, he'd still learn something, that he'd have to search for Paul Cézanne someplace else.

Unfortunately, the narrow rue Matheron offered few good doorways from which to make his observations, so Westerbury settled on a corner, where he stood in the hot sun for almost an hour. During that time, the only people who passed through the street were an old woman carrying a basket to market, and a man in a bowler off to do some business. Just as Westerbury was about to give up, the Cézanne boy came running out of a doorway. Westerbury's heart leaped as he quickly hid behind a building. They *were* there. When he peered around the corner again, he saw the mistress, armed with a marketing basket, following her son. Happy lad. His father must be nearby. Westerbury pasted himself up against the wall and thought. If there is food-shopping, they must be planning for dinner. Dinner for Mama and Papa and Son, in an hour or so. He was dying of thirst. He'd have plenty of time to get a drink.

Just one for Solange, his dear girl; that had been his intention. Just a little something to buck him up for the battle. Then Westerbury dedicated a second drink to science and its practitioners, and a third to Sir Charles Lyell, the greatest of them all. He found that the creamy green liquid went down so well, when you had the time to sip at it, that he had to order another. Who cared if the barkeeper gave him a suspicious look as he got out the bottle and water again? He had no other customers, and Westerbury wanted more. He watched impatiently as the man poured a bit of the absinthe into a tall glass. As soon as he was done, Westerbury added a spoonful of sugar and mixed in the water.

Fortification, that's what was required. So he wouldn't give in. So he'd be the avenger, the truth-seeker. As long as they let him. That thought brought him up short. And, indeed, when he glanced behind him, he spied a gendarme peeking in the window of the café. Their eyes met, but the policeman did not enter. Instead, without giving any indication of whether or not he recognized Westerbury, he left. Time to move on. Westerbury sent some coins clattering across the zinc counter and left. He made sure no one was trailing him, then headed back toward the rue Matheron.

When he turned the corner, he saw Cézanne almost immediately, ambling toward his townhouse, carrying a large bouquet of flowers. How homey, Westerbury thought, how gallant. How disgusting! A rage tore through him, driving him toward Cézanne. "Murderer! Coward!" he shouted. By the time he reached the startled artist, his hands were poised to take him by the neck and strangle him. Cézanne threw the flowers aside. He grabbed Westerbury's arms, and, with surprising strength, pulled him away.

"Say something!"

Cézanne remained mute, holding on to Westerbury with an iron grip.

"Say something. Confess. You did it!"

"No," Cézanne shook his head, "no."

Westerbury managed to push him up against a wall. "Let go of me!" Westerbury demanded, and amazingly, Cézanne did just that.

Westerbury's hands clenched with fury. He threw a punch right in the artist's ugly face.

Cézanne did not move. So Westerbury threw another, this time drawing blood from the murdering coward's nose. Still Cézanne remained motionless.

"What is wrong with you? Talk to me. Tell me what you did to her!"

"Nothing. I did nothing." The artist began shifting his head from side to side. Seeking help? Or making sure that no one was about to hear them? What did it matter to Westerbury? He had him now.

"Oh yes, that's right. When Solange was a mere girl, you did nothing. You scoundrel. Nothing!"

Cézanne swallowed hard, and looked straight at Westerbury. "I'm sorry," he whispered. Westerbury's arm shot out in an attempt to take another strike at Cézanne's face. This time the artist fended off the blow, but still did not hit back.

"What's wrong with you? Do I need to knock it out of you?"

"I didn't remember. And when I found out—"

"You killed her!" Westerbury's next blow was again blocked by the artist's strong arm.

"No, no. I couldn't. Never."

This time Westerbury aimed for Cézanne's belly, and knocked some wind out of him. When Cézanne bent over to cover the pain, Westerbury hit him in the head again, sending him reeling to the ground. With a yelp of pain he realized he had struck so hard that he might have broken something in his hand. So he began to kick Cézanne on his legs and back, while the artist tried to protect himself by rolling into a ball.

"Tell me the truth!" Silence again. Why was the idiot taking the punishment and not striking back? Westerbury drew back, breathing hard.

"Tell me the truth!" he roared. You could not engage in an honorable duel if only one of you was manly enough to fight.

Cézanne peeked out from hands cupped around his face. "I told you. It wasn't me. I couldn't kill anyone."

Was he supposed to believe the lying coward? Before he was able to strike another blow, Cézanne scrambled on all fours to the wall of the house across from his own and turned around to face his assailant, his legs folded up against his body. "You knew before she died that she did not love me. You knew, didn't you?"

Cézanne was begging to have his humiliation confirmed. "Love you? Love *you*?" Westerbury retorted. "Of course I knew!" He kicked hard at the artist's calves. Cézanne did not even cry out.

He did not have to because, before either of them noticed, they had company. Franc pinned Westerbury to the wall, in one swift straight-arm motion, while a gendarme pulled Cézanne to his feet.

"You were supposed to stay out of trouble," Franc said, and smiled, showing the full range of his hideous tobacco-stained teeth.

That smile so enraged Westerbury that he grabbed at the inspector's hair, pulling it hard. He only reached the greasy mane because his arm was longer than Franc's, but certainly not stronger. The brute punched him in his side so hard that he nearly vomited with the pain.

"Let him be." Westerbury heard Cézanne's voice through the ringing in his ears. "Let him be. We were just talking."

"Just talking, huh? I should take you in too. Lucky for you that you have a rich father." Franc's voice was full of disdain.

Through blurred vision, Westerbury saw Cézanne meekly picking up the flowers. Even though he had a rich father, even though he was a native, the lying, murdering coward did not try to challenge Franc.

"Are you going to fight me, or just walk back to the prison peaceably?" The burly inspector still had Westerbury by one shoulder. Franc pressed him hard against the stone wall and shook his fist in his face.

Westerbury glanced down at his limp, helpless hands, one bloody and starting to swell, the other streaked with black pomade, the symbol of his tragically ephemeral victory against the French police. What choices did he have? Get beaten to a pulp, or surrender. So he stepped ahead of Franc, holding himself with the rectitude born of dignity and honor, as he marched back to his own cruel purgatory. Perhaps this time the dim-witted Arlette would be smart enough to come looking for him and get him out.

30

THE SCENE WAS ALL TOO FAMILIAR. Franc and Westerbury blustering away at him. This time together, in his chambers, replete with mutual recriminations. Martin sank back in his chair. God, he was weary.

"Where's Old Joseph?" Franc demanded. "We've got him here. Let's get him to confess right now and have it all written up nice and official." The inspector was so eager to put Westerbury away that he had not moved from the doorway that divided Martin's office from the foyer.

"I sent my clerk out for a long lunch because we had no witnesses scheduled for today," Martin said evenly. He could not imagine what would make Franc think that Westerbury was about to confess to anything. "As for you," he said to the Englishman, who was sitting in one of the witness chairs across from his desk, "let's see what we are going to do with you."

"I've done nothing wrong, I told you. I just tried to find the murderer, which is more than I can say for either you or that brute over there." Westerbury's eyes were glazed over. He had been drinking again.

"He claims he's done nothing!" The inspector scoffed. "I told you that we saw him kicking the artist right in the middle of the street. Assault, disturbing the peace, disobeying the conditions of his release, and assaulting an officer of the law."

"Just defending myself. Trying to hold you back by your greasy hair." Westerbury held up his pomade-streaked hand for one and all to see.

"Why, I should—" Franc made a lunge for the Englishman.

"Stop! Enough!" They were like two children, the one the school-yard bully, the other the weakling, driven by drink to challenge him. "Is Cézanne going to press charges?" Martin had to insert some rationality into the proceedings and get them away from him.

"No! He wouldn't dare." This was Westerbury.

"That," Martin said coldly to the Englishman, "is most certainly not for you to decide."

Martin turned to his inspector. "Did you talk to him? Does he want to press charges?"

"No, he's just as cowardly as this one. Maybe getting a bloody nose scared him. Give him time to think it over, though. I bet he'll come running to you, complaining." Franc's legs were set in an open stance, ready to pounce and pound.

No complaint, then. Martin sighed. He had a number of choices. He could fine Westerbury on the spot, throw him in jail, or wait for someone to file charges.

Martin reached for his pen, still not sure what to write on the order, when Westerbury decided his own fate.

"You know as well as I do that he did it," he pleaded with Martin. "You read the letter. She hated him. She hated him for what he saw twenty years ago. He watched her being raped and—"

Suddenly there was silence. Westerbury stopped short, no doubt realizing his blunder. Martin gripped his pen. He had kept his word to the Englishman by downplaying the importance of the letter in his conversation with his inspector, and the idiot had let the cat out of the bag. Without even looking up, he knew that Franc was staring down at him. Keeping his hand as steady as he could, Martin began writing. "Mr. Westerbury, we'll keep you in prison for forty-eight hours, which should give you a nice long time to reconsider your actions. The next time it will be for much longer, at least a week, I guarantee you." All he could think about was what he was going to say to Franc once they were alone.

Westerbury was on his feet. "I will die for her if I have to." The chivalrous knight's last stand—and a feeble one at that, considering his ineptitude.

"There's a gendarme outside?" Martin's mouth had run dry. He had to get Franc out of the room.

"Yes." The inspector's gaze had never let up.

"Tell him to take the prisoner away. We can catch up when you are done."

The inspector nodded. He stood stock still for another moment, making sure he communicated the full depth of his displeasure. Then he grabbed Westerbury by the shoulder and began shoving him out the door.

As soon as they were outside of his chambers, Martin opened his cabinet and searched frantically in the folds of Solange Vernet's dress for her letter. When he found it, he grabbed the envelope and placed it on top. He slammed the door closed and replaced the key in his desk, beating Franc's return only by an instant.

The inspector returned, eyes narrowed, fists slightly clenched, as if he were about to "soften up" some petty criminal. It took a supreme act of will for Martin to remind himself that he was not charged with anything. Yet. He rose to speak first.

"As I told you, I promised Westerbury that I'd try to keep the contents of the letter confidential for as long as possible." His heart was pounding so hard that he was sure that Franc could hear it.

"And you also told *me* that it contained nothing important, no new information."

"I am not sure it does."

"Well, Westerbury thinks so. And it seems like you trust a criminal more than you trust me." The inspector was so enraged that bits of spittle were flying onto his chin.

"That is not so. I was trying to keep my word. And I am not sure the Englishman is a criminal. Being a pompous ass is not yet a crime, as far as I know."

"Being a murderer is."

"I am not convinced he did it."

"Then who did?" Franc shouted.

"I don't know."

"Well, I do. It was one of them."

"And your proof is?" In the midst of battle, Martin somehow was finding the nerve to hold his own.

"Let me see that letter." This was more than a demand, it was a threat.

"I am not sure it will tell you anything."

"I'll decide that."

"No, I will."

"When the Proc returns—"

"When the Proc returns, what?"

"I'll tell him not only about how many qualms you, supposedly a judge, had about jailing a murder suspect. I'll also tell him about a certain deserter that we found in the woods."

So there it was, out in the open. Franc knew, or at least suspected, that Martin had helped Merckx to escape, and was quite willing to use this information against him. In the days since Merckx's death, when Martin had allowed himself to face up to the worst that could happen to him, he had known this. Still, hearing Franc say it sent a cold wave of fear through his chest into his stomach.

"That is an entirely different matter." Martin was hanging on to his desk to keep his hands from trembling. He had to make a show of not backing down.

"I think whether or not one is worthy of being a judge is all one matter. And," Franc lowered his voice, "one of the ways to be a successful judge is to cooperate with the police, not fight them, not try to solve the case on your own. You still have a lot to learn. Wasn't that our deal, that we would work together?"

Martin could almost breathe again. They were both stepping back. In the last few days, ever since they had killed poor Merckx, he had found that he much preferred the cajoling Franc to the threatening one. He let go of his desk.

"You're right, of course. You're right. I was just trying to keep my word. There are things in the letter that Westerbury found humiliating. Very personal things. We had made a deal. He would tell me where the letter was, if I kept the promise to him not to tell anyone about it unless I had to. I trust that you will not reveal the contents unless it's absolutely necessary." He did not even wait for any response from Franc, before continuing. "Trying to keep it to myself just shows my lack of experience. Again. My first murder case, all that." He had to stop babbling. It made him seem too desperate. Martin moistened his lips with his tongue. "It should be right here with the other evidence." For the second time in less than five minutes, he retrieved the key from his drawer and opened the cabinet. Martin reached for the envelope, and willing his hand not to shake, gave it to Franc.

"As you'll see," Martin said, "it explains why Solange Vernet never had any real interest in Cézanne. It is fairly clear that they were never lovers, although he was infatuated with her. You can tell me if you see something in it that I may have missed." Martin winced when Franc yanked the letter out of the envelope. Both were composed of thin lavender-scented paper. Neither would last long under such rough scrutiny.

Franc took one look and stuffed the pages back into the envelope. "May I take it with me down to my office?"

Martin was stunned. He had never expected Franc to ask such a thing. He felt caught between what Merckx had gotten him into and his duty to Solange Vernet. Letting the letter go, even for an afternoon, felt like a violation.

"I'm a slow reader. You know, I don't have your learning." Franc opened his arms as if he were pleading. "Other judges, those I consider my friends, take this into account." The humble pose. Which Franc was he to believe? The bully, the tutor in the methods of crimes and misdemeanors, or the man of the people working his way up to a position of respect? Martin had witnessed the appearance of all three during their short, heated confrontation.

"I've handled other evidence, you know." Franc was relentless. "From judges that know and trust me. Judges who are not always on their high horse."

"You know I'm not like that." This came out before Martin could stop himself. Sometimes it felt like Franc had him on a string, as if he were some limp marionette jumping to orders.

Franc waited for an answer. Martin cleared his throat. He stared at the letter, filled with Solange Vernet's delicate script, encased in Franc's thick, hardened hands. He could not let the letter out of his chambers. He could barely let it out of his sight. Yet he had just handed it over. He had to figure out a way to get it back.

"Well?"

"I've an idea." For a moment Martin feared that, in his panic, his mind had stopped. "The paper is rather flimsy and wearing down. It would be safer to keep it here. Joseph is due back any minute. You know how fastidious he is. He's just the right person to handle it. I'll have him copy the entire thing for you. That way, we'll both have more time to go over it. Then we can put our heads together and see what we come up with."

This was such a reasonable solution that he could not imagine how Franc could reject it. And yet the inspector hesitated.

"I'll send Joseph down as soon as he is done. You should have your copy well before supper time."

Martin swallowed hard and held out his hand. He was sweating from every pore in his body.

"Yes, and then I can see if there is something you missed," Franc said.

"Right, exactly." Martin almost sighed with relief when Franc gave the letter back to him. His damp fingers stuck to the envelope as he gingerly placed it on his desk.

"All right, then." Martin looked up at his inspector. It was time for Franc to go away.

"All right? Nothing else? What did Zola have to say?"

Why hadn't Martin thought of that? Any account of the Zola interview might serve to placate his inspector. "Actually he said nothing, except that he *knew* Cézanne was innocent. He spent the whole time defending his friend. The reason *we* are supposed to believe both of them is that the artist swore to his innocence on the banks of the Arc, which is a kind of sacred place for them." Martin had added that last little bit for effect, and it evoked the reaction he hoped for.

"Phffff." Franc blew out a gust of contempt. "And who would believe either of them?"

"Yes, exactly," Martin said, practically collapsing into his seat. He had not mentioned the telegram, and he hoped to God that his clerk wouldn't either. "And the boy, the little messenger." Martin at least had to try to play the role of a superior.

"Nothing." Franc sounded so damned unconcerned. Martin did not have the will to ask him about the gloves or the knife.

"All right, then," Martin said for the second time, desperate to be left alone. He did not want to wipe away the sweat on his face in front of Franc.

"Sir, I think I was out of line."

"Yes?" Martin looked up.

"About the deserter. Just because he was your friend—" The threatening scowl had disappeared.

Martin put up his hand as an acceptance of the truce. "We both got a little heated. We're both under a great deal of pressure. A double murder case."

"That could make us or break us," Franc said, echoing the words he had first uttered on the wagon carrying Solange Vernet's swollen corpse back to Aix. The words that had sealed their partnership.

"Right, that could make us or break us." Martin repeated Franc's pledge with neither hope nor conviction.

"Well then, sir," Franc said with a tip of his cap, "I'll be off. Down with the boys waiting for the letter."

"And keeping a man on Cézanne."

"Oh yes, of course, a man on Cézanne."

At least they agreed on something.

31

"LOOK, MAMAN, THERE ARE FLOWERS BY the door." Paul Jr. put the basket of fruit and vegetables on the step and picked up one of the blossoms.

"Let me see," Hortense said as she searched in her bag for the key.

"Here's a blue one." He held it up to her. "There are white ones too. They're really little."

Hortense examined the four perfectly symmetrical, delicately colored petals. "This has fallen off a *hortensia*," she told her son. "It's actually a very large flower." Had Paul brought her hortensias? She smiled to herself as she opened the door. He knew they were her favorites.

Once inside, Hortense and Paul Jr. discovered a trail of tiny blossoms leading to the kitchen, where they found Cézanne, sitting at the table pressing a bloody towel against one side of his face.

"Paul!" Hortense gasped. "What happened?"

"I got you some flowers," he said, gesturing toward a vase that held a bedraggled bouquet.

"Papa!" their son ran over to peer into his father's face. "Did you get into a fight?"

"You might say that."

Paul's sanguine air infuriated Hortense so much that she could hardly speak. Her son, on the other hand, was happily excited at the thought that his father had done something that he had been told not to do a thousand times.

"With whom, Papa? Who was it?"

"The Englishman. You know, the one who puts up all those posters about his lectures. The so-called science professor."

Hortense shook her head as she tried to catch Paul's eye. He shouldn't be saying these things in front of their son.

"Why?" Paul Jr. persisted.

"A disagreement. Over whether he or my old friend Marion was a better geologist. And we both know the answer to that question, don't we?" Cézanne winked at Hortense, proud that he had come up with such a clever story. What a fool he was.

"Let me look at you," she stepped forward and removed the cloth from his face. "Oh, my God!" The flesh around his right eye was swollen and purple, and there was blood on his cheek. "Did he cut you?"

"No." Cézanne wiped the cloth across his face. "It's just from my nose."

Just the nose? "And your hands?" Those precious hands. He couldn't stop painting now.

Paul held them up one by one and spread his fingers. Not a mark.

"You hit him back, though, didn't you, Papa?" Obviously, Hortense was not alone in wondering what kind of fight it could have been.

"Sure, and sent him packing too. Which I am about to do with you in a minute. I can tell your mother wants to talk to me alone."

"No, I want to hear more!"

Cézanne got up and kissed his son on the forehead. "Go now. We'll call you for lunch and talk then. So stay outside and close by."

"All right. But promise—"

"Off with you." Paul said, as he gave his son a friendly shove toward the door.

They did adore each other. Sometimes Hortense feared that that was the only reason Cézanne put up with her. But why did she have to put up with him?

"Hortense—"

"You don't have to seem so self-satisfied about this. What happened? Did he come here? Was he in our house?" She started toward the hallway to see if there was damage in the other rooms.

"No, no." Cézanne stepped in front of her. "We met outside."

"You fought each other in the street? What were you doing? You're a grown man. You belong to an important family."

"Hortense, sit a minute."

"No, not until you tell me." She wanted to pick up a plate and smash it over his shiny bald head.

"Sit, please."

He lowered himself into a chair, wincing just a bit as he settled in. If she was going to get any explanation, she saw no recourse but to sit and listen.

"Its all become clearer now," he began.

"Oh, he's knocked some sense into you?"

"You could say that."

"And you didn't even bother to hit him back."

"Maybe I deserved it."

"Why do you say that?" Although she could certainly think of some reasons of her own.

"It may be a kind of contrition, you know, like when you go to confession in the Church. For all the wrongs I have done."

"Stop speaking in riddles. I want to know what the fight was about," she demanded.

"He accused me of hurting her."

"Hurting *her?*" That was laughable. Solange Vernet had floated through the world impervious to everything except her own selfish desire to surround herself with fawning admirers, fools like Cézanne.

"I did," he said quietly.

"I don't want to hear it!"

"That's what I've been trying to tell you. The past doesn't matter. We—"

"Where is he?"

"They took him away. I think he must be in jail."

"And if he's not, what if he comes back?"

He had the nerve to shrug. Somehow she had to bring him back to reality. "You know, Paul, the Englishman could be a murderer."

"I don't think so," he said quietly.

"Don't think so? If not him, who?"

"I don't know. Maybe him. Maybe not." He grabbed her arm. "If he did kill her, it was not because he was jealous of me. He told me that. Don't you see, *that means that I had nothing to do with her death. Nothing at all!*"

Hortense yanked her arm away. If only he cared as much about her! She got up and began unpacking the basket, shaking so hard that the plums tumbled onto the floor.

"Here let me help you," he continued in the same maddening, conciliatory tone. "We'll all feel better once we've had something to eat."

After their lunch of cold chicken, cheeses, and pears, it all caught up with her. She lay down on the salon sofa with a book and fell asleep. It was a dreamless sleep, which brought her to a slow awakening. Still groggy from her nap, she struggled to focus on what Paul was doing.

"Stay still, my dear. Just like that. Yes." She was too tired to care, so she did not move.

"There." He got up."I'm going to add a little green and it will be done," he said, and left the room.

Hortense stretched and sat up on the couch. At least he was drawing again.

When Paul returned, he sat down with her and showed her the sketch. On the right side of the page was the most beautiful drawing he had ever made of her. She looked sleepy, far away, and utterly human. On the left was a giant white *hortensia* in full bloom.

"You see, " he said. "You are my flower."

She did not know what to say. All she wanted was to preserve the moment, to feel forever the warmth that flowed from her heart. Paul reached over and kissed her lightly on the lips. Perhaps it would be all right after all.

Friday, August 28

[The Arlésiennes'] reputation for beauty is completely justified, and it is something more than just beauty. They are both gracious in demeanour and of a great distinction. Their features are of the greatest delicacy and of a Grecian type; for the most part they have dark hair and velvety eyes such as I have only seen hitherto in Indians or in Arabs.

—Alexandre Dumas, *Impressions of Travel: The Midi of France*, 1841

$$32$$

IT HAD TO BE PAST TWO. Although Martin had only been standing in front of Chez l'Arlésienne for minutes, it felt like hours. He had been anticipating this moment since the night before, when a raucous crowd of workingmen had thwarted his plan to have a quiet early dinner. They had been celebrating something or other, filling the air of the tiny restaurant with cigarette smoke and high spirits, making Martin feel like an outsider. If Clarie had not spotted him at the door, he would have slipped away. But she did not let him leave until he promised to come back today and share what was left over from the midday seating. This was to be their first meal together. Worrying about it had even taken his mind away from Merckx and the case for a while. Still, he had no idea what he was going to say. What he did know is that this little restaurant was the only place in all of Aix where he felt he could be himself. Perhaps because it was the one place where someone knew what he had done and did not condemn him for it.

Martin took one last deep breath before putting his hand on the handle and pushing the door open. Only one customer remained, a white-haired old man with a cane hanging over a chair. Too deaf to have been startled by the bell, he was counting out coins to pay for his meal. Clarie hovered nearby, ready to help him out of his chair. She looked up and smiled at Martin as she handed the bent-over little man his cane. Martin held the door open as he limped out of the restaurant. Then Martin and Clarie were alone. The Choffruts must have been in the kitchen.

"I've got things ready over there," Clarie said before striding over to a little table in the corner. The one farthest from the kitchen, where, three nights ago, he had made his confession.

"This looks good," he said, as he put his bowler on the chair beside him. "Good, yes, thank you." She had laid a platter of cold boiled fish and vegetables in the center of the table and spooned aioli on each of their plates. Too late, he realized that he should have been helping her into her seat. Clarie did not seem to notice.

"Come, eat, I'm starving," she said as she pulled herself closer to the table.

"Me too." He sat down. There was no reason to be so nervous today. No confession to make. No new elements of the case to hide.

Still, for a moment, neither of them moved.

"All right. Let's both agree to what is going on." Clarie picked up a spoon and began arranging carrots, potatoes, and fish on Martin's plate. "My aunt and uncle think one thing, and we think another." She paused, eyebrows arched, waiting for him to chime in.

Each time he saw her, she seemed more and more beautiful. Perhaps this is because he had grown accustomed to the way her nose tipped slightly upward after its long descent. Or, was it her dark, almond-shaped eyes, alternatively glimmering with mischief or shining with sympathy?

Martin coughed. "Yes, they are matchmaking and we are—"

"Friends," she completed his sentence while he was still searching for the right word. "And since there is so little time left before I go to Sèvres, why shouldn't we—"

"Have an intelligent conversation every once in a while." Martin surreptitiously wiped his clammy hands on the red-and-white checkered napkin lying in his lap. It was good to get it all out. To recognize that they were of the same mind about so many things, and that romance was out of the question. Because Clarie was leaving in a few months. Because she wasn't attracted to him. Although she had been very kind.

"Franc probably just went along with my aunt and uncle to get on their good side," Clarie continued, as she dipped a cold carrot into the aioli. "They are so worried about me."

"And you're not?"

Clarie shook her head vigorously as she chewed. "I'm excited about the school. And I can always come back home."

At least she has a home to come back to, Martin thought, as he plunged a piece of fish into the garlicky white sauce.

"Don't you long to get back to Lille?"

"No." Not the Lille of his mother's expectations and his memories of Merckx.

"You mean," Clarie said, "they don't have a young woman back there waiting to marry you? That's my aunt's greatest fear, that there is someone already." She smiled and glanced back toward the kitchen, where the clatter of dishes assured them that the Choffruts were still busy. "If you do," she whispered, leaning closer to him, "don't tell her until I leave for Sèvres, or she might ask Franc to find someone else to try and keep me here."

Martin found this less amusing than Clarie did. "Actually," he said as he slowly swirled a piece of potato around his plate, "before I left Lille I was almost engaged. The only problem was that I didn't want to be."

"Why?" She stopped, suddenly serious. "I mean, why were you supposed to marry her and why didn't you want to?"

"She is the eldest daughter of distant relatives to whom my mother and I owe a great deal. She's a handsome, fine young woman, but—" he did not want to be unkind to Marthe DuPont. "Her father's a monarchist. A rich, influential monarchist," he said, as if that would explain everything.

"And you don't love her."

"We're very different. She . . . for example, she took some poor souls to Lourdes this month on the National Pilgrimage." Martin stuffed the piece of potato into his mouth. He had said too much already. He certainly did not want to talk about the letter he had just received from Marthe, describing "her" poor and "her" sick, and begging him to come with her next year to witness the miracles.

Clarie gave him a wry smile. "Not loving her is enough of a reason not to marry. Anyone who describes his fiancée as a 'handsome, fine young woman' certainly does not love her."

Martin was shocked. Marthe DuPont would never have said such a thing. Neither, he was sure, would Solange Vernet. Perhaps Franc was right. This one was indeed a bit wild. Not for the first time, he caught himself imagining what she would look like with her dark hair unfurled from the Arlésienne knot she wore on top of her head. He focused on his plate. He was not used to the clamor of feelings that Clarie aroused in him, wanting to be nearer to her at the very moment he felt like pulling away.

"Sorry." It was Clarie's turn to concentrate on her plate as she toyed with her food. "This is not my affair. I know how fortunate I am. My father would never pressure me into an arranged marriage. I shouldn't have. . . ."

Martin was struggling to find the most gracious way to accept her apology, when they heard the bell. In walked Franc, setting off the all-too-familiar pounding in Martin's chest. How in God's name did his intrepid inspector always know where to find him?

"There you are," Franc said as he marched through the empty

restaurant right up to their table. "I looked for you at the Palais and decided to see if you were out and about."

"Hello Franc," Martin pushed himself to his feet. Before he had time to make the obligatory offer of a seat, Franc had pulled out the chair beside Clarie. "Do you have any more of that?" his thick, callused finger pointed at their meal.

Clarie got up immediately. "Certainly. Besides, you two probably want to talk for a few minutes alone."

Martin was about to protest, when Clarie hastily added, "It's all right. The aioli can wait, and so can I." She had her back to Franc and gave Martin a look which seemed to say more, a warning not to do anything foolish. Before she left, she touched Martin's hand ever so lightly to calm him down. This gesture did not escape the inspector, who winked at Martin as Clarie headed toward the kitchen.

Martin ignored him. He could barely stand to look at Franc's grizzled, hardened face. This time he was more irritated than frightened by his inspector's unexpected appearance.

"Look, if they've got something in the kitchen for me, I'll move over to another table and eat with the aunt and uncle," Franc said. "Don't worry. I won't ruin your tête-à-tête."

You ruined it already.

"I just wanted to tell you that I read the letter."

"And?"

"And I don't see anything in it that gets us anywhere. It's still either Cézanne or the Englishman. Who else?"

"You don't think the earlier rape is important?" As much as he resented Franc's presence, he knew this discussion was essential.

"Not unless Cézanne can identify the rapist. Did he say he could? What did he say about it?"

Martin sighed. "Nothing really. He claims he doesn't remember it at all, except that it could be the source of the nightmares that he put on canvas during those years. He may be telling the truth. He seems to be completely without guile. Maybe seeing Sophie Vernet violated unbalanced him in some way. Especially because he did not act to help." Martin shook his head. "I don't know. I don't understand any of this."

"Well," Franc shrugged, "even if he could remember something, fiddling around with the servants happens all the time. It's probably too old and too minor a crime to prosecute. You know that better than me. Certainly no one would commit a murder to hide it."

Martin clenched his jaw and poured himself a glass of water from the pewter pitcher that Clarie had set on the table. It was so like his hypocritical self-righteous inspector to describe the brutality of what had happened to the young Sophie Vernet as "fiddling around." Yet Franc was staring at him, waiting for confirmation.

"It is past the statute of limitation on rape," Martin finally conceded. "So you don't think the earlier crime is important?"

Franc pursed his lips and shook his head. "I don't think it gets us anywhere."

"Then what about the money?"

"What do we know about that?"

"Nothing." Another dead end.

"Then I say that we get the Englishman to confess."

"I don't think he did it. How could he, after he read that letter?"

"Oh, come now," Franc said disdainfully. "I've seen more murders than you. The letter doesn't prove anything. People are harder, more greedy, more evil than you think they are. But you'll learn."

Martin took a sip of water. Even though Franc was much more experienced than he, Martin did not agree with him. If Westerbury had any feelings for Solange Vernet—certainly if he felt the passion for her that he proclaimed to the world—the Englishman could not have felt anything but the deepest remorse. After their quarrel, he should have gone to her immediately, on his knees. He should have begged forgiveness.

"So let me try to get it out of him."

"No," Martin set down his glass, "I will not send a case forward with a false confession."

"Then you may not go forward at all." The words came out of Franc's mouth one by one, like drops of water plopping into a dark, hidden cistern.

Their eyes locked. Merckx again. Perhaps the only way out was to let Franc wrap up the case and get his promotion. But this would serve neither truth nor justice. And Martin still clung to the hope that if he solved the case, he could save himself.

"Aunt and Uncle say there's plenty." Clarie had reappeared facing Franc. "And they would like you to join them as soon as they get done in the kitchen."

"Then, in the meantime, why don't you sit down and start your dinner." Franc patted the chair beside him.

Clarie sat down without a word and picked up her knife and fork. *She's being polite for my sake*, Martin thought. So he followed suit. Clarie speared a piece of fish and began eating it.

"I didn't mean to interrupt anything. I'm sure you two have lots to talk about."

Clarie shrugged and kept chewing, keeping her eyes on her plate.

"I hope M. Martin hasn't been filling you up with stories about Zola and his godless novels," Franc said, persisting.

"Not yet," said Martin. He smiled at Clarie, trying to include her in the joke. But she would have none of it.

"M. Franc!" Henriette Choffrut called out in her lilting high-pitched voice.

At last.

The inspector got up and, without another word, tramped across the room. After he had shaken the hand of each of the Choffruts and taken his seat, Clarie leaned over to Martin and whispered "Godless novels! The hypocrite! Let's eat and get out of here."

They finished their meal in silence. Then Clarie cleared their plates and announced to her aunt and uncle that she needed some fresh air before they started on the preparations for the evening meal.

"Of course, of course." Henriette Choffrut's voice was higher and more excited than ever, as if she still believed that Martin was an attractive enough prospect to keep Clarie in Provence.

"Come," Clarie said to Martin as soon as they were outside. "Let's see if there is a place to sit on the square." Martin had to hurry to keep pace with her, as she led him to the Hôtel de Ville. Since the market was closing down, they had no trouble finding a bench under a plane tree. Across the way, farmers were shouting and laughing as they took down their stalls.

"I'm worried about you," she said as soon as they sat down. Her eyes shone with an urgency he had not seen before. "I don't trust him. I meant it when I called him a hypocrite."

Martin took off his hat and laid it on the bench. "You shouldn't be worrying about me. I should not be involving you in my mistakes." His fatal mistakes, his crimes.

"Was it a mistake to keep your oldest friend from a certain horrible death?"

"And to lead him into another."

"You did not do that. Franc did. Or his men did, under his orders. I heard them. I told you."

Martin sighed. Was it true that women could not understand the law? "Nevertheless," he insisted, "I am a judge, and I committed treason."

"Shhhhh." She put her finger to her mouth. "Never say that again."

Even though there was no one near them, he knew she was right. That sentence, overheard, could ruin him, or even cost him his life.

"And why did he come to the restaurant just now? How did he know where you were? Why is he trying so hard to be involved in your life?"

Even though her questions echoed his own, he tried to make light of them. "He's a police inspector. Knowing where people are is his job."

Clarie grimaced in exasperation, as if he was a child refusing to be reasonable. "Why did he come today? What was he telling you to do?" She looked like she wanted to shake him.

"We were just talking." He lowered his voice. "I don't believe that either of our suspects did it, while Franc is convinced—"

"I believe in you more than I believe in him."

"What do you mean?"

Amazingly, Clarie blushed. "Perhaps I have no right."

"No, tell me. You're the only person I've talked to about everything." In fact, Clarie was the only person he had talked to about anything.

"It's like with your friend the deserter. You knew what you had to do. You did what was in your heart. And you were right. You should trust what you are feeling."

"Yes, but Franc says that if I were more experienced I would see it differently. He thinks I'm naïve. He thinks that just about anyone is capable of committing murder."

"Oh, Franc!" Clarie sprang up from the bench and crossed her arms in disgust. "Haven't you been listening to me? What about you?"

"Me? Sometimes I just wonder why all this is happening now. One disaster after another. Sometimes," Martin said softly, "I'm afraid that, if this is what a judge is, I am not fit to be one. Just not up to it."

Clarie sat down again and peered into his face. "Don't say that. You've worked too hard to get where you are." She waited until a fruit dealer rattled his cart along the cobblestones past their bench before going on. "Have you ever thought that it is Franc who is not fit? The way he takes advantage of everyone. You are a far better man than Franc."

Despite his self-doubts, Martin was heartened by the passion in her eyes and the determination in her jaw as she spoke. He loved the fact that all her intensity was mobilized for his benefit. He had to smile.

"I'm serious!"

"I know." He nodded encouragement. He did not care what she was about to say; he just wanted to watch her saying it.

"And I know there are things you can't tell me and things I don't understand about the law. But I do know this: you are every bit as smart as Franc. But," she was hesitating again, measuring each word, "sometimes you are afraid to follow your instincts, when all you want is justice and you do not want to hurt anyone in the process. As for Franc," she frowned and began to speak more rapidly, "his instincts are not about justice. All he wants is to get ahead, to be the big man around town. He doesn't care who he hurts."

"Goodness." She really did dislike Franc.

Clarie's determination evaporated, replaced by shock and hurt. She pulled away from him. "You *are* laughing at me."

"No! No, it's just that. . . ." He didn't have the nerve to tell her what he was really feeling at the moment. That there was a chance that a girl like Clarie could really care about him.

"Just 'that'? Perhaps you are right. It's not my affair. What does a girl like me know about these things?"

"No, I didn't mean—"

Before he could continue, Clarie was on her feet again. He reached for her, but only half-heartedly. He had no right to hold on to her, so he didn't.

She walked away, her back straight and proud. Before Martin realized that he should run after her, Clarie had disappeared around the corner.

33

MARTIN DID NOT BOTHER GOING BACK to his chambers. What was the use? No new evidence awaited him. No witnesses. No one to talk to any longer. Why hadn't he listened to Clarie? Why had he allowed himself to become so entranced by his own selfish desires that he did not show her the respect she deserved? Yes, respect! Hadn't she always listened to him? Intently. Seriously. Had she ever smiled when he was trying to tell her what was in his heart?

Martin meandered through the quiet, sun-bleached streets until he stood in front of the cathedral where he had mourned Merckx. He dragged his feet along the cobblestones where flowers had lain broken and forlorn on the day they discovered Solange Vernet's body. He rounded the corner where Franc had parked the splintered gray wagon. He had no idea what he was going to do with himself for the rest of the day, until he heard a voice calling for him. "M. Martin, monsieur le juge, we have something for you." It was little Amélie Picard running toward him in her loose schoolgirl's pinafore, her brown curls bobbing up and down. "Papa went to find you at the Palais. You've got a telegram. It came an hour ago."

"From Paris?" Martin's heart leapt in his chest. Zola!

"Come," she took his hand. "Yes, a telegram from Paris. And it's very long. Papa could tell from the weight of the envelope. Long and expensive, he said. You must be very important."

Martin stopped. "Did your father take it with him?" Please, no, Martin thought, as the disastrous image of the ever-curious notary bandying Zola's message about the town overcame him.

"No, no. It is here. Maman has it."

"Good, good." Martin nodded sagely, hiding his relief. It took every bit of control he had left in him not to race down the street ahead of the child.

Mme Picard was at the entrance to the house, holding a light blue envelope. He wanted to grab it away from her and tear it open, but prudence required that he act like a judge.

"Here it is," Mme Picard said as she handed the telegram to him.

"Should I go try to find M. Picard? Has he been inconvenienced?" Swallowing hard, he barely managed to get these pieties out of his mouth. His mind was racing so far ahead of him. Was there any hope?

"Oh, no," she answered, with a wave of her hand. "He was on his way to the office anyway."

"Thank you, Mme Picard." Martin fingered the thin envelope. It did contain more than one page. He tipped his hat toward Amélie. "Thank you for coming to find me. Since it undoubtedly has to do with official business, I need to read it in private." Thankfully, the girl was so impressed, she almost stood at attention while he squeezed past her and her mother, and, with measured steps, climbed up the stairs.

As he soon as he was alone inside his room, he barred the door.

Then he threw his coat and hat on the bed, unleashed his collar, and tore the envelope open. He turned aside the first page to find the name of the sender. Zola! There was hope.

Martin flattened the telegram on his table and began to read.

PARIS 18 AUGUST 1215

M. BERNARD MARTIN

14 BIS RUE DES ETUVES

AIXENPROVENCE

ARRIVED THIS MORNING VIA ALLNIGHT TRAIN FOUND ARTICLE FROM LE PETIT JOURNAL 7 MAY 1868 COPIED BELOW

GLOTON

CHILD MURDER STOP WE HAVE LEARNED FROM ONE OF OUR CORRESPON-DENTS OF A HEINOUS CRIME THAT HAS TAKEN PLACE IN A SMALL VILLAGE NOT FAR FROM PARIS STOP THE BADLY DECOMPOSED BODY OF YOUNG LOUIS BERIOT THE 10 YEAR OLD SON OF FRANÇOIS AND JEANNE WAS FOUND IN THE BUSHES NEAR THE SEINE STOP HE HAD BEEN KIDNAPED TWO WEEKS BEFORE STOP ACCORDING TO OUR SOURCES HE WAS STRANGLED SOON THEREAFTER STOP YET THE KIDNAPER DEMANDED A HANDSOME RANSOM PROMISING THE BOYS PARENTS THAT HE WOULD BE RETURNED TO THEM ALIVE STOP FOLLOWING THE ORDERS OF THE KIDNAPER WHICH THEY RECEIVED BY POST THE BERIOTS TOLD NO ONE ABOUT THE MISSING CHILD UNTIL TWO DAYS AFTER THEY HAD LEFT THE RANSOM HIDDEN IN A CAVE NEAR THE RIVER AND THEIR SON WAS NOT RETURNED TO THEM

IT WAS ONLY UNDER PRESSURE THAT THE LOCAL CONSTABLE CALLED IN THE GENDARMES TO HELP WITH THE SEARCH STOP IT TOOK THEM LESS THAN A DAY TO FIND THE GRUESOME REMAINS

DO THEY HATE US BECAUSE WE ARE RICH THE MOTHER CRIED STOP THEY HAVE TAKEN MY ONLY CHILD STOP FRANÇOIS WAS MORE STOIC STOP WE DID EVERYTHING HE ASKED STOP WE TOLD NO ONE AND WE PAID 10000 FRANCS IN GOLD COINS

THE POLICE HAVE FOUND NO CLUES STOP THE NOTE TO THE BERIOTS WAS MADE UP OF WORDS CUT OUT FROM THE LOCAL NEWSPAPER

WHO IS THE MURDERER STOP WILL HE STRIKE AGAIN STOP IN THE MEAN-TIME PARENTS IN ALL THE NEARBY VILLAGES ARE KEEPING CLOSE WATCH ON THEIR CHILDREN

THIS IS ALL I HAVE IN MY FILES ZOLA

The first thought that came to Martin was reasonable, logical. The money. This is where it came from. The ransom left in the cave was the sack of coins that the young Sophie Vernet had found in the room of the constable who raped her. Martin reread the telegram to confirm that, yes, he was sure that the same constable who had repeatedly abused her had tried to thwart the investigation of the kidnaping. He had to be the one who had murdered little Louis Beriot and left him in a cave to rot.

Suddenly, the idea that Solange Vernet's murder was connected to the kidnaping of little Louis Beriot took hold of Martin with the fierceness of a banshee howling in his brain. Unlike rape, there was no statute of limitations on murder, ever. It was a crime worth covering up at all costs. At the cost of changing your identity. At the cost of killing again, and again, and again.

Martin picked up the two pieces of thin, blue paper and examined the sparse, typed words, desperately hoping that they would dispel these bizarre suspicions.

And yet. How easy it would be to become someone else in the chaos of war. How easy to get a job as a constable in another part of the country when you were a heroic veteran. How easy it would be to fool someone as gullible, as naïve, as inexperienced as Bernard Martin. To keep him on a string, dancing to the rhythm of his master.

No! Martin slammed the telegram on the table. No! It could not be. He was just being too influenced by Clarie's words, by her passion.

Even she didn't mean to imply that Franc had committed any serious crime. She had just told Martin to follow his instincts. And yet, and yet. . . .

Martin thought his heart would be squeezed dry as his brain overflowed with images of Franc. Franc, jolly as they drove back from the quarry. Franc, saying that Solange Vernet deserved what she had gotten. Franc, so cavalier about the strangulation of the poor little messenger. Franc, unable to discover the boy's identity. Franc, so eager to blame Westerbury for the crime. Franc, who had murdered Merckx. Franc the chameleon, the would-be Vidocq, the man of a thousand moods and faces. Franc! This was instinct, all right. Instinct with a vengeance. It was mad. And it made sense.

Suddenly another image came to Martin. Charles Westerbury proudly displaying his hand as a badge of honor, a hand streaked with pomade from Franc's dyed-black hair. What if the dark pomade was not meant to cover age, but to create a disguise? What if it wasn't Cézanne's paint on Solange Vernet's missing gloves? What if they were stained with Franc's hair dye?

Martin lowered himself onto his bed and crossed his arms tight across his stomach. He began to sway back and forth. During those last terrible moments, Solange must have recognized her tormentor. But did she know why she was being murdered? Did she realize that she had signed her own death warrant all those many years ago, when as a young girl she declared "I know who you are" even though she knew nothing, nothing at all, about the kidnaping? Did Franc tell her why he was killing her? Or did he just strangle and knife her, in brutal triumph?

Martin got up and began to pace. If this were true, if any of it were true, his own role, the stupid and innocent part he had played, was all too obvious. Franc had been watching Solange Vernet for months, and waited until Martin was in charge. He was Franc's chosen dupe. These last two weeks—all planned and perfectly orchestrated.

Yes, Franc had been watching him, too. Otherwise, how did the inspector know where Martin was, always? How had Franc caught Merckx so easily?

Worse, not only had Martin been a dupe, he had stepped into a trap of his own making. Merckx's futile attempt at escape had played right into Franc's hands. If any of this were true, what a boon Merckx's arrival must have been, giving Franc the opportunity to commit a righteous, patriotic murder, while, presumably, guaranteeing Martin's continued pliability. Merckx! Martin's eyes filled with tears of pure and impotent fury. Everything was a garish, hateful blur. He grabbed his chair and threw it against the armoire.

The sound of the crash brought him to his senses. Breaking the furniture would do him no good. Martin picked up his chair and slowly straightened one of its staves, making it usable again. If Franc was the murderer, how could he, a judge who had committed treason, proceed against him? Yet, if Franc was the culprit, Martin had to get him. In order to do that, he had to think it through. Every conversation, every gesture, every piece of evidence. Martin had gone over everything that Westerbury and Cézanne had told him again and again. Now it was time to reconsider the words and deeds of his intrepid inspector.

Saturday, August 29

Then he looked at me, and I felt dazzled by the sensation of his eyes looking right into me, past me, deep in the future. There was a broad smile of resignation on his face.

Someone else will do what I haven't been able to do. . . . Maybe I'm just the primitive of a new art.

Then a sort of bewildered indignation passed over him.
Life is terrifying!

And I heard him several times murmuring like a prayer as the dusk was falling:

I want to die painting . . . to die painting. . . .

—Joachim Gasquet, *Cézanne:
A Memoir with Conversations*, 1921

34

"LISTEN, ENGLISHMAN. YOU MIGHT AS WELL confess. We're going to prove you did it. And then—" the brute made a chopping motion at the back of his neck. The guillotine.

"I did not do it." Westerbury met the threat with calm resolve, despite the fluttering inside his chest and the fact that Franc's head was almost touching his, smothering him with a miasma of rancid breath and spraying spittle. This time, at least, he knew there would be an end to it. Only hours to go. And when he got out, he had a plan. His bullish adversary had unwittingly given him an idea.

"I wish he'd let me knock it out of you! Any real judge would." This time Franc held up his fist.

"I will not confess to a crime I did not commit." After all, he *was* an Englishman, born to freedom and the rule of law.

The cell was stifling. Westerbury could hardly breathe, but he took pleasure in knowing that his inquisitor was sweating even more than he. The perspiration was practically dripping from Franc's nose and shaggy eyebrows onto his own. The heavier man could not last much longer. He would go away, just like the other times.

"Then let me put it to you this way." Franc stepped back at last. "Since it obviously was a crime of passion, all you have to do is confess to Martin and then tell the court how jealous you were. Tell them how that whore betrayed you with the artist. After all, no one around here really cares about your lover. She wasn't one of them. They'll probably let you off and send you packing back to England."

"She was not a whore. And I had no reason to be jealous." Westerbury had to defend Solange's honor. He was determined to prove, despite all that had happened, that he was still worthy of her.

"Really? She'd probably been a whore for a decade before you knew her."

This accusation was so beneath contempt that Westerbury did not even deign to respond.

"You're done talking, huh?" Franc moved away from the bed and shouted for the guard. When the door swung open, he delivered his parting shot. "Next week, when the prosecutor returns, it will be all over. There's nothing soft about him. So, if I were you, I would confess to the little judge right away, before they reassign the case. In fact, I'm going to insist that they do. They'll find a judge that will keep you here, with me, until you give in. And then," Franc grinned as he repeated the chopping gestures at the back of his neck. Finally, he slammed the door shut.

Westerbury slumped against the stone wall. Would they really take Martin off the case? At least he was honest and decent, if totally lacking in passion and imagination. Westerbury shook his head slowly; no, it was up to him. Charles Westerbury was going to show all of them how a man of passion, imagination, and science finds out the truth.

Westerbury got up and walked toward the ray of sunlight emanating from the tiny square window above his head. He raised his right fist and opened it slowly, revealing the long dark streaks that stretched across the fingers and palm of his hand. The gloves. Now he knew that there were two possible reasons for hiding them. They might indeed be stained with paint. Or—Westerbury shuddered—with pomade grasped from Franc's hair during Solange's final, terrible moments. This would explain why the inspector was so eager to make him confess, and why the bastard seemed to know so many details about how he and Solange had lived since their arrival in Aix.

Still, it didn't explain why Franc would need to kill her. Or what would drive Cézanne to murder Solange. Westerbury had to know, and was about to risk everything to find out. Risk his life, like a true gentleman, for Solange's honor. As soon as he got out, he planned to buy two pistols for the duel.

He stepped back and gazed at the window. If only he believed in heaven, then he'd have the solace of knowing that his angel was there, waiting for him. If only. But it was his great burden to be a man of science. The only thing he could be sure of was the existence of the world that lay right outside his cell. That was where he must seek his revenge.

35

MARTIN STOOD STARING AT THE LAW books that lined one wall of his office. These were the heavy tomes that his mother had sweated, saved, and begged for, the books for which she had mortgaged his life to the DuPont family. He had no time to make any provision to pack them, and he was not sure he would ever be able to come back for them. It couldn't be helped.

Before sitting down at his desk again, Martin peered out his window at the Palais square. No gendarmes, no Franc. Just ordinary people going about their noontime business. Had Franc put someone on his trail this morning? Martin had no way of knowing. He had only taken precautions once—when he had gone off to Mont Sainte-Victoire in search of Solange Vernet's letter. At all other times—Martin slammed his fist against the window frame in frustration—he had been completely careless, unaware and gullible.

He was working on two completely different reports. The first was to go into the official dossier, a catalogue of the material evidence and summaries of all the interviews and interrogations. He'd leave it for Old Joseph to deliver to the prosecutor on Monday morning. Martin planned to end this report with the argument that the evidence was inconclusive, that neither Westerbury nor Cézanne should yet be charged with the crime.

The second notebook was going with him, his personal record of the investigation, and of each and every encounter with Franc.

He should have had no trouble in putting together these reports. They were the *sine qua non* of his profession: the ability to gather, analyze, and synthesize evidence and present detailed, logical arguments. Nevertheless, he was stalled. The argument for inconclusiveness in the dossier was a half-truth. The conclusions he was coming to in his own notes were deeply humiliating. Each passing minute made him more and more certain that Franc had murdered Solange Vernet, the boy, and Merckx. By Monday afternoon he'd be searching through the police records in Paris to find out more about Alain Duprès, the dastardly constable of Bennecourt. Then he'd go to the military registry to trace the career of the self-proclaimed hero, Albert Franc, and the presumably "dead" Duprès. If Martin established that Franc and Duprès were one and the same man, he intended to bring the proof back to Aix, no matter what the consequences.

Hearing noises in the hall, Martin slipped his personal notebook into a drawer. He was rolling down the sleeves of his shirt when Franc entered the room.

"One of the boys said that you wanted to see Westerbury before we released him. I've got him here."

"Right. Please bring him in." It must be three o'clock, the hour when the Englishman's sentence was to be completed. Martin needed to hurry if he were going to finish before nightfall. "I didn't notice the time," he explained, without looking up, afraid that any expression on his face might give him away. "I've been summarizing for the Proc."

"I can see that," Franc said, as he scrutinized the papers that covered the desk.

Martin ignored this rudeness. If he did not talk, Franc would eventually have to go away. Tomorrow, Martin thought, tomorrow when I get on the train, I will finally be free of him.

"Jacques," Franc called out to the young gendarme, who was guarding Westerbury in the hall. Franc took hold of the prisoner in the foyer and gave him a shove into the office.

"Mr. Westerbury, sit for a minute." Martin kept his head down, going through the act of organizing his papers.

Westerbury complied, silent for once.

"Franc, I assume the release is in order and Westerbury can leave from my office?"

"Yes. But I don't understand why."

"Very well." Martin fashioned his face into a mask of immobility before facing his adversary. "I just need a moment to ask our witness a few questions for clarification. You may leave."

As he had done forty-eight hours before, Franc lingered stone-faced in order to convey his disapproval. When he got no reaction, he left, shutting the door to Martin's chambers with a bang.

Franc's departure revived the Englishman. "You don't look well," he observed, with a tone of inexplicable satisfaction.

"I'm fine." Martin did not need solicitude from a man who had certainly done his part to make life difficult.

"At least you've got the window open today. May I?" Westerbury got up and made his way around Martin's desk. "Nice view."

"Sit down."

"My, we are irritable."

And Westerbury was more annoying than ever. Martin had expected to confront a creature of pity. Instead, the Englishman had a gleam in his watery blue eyes and a lilt to his step. Was he up to something? Or had he finally been undone by the tragedy that he had helped to bring about?

"Sit."

"As for me, I'm beginning to get used to French justice. All I need is the fortification of a good meal and I'll be tiptop. I'm sure Arlette will provide me with one as soon as I walk in the door."

If Westerbury was determined to carry on a conversation all by himself, Martin was not about to oblige him. He did not have the time. "Sit," he insisted. After Westerbury finally took his seat, Martin approached him in order to talk quietly. "Answer me one question. Before you were arrested, had you or Solange ever noticed or met Franc?"

"No." Westerbury's response was quick and definite.

Martin crossed his arms. "I thought you might want to think about that before answering. I'm talking about all the time since your arrival in Aix."

"And I said no. I have thought about it."

Martin took a few steps away from the Englishman to get a better view of him. "Mr. Westerbury, is there something you are not telling me? It could help your cause."

"No." Again too quickly.

There obviously was something. The man was such a fool. "You realize that I can hold you for another forty-eight hours until you answer my questions fully and truthfully?"

Westerbury did not object. He did not even deliver an oration about his rights as a genius and an Englishman. He only shrugged.

"Did Franc or his men beat you? We do not allow that in French law."

"No more brutality than usual. I have no need to complain." Then he actually smiled. What had happened to him? At least the whining, self-pitying Westerbury was predictable. But this creature?

"You cannot go on bothering the Cézannes."

"I don't intend to."

"Then what is it that you do intend?"

"To do what I have to do." Martin was about to object, when Westerbury hastened to add, "No more street fights, you have my word. I have had time to think in prison. I can't go about like a madman. I have to go forward with my life. That is what I intend to do."

Martin did not believe him. "There isn't any more you can tell me? I am writing the report for the prosecutor right now. It will go better for you if you don't keep any secrets."

Westerbury shook his head slowly from side to side, still wearing that annoying, superior grin.

Martin returned to his seat and took up his pen. There was nothing to do but dismiss the idiot. "Mr. Westerbury, you are a grown man. You will have to face the consequences of your actions."

"I already have." Martin looked up to confirm the change in tone. For just a moment a shadow of regret passed over the unnatural brightness of the Englishman's demeanor. Then it disappeared. "And I will continue to face them in the future," Westerbury added. "May I go now?"

"Leave." Whatever the Englishman was planning to do, Martin would not be around to see it anyway. "Go," he almost shouted. Martin made a point of not looking up from his papers as he sensed Westerbury going through the motions of picking up his hat, tipping it toward him, and departing.

As soon as he heard the door close, softly this time, Martin threw his pen down. He got up and paced back and forth until he worked off his irritation.

Under the pressure of time, Martin wrote steadily for the next few hours, until an unexpected visitor interrupted his work.

The gendarme Jacques announced her arrival. "I'm sorry, sir. There is a woman here. She insists on seeing you. Almost hysterical. She says it's a matter of life or death."

Clarie? Could Franc have gotten to Clarie somehow and threatened her?

"Show her in immediately." Martin rose, ready to sweep her into his arms, comfort her, and take her to Paris if necessary. He was more disappointed than relieved to see that the woman in question was Hortense Fiquet. He retreated as she rushed toward him.

"Monsieur le juge, you must see this. You must do something. We can't deal with it any more. Cézanne is innocent."

Martin signaled to the gendarme to leave and close the door, then he asked Hortense Fiquet to try to calm herself. One of the buttons on the front of her dress was undone, and strands of straight dark hair were falling around her plain, frightened face.

"I cannot calm down. You must stop this Professor Westerbury. He won't leave us alone." She was clutching a small, white folded piece of paper to her chest.

"Let me see what you have there." He held out his hand.

She gave him the note. When he unfolded it, he almost gasped. It contained only two lines. The first from the letter that Solange Vernet had written to Westerbury, repeating the accusation she had made against her brutal tormentor; the second from the message carried to the Vernet apartment by the dead boy. "I know who you are. Please meet me at the quarry. C."

"Who brought this to you?" he asked sharply.

"Their maid. I mean, his maid."

Arlette LaFarge. "When?"

"Just minutes ago."

She wanted to say more, but he would not let her until he had the answers he needed.

"Where is Cézanne now?" He did not want another murder on his head.

"Somewhere off the Le Tholonet road. He hired a donkey early this morning and went to paint the mountain."

"Then he has not seen this."

"No, I told you, he left hours ago and won't be back until dark." She kept twisting her hands together in anxious little circles.

"You got this just minutes ago? And the maid brought it to you?"

She nodded, keeping her eyes on his face, waiting for his reaction.

"You did the right thing in coming to me, " he assured her. "Did the maid say anything else? Did she say when Westerbury wrote this?"

"She told me he said to wait an hour before she made her deliveries. That's all."

Deliveries? More than one? And why an hour? What was the madman up to?

"Did she say where else she was going? This is very important." The urgency in his voice made Hortense Fiquet take two steps back, away from him.

"Yes, I was furious. I wanted to talk to her. I wanted to go see the Englishman myself. But she told me that he had already gone and that she had promised to deliver the two notes within fifteen minutes of each other."

"Did the maid tell you where else?" He controlled himself enough to keep from shouting.

She shook her head, eyes agape with fear. "All I could get out of her is that she was going to the jail or to the courthouse. Wherever she could find him."

"Who?"

"I don't know. She just said it was a secret, and she promised her M. Westerbury that she would find him."

Martin very well knew who—Franc. Westerbury had somehow figured it out too. Or only half of it, for the Englishman was still deciding between two potential murderers. And he was waiting at the quarry for the one who took the bait. Martin pressed his eyes closed, trying to remember if there had been anything that Westerbury had said or done that afternoon which should have warned him. The only clue had been the Englishman's uncharacteristic self-control. Obviously he had decided to keep his own counsel and take things into his own hand. To become the hero of his own tragedy. What a fool.

"Well, what are you going to do about it? This must stop. I can't—" Hortense Fiquet had gotten her nerve back.

"Thank you." Martin interrupted her in mid-sentence. "You don't need to worry. I will deal with this immediately. Westerbury will not bother you again."

"Yes, but you do see, don't you that—"

"Please, Madame Fiquet, you were right to come to me. Now I have to do my part. A man's life may be in danger."

She would have said more if Martin had not taken her gently by the arm and escorted her into the hallway. "Do you want a gendarme to walk you home? Do you feel unsafe?" he asked.

She smiled. It did not take a great deal of concern or attention to please her. She shook her head. "I'm all right. But I will expect to hear from you." Her gray eyes were searching his, begging him to take her seriously.

"Yes, yes," he said as he moved her toward the staircase. Where was Jacques? The idiot disappeared on the one occasion when he could have been of use. As soon as Hortense Fiquet started down the stairs, Martin leaned over the railing and called out for the gendarme. Jacques's name echoed throughout the empty courthouse, to no avail.

Martin went back to lock the door to his chambers before hurrying down the staircase, overtaking Hortense Fiquet, who let him pass without a word. He rushed out the back door of the courthouse, where Jacques stood guard, and hurried to the prison yard, where the veteran François and two other men were playing cards.

"Is Franc around?"

"No." François took a cigarette out of his mouth and stood up at attention. "Some woman gave him a note and he rushed off, even took one of the horses."

"Do you know where he went? Do you know what the note said?"

"No, he put it in his pocket."

To be destroyed later, no doubt. "Fetch me a horse," Martin commanded. "And saddle two for yourselves. We have to go to the quarry immediately. Franc's life may be in danger." He only said this to rally the troops. It was the Englishman, the gallant fool, that he was actually worried about.

"Why do you say that?" one of them said stupidly, still not budging.

"The murderer may be waiting in the quarry for Franc." They still did not move. Martin could only imagine what Franc, their leader and comrade, had been saying about him. "You and you," he pointed at the tall veteran François and a burly gendarme, who was still sitting by the pile of cards. "Go! Now!" he yelled.

He was wondering what he would have to do to get them to obey, when François waved to his comrade. "Come on, Jean. If what he says is true, we'd better help Franc."

If what he says is true. Martin had not time to deal with their insubordination. He needed their help to pull Westerbury and Franc apart.

"I'm going up to my chambers to get my hat," he announced, as he started back to the courthouse.

When Martin reached the grand atrium, he slowed down. How many more times would he run his hands along the polished wood railing, ascending this staircase to his chambers? He took in the main hall bordered by the courtrooms. This had all lain before him, with the promise of a calling that he had tried so hard to live up to. If Franc killed Westerbury, what would happen to Martin? At the very least, his career would be over. And Franc would surely get away with everything. This outrage propelled Martin onward. He unlocked his chambers, slipped inside, and grabbed his hat.

By the time Martin returned to the prison, the horses were ready. With Jacques's help, he mounted one and told the men to follow him. Martin was not a good rider, but he rode as fast as he could, urging his horse in the direction of the quarry. At this very moment Westerbury might be dying. At this very moment Franc might be killing again. Martin beat the animal as he never had beat any horse before. Still the gendarmes easily kept up with him. When they were halfway up the

Bibémus road, they heard two shots ring out in quick succession. Martin's horse reared up, and, as he tried to regain control, he shouted to the men to go on ahead of him.

A moment later, Martin dismounted where he and Franc had left the gray, splintering wagon less than a fortnight ago. He tethered his horse to a tall pine tree and raced to the top of the quarry. Below him François was kneeling beside Franc. Not far away, Jean was kicking Westerbury.

"Stop!" Martin shouted as he scrambled down toward them. "Leave that man alone!"

"He shot the inspector!" The burly gendarme looked stupider than ever.

"Stop now, or I will see you in court!" Unless they were going to kill him, Jean had no choice but to obey Martin's order.

Martin crouched down near Franc's body.

"Look. Look what that bastard did," François cried out. "He shot him twice."

The side of Franc's head and his chest were soaked with blood. His hand was still wrapped around a bloody knife. Martin guessed that Franc had been shot at close range, his body propelled backwards by the force of the bullets. In spite of his mortal wounds, the inspector kept trying to talk. Martin thought he heard the word "whore."

"Whore," he repeated to François. "Did he say anything else?" Martin asked, as he frantically divided his attention between Franc and Westerbury, whom he needed to protect from the gendarmes' fury. "What else?" he demanded again.

François kept staring down at his dying friend and protector.

"This is important," Martin insisted again. "It could be evidence in the murder trial." Evidence that he hoped to use against Franc, evidence that he wanted to engrave in the gendarme's memory.

"I think he said, 'I made her a whore.' I don't know what that means."

"And?"

"And! What else do you want. Can't you see he's dying!"

Franc's muttering had become an unintelligible rasp, as his face contorted into a grimace of pain. He was leaving the world in a fit of rage.

Martin got up and patted François on the back. "Do what you can for him," Martin said before going over to the foolhardy Englishman. As soon as Martin saw him, he knew that Westerbury would not survive his own rash acts. His chest was also covered with blood, and he was breathing in short labored gulps. In his left hand, he was clutching a pistol. Another lay beside him.

"Leave me alone with him," Martin told the gendarme. "I need to ask him some questions. Go see about Franc." As soon as Jean left, Martin knelt down beside Westerbury. "What happened?" Martin said the words softly and distinctly. He needed to penetrate through Westerbury's pain before death overtook him.

Westerbury's eyes flickered open. "I shot him, old boy. I shot him. He killed my Solange and I. . . ."

"How did you know?" Martin asked, as he placed his arm under the dying man's head.

"The gloves," Westerbury made an effort to raise his right hand. "The stains, his hair, on the gloves." He let out a moan that was almost a shout. "I was going to duel for her. Her honor. Like a man. But he kept . . . coming at me. . . ." Westerbury panted for breath in little whimpers. "He said she was a whore . . . always had been . . . I think he was. . . ." Again he stopped, and his back arched in pain.

"The constable at Bennecourt. Yes, I know."

"If you knew. . . ." Westerbury whispered. There was little time left.

"I just found out myself. I am going to Paris to look up his records."

"Then this, this was all in—"

"No, no, not in vain," Martin spoke louder. He could not let the Englishman die believing that he had died for nothing. "I would not have gotten as far as I have without your help. And I am not sure that I could have found enough proof to prosecute him. He was a powerful man."

"Was?"

"He's dead."

"I did it, then. For. . . ."

"I know." Martin said, as Westerbury grimaced in agony. He lifted the Englishman's head closer to his own. "You did it for Solange. For her honor. She deserved such a gallant defender." This was all puerile. But he did not know what else to say. And somehow it felt right.

Westerbury slowly raised his eyes. They stopped flickering. Had Westerbury heard him? Had he been able to offer any comfort?

Then he heard the words, "for Solange," and he felt the weight of the Englishman's head on his arm, as it rolled to the side. The blood dripping from his mouth was the sign that he, too, was dead.

Martin waited until he was sure he could speak with a steady voice before standing up. "Dead. Both of them," he pronounced. "The Englishman waited for Franc with a pistol. Even so, Franc was strong enough to attack with his knife."

"Good. Good," said Jean. "At least he got the bastard back."

"Yes, he did," Martin responded quietly. "Yes, he did."

"So the Englishman was the killer after all, just like Franc said," François chimed in.

"No, no, he wasn't." Martin was not going to lie to them.

"Then who?" Jean approached Martin with fists clenched.

"Let's worry about that later. For now, we must get Franc and the Englishman back to Aix. You two go back and get a wagon. Remember to bring blankets to wrap the bodies, and have someone go find Dr. Riquel. I'll stay here and watch over them." The two gendarmes hesitated for a moment, as if they wanted to continue defending Franc's honor. "Go," Martin insisted. "We need to be back in town before dark. You are much better riders than I am."

The admission satisfied Franc's loyal comrades enough to send them on their way. They prided themselves on being men of action, ready to kill if necessary. Yet it was Martin, the man of reason, who was in command. And, now, he realized, a man of feeling as well. At the moment, too much feeling. He needed to be alone.

After the men left, Martin climbed up on a boulder. He did not have the stomach to stay close to the two dead bodies. To smell their remains. To shoo away the flies. It would be better to look ahead, he told himself. Now that he had a future.

When he raised his eyes, Martin was surprised to discover that he could see Mont Sainte-Victoire, rising above the reddening boulders and the mournful parasol pines. The sun was only beginning its long, slow, summer descent behind him. Its waning rays covered the mountain with pale, radiant colors: pinks and blues, yellows and greens, oranges and white. Somewhere near the foot of the mountain, Cézanne was rolling up his canvas and tying his easel to a donkey, oblivious to the fact that he had won. He, not Westerbury, would be left to conquer the mountain.

Tomorrow, Martin would catch the train to Paris to find the evidence to prove Franc's guilt and Westerbury's innocence. He'd leave a note for Hortense Fiquet, assuring her that she and Cézanne would be left in peace. Above all, and before everything else, he would go in search of Clarie Falchetti. To tell her he was leaving for a while. And to beg her forgiveness.

Postscript

March 1886	Zola publishes *L'Oeuvre*, his novel about an artist.
4 April 1886	Cézanne sends Zola a curt thank-you for his copy. They never speak again.
28 April 1886	Cézanne marries Hortense Fiquet in a civil ceremony witnessed by his parents.
29 April 1886	The couple marries in a religious ceremony witnessed by Marie Cézanne and Maxim Conil.
	The newlyweds will soon start to live apart, Hortense spending as much time in Paris as possible.
23 October 1886	Louis-Auguste Cézanne dies, leaving his son an income of about 25,000 francs a year.

November 1895   Ambroise Vollard mounts an exhibit of Cézanne's paintings in Paris, arousing interest and some favorable reviews.

29 September 1902 Zola dies under mysterious circumstances. Cézanne weeps bitterly when he hears the news of his oldest friend's death.

Zola was a legend in his own time.

Cézanne is the father of modern art.

Bernard Martin, Albert Franc, Clarie Falchetti, Solange Vernet, and Charles Westerbury are fictional characters.

Source of Quotations

1. John Rewald, *Cézanne: A Biography* (New York: Harry N. Abrams, 1986), p. 156.

2. Nicolas Freeling, *Flanders Sky* (New York: Mysterious Press, 1992), p. 162.

3. Sidney Geist, *Interpreting Cézanne* (Cambridge: Harvard University Press, 1988), p. 99.

4. Cited in Alan B. Spitzer, *The Revolutionary Theories of Louis Auguste Blanqui* (New York: Columbia University Press, 1957).

5. Royer quoted in Pnina Abir-Am and Dorinda Outram, *Uneasy Careers and Intimate Lives: Women in Science 1789-1979* (New Brunswick: Rutgers University Press, 1987), p. 147.

6. Michelet excerpted in Susan G. Bell and Karen M. Offen, eds. *Women, the Family, and Freedom. Vol. I: 1750-1880* (Stanford: Stanford University Press, 1983), p. 171.

7. Ronald Meek, ed. *Marx and Engels on Malthus* (New York: International Publishers, 1954), p. 186.

8. Benjamin F. Martin, *Crime and Criminal Justice Under the Third Republic: The Shame of Marianne* (Baton Rouge: Louisiana State University Press, 1990), p. 2.

9. Sholem Asch, *The Nazarene*, trans. Maurice Samuel (New York: Putnam's Sons, 1939), p. 3.

10. Françoise Cachin et al., *Cézanne* (Philadelphia: Philadelphia Art Museum, 1996), p. 274.

11. Alexandre Dumas quoted by Lawrence Durrell in his *Provence* (New York: Arcade, 1990), p. 89.

12. *Joachim Gasquet's Cézanne: A Memoir with Conversations.* Trans. Christopher Pemberton (New York: Thames and Hudson, 1991), p. 224.